THE LION OF CAIRO

Also by Scott Oden

MEN OF BRONZE
MEMNON

For more information on Scott Oden and his books, see his
website at www.menofbronze.com

THE LION OF CAIRO

Scott Oden

BANTAM PRESS

LONDON · TORONTO · SYDNEY · AUCKLAND · JOHANNESBURG

TRANSWORLD PUBLISHERS
61–63 Uxbridge Road, London W5 5SA
A Random House Group Company
www.rbooks.co.uk

First published in Great Britain
in 2010 by Bantam Press
an imprint of Transworld Publishers

A CIP catalogue record for this book
is available from the British Library.

ISBNs 9780593061251
9780593061268

Addresses for Random House Group Ltd companies outside the UK
can be found at: www.randomhouse.co.uk
The Random House Group Ltd Reg. No. 954009

The Random House Group Limited supports the Forest Stewardship
Council (FSC), the leading international forest-certification organization. All our
titles that are printed on Greenpeace-approved FSC-certified paper carry the FSC logo.
Our paper procurement policy can be found at
www.rbooks.co.uk/environment

Typeset in 11.5/15pt Plantin Light by
Falcon Oast Graphic Art Ltd.
Printed and bound in Great Britain by
CPI Mackays, Chatham, ME5 8TD

2 4 6 8 10 9 7 5 3 1

Mixed Sources
Product group from well-managed
forests and other controlled sources
www.fsc.org Cert no. TT-COC-2139
© 1996 Forest Stewardship Council
FSC

To Robert E. Howard, whose tales of swordplay and sorcery gave inspiration to a kid from Alabama, and caused him to take up the pen in his own name.

Kan ma kan
Fi qadim azzaman

There was, there was not,
In the oldness of time . . .

Traditional Bedouin Rhyme

Prologue

The rasp and slither of steel died away, the sound lost to a wind that howled over snow-clad ridges, pouring into the passes and sheltered valleys of the high Afghan Mountains. Ruptures in the leaden sky – a sky that promised little succour from the long winter at the Roof of the World – allowed mocking glimpses of blue heavens and golden light. And a mockery it was, for the sun's rays did nothing to allay the knife-edged cold, which cut through leather and wool and thick cloth to freeze flesh and stiffen beards.

Still, the two men who faced each other on the winding trail to the crag-set village of Kurram paid no heed to wind, cold, or sunlight. Snow drifts or naked rocks made little difference to the two as they slowly circled, breath steaming with every panted curse, each seeking an opportunity to bring this struggle to its bloody conclusion. Both fighters sported ragged Afghan turbans and trousers, girdled robes of striped silk and grimy wool, and belts bristling with knife hilts; they were alike in height, but where one was thick-waisted with broad shoulders, a bull neck, and grey flecking his beard, the other was young and lean and as graceful as the Turkish sabre he held in his scarred fist.

'Baber Khan,' said he, his Arabic punctuated by an Egyptian accent. 'Make peace with Allah, for your time is at an end. The blood of Kurram is poor price for the blood of my master's servants but it is a price that must be paid.'

Muscles knotted in Baber Khan's neck as he twisted his head and spat. He wielded a salawar, the sword-knife of the Afghan tribesmen: two feet of shadow-patterned Damascus steel, older than Islam, with a single-edged blade that tapered to a diamond point and a hilt braided with leather and silver wire. A leering face carved of yellowed ivory glared from the pommel. 'Your master? Your master is a coward who sits atop his rock and plays at empire! Bah! Think you I do not know who you are, dog of Alamut? You may have killed a score of my Afridis, but I have killed a thousand of your brothers, a thousand of your so-called Faithful!' Baber Khan raised his salawar, eyes blazing. 'Come closer, my little Assassin! Come closer, and let me make it a thousand and one!'

The Assassin's temper flared; with a guttural curse, he leapt for Baber Khan, his sabre whistling in a vicious arc that should have struck the Afridi chieftain's head from his shoulders – had he not been expecting it. Baber Khan ducked and twisted, his teeth bared in a death's head grin as he lashed out at the overextended Assassin.

It was sheer reflex that saved the younger man's life. He glimpsed the descending salawar, watered steel burnished by pale winter light; he wrenched his body to the right and awkwardly threw his sabre into the path of Baber Khan's blade. Steel met steel with a resounding clash as the salawar – fragile though it seemed – shattered the Assassin's sabre near the hilt. The young killer screamed as the tip of the Afghan blade bit into his brow and sliced down his left cheek, missing the eye by a hair's breadth.

The Assassin staggered, clutching his bloodied visage. More than pain lanced through his skull. A crawling sensation shivered across his scalp and down his spine: *a thousand tentacles of ice seeking to pry their way into his soul.* His ears rang with phantasmal sound, with voices not his own: *howling, gibbering, cursing, screaming; voices filled with rage, with terror, with purpose . . . cold, murderous purpose.* His jaw champed, teeth grinding as his own fury blossomed. Did he survive the fearsome siege of Ascalon, the initiations of al-Hashishiyya, and the relentless hunt through the Afghan Mountains to bring the death his master decreed for the Afridis only to fall prey to a poisoned blade? *Not poison,* a voice mocked, stronger than the others; an ancient voice tinged with madness. *No, not poison.*

The Assassin's wrath cut through the agony, granting him a moment of absolute clarity. Rumours he had heard of Baber Khan's cruelty, of his insane recklessness, of a pact between the chiefs of his clan and the djinn of the mountains, suddenly made sense. It must be the salawar. By what deviltry he could not imagine, but its touch filled his head with visions: ancient and bloody scenes of carnage, of slaughter, and of betrayal. It called to him . . . the Assassin's body spasmed; he took a step towards Baber Khan and then fell to his knees, glaring up at him through a haze of blood and fury. 'That . . . that b-blade!'

'Yes! You feel it, do you not?' Baber Khan replied; he ran a thumb and forefinger along the edge of his salawar, collecting the Assassin's blood. His grim smile widened as he licked his fingers clean. 'It is the Hammer of the Infidel, and none can stand before it! What is your name, dog?'

'Assad,' the young Assassin replied. He sat with his head bowed, oblivious to the blood dripping down his lacerated cheek. The knuckles of his right fist were white where he gripped the hilt-shard of his sabre. *My birthright.* His lips writhed, nostrils flaring as he fought off the fearful paralysis induced by that devil-haunted blade by focusing on the broken steel before him. *My father's sabre!*

'The Hammer of the Infidel kills before ever the final blow is struck! Even the gentlest caress of the blade strips a man's resolve from him, leaving him naked and trembling at the edge of the Abyss!' Baber Khan laughed. 'Assad, eh? My brothers will know the name of the fool who thought to challenge the chief of the

Afridis!' He stepped closer and raised his salawar, its tip poised for a killing blow.

'A fine trick,' Assad said, glancing up, 'since your brothers are already in Hell!' The Assassin exploded with the unexpected desperation of a wounded lion. He launched himself at Baber Khan and drove the hilt-shard gripped in his right fist into the Afghan's groin. Blood spurted and steamed as the man's ferocious bellow turned to a shriek. The jagged length of blade bit deep; Assad sawed upwards, ripping Baber Khan's belly open to the navel.

Colour drained from the Afghan's face. He swayed, eyes widening in disbelief; with one hand he reached out and knotted his trembling fingers in the collar of Assad's robe. Baber Khan struggled to raise his salawar.

'Allah!' he croaked. 'How?'

Assad caught the Afghan's wrist and stripped the blade from his grasp. Touching its ivory-and-silver hilt sent white-hot wires of pain stabbing through the Assassin's muscles even as he felt something cold and heavy touch his mind. Something ancient. Something filled with hate. Assad recoiled, but gritted his teeth and kept hold of the salawar. 'I am al-Hashishiyya, you fool,' the Assassin replied. 'Where others fear the Abyss, the sons of Alamut embrace it. Now, let my master's will be done!'

Before Baber Khan could react, Assad drew the salawar across his throat in one smooth motion and then shoved the Afghan away. And Baber Khan, Lord of Kurram and chieftain of the Afridis – Baber Khan, who had earned the wrath of the Hidden Master of Alamut by slaughtering his emissaries – took one halting step and toppled to the ground, his last moments spent writhing in a slurry of blood and snow.

But the Assassin paid no heed to Baber Khan's death throes. He paid no heed to the cold or the wind or to the burning agony of the laceration bisecting his cheek. No, the Assassin's attention remained fixed on the long blade in his fist, on its pommel of yellowed ivory carved in the shape of a djinni's snarling visage. 'I am al-Hashishiyya,' he said to the glittering-eyed devil. 'I am Death incarnate.'

So am I, the devil replied . . .

The First Surah

Palmyra

1

The sun hung in the blood-red sky like a misshapen lump of copper, its edges blackened, its face radiating waves of excruciating heat over a landscape ravaged by war. Thousands of mailed corpses littered the streets of Ascalon: bodies frozen in the act of dying; hacked asunder; blades of steel and iron yet clutched in their fists. Tattered pennons once carried with pride by Ascalon's defenders now rustled like ghosts on the hot wind.

As a ghost, too, did the figure of a dark-haired child drift through the great mass of the slain, swinging a wooden sword in boyish abandon. With it, he lashed out at imaginary enemies, the flash of his pale limbs incongruous in this gore-blasted wasteland. He chased the wind, tracking zephyrs of dust through deserted courtyards and down winding streets; past fire-gutted buildings looted by victorious Nazarenes. The wind led the boy to the city's heart, to where a ruined mosque squatted in the middle of a broad square.

Here the boy stopped, tapping the ground with the tip of his sword. His brows drew together as he eyed the structure. Curious, he mounted the shallow steps and peered through the open doorway. Inside, shadows swirled like smoke from a funeral pyre; shafts of copper light lanced through ruptures in the domed ceiling. The boy caught sight of a figure pacing the periphery of the chamber, a lean wraith clad in a surcoat of grimy white cloth who warily avoided the murky daylight.

The boy's youth made him fearless. He crossed the threshold, his voice profaning the silence. 'What was this place?'

Instantly the silhouette stopped and spun towards the door, falling into a predatory crouch. It snuffled the air like a hound on the trail of a hare.

'Are you deaf?' the boy said. 'What was this place?'

'A tomb,' the figure replied, its voice hard and guttural, full of rage. It crept forward, still in a crouch. 'And a prison.'

The boy glanced around, disbelieving. 'A prison? For what? There's no door.'

'For a fell and terrible beast.' Closer it came. 'One that has not tasted flesh nor drank blood since before you were ripped squalling from your mother's womb, little one.' Closer, sidestepping a column of light. Menacing eyes glittered and sinew creaked. Still the boy displayed no trepidation; he stood motionless, unwilling to credit the stranger's words.

'What kind of beast?'

Now, with only six paces separating them, the figure straightened. This close, the boy saw a design in blood caking the chest of the figure's surcoat: a cross, red on white. The stench of death clung to it; the boy blinked, his nose wrinkling. The smell reminded him that perhaps he should be cautious.

'The worst kind,' it hissed. 'One that hungers!' The Templar threw its head back, howling its rage as it sprang on the startled child. Too late, the boy raised his wooden sword as searing cold talons dug into his throat . . .

2

Assad bolted upright, his hands reaching for a weapon even as he stifled a cry of alarm. Sweat beaded his forehead; his nostrils flared as flint-hard eyes swept the shadowy corners of the room. Beside him, his companion mewled in her sleep. With titanic effort, Assad forced himself to breathe and willed his muscles to relax. Slowly, he sank back down on the bed, closing his eyes as the thudding of his heart abated.

It was a familiar nightmare. Even though fourteen years had passed, memories of the fearsome siege of Ascalon still haunted him; memories of hunger and thirst, of roaring fires and strangling clouds of smoke, of corpses left to rot in the sun and the blond giants whose hellish machines shredded the city's ramparts like paper. An involuntary shudder ran through his body.

Assad sighed and opened his eyes. A faint breeze rustled colourful, sheer linen panels hanging from the narrow windows; outside, streaks of crimson and gold heralded the rising sun. The air crackled with heat even before the first searing rays struck fire from the plastered mudbrick walls of the oasis city of Palmyra.

Assad sat up and swung his legs over the edge of the bed. Though nearing forty, his body still bore the indelible stamp of a warrior: a scarred frame hard-woven with knots of muscle and corded sinew. Assad's features were sharp and angular; a not unhandsome face made sinister by the jagged scar that ran from the corner of his left eye to his jaw, visible even through his close-trimmed beard.

The movement woke his companion. She stretched, the damp sheet slipping to expose her small breasts and an expanse of round, honey-coloured hip.

'What time is it?' the woman, Safia, murmured, her hand caressing his back.

'Near dawn,' Assad said. 'Go back to sleep.'

Half his age, Safia was a sloe-eyed courtesan whose charms earned her a lascivious reputation in the bazaars of Palmyra. 'It's too hot to sleep,' she replied. Her hand slid around his torso and down his belly, stroking the hard ridges of muscle before falling lower still. She purred. 'Besides, the maiden would ride her favourite stallion once more before the sun rises.'

Assad twined his fingers in her tousled black hair; leaning down, he gave her a savage kiss before lifting her hand away from his groin. 'Not now. I have to be about my business.'

Safia sighed. 'What business could you have so early?' She rolled on to her back, watching Assad as he stood and padded across the rug-strewn floor to where their clothing lay.

'That's none of your concern,' he said. He found his long shirt and his white cotton trousers beneath a pile of diaphanous blue stuff that passed for Safia's gown, all discarded in the throes of last night's passion; he drew his trousers on, and then glanced about for his boots. These lay in the corner near a crumpled pile of cloth that turned out to be his ragged sash and turban, his once-black khalat – faded now to a deep shade of charcoal by sun and sweat – and an empty sheath of leather-bound wood. Methodically, Assad retrieved his things and finished dressing.

'You're a dour man.' Safia sat up as he bound his hair beneath his turban. One end he kept loose, a veil of sorts to muffle his mouth and nose from blowing sand. Or to hide his features from prying eyes. 'Have you no joy for life?'

Assad's face hardened. He stalked back to the bed; Safia flinched away from him as he knelt, his eyes fixed on the smooth flesh at the base of the courtesan's throat. 'For life, yes. For questions, no,' he said, reaching a hand beneath where he'd been sleeping.

Assad's fingers closed on a cold ivory hilt. Instantly, ropes of muscle stood out on his arm as contact sent shards of emotion slicing into his mind: hunger, longing, rage, pain, grief. And most powerful of all: an ancient sense of hatred. Nostrils flaring, Assad curled his lips in defiance. He brushed aside those razor-sharp vibrations, mastering them through sheer force of will. The spasm passed in the span of a heartbeat, leaving only faint echoes in its wake.

He glanced down at the weapon he extracted from beneath the bed: a salawar, the sword-knife of the tribesmen who lurked in the high passes of the Afghan Mountains; its sculpted pommel bore the fearsome visage of a djinni, fanged mouth open as it roared in silent fury. *The Hammer of the Infidel, the Afghans called you; the blade of Afridi chieftains – the blade of madmen. But what name did your creator give you, I wonder? What words did he speak when he filled you with his hate?*

Assad, known from Seville to Samarkand as the *Emir* of the Knife, rose to his feet. He slid the blade into its sheath and thence into the sash about his waist, his hand draped lightly over the pommel. He motioned to Safia as he crossed her bedchamber and opened the latticed door leading to the garden. 'Get dressed. It will soon be time for morning prayers.'

'Prayers?' she said. Unashamed of her nakedness, the courtesan crawled from the bed and followed Assad out on to the colonnaded portico. The air smelled of clean desert breezes, of kitchen smoke and baking bread. 'You don't strike me as a religious man.'

'Don't presume you know me because we've lain together twice,' he replied.

A ribbon of orange fire brightened the eastern horizon, presaging a day of unsurpassed brilliance, a day filled with heat and dust and chaos. Within the hour, the rising sun would sear away the cool shadows of the garden. The inviting *plash* of water in the fountain's blue-enamelled basin would become a sound of mockery; birds warbling in trellises of flowering jasmine would seek shelter in the eaves of ancient monuments. The only respite would be in the thin shade of a palm tree. Assad savoured the cool while it lasted.

'Will there be a third time? Or a fourth? Will you not return tonight and allow me the chance to know you . . . better?' Safia's fingers trailed down his arm.

Assad glanced sidelong at the petite courtesan. She stood with her legs crossed, her back arched and shoulders pulled back to emphasize her pear-shaped breasts. A ghost of a smile played at the corner of his mouth. 'Perhaps,' he said, looping an arm about her waist. He stroked her bare bottom before giving it a playful swat. 'Now go back inside before you take a chill.'

Safia laughed and spun away from him. 'Will I see you tonight?'

The gleam in Assad's eyes left little doubt. He watched her a moment longer as she pranced through the fretted door and into her bedchamber. When he turned away, however, the veneer of lust he so scrupulously maintained in her presence vanished; his scarred face reflected only cold and disciplined confidence. The surety of a killer.

Assad left by the garden gate. Safia's villa stood amid a warren of tight alleys bordering Palmyra's central bazaar. Built, she claimed, by the ancient Queen Zenobia, the place was obviously maintained through the largesse of her countless patrons – a fact which did not escape Assad's notice. Safia was a favourite of Palmyra's wealthiest sons, its princes, merchants, and shaykhs, men who had the wherewithal to keep her in lavish style; why, then, would she seek out the company of a man of *his* calibre: by all accounts a penniless freebooter with a violent reputation?

Had she been any other woman Assad might have chalked it up to simple boredom, a diversion from the endless parade of cultured fools who graced her bed. But not Safia. She was too calculating. *Why? What did she stand to gain?* Assad's eyes narrowed. He was prepared to depart Palmyra for Baghdad by month's end – to take the life of a man he'd been stalking for over a year – and it was not in his nature to leave unanswered questions in his wake. He would discover the truth of her motives, God willing, and he would do so this morning.

Assad threaded through the alley between the courtesan's home and the flaking walls of her neighbour's, who was away in Damascus on business with the Sultan (or so a garrulous watchman had bragged). Like most of the homes in Palmyra, Safia's villa was but a single storey, rising twenty feet from stone foundation to its decorative crenels of whitewashed mudbrick. Just over the low garden wall from the alley, a flight of stairs ascended to the flat roof.

Assad stopped. Though muffled by the villa's walls, he heard Safia's three Ethiopian slaves singing as they went about their morning tasks: from fetching water, to stoking the fire under their mistress's bath, to laying out a selection of her gowns. Carts rattled on the uneven paving stones of the bazaar; he heard the sharp crack of a hammer, a child's angry scream. He heard good-natured laughter as a knot of men passed by on their way to the public baths – the hammam. Closer, a dog raised a racket. Assad glanced back down the alley. Motes of dust turned golden with dawn's first light; soon, the muezzin would climb the minaret of Palmyra's main mosque to call the faithful to prayer.

Cat-like, Assad leapt, caught the coping of the garden wall, and swung himself over. He dropped easily; without a sound he darted up the stairs to the roof of Safia's villa. When the heat of high summer became unbearable, most of Palmyra's citizens retreated to their roofs to sleep or to entertain; Safia was no different. Her home sported a loggia of rich red cedar, pierced by rosette-shaped holes to take advantage of the fickle desert breeze. What caught Assad's attention, however, were the fluted copper shells, wind-catchers – malqafs – that provided ventilation for the interior of the villa.

And a way to listen to what was going on inside. 'Gossip holes', his old mentor Daoud ar-Rasul had called them. 'Become a man of few words and you need not worry,' he'd said. Assad crouched a moment near each one, his head cocked to the side as he listened for Safia's voice. At one, he heard the rattle of crockery; another, a man speaking in the liquid syllables of Africa. Assad padded to each in turn, placing his feet with care so as not to cause a noise. Finally, at the next-to-last malqaf, he heard Safia's smoky voice, faint at first, but growing in volume as she no doubt moved closer to the interior grille.

'. . . swear to you, by week's end I will have him wrapped around my littlest finger. Then, he will sing like a nightingale.'

'Take care with him,' a voice replied – male, but with a quality that hinted at effeminacy. A eunuch, perhaps? 'Do not give him cause for suspicion. This is not a man you can trifle with.'

'But he *is* a man, my dear, and men are my purview, not yours. I know them better than they know themselves. A man cares only for two things: his manhood and his ego. Stroke one or the other and he will show you much favour, but if you stroke both – ah, if you can stroke both then there is no secret he would not divulge, no confidence he would not betray. This Emir is no different. Honestly, I don't know where this fear you have for him comes from. He seems so . . . pliable.'

Assad heard the man choke and splutter. 'Pliable?' he said once he'd regained his breath. 'The old eunuch who manages your estate is pliable, Safia. The man who bakes your bread or blends your perfumes or fetches your slippers is pliable. The *Emir* of the Knife is far from it. He is a slayer of djinn, by Allah! They say he crossed the Roof of the World to study with a blind master of Cathay in the mysterious East; that he learned to kill with the slightest touch.'

'He touched me and I yet live.'

'Because he did not wish your death, you foolish woman! He serves the Lord of al-Hashishiyya!'

Safia made a rude noise. 'Al-Hashishiyya is a nest of thugs!'

'True, but they are dangerous nonetheless. If the *Emir* of the Knife means to kill the vizier of Baghdad, Safia, I need to know when.'

'Why this charade? If it will preserve your vizier's life, then why not simply kill this so-called Emir and have done? Have you no spine, Husayn?'

Husayn! Assad's lips curled into a humourless smile. He knew him after all – one of the vizier's lap-dogs who dabbled in secrets and schemes while posing as a physician from Karbala. The eunuch and Safia were thick as fleas on a Bedouin carpet, apparently. Now, he reckoned, the slut's advances at least made sense.

'We have tried . . .'

Assad stood; he dropped his hand to the hilt of his salawar, feeling the rage imprisoned in its ancient blade course through him. He'd heard all he needed.

3

'The man is uncanny!' Husayn said; his kohl-rimmed eyes never stopped moving. He was slender for a eunuch, his shaved head oiled and gleaming like an ivory dome. Gold glittered on his fingers and around his wrists. A crescent-shaped pendant of electrum and mother-of-pearl lay heavy on the breast of his black-and-gold damask robes. Fingering a strand of ebony worry beads, Husayn paced back and forth across Safia's sitting room, his slippered feet whispering on marble tile. 'Poison, betrayal, ambush . . . we have tried all of these things and have failed. It is as if he knows our minds better than we do.'

Safia reclined on a divan. Dressed now in a burnous of gauzy saffron linen, she petted a small grey cat that sprawled at her side. Feline and mistress stretched, languorous in the rising heat; the courtesan, at least, revelled in the trickle of cool air flowing from the malqaf grille overhead. 'Give me a vial of poison,' she said, offhandedly. 'I will put it in his wine tonight.'

A frown creased Husayn's forehead. 'You? You think you can succeed where better men have failed?'

'Of course. Did the Emir trust these "better men" of yours enough to sleep in their presence, or to eat and drink what their servants prepared? He trusts me this much and more.'

The eunuch stopped; ebony beads *ticked* together as he ran them through his manicured fingers, a sound like thoughts falling into place. He glanced over at Safia. 'Intriguing,' he said. 'You can do this?'

The courtesan's eyes turned to daggers as she caught the un-spoken implication of his question. 'I may be a woman, eunuch, but do not mistake me for the frail and retiring flowers of your master's harem! Your fearsome Emir would not be the first man I've killed, nor will he be the last!'

'Intriguing, indeed,' Husayn said, his fine brows knitted in thought.

Safia returned her attention to rubbing the cat's stomach, listening to its throaty purr, and ignoring the eunuch as he paced to the arched doorway of the sitting room. Beyond lay the courtesan's bedchamber, its incenses and perfumes barely masking the musky stench of sex. She would send for her girls after a while, and instruct them to tidy it up in advance of Assad's return, to decorate it in red and yellow silks and candles of crimson tallow. Tonight, she would greet this Assassin, this Emir, naked and glistening with fragrant oils. Safia lay back; eyes closing, she revelled in the moisture and heat that flared between her thighs. *And after I've taken my pleasure, he will die.*

She heard Husayn turn. 'If you are serious about this, I have an appropriate concoction already distilled, though it must be mixed with a more savoury wine than usual to hide its—'

A noise interrupted him: a soft *slish*, like silk parting under the keen edge of a knife. Then, silence. Safia waited for the eunuch to resume. *Merciful Allah! They clipped his good manners when they clipped his balls.* 'Hide what? Its taste?' She sat up just as Husayn's head slid from his shoulders; her eyes bulged at the sight of whitish vertebrae cleanly exposed and leaking marrow, at the twin jets of bright blood pumping from the severed arteries of his neck. The eunuch's head struck the marble tiles – a pulpy sound not unlike that made by a melon dropped from a table's edge – while his body remained erect a moment longer, even taking a staggering step towards her before collapsing.

Safia found her voice, screaming as Assad emerged from the shadow of her bedchamber. He stepped over the eunuch's twitching corpse with murder in his eyes and a ribbon of blood dripping from the blade of his salawar.

'Why . . . Why are y-you here?' She scrambled to rise, her eyes wide with terror; beside her, the cat hissed and shot off the couch. 'Why—'

Without breaking stride Assad caught her by the throat, lifted her bodily from the divan, and slammed her against the wall.

Another piercing shriek escaped around the iron fingers holding Safia aloft.

'Scream all you like. I've silenced your slaves, and who outside these walls would care what sounds come from the house of a harlot?'

She clawed at his hand. 'W-Why are you d-doing this? He . . . He was my physician!' Assad leaned closer, his scarred face merciless. He touched the tip of his salawar to her cheek. Safia shrank from the contact, trembling, and then crying out as tendrils of soul-wrenching hate imprisoned in that accursed blade wormed like maggots into her skull. 'There is no God but God,' she whispered, squeezing her eyes shut.

Assad ignored her prayer. 'Your physician was a dog I should have put down months ago. This is the day of your death, Safia, but you have a choice: answer me truthfully, tell me all you know and your death will be swift and without pain. Or continue lying to me and I promise you, you will linger in agony. The choice is yours.'

Her eyes flew open. 'Please, Assad! I—'

'Choose.' The *Emir* of the Knife pressed the blade into her cheek; his own eyes gleamed like chips of frosted obsidian.

'What . . . What d-do you wish to know?'

4

Safia went easily in the end, dying as the muezzin called for the noon prayer. Assad stood over her body, its beauty unmarred save for the narrow wound beneath her left breast where a knife-thrust had stilled her heart; he wiped clotted blood from his salawar using a scrap of cloth torn from the hem of her burnous, then he sheathed the weapon. He glanced from Safia to the eunuch's headless corpse. The vizier had more eyes in Palmyra than he would have imagined, at least a dozen, and all of them focused on *him*. Such ferocious determination to live was rare in the enemies of al-Hashishiyya, who often took no precautions beyond prayer, preferring instead to leave their fate in the hands of Allah.

A man with the will to live made Assad's work more of a challenge. So be it! He would accommodate the wretched fool. He would change his plans; leave for Baghdad today rather than at the end of the month. *But first* – he glanced from body to body.

Assad had been no stranger to killing even before he pledged himself to the Hidden Master of Alamut; he'd learned the art in the iron crucible of Palestine, fighting against the Frankish invaders who had seized Jerusalem. What his brothers of al-Hashishiyya taught him was to kill silently, quickly, and without remorse. Still, he felt a pang of sadness as he carried Safia's body out into the garden, where it would join that of Husayn and her three household slaves – along with wads of blood-soaked linen – at the bottom of the cistern which fed the fountain. Despite her treachery, she'd been a pleasant companion. Yet, pleasant or not, Safia had chosen her path.

Assad said nothing as he knelt and eased her over the cistern's brick-lined edge; he uttered no benediction as she splashed into the water with the others, offered no prayer as he levered the wooden cover back into place. With any luck it would be days before anyone discovered their whereabouts.

Assad did not linger. From the courtesan's villa he made his way south, to the most ancient quarter of the city. Afternoons brought a sense of indolence to the streets of Palmyra as men of all walks sought a cool drink and shade from the ferocious heat of the Syrian Desert. Shops closed; stalls were shuttered in the bazaar as men lounged under striped awnings, in courtyards, and in gardens. Women sweltered in their harems.

Assad's destination overlooked the crumbling ruin of a Roman hippodrome; it was a caravanserai with a dilapidated façade of peeling plaster, fretted windows, and a keel-arched entryway nearly three storeys high. Bearded faces peered down from the roof while inside muleteers and camel drovers sprawled in the shadow of a colonnaded arcade, some drinking wine and throwing dice while others dozed. Their charges, part of a caravan awaiting the arrival of a shipment of date wine, sat in the centre of the courtyard beneath a cluster of palm trees, bellowing and braying, tails twitching in an effort to keep the flies at bay.

None moved to stop him as he plunged through an open door and up two flights of rickety stairs to the third floor. Guards walked the gallery, at times leaning over the balustrade to stare into the courtyard; hard-eyed men wearing turban-wrapped helmets and mail shirts beneath their robes, they kept their hands well away from their sword hilts as the scar-faced Assassin passed.

'Farouk!' he called, throwing open the door to the caravan master's suite of rooms. His voice echoed down a short entry hall that widened into a guest chamber. The place was sparsely furnished with faded cushions and a low table holding a water pipe and a cupboard topped with an oil lamp. Reed mats covered the floor, and over these lay carpets woven in shades of blue silk and cream-coloured wool, ragged-edged and dusty. 'God curse you! Farouk!'

A man stepped through a curtain of wooden beads. He was Persian, his beard trimmed to a point, his round face hollow and etched with concern. A white skullcap shaded his bald pate; his embroidered kaftan bore stains of ink and wine. He glanced back the way he had come before hissing to Assad: 'Where the devil have you been?'

'Protecting our interests.' Quickly, the Assassin relayed what had happened at the courtesan's home. 'It was a shame I had to kill the woman, but as consolation at least our old friend Husayn will trouble us no longer. My plans have changed, Farouk. I need a good horse and provisions enough to reach Baghdad.'

Farouk, like Assad, was a servant of al-Hashishiyya, though the Hidden Master had never called upon him to take a life or to unduly risk his own. Rather, his worth lay in his relative obscurity. As a fixture on the caravan route between Palmyra, Damascus and

Cairo, Farouk helped shepherd the flow of information to Alamut, from messages hidden in plain sight, to missives penned in poetic code, to cryptic phrases muttered among strangers. He was accustomed to dealing with the carriers of information, not with the men who utilized it. Lines of apprehension creased his forehead. 'Wait, wait,' he said as Assad started to pace.

'A horse, Farouk. Send one of those sluggards in the courtyard—'

Gold flashed in the afternoon light as a gnarled hand parted the wooden beads of the curtain. Assad saw it and reacted; eyes blazing like slits of murderous fire, he clawed at the hilt of his salawar. His other hand tightened into an iron-hard fist. Farouk, who did not lack courage, caught Assad's arm before his blade left its sheath.

'Allah confound you! Wait, I said! He's here to see you!' The caravan master indicated the newcomer with a jerk of his head. 'He says he has known you for many years.'

Surprised, Assad recognized the man who stepped through the curtain, a man whose three-score-and-ten years weighed heavily on his narrow shoulders. Eyebrows as silvery and sparse as his beard met over his thin nose in a 'V' of disapproval. 'Were I your enemy,' the newcomer said, his voice like the scrape of sandstone on marble, 'and younger, you should be waking up in Hell, my young Emir.'

'Then praise be to God that you are not my enemy, Daoud ar-Rasul! *As-salaam alaikum.*' Assad sketched an elaborate bow, gracefully touching the fingertips of his right hand to his heart, lips, and forehead.

'*Alaikum as-salaam,*' the older man replied, smiling. 'And praise be to God, indeed. It pleases me to see you again, Assad.' A head shorter than the tall Emir, Daoud ar-Rasul – Lieutenant of Alamut and the voice of the Hidden Master – shuffled forward and embraced his protégé, kissing both cheeks.

'Why are you here, my friend?' Assad said. A faint smile could not hide his concern. 'You should be somewhere cool and agreeable, not sweltering in this godforsaken cauldron. Farouk, fetch our guest something cool to drink.'

Daoud held up his hand; gold winked again on his index finger – a signet ring, antique and massive, bearing as its seal a stylized eagle carved of lapis lazuli. 'Good Farouk has already been a most excellent host. You and I must speak on matters of grave importance, my young Emir. A chair, if you please, Farouk, then give us a few moments.'

The caravan master nodded, fetched a straight-backed chair from an inner room, and then hustled out of the door, leaving the two men alone in the guest chamber. Daoud settled himself, smoothing his grey khalat and his gold-buttoned undervest. Assad drew his sheathed salawar from his sash and settled on to a cushion at Daoud's feet, the weapon balanced across his knees.

The old man scowled at the blade, at its leering pommel. 'You still carry that abomination? Get it out of my sight!' He made the sign of the horns to ward off evil.

'As you wish,' Assad replied. He laid the salawar behind him, covering it with a spare cushion.

'If you had any sense you would cast that thing into the sea and take to carrying an honest blade again! I know of a smith in Mosul who could recast your father's sabre. Now that . . . that was a fine weapon.'

It was Assad's turn to scowl. 'What goes, Daoud? You didn't travel all this way to berate me over my choice of tools.'

'No. No, I did not, though you would be wise to listen to me.' The older man cocked his head to the side. 'You are Egyptian, are you not?'

'After a fashion,' Assad replied, his scowl deepening. 'Born in Cairo, though I have not laid eyes on the Nile's banks in a score of years – but you know this, my friend, even as you know why.'

The Lieutenant of Alamut nodded, stroking his beard as though recalling pieces of a long-forgotten tale. 'Age cripples more than a man's muscle and bone . . . it wreaks havoc with his memory. I pray you live long enough to understand.' Daoud lapsed into silence. A dozen heartbeats passed before he again stirred. 'I was a boy when Ibn al-Sabbah – peace be upon his name – ascended to heaven, and I have lived to see four of his noble bloodline assume the mantle of Hidden Master. All have had their faults, but we excused them because they were the descendants of Ibn al-Sabbah – peace be upon his name. Our new master is no different.'

'He has ruled Alamut for less than a year,' Assad said. 'What flaws could he have developed so soon?'

'Only one and it is beyond his control: youth. Our new master is very young, Assad. Young and brimming with dreams and ideals not yet tarnished by disappointment or grown faint with age. But for all that we might hold him to blame for his boyish exuberance, he remains a scion of Ibn al-Sabbah – peace be upon his name – a cunning diplomat and a ferocious leader. He prides himself on recognizing a man's strengths. Where his father looked at you and saw merely a weapon, he claims to see something more. A capable man, a man he believes he can trust with a delicate task.'

'Am I not already tasked with visiting his wrath upon that dog of a vizier in Baghdad?'

Daoud's features twisted in a moue of distaste. 'Our enemy in Baghdad deserves a slow death, true, but regretfully he has earned a reprieve for now. Your plans have well and truly changed, Assad. The Hidden Master wishes you to go to Cairo.'

'To Cairo? What the devil for?'

The older man's eyebrows inched up. 'Do not forget yourself, Emir. Do not forget what you are, or whom you serve.'

Assad looked away, nostrils flaring. He clenched his jaw to keep his anger in check. 'I . . . I spoke without thinking. You chasten me, and properly so. But the question stands, Daoud: why does our master wish me to journey to Cairo? And why now?'

'To forge an alliance. Did you know,' Daoud began, 'that the Fatimid Caliph of Cairo and the Hidden Master are of a similar age? My spies tell me the Caliph reached his majority a year or so before our master. Thus, had it not been for a schism dating back to the days of Ibn al-Sabbah – peace be upon his name – these two young lions might well be allies today. Perhaps even brothers. Can you imagine, Assad, what power we would wield if Alamut and Cairo were as one? We could cast down the Sunni Caliph of Baghdad, drive the Turk back beyond the Black Sea, and reclaim Jerusalem from the Infidel!' As quickly as it appeared, excitement dissipated from the older man's visage. He looked down at his gnarled hands, twisting his signet ring to stare at its engraved stone. 'And so it would be, but for a decades-old squabble over succession. Our enemies unite while we revel in our division. Our master, at least, has his freedom. The Caliph of Cairo is much beloved by the folk of that city, and yet he remains little more than a prisoner in his own palace, or so my spies tell me. Kept alive as a figurehead by overly ambitious men.'

'And what will my presence accomplish?' Assad grunted. 'You know as well as I that if this young Caliph were a vigorous man then perhaps I could aid him in recovering his birthright by spilling the blood of his jailers. But it's more likely that he's a degenerate wretch like his forebears. No amount of diplomacy or bloodshed on my part will give a man such as that the spine he needs to rule. This is a lost cause wrapped in a fool's errand, Daoud. Surely our master must see it, too?'

Daoud leaned forward. 'As I said: he is young, Assad, and often the young see things their elders cannot – or will not. He does not believe in lost causes or fool's errands, but he does believe in you, my friend. He believes in the *Emir* of the Knife. Go to Cairo as Alamut's emissary. Use your formidable skills to strengthen the Caliph's position and dispose of any who would do him harm. But – and this is critical, Assad – the Caliph *must* know who it is that aids him. His enemies . . . let his enemies speculate. Sow fear among them as you will, but impress this upon the Caliph: say that Alamut stands ready to forgive our long-held grievances, to mend the rift that divides us.'

'And if the Caliph wishes no dealings with Alamut?'

Daoud shrugged. 'What he wishes is irrelevant. Caliph Rashid al-Hasan and the Hidden Master *will* be reconciled. His survival – and ours – depends on it.'

Assad said nothing; his fingers tapped a staccato rhythm against his thigh. For over a year he'd done nothing but plot the demise of the vizier of Baghdad – an outspoken enemy of al-Hashishiyya who pressed his allies to call for a jihad against Alamut. Already, a score of fedayeen, the Faithful, had died in straightforward attempts on the vizier's life, each failure revealing a little more of the palace's elaborate defences. Assad had used the fedayeens' sacrifice to weave a trap as delicate as a spider's web and no less venomous. And for what? To have his plans scuttled by a young man's idealism? Assad sighed. *Exactly so.*

Despite his annoyance, the Assassin dredged his memory for recollections of Cairo, a city he had not seen in two-and-twenty years: its sights and smells, the cadence of its native speech, the sound of its myriad bazaars. This hazy picture created glaring difficulties from the outset: what route to Cairo and in what guise; what would he need to establish himself in the city; what sources of information could he rely upon. His face became a grim mask as the difficulty of rescuing some Fatimid half-wit from his political betters sank in.

'Well, my young Emir?'

Assad glanced up. 'These spies you mention,' he said. 'I expect I'll have need of them. Send Farouk, too. Likely I'll hear no end to his complaints, but he's a good man and he knows Cairo. And gold, enough to open doors and loosen tongues.'

'You will have all you require.'

'It will not be an easy journey. I should make ready and leave as soon as possible; perhaps as early as tomorrow, but by week's end at the latest.' Assad retrieved his salawar and clambered to his feet, a thumb hooked in his sash. He towered over the frail Lieutenant of Alamut. 'You are as a father to me, Daoud ar-Rasul, and thus I pray you realize how impossible this burden you've laid across my shoulders is.'

Daoud glanced up; his eyes glittered with a measure of their old fire. 'Impossible? What one man deems impossible another might see as merely a challenge. Which are you, my son?'

'Ask me again on my return.'

The Second Surah
Into the City of Tents

1

A crash echoed from beyond the bolted door, metal clattering as though someone had let fall a heavy blade. Startled, al-Hajj glanced from his cluttered work table, the light from a pair of oil lamps glittering in his narrowed eyes. He cocked his head to the left, listening . . .

There it was again! Fainter this time, less strident: the scrape of metal on wood.

Corpse-fingers stirred the hair at the base of al-Hajj's neck as he clawed through the riot of books, scrolls, and loose scraps of paper strewn across the table, searching for the curved dagger he kept near. Finding it, he slipped the blade from its worn leather sheath. 'Who goes?' al-Hajj bellowed.

No one answered.

Al-Hajj rose from his chair and crossed the darkened study, eyeing every chest, every cupboard, and every shuttered window as though it harboured murderous life. Thick carpets of patterned loom-work muffled his footfalls. Reaching the door, he drew back the iron bolt and flung it open. 'Who goes, I said?'

In the latticed gallery outside al-Hajj's apartments – on the fourth floor of a caravanserai owned by a consortium of cloth and silk merchants – a young Armenian slave in a long white shirt crouched on the polished hardwood. The gallery overlooked a garden courtyard where night lamps of gilded copper set amid the foliage gave off a dim, buttery glow; a cool breeze redolent of the Nile rustled the spiky fronds of date palms and set shadows to dancing.

At al-Hajj's sudden appearance, knife in hand, the Armenian boy gave a bleat of terror and fell prostrate on the gallery floor. A silver platter etched and inlaid with enamelled leaves lay by his elbow; near his hand were a matching goblet and an overturned bowl of dates. A sweet aroma rose from puddles of spilled pomegranate juice. Al-Hajj scowled, feeling the fool at this, the obvious source of the noises. 'Why are you skulking around, boy? What devil's work are you about?'

The slave – a eunuch, twelve years old and newly gelded – glanced up, tears sparkling on his long eyelashes. 'M-Master told . . . b-bring refreshments you,' he said, his Arabic barely comprehensible. 'T-Tray . . . slip . . .'

Al-Hajj stepped over the threshold and looked out into the gallery. The boy's master, Ibn Zayid, lived on the floor above; he was a pinch-faced old gossip, a dealer in silks from distant Cathay, and as suspicious a man as any al-Hajj had ever met. Ibn Zayid's current obsession was with the source of his neighbour's wealth; he could not fathom how a lowly seller of trinkets and gimcracks who rubbed elbows with the beggars outside the ruined mosque of al-Hakim could afford to live under the same roof as he, a prosperous merchant. Al-Hajj sighed, shifting his gaze to the slave. Even pale with fear he was a handsome young thing, tall for his age and full-lipped, his dark eyes smudged with kohl. Like the refreshments he carried, the boy was an offering.

Al-Hajj had no servants of his own, no slaves a would-be enemy might compel to betray his secrets; here, for the second time in half a year, Ibn Zayid – whom Allah had not graced with subtlety – was presenting him with one, a slave easily turned. Al-Hajj well recalled the merchant's first attempt: a comely Hindi girl from the Malabar Coast, lithe as a dancer, her silken tresses scented with cinnamon and rosewater. Not lightly did he refuse *that* gift, but refuse it he did – and in a fit of pique the old fool sold her off to a Syrian whoremonger who catered to the perverse. Nor, he reckoned, would the boy's fate be any different, for Ibn Zayid was not a man accustomed to feeling the sting of defeat. A flash of rage reduced al-Hajj's crinkled eyes to slits.

He knelt, gathered up platter and goblet and placed them inside his door, his knife with them. The slave retrieved the dates and piled them back in their bowl. The older man winked; a smile softened the hard lines of his face. 'I'll take that. Go back to your master and thank him for his hospitality. Tell him it's that very sort of kindness which makes living in such a fine establishment worthwhile. Do you understand?' Hesitant, the boy nodded. Al-Hajj rose. 'Good. This last bit is most important: tell him, God willing, I shall repay him in kind. Off with you, now.' Al-Hajj retreated into his apartments, slammed the door, and shot the bolt.

Alone, al-Hajj's anger turned cold. He sagged against the arabesqued door jamb, shaking his head. *That old fool will need to be dealt with, and soon, before his suspicions become tittle-tattle in Cairo's bazaars.* For, in this instance, Ibn Zayid's suspicions were well founded. 'Al-Hajj' was not his true name, nor did his supply of silver come from hawking trinkets along the Qasaba – though that's how he spent the better part of his days. No, the man known as al-Hajj dealt in a far more precious commodity: the flow of information; the gathering of secrets.

A small part of him pitied Ibn Zayid. Those whose cause al-Hajj served did not suffer intrusions into their business lightly. Renowned for their patience, their cunning, his employers waged a war of terror against their oppressors – Moslem, Nazarene, or Jew; they were masters of disguise who could hide among their enemies for months if need be, watching and waiting for the perfect time to strike. They had many names – as many names as the sky had stars – but their most potent appellation was the one that struck fear in sultan and slave alike: al-Hashishiyya, the Assassins, that glorious sect whose princes ruled from the unassailable heights of Alamut.

Like his anger, al-Hajj's pity faded and turned cold. He dropped the bowl on the carpet beside the platter, straightened, and returned to his work table. The tools of his trade spread across the age-worn teak: letters of introduction, of credit, and of personal business; inventory lists; ledgers showing expenses and sums; sealing wax and signets; blank sheets of fine Samarkand paper; an abacus. More than mere props, the items contained messages, some couched in superfluous gossip, others in a dizzying cipher of numbers. Ibn Zayid's death sentence would travel across the city in the same manner, as a letter to a colleague bemoaning losses in the silk market followed by a column of sums that, when matched to corresponding letters in Arabic, spelled out the old man's name. 'A petty crime,' he would mournfully tell Ibn Zayid's sons. *And Allah protect the fools from their own curiosity.*

Al-Hajj resumed his seat. He selected a square of heavy paper and took up his pen, dipping it into an antique ink-pot of Egyptian alabaster. As he began to craft his letter, however, two sounds intruded on his concentration, both sinister in the pervasive silence of the study: the creak of a wooden shutter and the soft hiss of steel on leather. He scowled, his hand going to his knife and finding only an empty sheath. *Blessed Allah, I left it by the door!* Al-Hajj turned . . .

. . . and saw a deadly apparition: a tall figure, lean as whipcord and clad in black from sole to crown. Around him, shadows parted and swirled like an infernal cloak; only his eyes were visible, and they blazed pale and fanatical. With blinding speed the apparition closed on al-Hajj, his movements predatory and graceful, the steel in his fist a blur.

Paralysed, al-Hajj watched in horror as the blade streaked closer. He kept his shutters latched; he was on the fourth floor . . . by the Prophet, who would dare? 'Who . . . ?'

And then, pain. Searing pain. It blossomed in his chest, ripping the breath from his lungs and robbing him of speech. Bone and wood crunched together. Al-Hajj could not yell; he could not curse; he could not cry out to God for succour. All he could do was writhe against the spike of cold fire that held him fast against his chair.

The apparition's eyes – *Death's eyes!* – transfixed him like lances of pale fire, staring through him with naked contempt. He leaned over, his head mere inches from al-Hajj's ear, and whispered: 'The boy was an unexpected diversion. I should thank him. Quickly, my friend. We know you are not alone in Cairo. Tell us what words will bring your comrades out of hiding.' His accent betrayed a Syrian descent. *Syrian . . .*

In agony, al-Hajj glanced down at the long knife protruding from the centre of his chest, blackened blade shimmering with blood. Its design was Frankish, with a simple bronze cross guard and a grip of sweat-stained leather. Al-Hajj wanted to reach out and grab it. He wanted to tug it free and hurl it in the bastard's face, but his arms were leaden, immobile.

'Come, my friend, speak the words,' the intruder whispered, his voice as soft as silk.

Silk. Al-Hajj blinked, tasted blood; he shivered as a chill crept up his body, as the pain in his chest and back ebbed. *God willing, I shall repay him in kind.* 'A-Ask . . .' he managed. His lips peeled back in a scarlet smile. 'Ask . . . old . . . old man . . . u-upstairs!'

The intruder straightened, eyes narrowed. His fingers flexed around the hilt of the knife; his other hand lay heavy on al-Hajj's shoulder. 'No matter. We will find them as we found you, my friend. The dead keep no secrets.' Bone grated as the intruder wrenched the blade free of al-Hajj's spine, twisted it, and sent the tip plunging into his heart.

The man who called himself al-Hajj stiffened, his mouth opening in a silent scream.

2

The caravan road cut across the Sinai like a dusty scar. Leaving the Red Sea port of Aqabah it followed ancient Bedouin trails from well to well, curling along the gorges of the Wadi al-Arish where scrub and thorn grew in the beds of long-vanished rivers; at al-Suweis, beneath the frowning heights of Jebal Ataga, the road passed a broken obelisk – its surface pocked from centuries of exposure and abuse – marking the eastern frontier of the Fatimid Caliphate of Egypt.

Assad reined in his horse and waited for Farouk to join him. The Persian's business interests often brought him to Cairo by the same road; thus, he had contacts seeded all along the route – men who listened to the news of the day and remembered those bits and pieces they knew might interest him. He repaid them in kind, or less often with gifts of precious balms, fine fabrics, or silver coin. They never suspected he was anything other than a man in love with gossip and small talk.

The road out of al-Suweis was choked with travellers, a polyglot of merchants, tradesmen, and pilgrims; three distinct caravans – one from holy Mecca, one from Damascus laden with incense, and one from Mosul bearing carpets and fine bronzework – fused into a shambling mass of men, horses, and camels. Hundreds of feet and hooves kicked up a chalky haze which refused to dissipate. It stiffened men's hair and beards and masked their faces until the passing host seemed less than human, a cavalcade of raucous spirits bound for Hell.

Assad's chestnut mare whinnied, favouring its left foreleg. He dismounted and stroked the animal's neck, murmuring to keep it calm; he knelt and raised its leg to inspect the hoof. Assad gave a sour grunt. Not only had a sliver of rock wedged itself against the mare's sensitive frog, but the horseshoe itself shifted in his grasp. Carefully, he pried the stone out and tossed it aside. The loose shoe would have to wait.

Assad straightened as Farouk, astride a roan gelding, cantered up. They were a month out of Palmyra and already the Persian looked healthier than Assad had ever seen him; he wore white trousers and a girdled kaftan beneath a cloak of finely woven blue cotton. His turban, too, was blue, with a fold under his chin to protect his nose and mouth from blowing sand. A scimitar hung from his saddle horn. 'Trouble?'

'She needs to be shod over again, this time by a farrier who knows his business. By Allah, the man who put this shoe on was a pox-riddled village half-wit.' Assad brushed away a rime of sand and dried sweat crusting his khalat, and then hitched at his sash. He rested a hand on the hilt of his salawar. 'What did your man at al-Suweis have to say?'

'Nothing good,' the Persian replied. 'He has received no word from Cairo, spoken or written, in well over a month. Passing strange, he says.'

'Perhaps they had nothing to remark upon. What news from other travellers?'

'Aside from prodigies and portents?' Farouk shrugged. 'Just the same garbled tales of pestilence and war. The Bedouin claim to have seen winged djinn in the guise of great vultures circling Jebal al-Far'on, the Mountains of Pharaoh. Others have heard the voice of the Father of Terror speaking in riddles from beneath the sands of Giza. *Bismillah!* What is the truth of it? Some say the Sudanese mercenaries have risen against the vizier and now occupy the port of Fustat; others say that Turkish soldiers set fire to that district, and that it burned for three-score-and-two days before Merciful Allah snuffed the flames in a sandstorm.'

'Likely the truth lies somewhere in the middle,' Assad said. He glanced back the way they had come, squinting through the dust to catch a glimpse of the heat-ravaged landscape through which they toiled. 'How far is it to Cairo?'

'*Inshallah*, three or four days once we break through this rabble.' He indicated the mingled caravans with a toss of his head. 'But a week or more if the khamsin arises.'

'The khamsin!' Assad spat. Those winds, born in the wastes of the Sahara, arose every spring to disrupt the cool north breeze and scourge the Nile Valley with sand and heat and madness. 'Then let us ride as though Shaitan himself dogged our path and pray our good fortune holds.'

'Pray or not, it makes no difference.' Farouk shrugged again, a gesture of resignation. 'God does not listen. If He did, I would be in a shaded garden smoking my pipe, a cool drink at my elbow, and a pair of girls to dance for my entertainment. No, my friend, prayer is useless when God turns a deaf ear to you.'

Wood and leather creaked as Assad swung up into the saddle. 'With your endless nattering,' he said, shaking his head, 'a deaf ear would be as a gift from heaven.'

3

Beyond al-Suweis the Eastern Desert began, an abode of jackals and of vultures and of desperate men. Under a white-hot sky, towering ridges of red and gold sandstone as sharp as knapped flint lorded over shifting dunes and plains of loose scree. Pools of shade existed at the small wells along the road, under dusty palm trees or stunted acacias; though at times brackish and hot, the water in these wells at least was palatable.

Assad set a punishing pace. For three days, he woke Farouk in the frigid hours before dawn and kept him in the saddle until well after dark; during the hottest part of the day, however, Assad yielded to the Persian's experience and they sought whatever shade lay close at hand. Never too long a lull, a few hours at most; then, after bolting a handful of dried dates and washing it down with a ration of blood-warm water, the pair resumed their course.

And so it was on the afternoon of the fourth day. Riding single file, Assad frowned as Farouk drew rein and stopped. The Persian glanced over his shoulder and smiled. 'Look there,' he said, pointing ahead and to the left.

Assad shaded his eyes against the westering sun and studied the horizon. He saw nothing in the shimmering heat but the gleam of sunlight on distant outcroppings of limestone, their formations jutting from a sea of tawny sand. 'Are you addled? There's nothing out there but desert.'

'Look closer.'

Assad, though, looked askance at the Persian.

'Go ahead, look closer, my friend.' Farouk gestured again. 'There, to the southwest.'

'We're wasting time,' Assad replied, but he did as Farouk asked, peering in the direction indicated. He saw the shimmer . . . the too-bright gleam of sunlight . . . too bright and too regular . . .

'What the devil is that?'

Farouk's smile widened. 'This time of day, the sun strikes just so from the minaret of the mosque of al-Jamali, at the crest of the Muqattam Hills—'

'—overlooking Cairo,' Assad said, exhaling.

'Overlooking Cairo, indeed. Praise Allah, for He is deserving of praise. Our journey is nearly at an end.'

The Assassin nodded. 'Our journey, perhaps, but our task is just beginning. Come, my Persian friend!' He spurred past Farouk, coaxing his mare to a canter. 'We're wasting daylight!'

With each passing mile signs of habitation became more in evidence, from the round black tents of the Bedouin to distant sounds of quarrying in the Muqattam Hills. Each ridge the pair crested revealed more of the Nile Valley. Like every good Egyptian, Assad learned as a child that the Nile was Africa's jugular; waters rich with nourishing black silt coursed from the country's heart to its head. In the south, the Nile was a strip of fertility like a long and narrow oasis bounded on either bank by escarpments and harsh desert. In the north, the river fanned out into six tributaries that fed the lakes and marshes of the Delta before emptying into the pale surf of the Mediterranean. Cairo sat astride the point of confluence, where north met south.

From a spur of the Muqattam, with the sun a ball of fiery copper just above the western horizon, Assad glimpsed the city of his birth again. Medinat al-Qahira, men called it, the Victorious City; ringed by fields and canals, Cairo seemed smaller than he remembered – a walled enclosure pierced by half a dozen gates, the marble domes of its mosques and palaces ablaze in the fading sunlight, its crooked streets lost in shadow. Outside the walls he noticed signs of the city's growth: markets and mausoleums, villas and lakeside gardens, all stretching south along the road to Fustat, Cairo's port, a vile-seeming jumble of mudbrick and old stone that hugged the Nile's bank like a babe on its mother's teat. Well beyond the river's western shore, Assad yet discerned the majestic peaks of the Jebal al-Far'on – the Mountains of Pharaoh: those monumental pyramids consecrated to the infidel kings of Old Egypt.

'They say he who has not seen Cairo has not seen the world.' Farouk's saddle creaked as he shifted his weight. A northerly breeze sprang up, spiced with the scents of orange blossom and Nile mud.

'I've seen the world,' Assad replied. He stared up at the fading red-gold sky. 'Cairo pales beside it. When I was a boy, I remember the Cairenes had a custom of barring the gates of the city from sunset to sunrise. Is this still so?'

Farouk nodded. 'It is, but the city's wardens have grown lax. A small coin will buy entry after dark, with no questions asked.'

'Their negligence will be to our benefit, then.' The Assassin nudged his mare forward. 'Have you a safehouse in the city?'

'Not quite.'

4

Stars flared in the firmament as Farouk guided them to their destination, a caravanserai squatting in sight of Cairo's torch-lit northern gates. Called Bab al-Futuh and Bab al-Nasr – the Gate of Conquests and the Gate of Victory – they were the traditional beginning and ending of any Fatimid general's campaign. He marched out through the former to do his Caliph's bidding and returned through the latter, or he returned not at all.

'I remember none of this,' Assad said, a toss of his head encompassing the tall stone buildings – caravanserais and commercial warehouses – with their sculpted lintels and narrow windows that lined the right-hand side of the wide Street of the Caravans, interspersed with lesser houses of brick and painted stucco; some boasted small, manicured gardens. 'Twenty-two years ago all of this was a parade field.'

'Time is a most diligent soldier,' Farouk replied. 'It marches on without respite and without care. Who can say? In another twenty-two years this might be a parade field yet again. Only Allah in His infinite wisdom knows these things.'

As far as Assad could tell, nightfall brought no appreciable lull to the business along the Street of the Caravans. Torchbearers and armed guards accompanied men in fine robes as they went about arranging the division and distribution of goods, their slaves darting from warehouse to warehouse with messages and bills of lading and contracts for ratification. The Caliph's market inspectors were never far behind, assuring that weights and measures were accurate and that they paid in full the taxes the Prince of the Faithful levied on imported goods. Lesser merchants met their peers in the shadow of the great mercantile houses, sitting together on cushions to share news along with bowls of date wine and pipes of hashish. Some of these men greeted Farouk by name.

'*As-salaam alaikum*, brothers!' the Persian said. 'Seek me out later in the week, my friends! I have a shipment of incense coming,

the finest in all of Arabia! I will give you good prices, no? You, boy!'
Farouk called out to a young slave. He fished a small coin from a
pouch at his belt and flipped it off his thumb. 'If your master
allows, run ahead to the inn of Abu Hamza and tell that
honourable fellow to expect company this evening! Tell him
Farouk of Palmyra sends his compliments!'

The boy caught the coin in mid-air and sprinted off without
waiting for his master's approval. Farouk dismounted; Assad
followed suit, trusting that the Persian had good reason for it. He
stood by silently, holding the reins of both their horses as Farouk
ambled over to a knot of men who sat near the entrance to one of
the more affluent caravanserais, arrayed on carpets and cushions
beneath an arched window. Sweet smoke coiled from their water
pipes as they watched the evening market unfold, ever curious.
Farouk greeted them warmly.

'My friends! Khaled, you're looking well! How is your son,
Umar? What goes, brothers? I heard rumours in Palmyra, tales of
riots and ill omens and of flames devouring the city! I hurried
ahead of my caravan to see for myself, to salvage what I could. Yet
here I stand, looking upon a pleasant gathering of learned men.
Allah smite those who would speak such lies in my ear!' The men
jostled and moved aside, making room for Farouk to join their
circle. The Persian crouched beside Umar. He was the eldest
among them, a grey-bearded man, thin and elegant in his white
galabiyya and turban-wrapped tarboush.

''Twas not wholly lies, Farouk,' he said. 'For a time we thought
the End of All Things had indeed come.'

'Aye,' the others echoed. 'Hearken, by the blessed Prophet,
Umar speaks true.'

'You must tell me this tale, Umar!'

Assad shifted, watching the street as he eavesdropped on their
conversation. He assumed the role of Farouk's bored bodyguard,
adjusting his stance and manner so that passers-by who noticed
him would see precisely that: a freebooter marking time until his
master no longer needed him.

Water burbled as old Umar took a draw from his pipe, held it, and then exhaled, the cloud of smoke wreathing his head. 'Do you know, Farouk, that among the warlike Mamelukes, the White Slaves of the River who guard the Caliph's person and make his slightest wish a reality, there are two great companies: one whose ranks are filled with Turks, and another whose members are Circassians from the distant Caucasus? They are slaves, aye, but they are renowned as much for their loyalty as for their prowess at arms. Still, nigh upon two months ago the unthinkable happened; one of the Caliph's Circassian Mamelukes, a young man full of vigour and pride whose name escapes me, fell from favour and was dismissed from his post at the Caliph's side. What his original infraction was, I know not, but—'

Khaled, a sallow-faced man with a bristling black beard and suspicious eyes, interrupted. 'He was a Circassian. That sort needs no reason to flaunt God and the Prophet.' The other listeners hissed Khaled to silence.

Umar continued: 'Whatever his sin, he compounded it by going forth into Fustat and carousing with a decidedly seditious element, men who hate peace and good order as Allah hates the Infidel.' Umar leaned closer. 'They convinced this malcontent to re-enter the palace and sheathe his sword in the Prince of the Faithful's breast! Can you countenance such a thing? And his fellow Mamelukes who were guarding the doors to the Golden Hall that day, they allowed him to pass! My nephew – you remember him, Farouk? He was the one who bought half your last shipment of incense – he was there to petition the Caliph for a lessening of our taxes and saw the whole sorry episode unfold. What with all the courtiers and eunuchs twittering about the throne, he said this godforsaken Circassian got as close to the blessed Caliph as I am from you before someone took note and raised an alarm.'

'Allah's mercies upon his keen eye, whoever he is,' Farouk murmured, a sentiment echoed by others. Assad noticed several other men, merchants and caravaneers, had wandered over and now stood at the periphery, listening as Umar told his tale – one they had doubtless heard a thousand times over. Still, the old man relished their attention; he paused for dramatic effect and took a long drag from his water pipe.

'Who stopped him, this godless Circassian?' someone asked. 'Was it a great cavalier or a cunning servant?'

Umar shook his head. 'It was the vizier himself. The Circassian was so intent upon the Caliph – almost as if he was blind to all else, my nephew said – that he did not see the vizier approaching on his right hand. Without a word, that worthy man snatched the Mameluke's own dagger from his girdle and drove it into his heart!' Umar pantomimed the killing, tugging a curved knife from his belt and stabbing the air. 'Once! Twice! Thrice! Until the infidel lay dead at his feet.' Feigning exhaustion, the old man dropped the knife into his lap. 'Well, it was chaos after that. The Turkish Mamelukes blamed their Circassian brothers for this lapse in the Caliph's defence; the Circassians blamed the accursed Jews and Nazarenes lurking in Fustat for corrupting one of their own, and the vizier blamed the lot of them – whence spring your rumours of riots and fires, Farouk. For a month, Fustat ran red with blood as Circassian, Jew, and Nazarene fought one another, looted, and destroyed. Finally, acting on the blessed Caliph's behalf, the vizier sent Sudanese mercenaries into Fustat to quell the riots, then expelled all the Mamelukes from the palace! The Turks were ordered to garrison Cairo's gates, while the vizier reduced the Circassians to a wretched existence as mere foot soldiers in the urban militia.'

'Surely, though, the vizier would not leave the palace undefended?' Farouk said.

'Allah forbid! No, that task has gone to another band of mercenaries called the Jandariyah, Syrian Arabs hired out from under the very nose of the Sultan of Damascus, God curse him . . .'

Assad turned slightly and stared at the back of Farouk's head. *But what of the Caliph,* he wanted to ask. The whole story sounded almost too pat, too convenient, as though someone in the palace –

indeed, in the Caliph's own circle – had engineered it as a way of removing the threat of the Mamelukes. As Umar had said, these slave-soldiers were fiercely loyal to their master and would have presented a major stumbling block to an enemy who sought to remove the Caliph. Handily, someone circumvented them and put mercenaries in their place. But who? The vizier? The commander of the army? Some faceless chamberlain who preferred the anonymity of the shadows? Or could it truly be as simple as a dis-graced Circassian seeking to expunge the stain on his honour with blood?

Assad needed more to go on. He—

A commotion behind him, from farther down the street, crushed his ruminations like a mace. He heard the approach of horsemen, their clatter all but drowned out by a rising tide of voices – curses, cries of outrage, and the shrill screams of unseen women: '*Al-Dawiyyah! Allah yil'anak! God curse the wretched Infidels! Al-Dawiyyah!*' Assad spun; harness rattled as his and Farouk's horses whinnied and tossed their heads, spooked by the sudden cacophony. '*Al-Dawiyyah!*'

The Assassin spotted a squadron of cavalry cantering towards the Gate of Victory; most of the horsemen were Sudanese, lightly armoured lancers wearing the black cloaks and turbans of Fatimid soldiery. The two men they escorted, however, were neither Arab nor Moslem. They were Franks: mailed knights astride great prancing stallions, their white surcoats sporting the blood-red cross of the Order of the Temple.

Al-Dawiyyah. Templars.

The sight of that hated symbol of Nazarene arrogance brought a curse to Assad's lips. A dream-image flashed through his mind: *a design in blood caking the chest of the figure's surcoat: a cross, red on white. The stench of death clung to it . . .*

The Assassin's fingers curled around the hilt of his salawar; the hate radiating from that blade paled against the naked fury already coursing through his body. Assad's eyes blazed. His jaw clenched and unclenched. He wanted to rip into their bellies and tear out their entrails, hack them apart as they had hacked apart defenceless captives at Ascalon. Assad wanted to drink Templar blood.

It took every scrap of resolve he possessed to simply stand still and watch them pass – *let* them pass – when in his soul the spirits of long-dead friends cried out for vengeance. *Soon, brothers. Soon.* Slowly, finger by finger, he let loose his salawar as the cortège vanished into Cairo.

The Gate of Victory trundled shut, hinges squealing.

With a promise to break bread with them tomorrow, Farouk left his clutch of friends and went to stand beside Assad. 'A curious thing,' the Persian muttered. The tumult of the Templars' passage faded as men returned to their business, drifting back inside their caravanserais and warehouses, their moods darker. 'Come, let's be off.'

'No. I want to know what deviltry is afoot! Why is the Caliph consorting with the dogs of Jerusalem? In the name of God, who rules Cairo? Is that too difficult a question?'

Farouk shrugged, clapping Assad on the shoulder. 'We are tired. Perhaps we cannot see the truth of it? Come, let us repair to the house of Abu Hamza. A bath and a meal will no doubt foster much-needed clarity—'

'I have all the clarity I need. What I don't have are answers.' Assad passed him the reins of both horses. 'You go on ahead and ply your contacts. Find out what you can.'

'What of you? Where will you be?'

The tall Arab pushed past Farouk and headed for the Gate of Conquests, his mind already on the names Daoud had given him. When he looked back, his eyes were like slits of cold fire. 'Plying contacts of my own.'

5

Behind Cairo's walls, in the sumptuous East Palace of the Fatimid Caliphs, the most powerful man in all of Egypt contemplated his next move. He studied his adversary closely, recalling the adage that a weakness of the body did not necessarily translate to a weakness of the mind. His adversary, perched on a divan across from him, was a wizened old eunuch, sharp-featured and pale, his bulging belly and pendulous breasts hidden beneath a loose galabiyya of finely woven black linen. He watched as the eunuch's palsied hand hovered over the game pieces arrayed between them. *Weak in body, not weak in mind.*

Lamplight gleamed from the edges of the elegant shatranj board, its squares fashioned of milky alabaster and deep green tourmaline. Pawns of ivory and silver confronted those of ebony and gold, while tall horsemen, crenellated rukhs, stately elephants, and bearded wazirs defended their jewel-encrusted shahs.

With excruciating slowness, the eunuch selected an ivory elephant and used it to capture one of the man's ebony pawns, adding it to the four he already possessed. 'It is not always flash and glitter that wins a battle, vizier,' the eunuch said. 'Sometimes, victory can be achieved through the simple act of attrition.'

'You are as predictable as the Nile, my old darling,' the vizier, Jalal, said. He moved one of his rukhs into position to threaten the eunuch's shah. 'And you know nothing of battle.'

The eunuch smiled, his teeth yellowed kernels. 'Ah, the blessed river may be predictable,' he said, 'but does that make it any less dangerous?' Deftly, he drew a horseman back to protect his shah. 'Tread with care, my friend.'

Jalal sat back, studied the board. He was a tall man, lean and dark, with heavy-lidded eyes and a sensuous mouth that lent his predatory features an aspect of wanton cruelty; traces of grey flecked his goatee. Clad in a silken robe girdled with satin brocade and a pearl-sewn turban, he reclined easily on his cushioned divan and reached behind him, past the remnants of his evening meal, for a goblet of wine. Slave and master sat beneath a colonnade, on a marble portico overlooking one of the palace's many small gardens. Delicate lamps of gilded glass hung from the branches of willows and sycamores, casting bands of light and shadow over a cobbled path that wound past the burbling fountain. A chorus of crickets drowned out the sounds of Cairo settling in for the night.

Jalal glanced up. 'How is our Caliph this evening, Mustapha?'

'Restless,' the old eunuch replied. 'For days he has wanted no more of the opium pipe, so this night we were forced to mix the juice of the poppy with his wine instead. He sleeps, but fitfully. I do not know how much longer we can continue this, Excellency. Al-Hasan grows resistant to my arts.'

The vizier's eyes narrowed. 'How comes this resistance? You're giving him the full measure, are you not?'

'The full measure and more besides, when he will take it. His dreams are the culprit, Excellency. They give him hope, and in hope he finds the strength to resist. As Allah is my witness, I fear the day is coming when he will try to assert his authority over you, when he will seek to truly reign as Caliph and not simply as a figurehead. His dreams tell him this. He also dreams of his Circassian friend, the one you killed before his eyes, and he demands we send for a Sufi to aid him in interpreting these visions. I do not know how much longer we can deny him, Excellency.'

Jalal sighed, picked up a captured pawn, and studied the detail. It resembled a tiny Mameluke, carved from African ivory and accented with fine silver, clutching sword and shield as it awaited the hand of its master. *Ready to die like a good slave.* 'Perhaps,' he said after a moment, 'it is time our poor young Caliph is stricken with the illness of his forefathers.'

Mustapha arched an eyebrow. 'So soon, Excellency? Are you prepared for the chaos his death will engender? The common folk love him . . .'

The vizier returned the pawn to the table's edge. 'And so? Who among the peasants would dare thwart me? Who among the courtiers and officers, for that matter? Not the Jandariyah, for their captain answers to me alone. Not the Turks or the Circassian Mamelukes, for we have winnowed their ranks and thrust their leaders to the margins of influence. All that remains are the Sudanese mercenaries – a contentious lot, to be sure – but so long as their prince, Wahshi, is well paid he will do as I command. Allow the Caliph to linger for a month, Mustapha, and my position will be unassailable. I *will* be Sultan.'

The old eunuch nodded. 'So be it, Excellency. By week's end, our dear al-Hasan will be in the grips of a terrible fever. No doubt mortal.'

'Sometimes,' Jalal said, his lips curling into a devilish smile, 'the answer to a problem is profoundly simple.' He reached out and decisively moved a humble pawn forward to capture one of the eunuch's elephants.

Mustapha sat up straight. The remaining pieces on the shatranj board assumed an ominous symmetry. 'You're using Dilaram? Oh, you are a cunning one, Excellency. Cunning, indeed. But is it enough to be cunning? That is the question—'

Before Mustapha could continue, however, another eunuch interrupted – this one well muscled and as black as the Abyssinian night, his skin in marked contrast to his red silk pantaloons and gold-scaled vest. He abased himself on the cold marble beside the vizier.

Jalal glanced over. 'Speak.'

'Two men have arrived in Cairo seeking an audience, Excellency. Franks, from Jerusalem, under a banner of peace. They are . . . they are Templars, Excellency.'

Both the vizier and Mustapha's eyes narrowed with suspicion. 'Surely a ruse,' the old eunuch said, tugging absently at the loose flesh under his chin. 'When have those Infidel jackals ever honoured a flag of peace? I would wager they are not Templars at all, but Assassins.'

Jalal gestured for silence. 'What are their names?'

'Hugh of Caesarea, Excellency, and with him a man called Godfrey. They claim to be messengers from King Amalric, bearing grave news. More they would not say. Shall we execute them or imprison them, Excellency?'

After a moment's pause, Jalal responded with a brusque shake of his head. 'Neither. Escort them to the Golden Hall. I will speak with them before I pass judgement.'

'Hearkening and obeying, Excellency.' The Abyssinian eunuch salaamed and hurried off to do the vizier's bidding.

Jalal looked back at the chess board. 'So, my old darling, you were saying something about cunning?'

6

The twin minarets of the mosque of al-Hakim, whom men called the Mad Caliph, gleamed like naked bone against the night sky. This ruined edifice – long since abandoned as a place of worship – straddled the walls of Cairo between the Gate of Conquests and the Gate of Victory, its covered galleries and sharply crenellated bastions indistinguishable from the city's own ramparts. A crumbling portico jutted into a broad unpaved square where by day fruit-sellers and garlic merchants set up their stalls; by night, square and mosque were the abode of beggars.

Cairo had its share of mendicants and fakirs – gadflies who cajoled travellers or spun exotic tales in exchange for coin – but most of those who clustered about the mosque of the Mad Caliph were truly wretched, the diseased and the insane whose existence depended upon the whims of Moslem generosity. Few regarded them as human; most paid them little heed. The blighted aura of pestilence and death that clung to the mosque of al-Hakim provided the perfect camouflage for an agent of al-Hashishiyya.

The spies of Alamut hide in plain sight, my young Emir, Daoud ar-Rasul had said. *Chief among them is one called al-Hajj, the Pilgrim. He lurks near the old mosque between the gates, posing as a poor merchant even as he watches the comings and goings. When you find him, speak thus in the tongue of Persia: 'Sharp-eyed are the eagles in the minarets of Nizar', and he will know you as a comrade of the Hidden Master . . .*

Assad stalked across the square, slow and predatory. A thin mud of trampled fruit and excrement squelched underfoot; clouds of stinging flies arose with each step. During the day, merchants paid a few bits of silver for a man to wander the market and sweeten the air with a censer. After nightfall, however, the incense faded, leaving behind a ghastly stench of human waste and rotting garlic. None of the beggars picking through the offal left behind by the fruit-sellers accosted Assad, nor tried to bar his way; one glance at his scarred face, at the deadly gleam in his eyes, at the well-worn hilt of his salawar, was enough to convince them to mind their business.

Assad remembered this place from his childhood, though he rarely had occasion to travel into this quarter of the city. His father had died when he was a boy; he and his mother – a laundry-woman – had joined the household of his uncle, a well-respected cadi who lived outside the Zuwayla Gate, on the road to Fustat. The old gatekeeper of the house, also called Hakim, loved to regale him with bloody tales of his namesake, the Mad Caliph. *He lives inside his mosque,* Hakim would say, his wide eyes bloodshot and glassy, breath reeking of wine. *And it is to his mosque that ghûls and djinn bring the hearts of children who do not recite their Qur'an properly. Do you know your Qur'an, boy?* Assad's lips thinned in a half-smile. Hakim and his stories were one of the few fond memories he had of Cairo.

Flakes of old limestone crunched underfoot as the Assassin ascended the steps of the mosque's portico. Sickly light streamed out through a yawning archway that led into the interior, giving him enough illumination to see – and to be seen. 'I seek al-Hajj!' he said to the beggars clustered beneath the portico. 'Is he here?' The ragged figures flinched and yammered at the sound of Assad's voice. They shrank from him and slunk away, or simply crouched against the wall with their faces averted.

Assad passed beneath the arch and entered the mosque's court-yard. Ancient columns like palm-trunks hewn from yellowed marble held up the decaying arcade; a century and more of filth and neglect caked the floor while the soot of countless small fires blackened the walls. Beggars stirred at his intrusion, their fear giving way to annoyance; from the shadows he caught the glint of rheumy eyes and heard muttered voices. A mad cackle echoed about the courtyard before it degenerated into a fit of coughing.

'Al-Hajj!' Assad called out. Pox-scarred faces glared at him. 'Gold to the man who can show me to al-Hajj!'

After a moment, a voice bellowed in return: 'Who wants to know?' Assad's head turned; across the courtyard, in the corner where a fire burned beneath a mottled pepper-pot dome, six men sat apart from the other beggars, dicing for scraps of fruit. In appearance they were as thin and ragged as the rest, but their faces lacked any hint of insanity. The one who spoke canted his head to one side to stare at Assad with his good eye, black and glittering. His other was nothing but a scarred socket.

'Are you al-Hajj?'

'Who wants to know, I said!'

Assad moved out from beneath the arcade and walked towards them, his temper checked by the thinnest thread of reason. 'I am but a messenger, sent by an old friend of al-Hajj.'

'Bah!' The one-eyed man grunted. 'That whoreson has no friends!'

'You know him, then? Do you know where I can find him?'

'Aye on both scores, praise be to Allah. I know him and I know where he is.' The men around him stiffened as Assad drew closer, their hands dropping from sight. Whoever this man was, with his wiry russet beard and fey locks escaping from beneath a sweat-stained scarlet turban, they thought him important enough to defend.

'Take me to him. I'll make it worth your while.'

'I doubt it not, but he is easy enough to find on your own, stranger. You need only go south, out of the Zuwayla Gate, and follow the road to Ibn Tulun's mosque on the outskirts of al-Karafa cemetery. You know it? Good. Ask anyone there, and they will show you al-Hajj's grave.' The men around him chuckled. 'Tell him Musa sends his regards.'

'Musa, is it?' Assad's hand dropped to the hilt of his blade as he took a menacing step towards the one-eyed beggar. 'Do you think it wise to toy with me, Musa?'

To his credit, Musa did not flinch. 'I don't know you, stranger, as you don't know me. Perhaps humour at your expense is unwise, but so is assuming I have lied to you. Al-Hajj has been dead a week now, knifed in the caravanserai where he dwelt, not far from here. I found him myself.'

'Are you certain it was al-Hajj?'

Musa tilted his head, showing Assad the burned-out socket of his eye. 'Though I have but one of these left, I can still tell a man I've broken bread with from one I haven't.'

'Who killed him?'

'Only Allah, in His magnificent wisdom, can answer that.'

Assad said nothing, his face a mask carved of cold stone. He dipped two fingers into the sash at his waist and brought forth a small linen bag; coins chinked as it struck the ground in front of Musa. 'My thanks.' With that, Assad turned and retraced his steps from the ruined mosque.

7

Musa watched the stranger leave; he reached down and picked up the bag, holding it for a moment, weighing it in the palm of his hand. His good eye narrowed to a slit. With a sharp gesture, he summoned a pair of his men closer. 'Follow him. Find out who he is and what his business was with al-Hajj.'

Silently, the children of the Mad Caliph drifted out after the stranger.

8

Three-quarters of an hour later, Jalal left the palace courtyard – and left Mustapha shaking his head, grumbling at how the vizier had beaten him in six moves. 'Predictable, as I said,' Jalal had said, smiling at the old eunuch who had been his tutor and mentor as a child. That smile faded now as he padded down a dim tapestry-hung hallway, bracing himself for his audience with the Templars.

Templars! A foul taste filled Jalal's mouth at the thought of those Infidels breathing the rarified air of thrice-blessed Cairo. What was that Nazarene, Amalric, playing at? Of course, the King of Jerusalem had sent messages to Cairo in the past – from offers of friendship and alliance to outright threats and blandishments – for the pig made no secret of his desire to add Egypt to his demesne, by war or by wiles. But grave news delivered on Amalric's behalf by the most devout enemies of Islam? To Jalal, that smacked of a less-than-subtle deception.

The vizier passed through doors of polished teakwood bound in straps of arabesqued gold, guarded by Syrian mercenaries in spired helmets and coats of gilded mail, naked swords gleaming; chamberlains, servants, and eunuchs scurried clear of his path, bowing low. The East Palace was no single structure; rather, it was an aggregation of palaces and mosques, a labyrinth of courtyards and galleries, vaulted corridors and ivy-shaded arcades. At its heart – and indeed at the spiritual heart of all Fatimid Egypt – lay the Golden Hall of al-Mu'izz li-Din Allah.

Built for the first Fatimid Caliph whose name it bore, the

Golden Hall stood as a testament to the wealth and power of the Princes of the Faithful and True Successors of the Prophet Muhammad, a bastion of Shi'ite glory amid a sea of Sunni heresy. Jalal gained entry through a small side door that opened on the curtained alcove housing the Seat of Divine Reason, the throne of the Caliph. This rested beneath a canopy of golden Mosul silk, sewn with pearls and precious stones, on a stepped dais of pale white marble – a chair of gilded teak and ivory cushioned in white velvet. Jalal gazed upon it with a lust that transcended the flesh, his face growing hot with desire. *Give me a month! A month and my position will be unassailable! I will be Sultan!* The vizier's covetous eyes lingered over his master's throne a moment longer before he pushed past the silken curtain and entered the Hall proper.

Domed in gold-filigreed alabaster and paved in the same snowy marble as the dais, the cavernous Golden Hall was deserted save for the Abyssinian eunuch and a score of the mercenary Jandariyah, all of whom scowled with open contempt at the two awe-struck Templars – the first of their accursed kind to gain admittance to this holy sanctuary. Nor was the grandeur of their surroundings lost on them. The pair described slow circles, whispering to one another in coarse Norman French, their blunt faces tilted heavenward as they tried in vain to calculate the wealth on display around them. Empty scabbards clanked against their mailed thighs, the sounds amplified by the Hall's perfect acoustics.

'Hearken!' the eunuch barked in Arabic, a tongue the two Templars evidently understood. 'His Excellency Jalal al-Aziz ibn al-Rahman, vizier of Egypt!' He prostrated himself, and the soldiers followed suit; only the Templars remained standing, though they paid Jalal his due respect after the fashion of their people, with a curt bow. The Abyssinian, his dark face a mask of scorn, arose and gestured to the Franks. 'Excellency, I present you the Amir Hugh, who styles himself a prince of Caesarea, and his companion, Godfrey de Vézelay.'

Jalal arched an eyebrow. 'Templars? Your order is well known in Cairo, and not for its good works. You risk much by coming here. What is this grave news you claim to carry?'

Hugh of Caesarea stepped forward. The Frankish knight was a bull of a man, short by Jalal's standards but thickly muscled; great blond moustaches drooped from the corners of his mouth. 'My lord,' he said in crudely accented Arabic, his voice echoing off the walls with their scalloped niches and frost-white columns. 'We come to you in peace and in the hour of your need!'

'And what need is that?'

Hugh glanced at his companion, Godfrey de Vézelay, a saturnine, black-haired Frank with pox-scarred features and eyes as flat and lustreless as those of a crocodile. A ghost of a sneer curled his thin lips. 'God's teeth, man! Are you so busy plotting amongst yourselves that you have no spies in Damascus? An army from that accursed city marches on Cairo as we speak!'

From all about came sharp intakes of breath, followed by curses and deprecations and offers from the soldiers to remove the Frank's lying tongue. The vizier stilled them with a gesture. 'I warn you, Infidel,' he said, a dangerous purr in his voice, 'truce or no, you play a game that can only end with your death. My patience has its limits . . .'

Hugh's face darkened. 'We play no games with you, Saracen. Upon our oaths to God, we speak the truth! A Damascene army blessed by Sultan Nur ad-Din himself is bound for Cairo. What's more, that Kurdish devil Shirkuh – the Sultan's own lap-dog! – commands it, and with him comes a man you know all too well: your predecessor, Dirgham.'

For an instant, the vizier forgot the rules of decorum. His arm shot out; his fingers knotted in the coarse fabric of the Templar's surcoat. 'Dirgham? Are you certain?'

'He marches with Shirkuh, by God! Doubtless he is the instigator of all this as well. A dozen times since seeking asylum in Syria has Dirgham petitioned King Amalric for an army, one he could use to recover what you stole from him . . . control of Egypt. And a dozen times King Amalric has refused him. Shirkuh, it seems, is more easily swayed.'

'Shirkuh easily swayed? Not likely. If what you say is true, then no doubt the dog-Kurd has his own reasons for aiding Dirgham.' Jalal loosed the Frankish knight and stared at nothing, his eyes as cold and hard as the stone underfoot. *Dirgham!* The name was anathema in Jalal's presence, expunged from the tongues of courtiers by the promise of violence and blackened in popular memory by the spreading of horrific tales. *Dirgham!* That father-less son of local Arabs had been a relic of Rashid al-Hasan's father's reign, a minor chamberlain who wormed himself into the young Caliph's confidence. He played the role of teacher, declaim-ing to the world that he only had Rashid's best interests at heart even as he plotted to strip the boy of his power, if not his life. Three years past, in the opening gambit of his drive to become Sultan of Egypt, Jalal's mercenaries dismantled Dirgham's network of support, killing or discrediting all his allies until the man had no choice but to flee Cairo in the night – a step ahead of the executioner's sword. 'And now he's back, may the jackals gnaw his liver!' the vizier muttered. He glanced suddenly between the two Templars. 'What does Amalric seek to gain from this? Why would he send you to warn us?'

'He seeks peace,' Hugh said, 'and an alliance against Nur ad-Din. The Sultan of Damascus grows too strong for Amalric to resist on his own, even with the power of the Temple behind him, and our fellow Christians are too busy scheming against one another to recognize the threat he represents. Thus, King Amalric offers his hand to you in friendship. Should you wish it, Jerusalem will come with all due haste to Cairo's defence.'

'And you, Templar? What do you and your brothers hope to gain?'

'Our master, Arnaud de Razès, is charged by the Pope himself with protecting Jerusalem and the Holy Temple. Sometimes, that protection must be bought or bartered for. In truth, aiding you and your filthy Saracens betrays our oath to God, but harsh times often require harsh measures. If our master commands it, we Templars will fight for Cairo as we fight for Jerusalem.'

Jalal turned his back on Hugh and walked a short distance away, his arms folded across his chest. Slender fingers plucked at his goatee. He believed the Templar spoke true, that an army from Damascus was marching on Cairo; that Shirkuh commanded it and Dirgham travelled in its train. And he was certain, too, that a Nazarene army stood upon his doorstep, snuffling like a jackal after the lion's scraps. Of course he believed the Templar. What fool would craft such an elaborate lie? But a tremendous chasm existed between belief and trust. Amalric had other motives besides peace, of that Jalal had no doubt. And yet, he and Amalric did share a common enemy in Shirkuh ibn Shadhi: a devout Sunni who lumped Fatimid and Frank together in the same pile of offal. Jalal, though, preferred to look at it in terms of his nascent bid for the sultanate: whose friendship would prove most advantageous in the coming months? Damascus or Jerusalem?

'What exactly would Amalric bring to this union?' Jalal said, turning.

'Eleven hundred knights,' Hugh replied, 'and eight thousand men-at-arms. We would require from you supplies and forage, and a secure base from which to operate should Shirkuh decide to prolong his campaign beyond a single engagement.'

Jalal nodded, lapsing back into thoughtful silence. His own forces were weak and divided. Besides the Jandariyah, a thousand strong, he knew Wahshi, Prince of the Sudanese mercenaries, would answer his call with five thousand savage fighters; he could reconstitute the White Slaves of the River from the two thousand Circassians he had exiled to the ranks of the urban militia and the three thousand Turks who now defended Cairo's gates. And, if Allah smiled upon him, perhaps he could assemble a draft of levies from Fustat to serve under the Sudanese . . .

And perhaps the waters of the Nile will turn to wine! In a moment of sickening clarity, Jalal realized he had no hope of defeating either army with only the forces at his disposal. He needed an ally. *But who? Not Shirkuh. So long as Dirgham remains alive, he and his master in Damascus are a threat to my plans. It must be the*

Franks, then. The vizier hid his disgust at this decision with a smile.

'We are beset by a common foe, it seems,' he said at length. 'One that would see us both driven to extinction. Therefore I see great benefit in an alliance between Cairo and Jerusalem, a pact of friendship and mutual defence against Damascus. If Amalric can offer his hand freely and without expectation, then surely I can accept it with graciousness.' Jalal extended his hand to Hugh of Caesarea. 'We welcome your lord's aid.'

The Templar clasped his hand and matched the vizier's smile tooth for tooth, a gesture Jalal presumed as insincere as his own. 'We must move quickly then,' Hugh said. 'Shirkuh's strength is in his speed. For all we know, he has crossed Sinai already and is lurking in the desert east of here. Among my possessions is a dovecote of pigeons. If it pleases you, have your man fetch it while I prepare a message for King Amalric.' The Templar's smile widened. 'He awaits your answer at Bilbeis.'

Thirty miles north of Cairo, Bilbeis stood at the head of the ancient caravan road that connected Egypt with southern Palestine. But if Hugh of Caesarea meant to startle Jalal with that revelation he was surely disappointed. The vizier hid his consternation behind a bland smile. Already his thoughts were elsewhere, focused on weaving knots of deception around this new-found alliance. Once the game had played out, once victory over the Damascenes was assured, these knots would become useful in strangling Frankish ambitions. *Cairo's body is its weakness, not its mind. Not its mind.* The vizier motioned to the Abyssinian eunuch. 'This one will see to your needs. Please, my friends, I pray you accept the Caliph's hospitality, at least until your lord arrives.'

Hugh started to speak, but Godfrey de Vézelay cut him off. The taciturn Frank stared at the vizier as though trying through an act of will to crack open his ribs and peer into his heart. 'Are we to be privy to the Caliph's counsel, Lord Saracen, or is it his intent to simply fob us off on his underlings?'

Jalal's smile never faltered, though his eyes betrayed no trace of humour. 'The Caliph's counsel is none of your concern, Templar, and in matters of war it is customary for the amirs of the land to meet in congress. When I convene them on this matter, if you are in attendance it will be by the grace of Allah and my own good humour. See they are well cared for!' he ordered the eunuch, who bowed low. Then, with a curt nod to his guests, Jalal spun and retraced his steps from the Golden Hall.

Neither he nor the Templars noticed the kohl-dark eyes glaring at them from the depths of a shadowed niche.

9

The vizier's departure signalled a general exodus from the Golden Hall. The Abyssinian eunuch gestured for the scowling Templars to accompany him; he escorted them through a pair of mammoth gilded doors, each as tall as ten men. The soldiers followed in their wake. The rustle of cloth and leather and the clash of harness all abruptly ceased as those vast portals clanged shut, the reverberations fading until silence once again ruled the Golden Hall of al-Mu'izz li-Din Allah.

Had someone remained behind, after a score of heartbeats they would have heard a faint *snick*, followed by the silky grate of oiled stone as a section of wall inside the shadowed niche – decorated with a frieze of geometric shapes and Arabic script – swung inward. A moment later they would have marvelled at the sight of a woman inching forth, young and as slender as a Nile reed, her face pale with dread. She wore a gown of soft grey linen beneath a blue mantle embroidered in silver and a shawl of gold-fringed silk; her slippered feet made hardly a sound as she crept into the open, smoky eyes flickering from the door to the curtained alcove where stood the Caliph's throne.

The young woman trembled violently, as much from anger as from fear. She hadn't meant to eavesdrop – it was mere curiosity and the whim of Allah that put her in that niche in the first place – and yet she could scarce credit what she had heard, what she had seen. The vizier, a man the Caliph entrusted with good governance, treating with the enemies of God? Forging alliances with the Nazarenes against fellow Moslems? And, most blasphemous of all, committing such treachery in the very shadow of the Seat of Divine Reason? 'Most Merciful and Compassionate Allah,' the woman, Parysatis, whispered in her native Persian, 'why could I not have been born a man?'

A man, she reasoned, could have gone forth and shouted the vizier's perfidy in the streets, railed against it in the squares and the souks. Yet, as a woman, whom could she tell? Whom did she know in a position of authority, powerful enough to denounce the vizier? Certainly not the eunuchs of the Caliph's harem, where she was the most minor of concubines, one girl in a hundred, who ostensibly only left its confines when the Prince of the Faithful required a beautiful puppet for the evening. Often, she rejoiced in the fact that her keepers were an incompetent lot; their benevolent neglect allowed her to slip away and explore the warren of ancient and largely forgotten passages hewn into the palace walls – passages she had heard spoken of in tales, but whose existence she discovered quite by accident. Still, those same eunuchs, with their power on the wane, would likely kill to possess her secret: a network of spy holes that even the vizier seemed unaware of.

If she could not tell the eunuchs, then whom? The Caliph's aunts, perhaps? Parysatis almost laughed at that. No, those harridans were too busy plotting against one another to care what went on outside the harem walls. Save for Yasmina, a slave-girl gifted to her by one of Cairo's leading courtesans, Parysatis was alone. Alone, and saddled now with damning information. Tears sparkled at the corners of her eyes. Who could help her? Whom could she trust to relieve her of this burden? The soldiers? Their officers? Who?

Why not go the Caliph himself?

The voice in the back of her mind was the voice of her father, a staunch Shi'ite nobleman of old Persian stock from Shiraz who had bequeathed her, his only child, to the Prince of the Faithful as part of his estate. She remembered him as a straightforward man, almost blunt. Two years in the grave and his memory was no less frank.

Why not go the Caliph?

Parysatis turned and stared at the silken curtain hiding the Caliph's throne from view, her eyes narrowing in thought. She knew a way to reach him: through a slender door hidden in the scalloped niche behind the Seat of Divine Reason, a passage that led straight to al-Hasan's apartments – but would he listen? And if he listened, would he act?

Why not?

Tears of frustration dried on Parysatis' cheek. Though she'd only been in Rashid al-Hasan's presence a handful of times, never had she sensed undue malice in the young Caliph. She thought him a just ruler, as achingly handsome as the cavaliers in the epic *Shah-Nameh*, and outspoken in his hatred for the Nazarenes of Jerusalem. 'He would not want this,' she murmured, shaking her head. The Caliph deserved to know what evils his vizier perpetrated in his name. *And I must tell him, for no one else will.* A growing sense of duty bolstered her resolve as Parysatis crossed to the gold-crusted curtain and twitched it aside.

Her breath caught in her throat at the sight of the Seat of Divine Reason, a relic of the Fatimid Caliphs who traced their lineage back to the Prophet Muhammad through his daughter, Fatimah. The Seat was said to have been the Prophet's own, the chair he used when he instructed his children and his followers in the ways of Islam, though adorned in later times with ivory and gold. The Seat had power; Parysatis felt it, her skin prickling as though the faith of the righteous and the pure emanated from the wood itself. It emboldened her, reassuring her that she was doing the right thing. With reverence, the young woman ascended the dais, veiling her face with the end of her shawl and keeping her eyes averted.

The niche at the back of the dais was indistinguishable from the others in the Golden Hall, its stone similarly embellished and scalloped, covered in frieze-work and script. Its function followed that of other doors Parysatis had discovered; deep-cut geometric designs camouflaged the catch. To trigger it, one had only to know what to look for. Parysatis' hands moved over the carvings, applying pressure until a knot of stone gave way beneath her fingertips; she heard a faint *click*, and with hardly any effort she pushed the narrow door open and stepped inside.

She gave thanks, for once, at being born a woman; a man, even one of slighter build, would need to stoop and turn sideways to negotiate that tight space. The air was heavy and stank of brick dust and old plaster. From deeper down the passage slices of lamplight trickled through sporadic spy holes, each a tiny slit used to observe hallways and chambers; they did little to relieve the stygian darkness.

Parysatis exhaled. *What if I've misjudged him? What if the Caliph is in accord with his vizier?* She glanced over her shoulder at the gleaming seat of Fatimid power. She could flee easily enough, leave the Golden Hall and make her way back to the harem with no one the wiser. She could put this night from her mind . . .

. . . but for her father's voice, scolding and resolute. *Do you want the enemies of God to triumph, little bird? Then do nothing.*

Parysatis exhaled again and stepped beyond the threshold, suppressing a thrill of terror as the door's counterweight closed the portal behind her. 'Someone must tell him,' she whispered, her voice explosive in the tomb-like silence. 'For good or ill, someone must tell him.' *Merciful God, let it be for good!*

The young woman moved with all haste after that, her footing swift and sure as she sidled down the passage. Night sounds seeped in from the various spy holes: the clash of mail and a sulphurous oath as a guard jerked awake at his post; low moans and the rhythmic creak of a divan; a door latch rattling; faint voices. Parysatis frowned. The voices came from on down the passage, from its terminus at the Caliph's apartments.

Parysatis moved now with exaggerated care, drawing close to

the end of the passage, to the smooth stone door wherein a slit was set above the level of her eyes. The voices grew in volume, their muffled words sharp with anger; one she recognized instantly: the vizier.

Prudently, the young woman kept her hands clear of the door's bronze latch as she raised herself on the tips of her toes and peered out of the spy hole.

10

From the mosque of al-Hakim, Assad made his way south along the Qasaba, a serpentine street of markets and bazaars that sliced down the centre of Cairo, as jagged as a sword-cut. This part of the Qasaba between the Gate of Conquests and the square which divided the East and West Palaces – called the Bayn al-Qasrayn – doubled as a processional avenue; it was broad and paved, covered by a high ceiling of wood and palm-fibre matting to protect passers-by from the ferocious Egyptian sun. At intersections, the ceiling soared into domes of once-white stucco, soot-stained now and forever flaking.

Though the hour was growing late, merchants yet sat cross-legged in front of their stalls, extolling the quality of their wares to potential patrons: those off-duty soldiers and labourers who sought food, wine, and diversion. The smells of boiling oil, grilled meat, and spices filled the air; Assad heard the tinkle of a sharab-seller preparing his sherbet concoctions, the fruit juices no doubt sweet and ice-cold. Other men hawked crocks of thick Egyptian beer or flasks of khamr, a wine made from lightly fermented dates. Silvery laughter accompanied by the discordant music of flute and sitar came from latticed casement windows, mashrafiyyas, over-hanging the street, from silk-hung rooms where courtesans plied their trade.

Assad wove through the crowd. His stained khalat and ragged turban rendered him virtually invisible, another labourer, perhaps a caravan guard to judge from the hand draped over the ivory hilt of his long knife. Either way, a man down on his luck and barely worth notice. Twice, companies of Sudanese mercenaries in swirling black cloaks and glittering mail forced him to the edge of the street; the soldiers roared and sang, swaggering along with no pretence at discipline, like men too confident of their place. *Who owns them, the Caliph or his enemies?*

Would even al-Hajj have known? Though the would-be merchant might have been a useful asset, Assad didn't waste time fretting over his loss. Alamut had other eyes in Cairo, according to Daoud: one further south, a Qur'an-copier in the warrens of Old Fustat; and another closer at hand, a woman, a courtesan in the Soldiers' Quarter between the East Palace and al-Azhar Mosque. Either of them could provide the information he needed.

The woman first, then.

Assad veered off the Qasaba and plunged down the tangled labyrinth of side streets and vile-smelling alleys that led into the Soldiers' Quarter. Here, the bulk of the Caliph's troops made their homes, living with their families in tenement-like barracks of dirty brick. The ground floors also housed those businesses that catered to a soldier's needs: ironmongers and leather-workers, tailors and carpenters; the jewellers who made trinkets for their wives and daughters, and the scribes who recorded their wills.

Despite his long absence from Cairo, his destination was not difficult to find. The name Daoud had given him – al-Ghazala, the Gazelle – was well known to the men of the Soldiers' Quarter. Thus it was only a small matter to ask for directions to the House of the Gazelle. Merchants at the first two stalls shooed him away, embarrassed; the third flashed a sly smile. He was a round-faced tailor, and he glanced about to make sure none of his wives hovered near before directing Assad to the Street of Perfume Makers.

'Beware, my friend,' he hissed. 'She is . . . enchanting.'

The Street of Perfume Makers was a narrow lane in the very shadow of al-Azhar Mosque, its foundations as old as Cairo itself. From behind high walls Assad heard faint music and laughter as families passed the evening in their courtyards; palm trees and sycamores rustled in the light breeze as he padded down the deserted street. He found the House of the Gazelle easily enough, identified by a stone carving of that animal in full flight inset into an otherwise blank wall of mudbrick and golden stucco. Casement windows of fretted mahogany jutted out over the street. No light seeped through the latticework; no sounds save for the silvery tinkle of wind chimes. Assad moved to the mouth of the alley that led to al-Ghazala's door and paused, his head cocked to one side.

The sensation of hidden scrutiny raised the hairs on the back of his neck.

Assad glanced back the way he had come; he saw nothing. His eyes raked the second-floor windows across the street, then sought to pierce the gloom of the lane ahead, and ended up peering into the depths of the alley. Assad relaxed his muscles, unfocusing his vision in order to see without really seeing.

Shades of grey replaced the darkness. Wan light trickled in from overhead, a hooded lantern on a neighbouring rooftop perhaps; regardless, the narrow alley was empty as Assad crept down it, the hard-packed dirt swept free of refuse. *It wouldn't do to have clients stepping in filth.* He reached the darkened entryway, empty iron sconces flanking a red-daubed door.

Assad frowned.

The Gazelle's door stood ajar.

Carefully, he eased it open and slipped inside. A short hallway cut back to the left, ending in a keel arch that opened on the house's central courtyard. A night lamp flickered in its niche; the tinkling of chimes was the only sound to relieve the brooding silence. Where were her slaves, her guards? Surely a courtesan of the Gazelle's supposed influence employed a door warden at the very least?

Balconies ringed the courtyard, their delicate lattices upheld by marble columns scavenged from across the Nile: lotus-bundles carved with animal-headed figures and strange symbols that hinted at immense antiquity. Broken glass crunched under Assad's booted heel as he descended the trio of shallow steps to the court-yard floor; couches and divans, no doubt meant for entertaining, lay broken and scattered about the edges, their pillows shredded. Near the courtyard's centre, Assad saw splashes of what looked like dried blood. *What the devil . . . ?*

He stopped as four figures emerged from an interior room. Three were Arabs, gaunt men in long thread-worn shirts; their dark faces were lean and sharp with the hunger of opium addiction. The fourth was Ethiopian, a shaven-headed giant of a man in ragged trousers and a leather vest. Tribal scars ridged his muscular breast and cheeks: random whorls and lines that doubt-less wove spells of protection across his flesh. He alone noticed the stranger standing in the middle of the courtyard, and he silenced the others with a low growl.

'What have we here?'

'The Gazelle,' Assad said. 'Where is she?'

The Ethiopian gestured to his companions. The Arabs fanned out around the courtyard, one to the right and the other two to the left. 'We ask the questions, dog!' He tugged an iron-headed mace from his belt. 'Why do you seek the whore? She is a spy and a blasphemer, a cursed Ismaili, may Allah smite her with pestilence and plague! Are you another one of her followers? Are you a cursed Ismaili spy, too, dog?'

Ismaili, a follower of Isma'il, was one of the many sobriquets of al-Hashishiyya. So that was it. Someone must have discovered the Gazelle's connections to Alamut; perhaps al-Hajj's as well. *But have they slain her?* Assad glanced around at the Arabs. They were harafisha – street thugs – useful as extortionists among the beggars and the shopkeepers but ineffective against anyone with a back-bone. Predictably, two moved to flank him while the third circled behind. Knives gleamed in their fists as they edged closer. When

Assad did not deny his accusation, the huge African's lips peeled back in a sadistic grin; he slapped the haft of his mace into his open palm.

'Nowhere to run, Ismaili dog.'

'True,' the *Emir* of the Knife assured him, 'there's not.'

Without warning, Assad sprang to his left. Steel flickered as he swept his salawar from its sheath and, in the same motion, ripped it across that Arab's unprotected belly. Hatred flowed from the blade. Hatred and fear. The wounded man stumbled, screaming as loops of glossy purple viscera suddenly spilled into his hands. Assad caught him by the scruff of the neck and hurled him at the Ethiopian. Both men went down in a welter of blood and limbs.

Assad wheeled as the two remaining Arabs converged on him, bellowing curses, their bare feet slapping on paving stones and their knives upraised. Another man might have simply put his back to the wall and awaited their onslaught, but not him. The blade in his fist sang as he lunged for the nearer of the two.

They met halfway; Assad batted aside the descending knife and rammed his salawar through the Arab's chest, skewering him like a pig on a spit. Savage exultation poured into him; each death brought with it a sensation of invulnerability, as though he were beyond human. Laughing, the *Emir* of the Knife twisted and flung the dying man to the ground, the weight dragging his salawar free.

The remaining Arab's eyes opened wide with fear. He hesitated, and likely this moment of weakness saved his life: he skidded to a halt as Assad struck. It was a rising backhanded slash, one that should have laid the Arab open from crotch to sternum. Instead, the tip of Assad's salawar scraped bone as it sliced up through the man's jaw and into his cheek, bisecting the eye in its socket. The Arab screamed; he reeled away, bloody fingers clutching at his ruined face.

Before Assad could deal the death-blow, however, the enraged Ethiopian gained his footing and barrelled into him, a collision of muscle and sinew that sent both men crashing to the ground. The impact jarred Assad's salawar from his hand; it skittered across the stones of the courtyard and came to rest not six feet away, against the base of a column.

On the ground, the two men thrashed and rolled like dogs scrapping under their master's heel; they scrambled after Assad's blade. The Ethiopian spat curses in his native tongue. He grasped and tore at Assad's throat in an effort to find murderous purchase, iron fingers gouging bloody furrows in the flesh. Assad threw up one arm to protect himself; the other hammered at the Ethiopian's jaw and neck until blood started from his nose. One blow rocked that shaven skull back, and for an instant the grip on Assad's throat slackened.

It was the opening he needed.

'Dog!' He broke the stunned Ethiopian's hold, caught him by the chin and the back of the neck. In one sharp, smooth motion, Assad wrenched the African's head around, twisting it over his left shoulder until vertebrae snapped like rotted wood.

Assad kicked the twitching corpse aside and spat blood. His turban was gone. Sweat dampened his black hair, stinging the wounds the Ethiopian's fingernails had scored in the skin of his throat. His chest heaved beneath his torn khalat as he cast about for the wounded Arab.

Assad spied him across the courtyard, standing in the keel arch that led out into the alley, a scrap of cloth pressed to his lacerated face. The Arab steadied himself with an outstretched hand as he risked glancing over his shoulder. The sight of the blood-smeared stranger still alive unnerved him. Croaking in terror, the Arab staggered from the House of the Gazelle.

'Damn you!' Assad lurched to his feet, snatched up his salawar, and gave chase.

Fear lightened his quarry's step; no doubt it even made him forget the agony of his wound, for the Arab had already cleared the alley and was scuttling down the Street of Perfume Makers even as Assad reached the door. Still, the Assassin was confident he could run the man to ground. *And take him alive.* Though merely a hireling, the Arab doubtless had a few of the answers Assad needed . . . and the name of the man who hired him would make an excellent start. With a name—

So intent was he on running down the fleeing Arab that Assad missed the sound of footsteps in his wake. He missed the sudden stench of rotting garlic, and the peculiar whistle made by a stave of knotty acacia streaking through the air. The stave, however, did not miss. It smashed into the back of Assad's skull with terrible force. The blow drove Assad to his knees in the dust of the alley; explosions of light flared before his eyes and his vision swam. Blindly, he lashed out behind him with his naked salawar, felt it cleave flesh. A man screamed and fell back.

Yet, Assad's reprieve was short-lived. Off balance, gripped by sudden nausea, he struggled to regain his footing. He shook his head to clear it, wincing at the slivers of pain that threaded through his skull. The Assassin glanced up as a darker shadow crossed his path. He had the impression of an eye socket, scarred and empty, even as the crack of a cudgel sent him sprawling into a deeper night.

11

'The Nazarenes are at Bilbeis!'

In a towering rage, the vizier of Egypt paced the rug-strewn floor of the sitting room – the antechamber of the Caliph's apartments where his chief eunuch held sway. Silken tapestries hung between scalloped niches; a scattering of couches provided intimate spaces for conversation and for plotting. From one such couch – of lustrous ebony with cushions of red and gold brocade – Mustapha's eyes slid continually to the archway, expecting at any moment for Jalal's tirade to rouse the Prince of the Faithful. 'What? That's impossible.'

'I thought much the same, but at Bilbeis they are!' The vizier stabbed an accusatory finger at the old eunuch, who flinched as though struck. 'Where were your spies, you old fool? How often have you boasted that nothing goes on along the length and breadth of the Nile that escapes your notice? Then you must be blind and deaf! By Allah, a Nazarene army crosses our borders and we know nothing of it until they send messengers! Messengers!'

'Please, Excellency, lower your voice! I beg of you!'

'Lower my voice? Yes, I would hate to wake our lord and master from his much-needed slumber! May God fill his grave with fire! I ask this for the last time: where were our spies?'

'Our spies . . .' Mustapha spread his hands in a gesture of resignation. 'Our spies were where we left them . . . in the fields or in the markets. Therein rests our folly. Our spies did not fail us, Excellency. We failed them by not plying them as we should, by not offering bounties on information or sending out trusted men to harvest their knowledge. Indeed, so focused are we on what goes on behind these walls that we have forgotten there's a much wider world beyond – a world that would not weep if our beloved Egypt came to an abrupt and bloody end.'

Jalal stopped pacing. Spoken aloud, the words of condemnation served as a damper to his anger. The blame was his. *He* had miscalculated. *He* had ignored the distant threats of Damascus and Jerusalem as he pursued the mantle of Sultan with single-minded intensity. And he had very nearly been outfoxed.

'Rather than assigning fault,' Mustapha was saying, 'we should be concentrating on how best to extricate ourselves from this predicament.'

'Extricate? No. We should treat this predicament for what it is.' Jalal's eyes narrowed in thought. 'A shatranj match.'

The eunuch frowned. 'Excellency, this is no game—'

'A shatranj match it is, my old darling,' the vizier said, his tone brooking no dissent. 'Between Shirkuh and myself, and that wily Kurd is an acknowledged master. A master sets his pieces for his opening gambit, his tabiya, prior to going on the offensive, but which tabiya is he playing, eh? The Sword? The Slave's Banner? The Wing?'

'We cannot know for certain until all his pieces are in place.'

'True, but we can divine his plan from previous actions. Twice has Shirkuh come against us in as many years, and twice has that dog of a Kurd followed the same path: he skirts to the east of Nazarene lands, slips past the Frankish garrison at al-Karak, and then rides southwest from the tip of the Dead Sea. By Allah, his cursed horsemen outstrip the wind! Once across Sinai, he'll make for Atfih on the east bank of the Nile.' Jalal grew more animated as he spoke; his pacing resumed. 'At Atfih, Shirkuh will allow his army a day or two of rest. The men of that town will greet him as they always have, as a brother. He will loot their granaries, their markets; his soldiers will take what they want. All the while, that fool Dirgham will make wild promises to the local grandees to "free" them from my tyranny and claim he will restore the Caliph to his rightful place.'

'How will you counter, Excellency?' Mustapha asked.

'Give them no place to rest,' Jalal said. He turned sharply. 'Bar the gates of Atfih. Deny Shirkuh its granaries and markets. Deny Dirgham his easy audience.' The vizier smiled, thin and predatory. 'And, to slay a second bird with the same arrow, I'll relegate this task to the White Slaves of the River, to the Mamelukes. If they fail, it will save me from having to oversee their destruction; if they succeed, they will feel obliged towards me for having chosen them for such a grand task.'

Mustapha nodded. 'And if they switch their allegiance to Shirkuh and join his army?'

'Then their wives and children will pay for their perfidy,' Jalal said, a dangerous gleam in his eyes. He had no compunction about lining the road between Cairo and Atfih with the crucified bodies of the Mamelukes' loved ones – after first handing them over to the Sudanese for sport; he would make sure they knew it, as well. 'Tomorrow is Friday. I'll convene a council in the afternoon to brief the amirs of the army. Summon the commander of the Turkish regiment, that heathen Gokbori. It is to him we will give this task. We—'

Mustapha jumped to his feet, motioning the vizier to silence. A brusque nod of the old eunuch's head revealed the reason: Jalal turned to see the Prince of the Faithful stagger through the arch leading from the heart of his apartments. Mustapha prostrated himself; the vizier salaamed.

The Fatimid Caliph Rashid al-Hasan li-Din Allah was still a young man, not yet twenty-five, but his features bore the stamp of premature age and the veneer of dissolution. Beneath loose trousers and an open robe of white silk, the Caliph had the broad shoulders and narrow waist of a swordsman. His frame, though, displayed a gauntness that bordered upon emaciation. Knobs of bone, gristle, and sinew protruded from his jaundiced skin. Threads of grey wove through his wiry goatee, through his unkempt hair; bloodshot eyes stared out from hollow sockets. 'I heard voices, Jalal,' he said, thick with sleep and opium. 'What goes?'

'A thousand apologies, master,' the vizier said smoothly. 'We were debating the merits of a land dispute at Atfih, and my zeal must have got the better of me. The hour is late. Come; let me see you back to bed.'

Rashid shrugged off his solicitous hand. 'No. I am glad you came, Jalal. I would put a question to you.'

'Ask anything of me, master, and I will answer to the best of my abilities.'

'Who rules Cairo?'

The vizier blinked. 'Pardon, master?'

'You heard me. Who rules here? Am I not Cairo's lord and master? Am I not the Prince of the Faithful and the True Successor of the Prophet?' Rashid's face was feverish, glazed with sweat; he swayed and caught the carved arch for support.

'Indeed you are, master.' Jalal bowed again, more to hide the sneer that came unbidden to his lips than from any sense of respect. 'You are all this and much more. You are the Light of Islam and the Lion of the Faith. You—'

'Then why do my own eunuchs refuse to heed my commands? Why do I not recognize those men who guard me?'

'Your eunuchs are like grandmothers, Most Excellent One.' The vizier shot a perturbed look at Mustapha as the old eunuch drew back to a sideboard. There, he set about preparing a fresh draught of khamr; taking a crystal vial from the sleeve of his robe, he upended its contents into a silver cup. Jalal cleared his throat. 'And you do not recognize your guards because I frequently rotate them, to keep plots from hatching out among the army factions. Though charged with your defence, the soldiers who guard you also constitute your greatest enemy, master. Have you forgotten the Circassian?'

'Aye, Othman!' Rashid said, striking the stonework with a white-knuckled fist for emphasis. 'I thought he was my friend!'

'A friend is not one who desires your doom, master. Othman wanted you dead. He was there to put a dagger in your heart, and it is only by the grace of Allah that he told his plans to the whore he was with the night before, and she to one of my men.' Indeed, the vizier had spoken that lie so often he almost believed it himself. Othman, chosen to be Rashid al-Hasan's companion and body-guard because they were near the same age, had proven too headstrong, too inquisitive; in all, he was a terrible influence on the man the vizier planned to supplant. Yet, replacing the Circassian had only served to inflame his wayward sense of honour. When Othman gained entry to the palace the morning of his death, he was on a mission to visit ruin upon the vizier. Fortunately, the fool had blabbed his plan to his mistress the night before. And the Circassian's mistress was in Jalal's employ. *A close call, that.* 'I swear before God he was no friend of yours, master.'

The vizier's words had a pronounced effect on the Caliph. The young man sagged heavily against the wall, his balled fists relaxing, losing their white-knuckle rigidity. Jalal feigned pity as he offered the Caliph his arm to lean on; gratefully, Rashid accepted.

'How could I have been so wrong about him?'

'You see the best in all men, Most Excellent One,' Jalal said. 'Unfortunately, the soldiers of Cairo are dogs, petty men who scheme and connive behind your back – men like Othman, who would kill you simply to further their own ambitions. May Allah most high scourge them for their insolence!'

'He haunts my dreams. I see Othman's face in the shadows, Jalal. He tries to speak, to reveal some terrible secret that has driven him from the grave, but he has no words. Only blood spills past his lips. What does it mean?'

'I cannot say, master,' Jalal said. Arm in arm, they shuffled down the corridor to the Caliph's apartments. Mustapha followed, bringing with him the cup of drug-laced khamr.

Rashid al-Hasan dwelt in sterile splendour, in rooms as cold and as opulent as the tombs of his predecessors. Amid the silks and silver, the heavy gold and jewelled damasks, stood tastefully arranged islands of furniture: armoires of fine cedar beside divans of polished teak, chests of gilded sycamore sitting atop tables inlaid with ivory and mother-of-pearl. Glass and crystal twinkled in the yellow lamplight.

Only in the Caliph's bedchamber was there the slightest hint of the young man's personality: a riot of potted ferns lent the room the aspect of a garden; lamps sporting panes of gold-tinted glass gave forth a glow that emulated pale sunlight. Rather than tapestries, frescoes depicting a Nile hunt decorated the walls, while the floor was an elaborate mosaic: hundreds of small carved beetles taken from the ruins across the river were set among colourful tiles and semi-precious stones. Beside the Caliph's lion-footed bed, whose sheer linen panels rustled in a faint breeze, sat a small table; on it, a Qur'an with a gold-stitched leather cover rested beside a tall water pipe of brass and silver, its patina dulled from use. Latticed doors standing ajar opened on a small fountain court, high-walled and private; jets of water burbled in the marble basin of a lily pond.

Jalal helped the Caliph to the edge of the bed and motioned Mustapha forward. 'Drink this, Most Excellent One. It will help you sleep.'

Rashid took the cup, tossed back its contents, and grimaced at the sting of raw date wine. He settled back into bed with a weary sigh. 'Find me an interpreter of dreams, Jalal,' he said. 'An astrologer, a wise man, a Sufi – I care not, so long as he knows what he is about. I leave the details to you, as always, my good vizier.'

Jalal took the empty cup from the Caliph's hand and suppressed a smile of triumph. 'Master, I—'

Rashid waved him away, his eyes already closing. 'Just . . . Just see it done, Jalal.'

The vizier inclined his head. 'As you wish, O Prince of the Faithful.' He and Mustapha left together, retracing their steps to the antechamber. Jalal remained dangerously quiet.

12

The wait was interminable.

Parysatis stood on the tips of her toes until her calves ached; she turned her head this way and that, peering through the tiny slit in an effort to see more of the spacious antechamber. *He has guards and body servants*, said the voice of Doubt in the back of her mind, *and they will be near at hand. What if he calls for them? What if the vizier lingers? What if the eunuch never leaves the Caliph's side?* A thousand scenarios played out in her mind as she waited in that dark passage, and all of them ended in her death. Cold sweat rolled down Parysatis' ribs.

Nevertheless, as much as she feared for her own safety, she feared for Rashid al-Hasan's more, especially after all she'd overheard this night. *He's at their mercy!* What's more, the memory of his gaunt face brought tears to her eyes. *What have they done to him?* The Caliph was sick, weak in body and confused in mind, likely from the cruel diet of poppy juice and hashish his eunuchs foisted upon him at the vizier's urging. Were they trying to kill him, or simply control him? Does it matter? For the sake of her father, who had loved the Fatimid Caliph with zealous fervour, Parysatis decided in that moment that she would do all she could to loose the vizier's hold on him, to strike off his shackles. It occurred to her, too, that if she succeeded, might Rashid al-Hasan not then set her apart from his other concubines? *Might freedom be her reward?* She dared not dwell too long upon it.

Parysatis stiffened at the sound of footsteps. Jalal and his eunuch, Mustapha, came into view. The look on the vizier's face nearly sent Parysatis fleeing from the passage. His eyes were fiery slits; deep lines furrowed his brow. He glanced back the way they had come. 'How long before the fever takes hold?'

It was the eunuch's turn to frown. He shook his head. 'I . . . I have not administered it yet, Excellency. That was but raw poppy juice. I thought perhaps with the Damascus problem that you would—'

Jalal spun. Faster than Parysatis could follow, the back of the vizier's hand cracked across the old eunuch's mouth, a meaty sound that made Parysatis cringe. Mustapha staggered. Blood trickled from his split lip; he clutched the Caliph's silver cup to his breast. 'You thought? *You thought?* You do not think, Mustapha! You do as I say! Nothing has changed! By month's end, I want that worthless son of a whore on his deathbed! Do you understand?'

Mustapha nodded. 'Y-Yes, Excellency.'

'Good.' Parysatis saw the eunuch flinch as Jalal clapped a hand to his shoulder. 'Forgive my outburst. It has been a . . . trying day.'

'Perhaps you should rest, as well.' Mustapha dabbed at the blood with the knuckle of his index finger. 'I could give you a draught . . . ?'

Jalal chuckled, as though something the eunuch said struck him as funny. 'No, my old darling. I think not.' He walked beyond Parysatis' field of vision. She heard the door open and harness rattle as the guards outside snapped to attention. 'Admit no one. Mustapha, make sure your charge stays quiet for the rest of the night.'

'As you wish, Excellency.'

The door thudded shut. Mustapha stood there a moment longer, his face an unreadable mask, and then he turned and shuffled off in the opposite direction. He, too, left Parysatis' cone of sight. She listened, not daring to breathe, at the sound of his retreating footsteps. Her whole body trembled. Already horrible beyond compare, her situation had just become measurably worse. *They do mean to kill him!*

Seconds ticked by. Hearing nothing, Parysatis' hands moved to the latch. 'Allah, give me strength,' she whispered as she pulled open the secret door and peered out. She saw no sign of the eunuch; the antechamber was deserted. Quickly, Parysatis left the passage, trusting the door to close of its own accord. Her slippered feet made little sound as she crossed the antechamber and plunged through the arch, her mantle swirling behind her.

She reached the Caliph's bedchamber out of breath, her heart thudding in her chest so loudly that surely the echo must reach back to the antechamber. The voices in her mind gibbered and howled in a blind panic. Fingers knotted in her shawl, she stepped over the threshold like a woman going to her doom.

Rashid sprawled atop the coverlet, pale as death. She saw his chest rise and fall; his muscles twitched as he responded to something in his dreams. Parysatis crept to the Caliph's bedside, knelt, and clasped his cold hand.

'M-My lord!' Rashid started at the sound of her voice, his head moving back and forth. 'My lord!' She put a hand on his chest and shook him lightly. Groaning, the Caliph writhed away from her touch. 'Please, my lord! You must wake, I beg of you!' But the Caliph only sank deeper into the cushions of his bed, as though to hide. *He's not asleep, he's unconscious. Drugged.*

Parysatis sagged. What was she going to do now? What *could* she do? *How can I help you if I cannot get through to you?* Her brow wrinkled in thought; idly, she reached out and stroked the Caliph's hair, pushing it back off his fevered forehead. In her eyes, he was no longer the cold and remote figure of the Prince of the Faithful; no longer the True Successor of the Prophet. His weakness made him mortal. Rashid al-Hasan was a man in need of aid, in need of a friend. 'I will find a way to help you, my lord,' she said, resolve replacing fear. Softly, Parysatis kissed the back of his hand. 'As Allah is my witness, I—'

The young woman froze as sounds drifted down the hall outside the Caliph's doorway: a muffled cough followed by the scuff of a slippered foot on stone. *The eunuch!* Parysatis shot to her feet, glancing frantically about for a place to hide. *Under the bed? Behind the potted ferns?* Then her eyes lit upon the latticework doors that led out to the courtyard. She bolted, barging through the doors then easing them back to where they merely stood ajar. Beneath an ivy-hung arbour, Parysatis pressed herself against the stone wall and waited; she peered through the lattice at the Caliph's bed and the hallway beyond. Presently, Mustapha padded into the room.

The old eunuch, his lip already beginning to swell, brought a fresh goblet, laced no doubt with whatever poisons the vizier had commanded him to administer. Hovering over the Caliph, he tried twice – both times more forcefully than Parysatis – but still had no luck rousing him. She saw him frown and carefully place the goblet on the table by the side of Rashid's bed where he was sure to see it if he awoke. Then, with a final glance around the room, the eunuch withdrew.

Parysatis leaned heavily against the wall, closing her eyes as she mouthed a silent prayer of thanks. She waited a few moments before prodding the doors open and returning to Rashid's bedside. Curious, she picked up the goblet and sniffed its contents. Khamr, as she suspected, but its pungent aroma masked a faintly sour smell. An oily swirl stained its surface. She imagined the Caliph waking in the grip of a dreadful thirst; in her mind's eye, she saw him reach for the goblet, drink from it, and unknowingly poison himself.

No, not this time! Parysatis carried the goblet into the courtyard and poured its contents out beneath a flowering shrub. She rinsed it thoroughly in the lily pond and refilled it with cool water jetting from the fountain. As she did this, however, something caught her eye.

In the courtyard wall across from the latticed doors, moonlight illuminated a now-familiar architectural feature: a scalloped niche, replete with geometric carvings, partially hidden by a poplar tree in a heavy terracotta pot. Parysatis frowned. Leaving the goblet on the fountain's edge, she hurried over to the niche. It was identical to the others; with a prayer to Allah, she squeezed around the potted poplar and ran her fingers over the niche's carvings, searching . . .

Her breath caught in her throat as a marble lozenge gave way with a sharp *click*. She pushed. Grating and groaning, the door swung inward on dry hinges to release a cloud of hot dusty air, the exhalation of a long-slumbering beast. *Another one!* But where did this passage lead? The niche was in the east wall; east was the harem. From harem to passage to Caliph's bed . . . Parysatis glanced over her shoulder. Had she found the secret way by which al-Hasan's ancestors smuggled women into their presence without anyone becoming the wiser? Or perhaps was this a way for the Prince of the Faithful to spy upon his many wives? Whatever the reason, the palace's current resident had long since forgotten its existence.

To Parysatis, it was as a gift from God.

She hurried back inside and returned the goblet to the Caliph's bedside. He would wake, and at least his own terrible thirst would not be his downfall. *I cannot do much, but I can do this.* She stroked his forehead. *So like a great cavalier.* He looked more restful than before, as though he knew someone was watching over him. The idea brought a hint of a smile to her face.

'I'll come to you again,' she whispered, 'and soon. Together, perhaps we can find a way to help one another.'

Reluctantly, Parysatis drew away; she closed the courtyard doors behind her and vanished into the new-found passage. No matter where in the harem it came out, it would be far better than having to cross the breadth of the East Palace.

13

'*Where is it?*'

He could not breathe. The dark-haired boy, barely thirteen, gasped as thick fingers dug into the juncture of his neck and shoulder, a thumb across his windpipe, forcing his back up against the unfinished wall of his tiny room; he smelled the reek of wine, the mingling of sweat and rich perfume. The boy writhed and fought against the hand trying to choke the life from him, but his struggles only served to anger his attacker even more.

'*Where is it, you ungrateful little bastard?*' *the man hissed, foul breath steaming the boy's cheek.* '*Your mother confessed you stole my dead brother's sword, though I had to beat the truth from her! Hand it over and spare yourself her fate! Stop fighting!*' *An open hand cracked across his mouth.*

'*I didn't steal it, uncle!*' *he replied, blood starting from his lip.* '*It's mine! You only want it back so you can sell it!*' *The boy's uncle – his dead father's brother, a cadi who dispensed Islamic justice from the halls of al-Azhar Mosque – was a rotund man, fond of wine and free with his coin. The fool had two wives, sisters hardly older than the boy, and both had a fondness for silks and gold, for perfumes and fine foods.* He might deny them their excesses, *he recalled Hakim saying,* if only his prick and his spine were not one and the same.

'*Sell it? You little idiot! Of course I plan to sell it! Do you think the meat and bread you eat comes to you by the grace of Allah? There is a price to your upkeep . . . and the price is that accursed sword! Now, give it over, if you value your precious hide!*'

Though young, the boy understood the sword's worth. It was more than just an heirloom. The work of a master from Herat, its single-edged blade, slightly curved in the Turkish fashion, had the blessings of the Prophet inlaid in delicate gold calligraphy; its hilt was of fine wood and bound in twists of Persian leather, ray-skin, and golden wire. It was a gift, *his mother had told him, tears sparkling in her eyes,* a gift from a great shaykh whose life your father saved. In turn, it saved his life many times over in the wars against the Franks. We must keep it safe and well tended, to honour him. *The boy's gaze flickered to the sword's hiding place, beneath a loose board under the pallet he slept on, in the tiny room at the rear of his uncle's mansion.*

The boy's uncle, who often boasted he could read guilt or innocence on the faces of those brought before him as surely as a learned man could read a book, followed his gaze and knew it for what it was. 'So-ho!' *A wicked smile split his ruddy visage. He let go of the boy, turned, and flung the pallet aside. The board skewed, revealing the cloth-wrapped sword. The man bent and retrieved the weapon.* 'There you are, praise be to Allah.'

'Leave it be!' *Tears of rage flooded the boy's eyes; he lunged for the sword and received only the back of his uncle's hand for his troubles. The blow knocked him into the tangle of his bedding. He flailed about as he sought to rise again, to continue the fight. The boy's fingers brushed something metallic. Desperate, he tugged it free. It was the little dagger old Hakim had given him, its pitted blade thin and straight. The feel of it, its weight and balance, sent a thrill down his spine; it lent him strength, afforded him courage. With an incoherent scream the boy threw himself at his hated uncle, raking the knife across the man's belly. The sensation of steel ripping cloth and flesh, the boy discovered, was more sublime than anything he could have imagined. So, too, his uncle's reaction.*

The man shrieked. He let go of the sword and stumbled back, eyes goggling with disbelief as his fingertips probed the wound and came away bloody. 'You dare touch me?'

'You dare disrespect my father!' *The boy scrambled over and caught up the fallen sword, knife held at the ready as Hakim had shown him.* 'And you dare disrespect my mother by trying to make her your whore!'

His uncle raged. 'No, she was my brother's whore! That ignorant fool had a weakness for well-used women! I thank the Prophet that he's dead and no longer a disgrace to my family! And you, you misbegotten little cur, you'll be my eunuch soon enough! Guards! My men will carve your pea-sized balls off! Then, when I'm done with you, I'll sell you to the slaves in the quarries! You and your bitch of a mother, too!' *The man reached for him.* 'Guards!'

The dark-haired boy stood his ground, his face screwed up in a rictus of hate as his uncle grabbed him by the throat. Before the cadi's fingers could constrict, however, the boy struck back.

Steel flashed. With every scrap of power in his narrow shoulders, in his thin arm, the boy rammed the knife in beneath the hinge of his uncle's jaw; angled upward, it punched through muscle and bone and lodged in his skull. The cadi's eyes stretched wide. His hands flew to his own throat as he tried to speak, to breathe. Nothing came from his yawning mouth save a fine mist of blood. The boy spat in his uncle's face and shoved him away as the bedroom door flew open.

It was Hakim. The grey-bearded old gatekeeper stood on the threshold and watched in stunned silence as his employer writhed at his feet, gobbling and choking on blood. His contortions weakened; soon, they stopped altogether. Quickly, Hakim shut the door. 'What have you done, boy?'

'He . . . He tried to t-take my father's sword, Hakim,' he said, the cloth-wrapped weapon tight against his chest. 'P-Punish me as you will, but I . . . I do not r-regret what I have done. It wasn't his to take, and I will kill the man who tries to do it again!'

Hakim stared at the cadi's sprawled corpse, his eyes pitiless, full of disdain. 'No. I won't be the one to punish you. Allah has made His will known. But listen. You must flee Cairo. Your uncle, he has powerful friends; friends who won't look kindly upon his murder. You have to go and go fast. Tonight.'

'W-What about my mother?'

'I'll look after her, boy. I promise you, she'll be safe and will want for nothing.'

'I . . . I don't know where to go.' Tears welled in the corners of his eyes. His blood-spattered limbs trembled; he looked thirteen again. Thirteen and scared. 'What do I do, Hakim?'

The man exhaled. 'I have a cousin in Ascalon. He's an ironmonger and he always has a need for new apprentices. I'll send you to him. He'll take good care of you, boy, as Allah is my witness.'

As Allah is my witness . . . As Allah . . . As . . .

14

Assad did not regain consciousness as another man might, by thrashing and jerking about; he did not groan, or curse, or call out for water. Rather, he came awake silently and lay still, allowing time for his senses to take stock of his surroundings. He knew who had attacked him, knew it with cold certainty; the recollection of an eye socket, scarred and empty, was yet vivid in his mind. *Musa and his beggars. But why? Robbery? If that were the case I doubt I'd be waking up. Why, then?*

The air was cool and moist, thick with the tang of mildew and of damp stone. Assad's khalat was gone; his boots, too; hemp cords bound him hand and foot. He lay on his side on a floor of blue glazed tile, his skull throbbing as he listened to sounds around him: the drip of water, the rustle of wings, and faint cooing of pigeons from far above. Closer at hand, he heard harsh whispers.

'You say he simply showed up?' This from a man whose voice carried the weight of years. The way he sharply pronounced each word reminded Assad of an old soldier, a leader of men.

'Yes, effendi.' He easily recognized Musa's voice. 'He came around the mosque looking for al-Hajj, so when he left I sent my men to watch him. They fetched me when they saw he was making for Zaynab's house.'

'Who were these dogs he killed?'

'Harafisha,' he heard Musa say, his tone one of disdain. 'Looters, most likely. He slew three. We let the fourth slip past us in the alley, and then ambushed this one as he came out.'

'And he is not an associate, not a contact?'

'No.' A woman answered him, her voice husky and strained as though she tottered at the threshold of exhaustion. 'I've never seen him before, as Allah is my witness!' *Al-Ghazala, I presume.* That she was indeed alive brought a small measure of comfort to Assad.

'Let's see what he has to say for himself, then.'

Boots crunched on the tile; Assad saw them from the corner of his eye: soft leather sewn with silver thread. One nudged him in the ribs just hard enough to roll him on to his back.

The man standing over him was neither tall nor bulky, though the strength of his compact frame was evident in his bull neck and the corded sinew of his arms. Beneath a plain green turban, coal-black eyes glittered with curiosity as he stared hard at Assad, surprised to find him awake. Assad stared back, unflinching. The man had a weather-beaten face that had seen too much – too much blood, too much grief, too much injustice; the grey peppering in his russet beard he wore like a badge of honour.

'Playing dead, eh? Do you know me, dog?' he said, gathering his robes of dark green and cream damask around him as he crouched. Gold shimmered from the pommel of a curved dagger thrust into his girdled sash. Musa came up to stand behind him. 'Do you know who I am? I am Ali abu'l-Qasim, whom the folk of Cairo call Malik al-Harami, the King of Thieves! You are trespassing on what is mine! Who are you, and why were you sniffing around the Gazelle's door, eh? Who were those men you killed?'

'Not looters,' Assad said, rising up on one elbow. He lay on the floor of a hammam, a bathhouse, long past its prime. Water trickled from a broken fountain, from ruptured pipes and cracked basins, following runnels in the tile to pool in the low places. Decades of grime and pigeon droppings stained the floors, while guttering torches left cones of soot on the tiled walls; the unsteady light didn't reach every corner, nor did it find the vaulted ceiling high above. 'Your palace, O King?'

'My torture chamber,' Abu'l-Qasim replied. 'Who were they, if not looters? Associates of yours?'

Assad shot a venomous glance at the man known as the King of Thieves. 'If I had to guess, I'd say your half-blind idiot there let one of al-Hajj's killers get by him.'

'Liar!' Musa spat and pulled a knife from his ragged belt. 'Give him to me, effendi! I'll make him sing for you!'

'Be silent!' Abu'l-Qasim snapped over his shoulder. To Assad he said: 'How is it you know al-Hajj?'

'I don't. As I told that one, I bear a message for him from an old friend.'

'And does this message have anything to do with the Gazelle?'

Assad pursed his lips. 'Perhaps. If she is here I would speak with her.'

'Would you?' Abu'l-Qasim straightened. His boot heels clicked as he paced, clearly agitated. 'And what would you say to her, were she here?'

'Mind your business, old man,' Assad snapped. 'Bring her, if she is here and all will be made clear. I mean her no harm.'

'*Y'Allah!* The dog has arrogance enough for ten men! Who is in whose power, eh? You make demands of me? Of Ali abu'l-Qasim? You dare tell me what I should do? Man, Zaynab al-Ghazala is my daughter, and anything you would say to her you can say to me!'

Assad's eyes narrowed. 'Your daughter?'

'She is the only child I have left.' Abu'l-Qasim stopped pacing. His hand moved to the pommel of his knife. 'And if your death will make her safe, I swear – by the blood of the Prophet – you will never see another sunrise. My patience is at an end. Who are you and what do you want with my daughter?'

Assad studied the man, searching Abu'l-Qasim's face for some hint of deception, for the barest wisp of dishonesty. He found only cold resolve. The muscles of the Assassin's jaw clenched and unclenched. Slowly, he nodded. 'Tell her this,' he said. 'Tell her the *Emir* of the Knife would speak to her.'

His words provoked the desired reaction. Musa paled and swore. Abu'l-Qasim stepped back, scowling with uncertainty; at the same time, Assad heard a sharp intake of breath come from one corner of the hammam. He craned his neck and saw a woman emerge from the shadows, unveiled, her chestnut hair confined by a shawl of dark silk; dark, too, was the fabric of her gown and robe, so that the outline of her body melted into the gloom around her. Still, Assad saw enough to know she possessed grace and un-common beauty.

Her eyes, though, were wide with alarm.

'T-The *Emir* of the K-Knife, you say?' She edged closer, her manner as skittish as her namesake. 'He is in Cairo?'

'Aye. He is closer than you would imagine.' Assad struggled into a sitting position. When he again spoke it was in Persian rather than Arabic, and he kept his voice low and calm. 'We serve the same master. A young shaykh of storied lineage who dwells on a mountain-top by the shores of the Caspian Sea.'

'Speak the words,' she answered in the same tongue, her voice trembling. 'If you are who you claim, you will know the words.'

' "Sharp-eyed are the eagles in the minarets of Nizar",' he said.

The Gazelle closed her eyes and nodded. 'Loose him, Father.'

Abu'l-Qasim looked askance at her. 'You're certain?'

'Loose him. He is an Emir of the Hidden Master. He is an ally.'

The King of Thieves glanced at Assad, concern fretting his brow. Finally, he said: 'Cut him free, Musa.'

Reluctantly, the one-eyed man approached. The Assassin sensed Musa's fear as he used his knife to slice the ropes, first his feet and then his hands. Assad flexed his shoulders, feeling the first pin-pricks of restored circulation. His head ached and blood matted his hair to the back of his skull. 'Fetch my things,' he growled. 'And if so much as one thin dirham is missing, you will pay with your other eye.'

Musa hurried to do the Emir's bidding.

Abu'l-Qasim came over to where Assad sat. 'I make no apologies for my rough treatment of you. My daughter's life is all that matters to me,' he said, extending a hand to help the Assassin to his feet.

'We have no quarrel, you and I.'

'Good.' Abu'l-Qasim nodded. 'I offer you my hospitality, and my protection, while you are in Cairo. Anything you need . . . '

'A place to sit and some wine would be welcome,' Assad said. He looked from the King of Thieves to Zaynab. 'And answers to my questions.'

'Of course,' she said. 'Follow me.'

15

By what rights Ali abu'l-Qasim called himself the King of Thieves, Assad did not know. Perhaps because those who stole for a living – from sneak-thieves and extortionists along the Qasaba to bandits and Nile smugglers – tithed him a portion of their gains, an illicit tax that in turn financed the collective apathy of the urban militia, old soldiers who earned their stipends policing the city's streets. Or perhaps it had something to do with his beneficence.

'Without my father, the city's tax collectors and usurers would doubtless have bled whole neighbourhoods dry,' Zaynab said. Assad shifted in his seat; she stood behind him and sponged blood from his hair, her fingers gently exploring the extent of his injury. They were alone in a chamber on the second floor of the caravanserai where the King of Thieves dwelt, that worthy having gone to make a quick circuit of his guards while Musa had yet to return with Assad's belongings. Unlike the hammam, this portion of Abu'l-Qasim's lair showed signs of better maintenance, with reed mats and carpets and tapestries of silk and wool stitched with sayings from the Qur'an. Sweet smoke coiled from censers hanging amid the oil lamps of an intricate chandelier. 'He ensures they take only what is proper and no more. Those under his protection prosper.'

'And your father, he . . . approves of what you do?'

Zaynab smiled. 'Which part? That I am a courtesan or that I collect information for al-Hashishiyya?'

'Both.'

'On the former: I am a courtesan, not a whore. Men pay for the pleasure of my company, for conversation, for stories, for songs. They pay because I appreciate the lies they tell about their lives, because I compliment their egos. If it goes any further, the choice is mine, alone, and coin is never a consideration. As for the latter: I learned of the teachings of Ibn al-Sabbah from my father, who is a devout Ismaili. Much of what I pass along to Alamut comes from him, from his countless eyes and ears.'

'How long have you been under your father's protection?'

'I am always under his protection,' Zaynab replied, a hint of rancour in her voice. 'But I have been dwelling under his roof again since the night after our enemies got to al-Hajj.'

'They came for you, too,' Assad said. It was not a question.

Zaynab exhaled. 'I was abroad on business that night. In the cold hours before dawn someone invaded my house. At least, I presume it was but one man. No one knows how he gained entry, for dawn found the doors and shutters still locked and bolted. This wraith, whoever he was, killed my maidservant instead. And she did not die easily. No doubt he thought she was the Gazelle, and then he prolonged her agony when the truth came out and she wouldn't reveal my whereabouts.'

'You're certain she did not break?'

'Why?' The Gazelle bristled. 'Do you doubt a woman has the wherewithal to keep her mouth shut? *Y'Allah*! The poor girl did not betray me.'

'Then who did? Who else is privy to the secret of your allegiance?'

'Only my father and Musa.'

'And al-Hajj. How close were you?'

'We weren't close at all. He knew as little about me as I know about him. We took great pains never to move in the same circles. Al-Hajj collected information from the folk of the streets, from the beggars at the gates, from the drovers and herdsmen; he worked the Qasaba, the souks, listening to the chatter of merchants and caravaneers, to the plaints of the soldiers who guarded them, while I limit my activities to courtiers and officers, a few ministers and a cadi or two. I supplement what I glean from them with whatever news my father might provide. Save for Musa, we had no mutual contact. Nor is it known in the streets that the mistress of the House of the Gazelle is also the daughter of the King of Thieves.'

'And yet al-Hajj is dead and you are living in exile. Someone *has* betrayed you, but to whom?'

'Our master's enemies are beyond reckoning,' Zaynab said. 'Fatimid, Abbasid, Sunni, Shi'ite, Nazarene, Jew, Yezidi . . . the men you killed tonight could have been acting on behalf of any one of them.'

Assad gave a derisive snort. 'No, those men were hirelings of the basest sort, local dagger-men and street thugs. Doubtless someone paid them to keep a discreet watch over your door but their greed got the better of them. Still, someone confided in them – they knew enough to identify you as an Ismaili spy.'

Assad felt a faint stab of pain as Zaynab roughly dried the gash on the back of his head. It was a flesh wound: bloody, perhaps, but innocuous and not worth stitching. A linen square, held in place with strips of cloth, would protect it until it scabbed over. She finished her work in stony silence, then: 'I give you my word: I have never flaunted my allegiance to al-Hashishiyya! Nor was it a spur-of-the-moment decision to send news of our dilemma to Alamut. I was at my wits' end . . .'

'Your dilemma is not why I'm here.'

Zaynab blinked. 'Then it's mere chance that brought you to Cairo?'

'Chance?' Assad replied. 'No. It's not chance at all. I'm here for a reason, and I sought you out – like al-Hajj before you – for information. What do you know of the Caliph and his predicament?'

'The Caliph?' Zaynab went to a sideboard and filled two goblets with wine from a stoppered jug. She handed one to Assad and drained the other, using the moment's respite to marshal her thoughts. Finally, she said: 'What is there to know? Though the common people love him, the Caliph is ever a marionette who is oblivious to his strings. Ten years ago, after his father succumbed to illness – though some say it was poison – a vizier named Shawar put little Rashid on the throne, a porcelain toy in gilt robes that he trundled out for festivals and parades. Otherwise, the men of court largely ignored the poor boy until a minor chamberlain, Dirgham, I think his name was, used him to seize the vizierate from Shawar. Dirgham claimed to have Rashid's best interests at heart, but still he kept him shuttered away and far from even a taste of autonomy. Rumour had it Dirgham planned to do away with the young Caliph and assume the mantle of Sultan, regardless of the chaos it would cause. Fortunately, he never got the chance. He fell victim to a rival of his own, a courtier called Jalal, who engineered a rather impressive coup. A tale went round that Dirgham was slain, but I know he fled to Damascus and there he remains, goading Sultan Nur ad-Din in hopes he will someday take action. Today, Jalal rules Cairo virtually unopposed, though still under the Caliph's auspices, while the Caliph himself stays, or is kept, in a drugged stupor.'

'What of Rashid al-Hasan's character? Have the drugs and the indolence left him a degenerate? Could he be trusted to rule well if someone lopped off the hands that were pulling his strings?'

Zaynab paused. 'With the proper guidance, perhaps. But why should that be any of our concern? Are the Fatimids not the sworn enemies of our Hidden Master?'

Assad made no reply. What's more, he knew his silence piqued Zaynab's interest; he could see it on her face. But, before she could probe further, Abu'l-Qasim returned with Musa in tow. Gingerly, his face pale and drawn, the one-eyed beggar carried the Assassin's possessions. Assad reckoned he must have handled the salawar; even sheathed, its touch opened a window on ancient bloodshed, ancient sorceries – a waking nightmare that would cause an unprepared soul to question his very sanity. 'You were clad in blood-stained rags, my friend,' Abu'l-Qasim said. 'I bid Musa fetch you fresh clothing. Nothing else has been disturbed.'

'My thanks.' Assad stood and accepted the bundle from Musa, who looked relieved to be rid of it. 'There is an associate of mine, a Persian merchant, staying outside the northern gates at the inn of Abu Hamza. He answers to the name Farouk. Can you fetch him here in the morning?'

Abu'l-Qasim nodded. 'Musa?'

'It will be done, effendi.' The one-eyed man bowed and made to leave.

'Wait,' Assad said. From his things, he removed a leather

almoner heavy with coin and tossed it to Musa. 'A gift to the beggars of Cairo. Tell them it is from the Hidden Master of Alamut, who wishes them long life and prosperity.'

Musa's good eye widened; he looked to the King of Thieves for guidance. 'A most generous gift, my friend,' Abu'l-Qasim said. 'Suspiciously generous, in fact.'

'Is alms-giving not expected of the faithful?'

'Alms-giving, yes, but not bribery. Come, my friend, I've lived long enough to know one from the other. What do you hope to purchase with this gift?'

'Good will,' Assad said. 'And it's my experience that men are more apt to give it when their bellies are full. So let them dine well, or has Cairo become a refuge of hopeless cynics?'

Abu'l-Qasim paused a moment and then nodded to Musa, who bowed once more. 'The beggars thank you, O Emir, as they thank your master.'

Assad turned back to his things. Besides his boots – freshly cleaned – and his sheathed salawar, Musa had brought him a thin white galabiyya and cotton trousers of far finer quality than those he had owned. At her father's insistence, Zaynab averted her eyes while Assad stripped and drew on these undergarments. Next, he donned a khalat of dark green linen, richly embroidered in gold thread, followed by a matching turban and a sash of silky black brocade. Into this, he thrust his salawar, its hatred subdued, like some great beast sated on blood.

'I must speak with al-Hasan,' Assad said. 'Soon.'

'How?' Zaynab asked. 'The vizier rarely allows anyone to see him, much less speak with him.'

'Ha! The vizier? That son of a whore is a despot,' Abu'l-Qasim said. '*Inshallah*, he will boil in the stews of Hell!'

'*Inshallah*,' Assad echoed. 'Tomorrow is Friday, is it not?'

'It is.'

'I trust al-Hasan has not yet broken with the tradition set by his forefathers of attending noon prayer at, where . . . al-Azhar Mosque?'

Zaynab shook her head, frowning. 'No, at the Grey Mosque, al-Aqmar. It's closer to the palace.'

'Excellent.' The *Emir* of the Knife's eyes narrowed to slits. 'Be they beggar or prince, all are equal in the sight of Allah. I would wager the Caliph believes much the same thing.'

16

Weeping blood, the wounded Arab staggered through crumbling archways and down the vile-smelling alleys of Cairo's Foreign Quarter – the infamous Harat al-Rum – where sounds of brazen revelry seeped from behind tightly shuttered doors. The Arab reeled in half-blinded agony and nearly collapsed in a dank alcove, his face a clotted mask of gore. His heart hammered in his chest; he gasped for breath, tasting blood and sweat as he licked his lips and peered behind him, as he had done countless times since fleeing the Street of Perfume Makers, and watched for any sign of pursuit. He saw no one. 'Thanks be to God,' he muttered, and was off again.

His destination lay in a square at the blighted heart of the Foreign Quarter, between a pair of ramshackle tenements assembled from the jetsam of other quarters, from scavenged brick and fire-blackened planks secured with a thick gesso of Nile mud. Their upper storeys out of plumb, these tenements leaned together like matrons sharing a secret; stout old timbers cut from a ship's keel kept them from touching. At their feet, in a weed-choked hollow littered with shards of pottery, a flight of rough-hewn steps plunged into the earth.

The Arab staggered into the square, making for the head of the stairs as a shadow rose from the tall grass. Steel glinted in the darkness. 'Nay,' the Arab gasped as the shadow moved to intercept him. 'Stay your hand, brother! It's me . . . Ya'qub! I must see al-Mulahid!

Quickly, for I am wounded!' The man stepped forward and scrutinized the Arab, Ya'qub. He was clad in black, his hands and exposed flesh daubed with lampblack; a fold of his turban hid all but his eyes from view, and these stared unblinking, glassy with the effects of hashish. Reluctantly, the sentry sheathed his curved dagger. He raised two fingers to his lips and gave an eerie whistle.

Trembling, the blood-smeared Arab descended the stairs into another world – one of antiquity beyond reckoning. He felt carvings in the stone beneath his outstretched hand; he had seen them enough by the light of day to know what they were: blasphemous reliefs of men cavorting with animal-headed demons, of salacious women worshipping at their feet and offering the creatures gifts of flesh and wine. Each rotting step bore him deeper into a lightless chasm, its air smoky and alive with unseen menace.

The stairs ended abruptly. Ya'qub's left hand brushed the edges of a jagged hole hacked into the wall, covered by a curtain of thick hide. He twitched this aside . . . and yelped as rough hands snatched at him, hauling him inside. 'Merciful Allah! Please! I am wounded! Guide me to al-Mulahid!'

In response, a voice growled: 'Where are the others?'

'I beg of you, brother: guide me to the master, and quickly! We—'

A lantern flared; quaking, Ya'qub watched a fearsome visage drift into the sullen light: a chiselled face as hard as stone and bronzed by the sun, clean-shaven, with close-cropped hair the colour of dark gold and eyes like the pale morning sky. *Al-Mulahid!* But the man to whom Ya'qub owed his allegiance was no son of the East; he was European – a Frankish convert to Islam known to his followers as al-Mulahid, the Heretic. 'Answer the question.' His Arabic was flawless, his accent Syrian. 'Where are the others?'

Ya'qub fell to his knees. 'Slain, master! Slain by the Devil himself!'

'You were tasked with watching the woman's house, nothing more. A devil should not have seen you, much less had the opportunity for bloodshed. How goes that, dog?'

'It was Akeeba's doing, master. He led us out of hiding and inside . . .'

Others figures emerged from the inky darkness. Black-clad fedayeen, soldiers of the Lord of Massaif whose mountainous fortress sheltered the Syrian branch of al-Hashishiyya. Their girdles bristled with dagger hilts and rage glittered in their eyes. The Heretic loomed over the cowering Arab, his face a cold and impassive mask. 'This devil of yours, what did he look like?'

'I . . . I did not see him well, master, but h-he was tall,' Ya'qub babbled. 'As tall as you, with a . . . a long s-scar down one cheek, and . . . and as dark as the pit of Hell! He moved like a thing possessed, never still! H-He . . . He struck the others down with . . . with a long Afghan knife!'

The Heretic's head snapped around. 'What did you say?'

'H-He had a . . . a k-knife.' Ya'qub quailed. 'Like the ones found among the tribesmen in the high mountains . . .'

'This cannot be coincidence,' muttered the man called the Heretic. He frowned, catching the Arab in his baleful gaze. 'You say he struck the others down, but not you?'

'No, master. Akeeba distracted him and I was able to get away.'

'You left your brothers to die, you mean.'

Ya'qub started. 'N-No, master! I escaped so as to bring word of this devil to you.'

'Devil? He was no devil,' the Heretic said, pale eyes blazing. 'He was but a man. Have you forgotten the words of our exalted lord, Ibn Sharr? "Go thou and slay," was his command to you when you joined us, "and when thou returnest my angels shall bear thee into Paradise. And should'st thou die, even so shall I send my angels to carry thee back to Paradise." Why did you not slay this man or, failing that, join your brothers in death? Did you doubt Ibn Sharr's word?'

The Syrians pressed closer to the quaking Arab, their hands on their knives.

'M-Master! I—'

'No! The time for excuses has passed,' the Heretic said. 'My command was simple: watch. Ibn Sharr's command simpler still: slay or die. You, who turned your back on Paradise, have failed both. What's worse, you may have led our enemy straight to us!'

'Please!' Ya'qub dropped to his belly. Tears mixed with the blood staining his cheeks; he clutched at the hem of the Heretic's khalat. 'I-I beg of you, m-master!'

'He is unworthy. Show him the door to Hell, brothers!' The Heretic turned his back as his fedayeen surged in, whetted knives flashing in the dim lamplight.

The Arab's scream died with him.

17

Once, the Heretic had been a soldier of Christ, one of a thousand young idealists gulled into joining the army of a crusading Frankish king, duped by fiery speeches and the promise of salvation. 'A man is born in sin,' he vaguely recalled the words of his elders, 'but in Outremer, even the unrepentant can come to grace.' Yet, those wise men – sinners all – had stayed behind, snug in their cathedrals and castles, while their burdensome sixth or seventh sons went off to die in search of God's grace.

And die they did. In droves. Some succumbed to disease, others to starvation; those who fate or faith had spared on the long road from Europe instead paid the butcher's bill outside the walls of Damascus, falling beneath a hail of Saracen arrows.

Twenty years ago, a foolish Nazarene youth died in the dust of Outremer, bereft of faith or salvation, the knowledge of his identity stolen when the sharp edge of a hurled stone collided with his skull; from this empty vessel of flesh and blood, the Heretic was born. His Syrian captors named him 'Badr', after the full moon shining over Damascus on the night of his rebirth, and set about teaching him what they believed was the one immutable truth under heaven: *La ilaha illa'llah.* 'There is no god but Allah . . .'

The Heretic, though, knew better.

Stone-faced, Badr al-Mulahid left his men to dispose of the Arab's body and ventured deeper into the underground warren. Through an open door, a winged scarab carved in the lintel, he passed into a room of mammoth columns, stalks of papyrus rendered in dark sandstone; widely spaced lamps revealed surfaces etched with figures of men engaged in the profane adoration of a seated queen. A temple to old gods, his mentor, Ibn Sharr, called this place, *a fitting lair for the Sons of Massaif.*

Badr knew this was more than a lair. Ibn Sharr had chosen these ruins for a reason. The Heretic paused near one column, staring up at the dim figure of a hawk-headed man wearing a bulbous crown, surrounded by vertical registers of strange writing. There was *something* here, something dark and primordial woven into the cryptic glyphs, a wellspring of long-slumbering power that only a cunning mind could unlock. Thus, while Badr spearheaded Massaif's campaign against the agents of Alamut, as a prelude to consolidating Syrian power in Cairo, his mentor pored over the strange carvings and artefacts in search of . . . what? Knowledge? Wisdom? Perhaps a weapon of such awesome power as to bring Alamut to its knees? That last was the Heretic's most fervent hope.

Though the Syrian and Persian sects of al-Hashishiyya shared a hint of common ideology – both followed the precepts of Ibn al-Sabbah – their political goals cast them into bitter rivalry. Alamut sought merely the destruction of the Abbasid Caliphate of Baghdad; Massaif sought the same, along with dominion over the Fatimids of Egypt and the expulsion of Nazarenes and Jews from Syria.

And we will have it, Alamut be damned! Ibn Sharr will see to that!

The Heretic's mentor exuded a mystery as old as Egypt's stones and as sinister as his name implied. Was he truly the Son of Wickedness, the devil of legend? No man among them could say with conviction, for about even the most mundane details – his true name, the line of his fathers, his land and people – Ibn Sharr

105

remained guarded; though innocuous, such crumbs of information could still wreck untold malice in the hands of an enemy. Thus, all his followers knew with any certainty was that the man who called himself Ibn Sharr was a magus in a nest of killers, the sorcerous right hand to the Old Man of the Mountain. For the Heretic, at least, that in itself was a sufficient pedigree.

Badr al-Mulahid traversed the long columned hall. At its far end a yawning doorway opened on a smaller room, where the carved visages of dead kings glowered out from niches in the soot-blackened walls. Another room waited beyond this, smaller still; fingers of ruddy light slipped past a curtain shielding its door. Even through the thick hide, Badr caught the salty reek of nitre, the aroma of sweet cedar oils, and an underlying hint of corruption: consequences of Ibn Sharr's explorations.

Quietly, the Heretic stepped into a chamber which must have served as a sanctuary in the dim and forgotten past. No doubt here Infidel priests had sacrificed the blood of innocents to their abhorrent gods. In the wavering lamplight, he could make out a cavalcade of figures covering the walls, animal-headed and profane, forever marching towards a glyph-etched alcove resembling a false door. The Heretic was not a squeamish man, nor was he overly superstitious. Yet, as his eyes fell upon a half-dozen desiccated bodies swaddled in age-blackened linen, a supernatural thrill raised gooseflesh on his neck. Furtively, he made a sign of warding against the evil eye.

Among these ancient corpses lay a relatively fresh kill: a naked young woman, a child of the Malabar Coast, her once-brown limbs now pale in death; the scarf which killed her remained knotted around her slender neck. The Heretic did not give her a second glance. She was merely a tool, a vessel, one his mentor called *al-saut al-maiyit*: the voice of the dead. Through her, Ibn Sharr could speak to the spirits haunting this place.

Low tables held the other implements of Ibn Sharr's craft: amulets of stone or gold or lapis lazuli, wall fragments bearing deeply incised images, candles, knives of copper and gold, glass vials and bundles of dried herbs, a mortar and pestle, ink-pots and loose scraps of paper. Incense burned in a small bronze chafing dish, its fragrance lost amid myriad stenches.

Ibn Sharr reclined on a silken divan before the false door. Lean and spare of frame, his hairless scalp gleamed like polished mahogany; he had a sharp face, hawkish, with deep-set eyes and a beard more grey than black. He did not look up as the Heretic entered, the weight of his attention focused on a worm-riddled skull cradled in his hands.

'We are as children compared to these ancients, Badr, unlettered and ignorant of what has come before us,' Ibn Sharr said after a few moments. He stroked the skull's leathery brow; his own face was no less gaunt. 'I have spoken with the ghost-kings of vanished Ubar, held congress with the ghûls of the Rub al-Khali, and scaled the treacherous slopes of Mount Lalesh the Accursed for but a fraction of the wisdom that is to be found here, in these forgotten crypts!'

The Heretic glanced about, his eyes narrowing. 'You have deciphered these carvings, then? And this wisdom you speak of . . . all of *this*' – he gestured at the glyphs and figures – 'can be turned against Alamut?'

'These carvings are but stories, Badr. Tales of principled gods and of pious men. No, the true wisdom is locked away here' – he tapped the skull – 'in the memories of those who came before us. But the spirits of the dead do not give up their secrets willingly. This one, he was a priest of the Silent Being, a god who loved truth and hated abomination. He has taught me much.' Ibn Sharr let his feverish gaze wander over the carved walls, over pagan gods and enigmatic symbols. 'Neferkaptah is the name of the one we seek.'

The Heretic's brow furrowed. 'Is . . . *he* here, among these husks?'

'No. His resting place is a day's journey upriver, in the City of the Dead on the west bank of the Nile. Ta-Djeser, it is called.' Ibn Sharr glanced sharply at his lieutenant, nostrils flaring. 'You have the stench of death about you, Badr.'

The Heretic bowed. 'An initiate failed us, my lord. I used his disgrace as a lesson to the others. But he brought disturbing news. Our enemy has reinforced.'

Ibn Sharr's eyes blazed. 'You are certain?'

'His three brother initiates were slain in the home of the last of Alamut's spies – and the only one we have yet to account for – by a scarred man who wielded a long Afghan blade. It is a peculiar detail and one that cannot be mere chance. I believe the *Emir* of the Knife has come to Cairo, my lord, and the Devil only knows how many of Alamut's fedayeen he has brought with him.'

Far from being perturbed, Ibn Sharr allowed himself a smile, nodding as though suddenly privy to a wondrous revelation. 'Rejoice,' he said, his dark robes rustling around him as he stood. 'Rejoice, for the gods have handed us the means to snatch a great victory.'

'A victory, my lord?'

'Indeed. By my art and by your skill have we not blinded Alamut's feeble master? Blind and soon deaf, Badr. To compensate, to keep from falling, he has foolishly thrust out his right hand. What does instinct tell you?'

'That we should deprive him of that outstretched hand!'

'And so we will, but carefully,' Ibn Sharr said, turning to his lieutenant. 'This Emir is your nemesis, Badr. As foolish as it would be to underestimate you, it would be equally lethal to misjudge him. He is like water on the fire of your soul, and he stands between you and the gates of Paradise. You must overcome him, if it is truly the will of the gods that we triumph here. For the glory of Massaif, my son, you must kill the *Emir* of the Knife. Kill him and bring me his corpse. O, what tales his soul will tell!'

The Heretic's eyes glowed with a murderous light. 'Then for the glory of Massaif, it will be so!'

The Third Surah

Destroyer of Delights

1

Dawn coloured the eastern horizon; overhead, the cloudless sky faded from lapis to turquoise, glazing with heat even as the sun's first blistering rays crept over the ridges of the Muqattam Hills. Golden light fired the domes and minarets of Cairo's innumerable mosques, surfaces of stone and carved stucco growing hot to the touch despite the early hour. A breeze whispering across the Nile brought little relief to the muezzins, those solemn men who rose from their beds to sing the adhan, the call to prayer, from balconies high above the city.

The song began at al-Azhar Mosque, where a gnarled old muezzin – blind and near crippled – clutched his great-grandson's arm for support, so frail that the breeze threatened to carry him off. Still, the greybeard's voice had power. The adhan rose from the depths of his thin chest and drifted over the city, its words lilting and poetic: '*Allahu akbar* . . .'

In turn, muezzins from every quarter of Cairo picked up the thread of the song, their voices commingling, merging into a single call to prayer:

> *God is most great.*
> *I bear witness that there is no god but Allah,*
> *And Muhammad is His Prophet.*
> *I bear witness that Ali is the friend of God.*

Come ye to prayer.
Come ye to salvation.
Come ye to the best deed.
God is most great.
There is no god but Allah.

'*La ilaha illa'llah . . .*'

And from his balcony high atop the minaret of al-Azhar Mosque, the ancient muezzin held the final note of the adhan longest of all. Hands gripping the railing, sightless eyes closed, he presented the picture of divine rapture even as the power of his voice faltered and failed, leaving him to sag against his great-grandson.

The haunting echo of his call drifted through a city gone eerily silent.

2

Groggy with sleep, Parysatis heard the muezzin's cry as it reached its crescendo and slowly faded away. She heard, but did not respond. The young woman lay on her back, her pillows scattered, a rumpled cotton sheet across her midsection. Exhaustion added to the despair already weighting her limbs; it required titanic effort for Parysatis simply to breathe.

She'd been right about the passage in the courtyard wall. Despite a series of maddening twists and turns, it delivered her back to the harem by way of a secret door in an unused bath inside the women's quarters – and blessedly close to her own tiny cell. A small triumph, to be sure, but bittersweet: the knowledge that she could reach the Caliph's side unseen – indeed, at will – only served to deepen an already overwhelming sense of helplessness. *What can I do?* It was a question to which Parysatis had no easy answers.

She pried her eyes open and looked around. Measured against

the sprawling space of her childhood home in Persia, in the hills above Shiraz, her room in the Caliph's harem was but a closet – ten paces each side with a curtained door of heavy brocade and a latticed window high up on the wall. Besides the bed, she had room enough for a colossal wardrobe of warm mahogany, a cedar chest, and a small ivory-inlaid table holding her cosmetics, along with a collection of delicate carvings – a family of horses – she had brought from home.

The size of her living quarters reflected her status as a minor concubine, while her position on the periphery of the harem, well away from the apartments of the Caliph's aunts, was intended as a slight. It was their none-too-subtle way of reminding Parysatis that she would never be anything more than an inconsequential rustic. She didn't mind their scorn; indeed, she even relished it. The less they thought of her, the less inclined they would be to meddle in her business. Now, however, the young woman cursed her own standoffishness. Either of those loose-lipped old whores would have made an invaluable ally.

Parysatis sighed, closing her eyes again. She wanted to sleep, to forget what she had seen, but she kept picturing Rashid's thin and wasted frame. The Caliph was alone, surrounded by enemies. He needed her. *Allah, guide me upon the right path . . .*

The sound of her door curtain rustling jerked Parysatis away from the threshold of sleep. She heard her young slave, Yasmina, enter; heard her *tsk* in disapproval. 'Come, mistress.' Yasmina spoke Arabic with a thick Egyptian accent. 'It's time you were up and about. Your prayers . . .'

'Remain unanswered.' Parysatis groaned as she struggled to raise herself up on her elbows. Through bleary eyes, she watched Yasmina place a heavy silver tray on the table beside her bed. She'd brought breakfast – a small loaf of bread with butter and honey, a wedge of cheese, a bowl of fresh dates, and a cup of warm khamr – along with towels and an ewer of water for her mistress's morning ablutions. Parysatis caught one whiff of the cheese and felt her stomach heave.

'You look unwell, mistress.' Yasmina frowned, unhappy that Parysatis had decided to get involved in matters beyond her reckoning. Barely fifteen, Yasmina possessed a maturity that belied her years. In a gown of saffron linen, thin and shapeless, she reminded Parysatis of the women who had followed her father's soldiers out on campaign – women of twisted sinew, sun-blackened, all trace of softness carved from their bodies by horrible privations; women who had borne too much death and suffering. Alone of any in the palace, Parysatis trusted Yasmina. Trusted her as much with her secrets as with her life. 'Did you not sleep?'

'I tried,' Parysatis said. Her voice dropped to a whisper so the women chattering in the courtyard outside her door could not hear. 'But I couldn't get him out of my mind. You weren't there, Yasmina. You didn't see him, didn't see how they treated him. Merciful Allah! I don't know what to do or where to turn . . . our lord is suffering and I can do nothing to aid him!' Tears of frustration spilled from the young woman's reddened eyes.

Yasmina sat on the edge of the bed and clasped Parysatis' hand. 'Please, mistress, if you're going to persist in this folly, at least let me go into the city and seek out she who gave me to you. She will know best what you should do.'

'How can a mere courtesan aid me?'

'The Gazelle is more than a mere courtesan, mistress,' Yasmina replied, a hint of defiance in her voice. 'She is acquainted with men of high repute, nobles who doubtless have long-simmering grievances against the vizier. She knows better than any the sort of man who could aid you in protecting the Caliph.'

'But what if she can't . . . or won't?'

'But she can! And I know she will, mistress. We have only to ask. If you are uncomfortable with me telling her what you've discovered, then I will beg her to come and talk to you in person. She will come! As Allah is my witness, I know she will!'

'Perhaps,' Parysatis said. 'But I must find a way to help the Caliph now, today, before the vizier and his minions can do him more harm.'

Yasmina fell silent; her chisel-sharp features – framed by long, straight hair like midnight silk – bore the stamp of single-minded concentration. After a moment, she said: 'If he is as ill as you say, mistress, we should seek a physician. Could a doctor not prepare a draught for you to administer . . . something to counteract any poison?'

Parysatis stiffened. *A physician!* How foolish was she not to have seen the obvious? In order for the vizier's minions to poison the Caliph, they would need to subvert the palace doctors, or more likely deny the physicians access until the toxins had a chance to settle in. But what if she made the physicians aware of the plot? Did she dare believe the answer might be as simple as that? 'A physician,' Parysatis said, nodding to Yasmina. 'I think you may be right.'

A rare smile brightened the younger woman's austere countenance.

Parysatis glanced about until her eyes lit upon the silver tray holding her untouched breakfast; she grimaced, her stomach churning as she reached for the mug of khamr and the cheese. 'Go find the Chief Eunuch. Tell him I am not feeling well.'

3

In a room on the third floor of Abu'l-Qasim's sanctuary, Assad answered the morning's call to prayer. It was not piety that compelled him. Indeed, save for rare occasions like today when he had a deception to prepare for, Assad had not performed the salat, the ritual prayers, in a number of years – not since a previous Hidden Master of Alamut had freed the followers of Ibn al-Sabbah from the burden of Holy Law.

Still, the Assassin rose promptly as a true believer should and made the proper ablutions before turning his scarred face towards

Mecca; clad in his white galabiyya, he knelt on a fringed rug of patterned wool. The practised rhythms of the salat returned easily enough: the recitations of '*Allahu akbar*' and the opening verses of the Qur'an, followed by a series of gestures and prostrations called rak'as; at the end, Assad muttered the Shahada, the Statement of Faith, and then lapsed into silence, presumably in private prayer.

After a long moment, he nodded, satisfied his actions would withstand the most rigorous scrutiny; he glided to his feet and went about making sure his appearance matched his performance. To get near the Caliph, Assad meant to adopt the oldest ruse in al-Hashishiyya's considerable arsenal: he would don the robes of a holy man, a Sufi. This sect of long-haired dervishes lurked in the corners and colonnades of mosques throughout the Moslem world; some sought oneness with God through asceticism, and others achieved it by embracing the mystic traditions and philosophies of Old Persia.

Assad had assumed the identity of a Sufi in the past – what Daoud ar-Rasul called 'taking the wool', after the coarse cloaks some members of the sect preferred – and he had done so in each instance armed only with a small knife, one easily secreted on his person, trusting he could do away with his victim and escape in the confusion. This time, he had to chuckle at the irony of it all: he was taking the wool in the name of peace, to save a man's life rather than end it; if things went awry he would need something much larger than a dagger to make good his escape – something large enough to stand out. God, it seemed, was not without a raucous sense of humour.

The Assassin caught up his salawar, sloughing off the surge of emotions emanating from the blade; he ignored the deep hunger, the yearning, the hate it created in the pit of his stomach – no doubt echoes of the lives it had cut short. Steel rasped on leather as he bared its killing edge.

Assad had seen few weapons in his lifetime to match the salawar's simplicity. Only three fingers at its widest, near the hilt, the weapon tapered gradually to a diamond point, its delicate appearance belied by the blade's thick T-shaped cross-section; this made it heavy and flexible, the perfect tool for piercing mail, flesh, and bone. Yet it was not a subtle weapon, not one easily concealed on his person. *It needs to be hidden in plain sight*, he reckoned. *But how?*

Wrapped in contemplation, Assad tossed the sheath on the bed. He rummaged through his meagre belongings and came up with a whetstone, an old cloth, and a small vial of oil. With these, he crossed the room to a cushioned window seat where the light was good. In time, the methodical *slish* of oiled stone against Damascus steel competed with the sounds filtering in from beyond the tightly latticed window screens.

Assad's perch overlooked an intersection of two narrow lanes, both deeply rutted and now clogged with foot traffic: porters swaying beneath the weight of baskets and bales; water-carriers with tinkling brass cups, their goatskins bloated and sweating; braying donkeys laden with goods and toiling under the reed switches of their young masters. Groups of veiled women chatted as they walked, guarded by cousins and uncles armed with walking sticks, bronze-skinned toddlers astride their shoulders. Runners threaded through the tumult, coarse linen tunics flapping. Their bare feet kicked up puffs of dust that added to the miasma of the street – a haze of sweat and musk, incense and offal, rancid fat and wood smoke that seemed to breed flies as punishing as those Moses called down from the heavens.

Beneath him, Assad heard a ramshackle souk blossom into existence, a rag-pickers' bazaar where men in colourless galabiyyas and filthy turbans squatted in the shade with their meagre wares spread before them. Sing-song voices rose above the clamour, hawkers touting scavenged pottery as new or poorly dyed cloth as the finest Damietta cotton; their endless palaver vied against the bleating of goats, the laughter of children, and the staccato paean of an itinerant coppersmith's hammer.

This was the city he'd forgotten. The city of his youth, its mesmerizing flow of humanity broken up by islands of commerce; he cared nothing for its noisy, shifting, restive, parti-coloured currents and, in return, it cared nothing for him. Who was he but one face among thousands? Across the breadth of the world, men might step aside and whisper his name with superstitious awe – *beware the* Emir *of the Knife!* – but to the city of his birth, Assad's existence was of no more consequence than a single grain of sand beneath the mighty pyramids . . .

The Assassin shook his head. He'd forgotten Cairo for a reason; its air, its water, its monuments, all of it made him as mawkish and self-indulgent as an old widow. Assad scowled; stone scraped against steel as he turned his mind's eye away from the maudlin and concentrated on the task at hand. The Caliph. How would he react upon learning that the Hidden Master of Alamut sought an alliance with him? Would the importance of it even register with him? *Still,* Assad thought, *I am sworn to defend him, to make him strong, and to sow fear in his enemies. But what if he is his own worst enemy . . . ?*

A soft knock at the door broke into Assad's introspection. He paused in mid-strop and glanced up as Zaynab entered. She moved quietly, clad in a gown of shimmering blue brocade that whispered with each step, a bundle cradled in the crook of her arm. The sight of Assad awake and sitting in the window, his scarred face cast half in shadow, caught her by surprise.

'I thought to find you still abed,' she said.

'There is too much to do.' Rising, he drove the point of his salawar into the windowsill and left it there, quivering. 'Have you brought the things I asked for?'

Zaynab handed him the bundle. 'Black woollen cloak, a belt, sandals. All of it used, but serviceable. Also an old Bedouin prayer rug and a copy of the Qur'an I borrowed from one of my father's more devout Berber guards.'

'Good. It seems Ibn al-Teymani shall live once again.'

'Who?'

'Ibn al-Teymani.' Assad glanced sidelong at her. Something in the tilt of Zaynab's head, in the way her delicate eyebrows arched in expectation, provoked desire in Assad. His rational side knew he was simply responding to her mystique; the Gazelle's livelihood depended on her ability to set a man at ease, to enter into his confidence quickly and unobtrusively. But Assad's irrational side, flattered by her attention, seized upon it and craved more. 'You've never heard of Ibn al-Teymani?'

'Never,' she replied. 'Was he a follower of the Hidden Master?'

'His messenger, more like.'

Zaynab sat at the edge of Assad's bed, stiff-backed and proper. From under a loose shawl of pale muslin her hair glistened like polished mahogany; she watched him open the bundle and examine the items one by one. 'And these things will make him live again? I sense the beginnings of what surely must be a profound story . . . or a profound ruse.'

Assad flashed a sharp smile. 'Both. "Ibn al-Teymani" is a ghost, a name I inherited from my mentor, Daoud ar-Rasul.' The Assassin let the sandals fall to the floor and then slipped them on. Woven hemp and old leather creaked; he flexed his toes, rocked back on to his heels and then up on to the balls of his feet. Nodding, he picked up the threadbare black cloak and shook it free. 'Daoud was never a soldier of the fedayeen. When the Hidden Master dispatched him, say, to Baghdad or Damascus, it was because he wished to send an undeniable message. As our enemies tend to be of the devout sort, Daoud made an art of taking the wool in order to get near them. He took to impersonating an Arab holy man, whom he called Ibn al-Teymani, and would attend mosque day after day; afterwards, he engaged those around him in conversation or debate – making sure the recipient of Alamut's message was among them.'

'And this bit of subterfuge well and truly worked, with no other form of persuasion?' Zaynab held her head just so, her curiosity tempered with scepticism.

Assad snorted. 'It well and truly worked for Daoud. When he would take the wool, he would become an Arab holy man to his very soul, a Bedouin son of the desert who was as pious as he was mad. For myself, I trust that whomever I'm speaking with understands his life hinges on my good will. I remember a time in Basra . . .'

Basra. After a decade, Assad recalled only fragments of it: narrow lanes of whitewashed mudbrick that reflected the too-hot sun; palm trees rustling in the constant breeze off the Persian Gulf; he recalled sitting in the bazaar, under a striped awning, where he sipped icy sharabs with the local cleric while the man's green-furred monkey bedevilled his neighbour's cats.

He recalled, too, the cleric's mosque: a small structure, rustic, built of gypsum-plastered brick and sandstone tiles. Despite its size, however, the cleric roared and thundered as vociferously as if he preached from the great pulpits of Baghdad. In almost every sermon he made a point of reviling and refuting the 'murderous fanatics of Alamut'. It was only a matter of time before his voice reached the ears of the Hidden Master. Rather than kill him, which would perhaps lend credence to the cleric's words, the Lord of Alamut sent Assad, posing as Ibn al-Teymani, to reason with him.

After days of getting to know the man, of learning his peculiarities and his passions, Assad came to his home one night with an irrefutable offer. Catching the cleric unawares, he hurled him to the ground and put a heel to his throat. He drew a knife with one hand and a bag of gold with the other. 'A martyr or a man of means,' Assad spat. 'Choose now!'

Zaynab's hazel eyes widened. 'Which did he choose?'

'The gold, of course. The man was no fool.' Assad chuckled. 'Some time later, his people asked him why the sudden change of heart, why had he softened his stance against the devils of Alamut; I'm told the cleric replied – and, mind you, without the slightest pause – that though our arguments were brief, they had great weight.'

The sound of Zaynab's laughter caught Assad off guard; it had a bright quality, like chimes tinkling on a cool breeze. He almost smiled; instead, he turned away, a frown creasing his brow. What was it that round-faced tailor had said? *Beware, my friend, she is enchanting.* The man had not lied.

Lapsing into silence, Zaynab stood and walked to the window, drawn by the gleam of watered steel. 'Is it true what men say about you? That you journeyed to the Roof of the World and destroyed a Prince of the Djinn over this knife?'

'Is that what men say?' The Assassin picked the empty sheath up off the bed and joined her by the window. He stood on one side, Zaynab on the other; between them, his salawar protruded from the sill, the silver wire in its hilt sparkling.

Zaynab raised her shoulders in a half-apologetic shrug. 'It is, but surely it must be an exaggeration.'

'No, there is a kernel of truth to it, but just a kernel. I did journey to the Roof of the World, into the peaks and passes of the high Afghan Mountains, but it was no djinni I fought. He was a chieftain of the Afridis, a madman who had waylaid emissaries of Alamut on their return from Cathay the year before. I was the assassin sent to avenge them.'

She shuddered as a chill passed through her. 'Alone?'

Assad leaned against the window frame, arms folded across his chest. 'Some tasks are best suited to a single man. I was a soldier before Daoud recruited me into al-Hashishiyya, but rather than sacrifice myself to kill a single man I instead took a different path. I killed them one by one, always leaving the bodies where others of the tribe could find them. Finally, when he had no more warriors left to sacrifice, the chief came for me. Armed with this. As you can see' – he tapped the scar bisecting the left side of his face with the tip of the leather-bound sheath – 'I did not escape unscathed.'

'And thus the *Emir* of the Knife was born,' she said. He watched as she extended her hand towards the leering pommel; he made no move to stop her as her fingers brushed the cool ivory, as her flesh made contact. The response was immediate. Zaynab gasped and recoiled, snatching her hand back as though the hilt were white-hot. She stared at Assad with terror in her eyes. 'Merciful Allah! What kind of deviltry . . . ?'

'Whoever forged it bound an insatiable hate into the steel.' Assad tugged it free, oblivious to the galvanizing rush of emotion, and held it up before his eyes to study the pattern of light and dark whorls running through the blade. 'It wants revenge.'

'Revenge against whom?'

'Only Allah can say for sure. Not even the Afghans recall for what reason their ancestors created it, only that it's a relic of the Time of Ignorance. The Afridis found it in the safekeeping of a prince of Kabul when they sacked that city. Their chief took the blade back into the high mountains and made it his own, an heirloom of power. But his sons, and the sons of his sons, were weak-willed and indolent. Whatever sorcery the ancients imprisoned in the steel had no trouble sowing madness among them. It needs a stern master, I've found.'

'But how can you stand to touch it? It's unclean!'

A grim smile curled Assad's lips. Carefully, he slid the blade home into its sheath. 'It brings me good fortune.'

The Assassin turned away from the window as Abu'l-Qasim shouldered through the door, gold glittering on his fingers, and his robes of cream and white rustling. Farouk followed in his wake, looking as though something had scared him from his bed. Assad grinned at the Persian. 'I see you've met our new host.'

'Yes, yes,' Farouk snapped. 'The mighty King of Thieves! *Bismillah!* Now that we are allies, he owes me for a shipment of incense his swine stole from me last year!'

'That was yours?' Abu'l-Qasim smiled broadly. 'You move a fine product, my friend. Perhaps we should speak of a joint business venture. Your wares, my guards . . . we split the profits equally. What say you?'

'And give you the opportunity to rob me twice?'

Abu'l-Qasim roared with laughter. 'By God! Persians are the shrewdest of men! This one saw right through me!' He clapped a hand on Farouk's shoulder, giving him a good-natured shake. 'I like you, Persian. Mayhap I'll even pay you what you're owed.'

'Allah's blessings upon you, O generous King of Thieves.'

'Indeed.' Abu'l-Qasim glanced sidelong at his daughter. Zaynab remained by the window, her hand clasped to her breast as though it still pained her. Tension crinkled the corners of her eyes; her gaze drifted back to the weapon clutched in Assad's fist. 'Is aught amiss?'

His question drew from her a terse rebuff. 'No. The morning grows late. We should be about our business.'

'And what is our business, eh?' Abu'l-Qasim turned to Assad. The Assassin, however, appeared lost in thought. He stared at his salawar, weighing it in the palms of his hands, eyes slitted in concentration. 'Assad. What goes?'

Assad glanced up. 'You have a network of spies. Send them out to hunt down the dog who escaped me last night.'

'You marked him well enough, I gather?'

'Well enough that he'll need a surgeon.'

Abu'l-Qasim nodded. 'I know a good many of them. I'll make the enquiries myself.'

'What of the bodies that were left behind?'

'I sent men last night to collect the corpses and feed them to the Nile. They recognized one of them, the Ethiopian. His name was Akeeba.'

Assad's eyes narrowed. 'Was he a rival of yours?'

The question brought a wide smile to the King of Thieves' face. 'Him? *Y'Allah!* He was a pig, a two-copper thug who terrorized the derelicts and degenerates of the Foreign Quarter. A rival? Bah!'

'Have your men ask around. See if this Akeeba might have boasted about his new employer. What of the urban militia?'

'What of them? They won't interfere, but we have a different problem in that regard.' He glanced back at Zaynab. 'Their new captain, Massoud, has noticed the Gazelle's absence. He's a Circassian, one of the White Slaves of the River. He also thinks himself a rakish cavalier. He's heard rumours and has now decided to make finding her his priority. The man is a fool, but a dangerous fool.'

'Can your people deal with him?'

Abu'l-Qasim deferred to his daughter.

'Massoud is more than a good man and an ardent admirer,' Zaynab said. She walked away from the window. 'When he served in the palace he was a conduit of information, though he did not know it. His concern is touching. I will handle him myself. I assume it's not safe for me to return home?'

'Not yet,' Assad said. 'Not until we have some idea who is behind this.'

Zaynab chewed her lip. 'Then you make it difficult for me to allay Massoud's concerns. I doubt, Father, that you'd allow him to pay me a visit in your den of thieves?'

'*Y'Allah!* Why not throw me to the jackals?' Abu'l-Qasim waved the suggestion away, scowling. Despite paying for their silence, the King of Thieves did not trust the militia or their new captain – the man's admiration for Zaynab be damned.

'Of course not. I will need some time to devise a way of contacting Massoud. Speaking with him in person would be best, but regardless I will concoct a tale to answer his most pressing concerns. Perhaps we can even use him to deflect rumours.'

Assad nodded and turned to Farouk. 'I want everything you can gather regarding the Templars: names, how many guards the vizier assigned to them, what portion of the palace they're housed in, where their horses are stabled, everything.'

'Templars?' Abu'l-Qasim's nostrils flared. 'What's this?'

'Two arrived last night, escorted by a detachment of Fatimid cavalry. I want to know their purpose.'

The Persian raised an eyebrow. 'Have they become targets?'

'*Inshallah.*'

'This might be more difficult than you imagine,' Farouk said. 'I have only limited resources inside the palace – a lesser steward, a man whose cousin's cousin is a guard, but no one of particularly high rank . . .'

'I can be of service in this matter as well,' Zaynab said. 'My acquaintances at the palace run the gamut, from Mamelukes to chamberlains to ladies of the harem. Let me try and get word to them. No doubt the appearance of Templars has stirred a hornets' nest in their midst.'

Farouk inclined his head, a gesture of respect. 'That would be most excellent, lady.'

'And while the rest of you are occupied with these tasks, I will see about getting close to the Caliph.'

Abu'l-Qasim shook his head. 'I still say you are wasting your time with that notion, Assad. The vizier – Allah's curse be upon him! – rarely lets the Caliph out of his sight. Like as not, his guards will skewer you before you can get too close.'

'Then perhaps . . .' Assad began, steel whispering on leather as he slid his salawar free of its sheath. 'Perhaps I'll get close to the vizier, instead.' Cold eyes stared past the blade. 'Have you a carpenter in your entourage, O King?'

Abu'l-Qasim frowned. 'I can find one.'

'Do so, and quickly,' Assad replied. 'I have an idea how I can hide this in plain sight.'

4

The old physician summoned to the harem found Parysatis huddled in her bed, damp-browed and dishevelled, the stink of vomit – of sour wine and cheese – fouling the air of her tiny room. He shuffled to her bedside and sat, a stoop-shouldered man with a bulbous nose whose hair, beneath a blue embroidered skullcap, was silver and sparse. The women of the harem knew him as al-Gid, Grandfather. 'What troubles you, child?' he said, placing the rigid leather bag of his profession on the floor beside them.

'I must speak with you,' Parysatis whispered in Persian, a tongue she knew he spoke. 'Alone.' She looked past him; he followed her gaze. The Chief Eunuch of the Harem, a native Egyptian called Lu'lu, stood in the doorway of Parysatis' cell – a tyrant moulded of tawny fat who swathed himself in gold, silks, and linens as fine as any worn by the women in his care. Piggish eyes outlined in kohl and green malachite held a glimmer of distress. Though not, Parysatis decided, over her health. No, the Chief Eunuch's sole concern was decorum: he insisted that his charges be demure, lovely, and, above all else, quiet. Sickness, which was ever the enemy of good order, upset his equilibrium.

Behind him, several women pressed close, along with a gaggle of lesser eunuchs and servants. An illness in their midst was as much a cause for concern as it was for speculation. Had a rival poisoned her? Maybe she had tried to poison herself? Perhaps she wasn't ill at all, but with child? In hushed voices, like the twittering of so many birds, the women wagered on the outcome, betting bits of jewellery on which vicious rumour would prove true.

The physician frowned. 'Leave us. All of you.'

'Go away, my flowers!' The Chief Eunuch waved the gawkers away. 'Go! We must have privacy!'

'You too, my friend,' al-Gid said, his tone sharp.

Lu'lu scowled; fleshy lips writhed, peeling back in a grimace of displeasure. Despite being a slave, the harem's master wasn't accustomed to taking orders from anyone less than the vizier himself. For a moment Parysatis thought he might rebuke the physician for his impudence, or worse, summon his guards and have the old man beaten. Ultimately, however, Lu'lu held his tongue. Even he knew better than to trifle with al-Gid.

The old physician watched in silence as the eunuch backed out of the room and pulled the curtain closed with a savage tug. Al-Gid grunted, a dismissive sound, and then turned to Parysatis. 'That one has grown too large for his own pantaloons,' he muttered in Persian. Gently, he placed the back of one wrinkled hand against the young woman's forehead, feeling for a fever. The sleeve of his crisp white galabiyya smelled of incense and old herbs. 'So, child? We are alone . . .'

'I . . . I m-must ask you a delicate question.'

The physician raised a bushy eyebrow. 'Must you?'

'Have . . .' Parysatis flushed, stumbling over her words. 'Have you seen him? The Caliph, I mean? Perhaps within the last week?'

'A delicate question, indeed.' Al-Gid propped his elbow on his knee and tugged at the small tuft of hair beneath his lower lip. 'What concern is this of yours, child? Did you have a dream?'

'Please!' Parysatis' fingers plucked at the hem of his sleeve. 'Please, Grandfather, have you seen him recently?'

'I saw him last week, during Friday prayers at the Grey Mosque, but I was not allowed near.'

'And how did he seem?'

Al-Gid sighed; absently, he patted her hand, his brows knitting together in concern. 'Not well, God's mercy upon him. In truth, his eunuchs and guards have kept him sequestered from me for some time now. Though for what reason, I cannot say.'

Parysatis squeezed her eyes shut, afraid of what her next words would conjure. Had she misjudged him? Would this kindly old man be her saviour, or would he become her executioner? *Allah preserve me!* 'It's not his eunuchs or his guards who are to blame,' she said in a small voice. 'It's his vizier.'

'Are you addled, girl? What do you mean? Here, look at me.' He grasped her shoulders and gave her a light shake. 'Look at me, child. Why would the vizier wish to keep me away from the Caliph? What purpose could . . . ?' But al-Gid did not finish his sentence. In a twinkling, apprehension gave way to cold clarity; while the years may have palsied the old man's hands, they in no way dulled his mind. It remained as sharp as ever as the cogs and mechanisms of suspicion shuddered into place. He knew of only one reason a vizier might wish to keep the Caliph's physicians at arm's length; an age-old reason that did not bode well for young Rashid al-Hasan: Jalal, like his predecessors, had ambitions to rule. All traces of warmth drained from al-Gid's features; his frown deepened and his eyes narrowed to slits of black fire. He leaned closer. 'How do you know this, child?'

'I overheard him talking to the old eunuch who rules over the Caliph's apartments.'

'Yes, Mustapha,' the physician said, nodding. 'And you are sure? You are sure *this* is what they talked about? What you accuse them of, child, is an abomination before God! Could you have mis-understood what was said . . . ?'

Parysatis shook her head. 'I heard the vizier as clearly as I hear you now, Grandfather. By month's end, he wants the Caliph on his deathbed! He ordered this Mustapha to see it done. Later, that scoundrel brought the Caliph a goblet of tainted wine. By the grace of God, I was there to pour it out. I replaced the wine with water from the courtyard fountain before—'

Al-Gid cut her off. 'You did all this under the noses of his guards and his chamberlains? As Allah is my witness, child, lie to me again and I will hand you over to the Chief Eunuch to be punished!'

Parysatis bolted upright, nostrils flaring. 'I have not lied to you, old man! I did these things!'

'How? The Jandariyah allow no one inside the Caliph's apart-ments without the vizier's permission! How did you—'

'You have heard the tale of the False Kaaba, Grandfather? The eunuchs speak of it, but in whispers and then only to frighten us,' Parysatis said. Her anger ebbed, and she sagged back against her pillows. 'They say once a mad Caliph ruled over Cairo, and in his madness he ordered passages cut into the walls, into the found-ations of this very palace. Where these secret paths intersected, the eunuchs say he caused his slaves to build a pleasure kiosk, a blasphemous mockery of the most holy Kaaba of Mecca. Those who knew of its existence he had strangled, their bodies buried in a cellar beneath his kiosk. For the remainder of his reign, this Mad Caliph would kidnap his newest concubines from the harem and drag them down into this hell he had created, there to despoil and brutalize them. Those who survived he either handed over to his loyal Mamelukes or drowned in a marble pool of wine.'

'And it was his own sister who finally ended his madness,' al-Gid said impatiently. 'Yes, I know it well. A fabulous legend, like something from the *Book of a Thousand Tales*. But what does that have to do with anything?'

'The Mad Caliph's passages exist, Grandfather. The palace is riddled with them. That's how I overheard the vizier's plans.' In short order, Parysatis unburdened her soul, relating everything to the dumb-struck physician – from how she'd accidentally discovered the first door over a year ago, in a deserted storeroom, to her nocturnal wanderings through those narrow paths between the walls where men once spied upon their fellows. 'At first,' she said, 'I sought ways out of the palace, ways to escape Cairo and return to my home in Persia. Later, when flight proved fruitless, I merely sought ways to escape the boredom of the harem.' Further, she told him what she had seen and heard in the Golden Hall, in the Caliph's apartments, and of the courtyard door that brought her back to the harem. 'It exits in an old bathing chamber the women no longer use, not a hundred paces from here.'

'Merciful Allah!'

Parysatis' voice grew thick with emotion; tears welled at the corners of her dark eyes and spilled down her cheeks. 'He is so close, Grandfather! So close, and I know not how to help him! Even now, I cannot say for certain I am doing the right thing by telling you any of this. But I do not know whom else to trust or where else to turn! I risk everything, for you need only say a word to the vizier and it will be as though I never existed. The Caliph will drink their foul poison and all will be for naught . . . !'

'No, child,' al-Gid said, his face solemn. 'You have done the right thing. I owe nothing to Jalal – may Allah's curse be upon him! The man is a scheming jackal who thinks himself well beyond his station. I do, however, owe my life, and the lives of my daughters, to Rashid's grandfather. He died before I could repay his many mercies; his son, too. Thus has his grandson inherited my gratitude, and my need to make things right in the eyes of God. I must get in to see him, child. Will you guide me by these secret ways of yours?'

Parysatis jammed the knuckles of her hand against her teeth; she dared not breathe for fear of upsetting the delicate balance. *Had she found an ally?* 'Can . . . Can you t-truly help the Caliph?'

'*Inshallah*,' al-Gid said, placing his palm over his heart. 'I will try.'

Tears cascaded down the young woman's cheeks; she sobbed and flung her arms around the physician's neck. 'Bless you, Grandfather!'

'Hush, child. We have much to do yet.' He disengaged from her embrace and nodded. 'Dry your eyes. Good. Now, lie back and feign illness. Nothing too dramatic.'

Parysatis sank down and composed herself. Her dark hair in disarray, her eyes red and puffy, and her skin pale: one could surmise that she perhaps suffered from a fever. Al-Gid nodded again.

'Allah's mercy upon us,' he whispered. Joints creaking, the old physician gained his feet and made his way to the door. He yanked the curtain aside, revealing a bevy of impatient and expectant faces – the Chief Eunuch's prominent among them.

'Well?'

'She is very ill, my friend. The poor girl has a fever which has caused a serious imbalance in her humours.' The physician glanced back over his shoulder in mock concern. 'I will need to bleed her.'

'See it done, then,' Lu'lu replied.

Al-Gid touched the eunuch's elbow and guided him a few steps away from the others. He kept his voice low, his face grave. 'My friend, you do not wish me to do this here. Her condition is such that she is liable to produce a copious amount of foul-smelling blood. I need a secluded place, one your slaves may easily scrub afterwards, and one that is well away from the other flowers of your garden. Is there not an unused bath near?'

'There is.' Lu'lu snapped his fingers; the gesture brought one of his lieutenants forward, a squat Sudanese eunuch in garish silks. 'See she is brought to the old hammam,' he said. He held the lesser eunuch's eye for a long moment before dismissing him to his task and turning back to face al-Gid. 'Find me when you are finished, physician. We must discuss today's improprieties.' Without waiting for a reply, the Chief Eunuch whirled and walked away, the harem women scattering before him like a flock of frightened pigeons.

Al-Gid's eyes were cold and narrow slits. 'Improprieties. Of course.'

Under the Sudanese lieutenant's direction, a cadre of guards – muscular black eunuchs in white silk pantaloons and vests of silvered mail, curved swords thrust into leopard-skin sashes – hoisted Parysatis' narrow bed on to their shoulders and carried the frightened woman to the deserted bath. Al-Gid walked beside them, and though she could not see her, Parysatis knew Yasmina would not be far away.

The cortège passed through unbarred doors of polished cedar – tall and ancient and set with delicate arabesques of silver and gold – and into the hammam proper. It was a relic of a time when the Caliph's women numbered well over three hundred, one for every day of the year; though deserted for a decade, the servants of the palace took great care to ensure the old bath did not go to seed. At its heart stood a vast room, an octagon of polished marble beneath a dome painted to resemble a cloudless sky, its apex pierced by clerestory windows. Motes of dust drifted through shafts of amber light that warmed the mosaic tiles underfoot. The pools and plunge baths were dry, the fountains silent; niches meant for towels and linens stood empty.

The eunuch guards gently lowered Parysatis' bed to the ground and filed out of the bath, leaving their Sudanese lieutenant behind. Al-Gid motioned him along. 'Go. I must have privacy.'

The lieutenant shook his head. 'My lord's orders,' he said. 'I am to remain as insurance against impropriety.'

'Impossible.' The old physician straightened; he towered over the intractable eunuch. 'Please, my friend. This is not something you should be privy to, especially if the sight of blood sickens you. It is liable to be messy.'

The African's nostrils flared; his lips peeled back in a sneer of contempt to reveal teeth long ago filed to points. 'I was not born a eunuch, Grandfather. My people were flesh-eaters before the Arabs came. I used to sit at my father's elbow and we would drink our enemies' blood like wine, so save your concerns for those other simpering fools! You are wasting precious time. I will remain, and there is naught you can say about it. Come and let us help the poor dear before—'

As Parysatis watched this stalemate unfold, Yasmina, who had tarried at the door, crept up behind the eunuch. She moved like a cat, lithe and silent, far more predatory than a girl of her years should have been. Parysatis saw her pause, kneel, and heft a thick pottery jar off the floor. Before she or al-Gid had a chance to react, Yasmina closed on the eunuch and swung the jar like a headsman swings his axe. There was an explosion of dust, and Parysatis winced at the sound of pottery shattering against the African's skull.

The eunuch dropped without a sound.

Al-Gid cursed. 'Merciful Allah, girl! What are you doing?'

Yasmina's eyes were hard as she knelt beside the unconscious eunuch. Quickly, she trussed and gagged him with his own sash. 'We can beg forgiveness later,' she said. 'Hurry, mistress.'

Parysatis, clad only in a thin linen gown, flung the covers back and leapt from her bed on legs made unsteady by a mixture of fear and hope. 'Stay and keep watch, Yasmina!'

Bare feet pattering on the tile, Parysatis crossed to the western corner of the bath, still in shadow. She motioned for the old physician to bring his bag and follow. The walls of the hammam had neither telltale niches nor deep carvings; rather, they boasted a variety of inlays, from enamelled lotus buds to traceries of ivy done in gold and precious wood, to magnificent birds fashioned of silver with cloisonné feathers and jewelled eyes – an iridescent jungle that should have surrounded a pool of sparkling turquoise water.

Easily, Parysatis found the hidden door's trigger: an emerald leaf veined in gold filigree. Depressing it caused a chain-reaction; the faint creak of a counterweight presaged the opening of a narrow section of wall. Hinges ground together like stones in a quern. Parysatis put her shoulder against the door and forced it wider still.

Al-Gid peered inside; he frowned at the walls of rough-edged brick. Motes of dust drifted through fingers of light seeping in from the spy holes. 'This is the way?'

'It will bring us to the Caliph's courtyard.'

The old man exhaled. 'Lead on, then, and may Allah bless us in our folly!'

5

A fretted screen of old teak concealed the Gazelle from casual view. She sat in one corner of the open gallery overlooking her father's garden courtyard, chafing at the seclusion forced upon her simply because others sought her death. It was unnatural, this hiding, no matter how palatable her surroundings. She wanted to do more than write letters and stamp out rumours. She wanted to do *something*.

Willows and palm trees rustled in the light breeze. Zaynab stared at the writing material strewn on the table before her. The art of gathering information was difficult even under ideal circumstances; it was virtually impossible through third parties and intermediaries. How could she trust the words of men she did not speak directly to? Still, she deferred to her father's wishes; Cairo's streets were unsafe until her enemies chose to reveal themselves. She had little choice but to make the best of it.

Her father had left her neither alone nor unguarded. In the courtyard below, heavily armed Berber mercenaries watched as an endless parade of cutpurses and sneak-thieves streamed through the gate, pressed into the King of Thieves' service as rumour-mongers and eavesdroppers. Upon returning, they reported their findings to her father's spymaster, a squint-eyed snake of a man who wore the distinctive blue turban of the Banu Zuwayla, a local Berber tribe long in her father's association. Slowly – too slowly for Zaynab's tastes – his reports trickled up to her.

She thumbed through the newest sheaf of papers, a litany of grief written in a startlingly fine hand. Half were petitions brought by her father's followers: a patriarch complaining of the thieves who had stolen his granddaughter's dowry; a mother looking for vengeance on the robbers who had beaten her favourite son; a distraught family hoping in vain to find the kidnappers who had seized their two youngest children. She read them dispassionately, seeking some word concerning the men Assad had killed in her home or the arrival of the two Templars. She found nothing, save a useless chronicle of half-truths, petty crimes, and innuendo. Nothing concrete! Zaynab cursed and slammed the papers down in mounting frustration. *Who are they and why won't they show themselves?*

The sound of footsteps intruded. Zaynab glanced up to see Assad approaching. He wore a simple linen shirt and the cloak of a Sufi, though his bearing and demeanour shattered the illusion he was a holy man.

'This is ridiculous,' she said by way of greeting. 'How can I be effective if I am kept shuttered away from my resources?'

Assad took a seat opposite the slender courtesan. 'Your father wants you protected.'

'Why? Because I'm a woman? *Ya salaam!*' Zaynab made a dismissive gesture. 'You can appeal to him. You, he might listen to. I need to get out for a while, to hear what my people are saying in the streets – firsthand, and not filtered through the perceptions of others. Am I not the eyes and ears of al-Hashishiyya in Cairo?'

'No. You *were* the eyes and ears of al-Hashishiyya in Cairo. Whoever betrayed you and killed al-Hajj very effectively compromised your worth to our master. Our enemies know your identity; it is only a matter of time before the rest of Cairo knows it as well. Your father's judgement is sound. You will stay put and stay hidden.'

Zaynab leaned towards him, her full lips curling into a sneer of disdain. 'Does it not frustrate you that our enemies seem more audacious than we are? That they kill our brothers and friends with such impunity? Does it not spark desire in your breast to do them one better?'

'This is no game of one-upmanship,' Assad said. 'It is a game of patience. I know better than to answer audacity with recklessness. We will wait them out, wait for them to make a mistake. And when they do, *inshallah*, I will send them straight to Hell.'

'You? When do I get to strike a blow?' Zaynab sat back with a frustrated curse. 'You're right, I'm sure, but I detest doing nothing. It makes me feel . . . useless.'

Assad picked up a loose sheet of paper. 'What have you discovered about the godforsaken Nazarenes?'

'Nothing! I have been at this all morning and only gathered two by-blow rumours: one declares them a pair of captured Franks brought to Cairo for execution; the other paints them as renegades seeking to betray their former lord.'

'Prisoners, even men of rank, are rarely allowed to keep their weapons and armour,' Assad said. 'And renegades would have doffed those damnable surcoats long before entering Moslem territory. Most likely they are emissaries from Jerusalem on some errand or another.'

'Of course they are, and I could find out more if you would but untie my hands.' Zaynab glanced up, a devilish gleam in her eyes. 'I could come with you to the Grey Mosque. It's only a stone's throw from the palace gates . . .'

Assad ignored her. He glanced down into the garden where thieves sprawled in the shade, propped on cushions like men of leisure. After a moment he stirred. 'Your best course of action is to wait, and to pray the messages you have sent make it through to your contacts in the palace.'

'A game of patience,' Zaynab spat.

Assad gave her a faint smile. He started to rise when a sudden commotion in the courtyard drew his attention; frowning, Zaynab followed his gaze. She saw Musa practically dragging another beggar through the gate. The mismatched pair hurried up the steps and into the gallery, the one-eyed man flushed and breathless.

'Mistress.' Musa salaamed; he turned to the other beggar, a sun-blackened Egyptian who self-consciously smoothed the front of his torn and filthy galabiyya. He reeked of stale sweat, piss, and onions. 'Quickly! Tell her what you told me!'

The beggar bowed. Tremors ran the length of his spine, causing his limbs to shudder and his head to twitch as though the fingers of a celestial puppeteer plucked at the strings holding him erect. 'Allah's mercy upon you, mistress,' he managed. 'Men came around . . . around the Nile Gate this morning, asking after you and more.'

'Not just the Nile Gate,' Musa added. 'I'm told they visited all of the gates.'

Zaynab nodded. 'Who were they?'

'I . . . I only saw three of them. The man doing the talking had an infected eye and claimed he was an old friend of yours, a carpet-seller from Aleppo. Other two were evil-looking villains, mayhap his porters . . .'

'And what were they asking?'

'If we'd seen you, mistress . . . or maybe a rough customer carrying a long knife with a djinni's face on the pommel.'

Assad grunted. 'They wasted no time.'

'They must be confederates of the men you killed last night,' Zaynab said, her fingers drumming against the arm-rests of her chair. Her composure slipped; spots of colour blossomed on her cheeks. 'He claimed to be an old friend of mine, you say?'

The beggar shuffled from foot to foot. 'Aye. He . . . He offered us a whore's weight in silver if we knew anything, but we told 'em to bugger off, mistress.'

'You did the right thing, my friend.' Zaynab's delicate nostrils flared. '*Y'Allah!* I weary of this game of patience we're playing!'

Assad smiled, cold and deadly. 'Then let us change the rules.'

'What do you have in mind?'

He nodded to the Egyptian beggar. 'Listen carefully and take my words back to your brothers at the Nile Gate. See it spreads to the other gates, as well. Tell them we will offer them one better: a whore's weight in gold to the one who brings this seller of carpets to us!'

'Alive?' The beggar flashed a decaying smile, his head bobbing.

'He is useless to us otherwise.'

Musa, though, shook his head and scratched at his bearded jaw. 'Mistress, your father—'

'I do not answer to my father!' she snapped. 'Not in this matter! Whoever this seller of carpets is, he and I have business to discuss! And I'd wager Assad has a few things to ask him, as well!'

'Oh, I have, indeed,' the Assassin said. Musa shot him a black glance but said nothing.

'Will you do this?' she asked the beggar.

The Egyptian nodded vigorously.

'Excellent.' Zaynab took up a silver pen, dipped it in ink, and wrote something on a scrap of paper. 'Here. Take this down to the man in the blue turban. He will give you a few coins and see you have something to eat before you go. Fidelity such as yours cannot go unrewarded.'

'Thank you, mistress.' And with a clumsy salaam, the beggar backed away, turned, and scurried for the stairs.

Assad grunted. 'Can that one be trusted?'

'As much as you or I,' Musa said.

'That's small comfort.' The Assassin turned and made to leave, pausing only to fix his stern glance on the courtesan. 'I will be back as soon as I can. Bide here and do nothing foolish.'

'I will be the picture of obedience,' she replied as he walked away. 'As Allah is my witness.' Zaynab watched him go and then turned to Musa. She picked a letter up off the table, the paper triple-folded and sealed, a gazelle impressed in the scarlet wax. 'Forgive my outburst earlier, dear friend, but this might be the break we've been hoping for. If you please, have this delivered to the commander of the Circassian Mamelukes, Massoud, immediately. It requires no answer.'

The one-eyed man nodded and accepted the missive.

'I have chosen a safe location in which to meet with him—'

'Your father won't be pleased.' Musa scowled. 'Nor will your Emir.'

'You will come with me, along with a detachment of my father's Berbers, of course. There is an inn in the Soldiers' Quarter run by an old campaigner called Ahmed the Crippled. Do you know the place?'

'Aye,' Musa said. 'The Inn of the Three Apples.'

'Good. Send a man to rent a room in Massoud's name.'

'I can't talk you out of going, can I?'

Zaynab shook her head. 'No.'

'Then I will see to both tasks myself. Allah grant me mercy if your father finds out.' Sullen, Musa bowed and withdrew, leaving her alone in the gallery.

Zaynab sank back into the cushions of her chair, a satisfied smile curving the corners of her mouth. 'Patience may be a fine thing,' she muttered. 'But I much prefer decisive action. Let our enemies be on the defensive for a change.'

6

Parysatis shortened her stride; she glanced back, and then paused to give the old man time to catch up. Pushing her sweat-heavy hair out of her eyes, she hissed: 'It's not far now! Hurry, Grandfather!'

Al-Gid gestured her on, wheezing through the dust. The air in the passage was chalky and hot, ripe with the stench of neglect. The walls around them were a jagged patchwork of dun-coloured clay peppered with bits of ancient stone – shoddy and unfinished, but for the immaculate masonry in those places pierced by spy holes. Their path wound serpentine, following the palace's ancient foundations. In places direct sunlight seeped in through slender apertures; al-Gid felt the touch of cooler air and heard the sounds of gurgling water and birdsong. He reckoned they were skirting the marble-paved courts that lined the route to the Caliph's chambers. Beyond, the passage twisted again, narrowed, and plunged into thick shadow.

'It's up ahead,' he heard Parysatis whisper, and as they rounded a corner al-Gid saw the end of the passage, diffuse light spilling through a pair of slitted holes. The door was a panel of featureless stone; near its right edge, some long-dead mason had driven in an iron staple, flecked with rust, to serve as a handle. Parysatis reached it first. She stretched up on to the tips of her toes, palms against the stone, and pressed her eye to one of the holes. 'He's still abed,' she said, breathless. 'He seems alone.' Her fingers reached for the iron handle.

Al-Gid caught her hand. 'Wait. Let me look.'

She glanced back, her dark eyes flaring with impatience, but stepped aside to give the physician space. 'Hurry. We may not have much time.'

The old man said nothing. He mimicked her movements to peer out of the narrow hole. Though partially obstructed by the trunk of an ornamental tree, the vista that stretched before him was one of casual familiarity; he recognized the greensward, the ivy-cloaked arbour, the fountain pool. How often in years past had he sat on its stone lip to dabble his fingers in the cool water? How often had the old viziers, Shawar and Dirgham, summoned him in the middle of the night to investigate an errant cough, an innocent sniffle? They each had used the boy in their own way, as a tool to leverage power, but they at least understood the need to keep the Prince of the Faithful healthy and alive. *Not so that fool, Jalal!* Al-Gid gritted his teeth against the rage that threatened to consume him. *Allah's curse upon that grasping swine!*

Through latticed doors, the physician could just see the too-pale form of the Caliph sprawled in his bed. Asleep or dead, the old man could not say. *Am I too late?*

'Please, Grandfather!' Parysatis' voice trembled. 'We must hurry!'

Al-Gid drew back from the door and nodded. 'Open it.'

Hinges grated as Parysatis tugged the secret portal open, revealing the slender trunk of a potted poplar that partially blocked the way. A breath of air stirred the dust at al-Gid's feet. Before she could rush out, however, the physician caught her by the shoulder.

'Stay here,' he said.

'I should come with you in case—'

'Do as I say, child. Stay here. Close the door. I will rouse him and gauge his lucidity. When it's safe, I will motion for you to come out. Do you understand?'

Parysatis did not respond. She stared plaintively across the courtyard, tears gleaming at the corners of her eyes.

He shook her. 'Do you understand?'

'Yes.' Parysatis blinked, closed her eyes. 'Hurry, Grandfather. He has need of you.'

His manner softened. 'Give me but a moment, child. But a moment and I will call for you. Do not weep. You have done us all a tremendous service. I swear by the Prophet, our Prince is going to want to thank you himself.' The old man smiled kindly in hopes of allaying her frustrations. 'Be strong.'

'Be careful,' she replied, wiping her eyes.

Al-Gid redoubled his grip on his bag, winked at her, and squeezed out of the door. He waited beside the poplar for it to *snick* shut. As it closed, however, it occurred to him that he had no idea how to trigger it from without, no clue which carving to press or which stone to manipulate. He could not even locate the spy holes in the deep niche with any confidence; still, he knew Parysatis watched him. He sensed the weight – and the impatience – of her gaze. With a nod, the old man turned and hobbled across the sward. He emerged from the truncated shadows of the courtyard's eastern wall, the cruel heat of the Egyptian sun heavy on his neck and shoulders, and quickly crossed around the fountain and under the arbour.

Inside, the physician felt the heat slough away. Above his head, the back-and-forth motion of silken punkahs – each one drawn by the hand of an unseen slave – sent cool jasmine-scented air swirling through the chamber. Greenery whispered in this artificial breeze. Amid the stalks and fronds, al-Gid caught sight of a familiar feline face, black as night with eyes of delicate topaz. He heard the cat's inquisitive *chirrup*. The physician crinkled his eyes. 'Greetings, Roshanak,' he muttered. 'I'm here to check on your master.' In response, the cat darted from among the plants and vanished under Rashid's bed.

The young Caliph had not moved. That he breathed brought a prayer of relief to al-Gid's lips, but the physician found the Prince of the Faithful's condition appalling; his skin stuck to his bones like that of a pitiful beggar. '*Bismillah!*' Al-Gid shook his head; he unslung his bag and sat on the edge of the bed.

'Great One,' he said, touching Rashid's shoulder. Despite the cool air, the Caliph's face and body glistened beneath a veneer of sweat. 'Great One. You must wake.'

The Caliph stirred. His muscles twitched; a spasm caused him to stiffen and fight. Ropes of sinew stood out in his neck as he clenched and unclenched his jaw.

'Please, Great One. Open your eyes.'

Slowly, he did as al-Gid asked. His eyes fluttered open, and then suddenly widened. The Caliph's body went rigid. Trembling fingers clutched at his bedding, at the hand that lay on his arm. 'A-Allah!' he croaked.

'A thousand apologies, Great One,' the old physician said. He kept his voice low, a soothing monotone. 'It is only me, it is only Harun. Old Harun.' Al-Gid used his given name. He repeated it over and again, smiling, trying to reach the Caliph through the fog of confusion that clouded his eyes. The physician had seen such looks before – in the faces of men too long dependent on opium. *They must be keeping him drugged as a prelude to poisoning him.* 'Come, Great One. Have you forgotten old Harun so soon?'

The Caliph blinked. 'H-Harun?'

'Yes, Great One. Forgive my intrusion, but I heard you might be unwell.'

'Harun.' By increments, the young Caliph's body relaxed;

he licked his cracked lips. 'My old friend. I have missed you.'

'And I you, Great One.'

Rashid coughed and struggled to sit upright, his dark hair tangled about his shoulders. 'H-Have you anything to drink?'

Harun al-Gid cast about until his eyes lit upon the goblet at the Caliph's bedside. If Parysatis spoke true it should be safe. Still, he took no chances. Al-Gid picked it up, dipped his smallest finger into it, and touched it to his tongue. Pure water – neither sweet nor cool, but potable. He nodded to the Caliph. 'Here, Great One. Let me help you.'

With the physician's aid, Rashid sipped from the goblet. The young Caliph drank a few swallows and then sank back down, his lips twisting into a grimace. 'A change from the wine I usually have in the morning.'

'Yes, Great One. We must discuss that. How do you feel?'

'My sleep is troubled,' Rashid replied. The cat, Roshanak, leapt on to his side of the bed, stretching and purring in greeting. Seeing her, the Caliph managed a thin smile; he raised his hand so she might brush up against it. 'I wake weary and cannot find respite from the dreams that plague me. Most days, that is my sole companion.' With a tilt of his chin, he indicated the water pipe sitting on the bedside table.

'Opium, still?'

The younger man shrugged, waving the physician's concerns away. 'But it doesn't matter. You must return to court, my old friend. You must resume your place.'

'I never left court, Great One,' al-Gid said. 'I was barred from seeing you by your vizier. No doubt so I would not raise alarm at how poorly they are treating you. Look at yourself, my young lord. Those who profess to serve you have allowed you to waste away; or worse, they themselves are the architects of your sickness.'

The Caliph frowned; he said nothing for a moment, his downcast eyes blazing with a measure of their old fire as he stared at his thin hand, knobby and fleshless. He clenched it into a fist. 'Perhaps you are right, Harun, but what of it? I have been a pawn of men like that since I was but a boy; men cut from the same bolt of shabby cloth, with their hollow promises and claims of concern. But what of it?'

'You mean you know your vizier intrigues against you?'

'All of them have,' the Caliph replied. 'Though Dirgham, at least, liked to play as though he had my best interests at heart. I assume Jalal is no different. So long as they do what's best for Egypt, I find I am content to go along with their charade.'

Al-Gid shook his head. 'Would it not be best for Egypt to be ruled by an incorruptible Prince descended from the Prophet's own daughter, and not by a gaggle of his scheming eunuchs and lackeys?'

'It would, but I am a realist, Harun. I may dream of seizing the reins of power and ruling like the Caliphs of old, but I have wisdom enough to apprehend the futility in such grandiose dreams. I would not know where to begin . . .'

The old physician leaned closer. 'You begin, Great One, by reclaiming your dignity. As Allah is my witness, you are the Prince of the Faithful, not some pipe-smoking derelict from Fustat! Act accordingly and a new-found respect for your person will follow. To be sure, others are aware of your plight, Great One. They work tirelessly on your behalf, but their work will be for naught if you succumb to indolence or despair – or to poison.'

'Poison?' The Caliph frowned. 'They would not dare.'

'Do not be so certain, Great One. Men desperate for power would dare much to gain it. You must not—'

The cat warned Harun al-Gid they were no longer alone. He saw Roshanak's ears flatten against her skull; feline muscles tensed. Something – someone – over his shoulder spooked her. *Parysatis?* Frowning, the old physician straightened, turned . . .

. . . and cried out as sudden and excruciating pain blossomed in his side, just below his ribs. Al-Gid twisted, his body contorting away from the impaling knife; he stared at the grinning countenance of his attacker: a eunuch, a narrow-faced Moor in the plain robes of a servant.

Al-Gid heard the Caliph's voice as if from the bottom of a well: 'Khadim! What are you doing?' The Moor, however, did not acknowledge him. Iron fingers knotted in the breast of al-Gid's galabiyya. Fabric ripped, and the old man was lifted clear of the tall bedstead; he felt himself floating.

For the span of a heartbeat, Harun experienced a sensation of peace, of silent calm. He looked back into the young Caliph's eyes, wide now with equal parts shock and outrage, and wished he had done more to warn him of the danger. And what would become of poor Parysatis, so like his daughters? *I should have told you about her.* Nearer, he saw the Moor's lips peel back as he bellowed . . . what? A curse? A warning? It mattered little. The heartbeat passed, and Harun al-Gid's world exploded into shards of white-hot agony as the Moor slammed him to the floor with enough force to shatter the bones of his pelvis.

As pain-laced darkness closed around him, the last thing Harun al-Gid saw with any clarity – beyond the Moor's upraised knife, wet with his blood – was the young Prince of the Faithful springing from his bed, one hand reaching for his water pipe.

7

The crunch of his old friend's bones, his piercing screams, galvanized Rashid al-Hasan. The Moor had Harun pinned to the floor, the knife in his gory fist raised high to deliver a killing blow. And for what? What trespass had he committed? Was concern for his well-being now a reason for murder? Rashid's rage boiled over, provoking the young man to action.

Bare-chested, the Prince of the Faithful rose from the tangled bed-linens and snatched up the first thing he saw: his water pipe. Inverted, it resembled an old Egyptian mace: a flaring tube of brass, inlaid silver, and gilded glass replacing a wooden haft; its weight coming not from a stone head, but from a core of lead in its base. Yellowish water sluiced over Rashid's knuckles.

'Khadim!' he roared. The Moor glanced back. Before he could react, the Caliph swung the heavy pipe with every scrap of strength locked away in his thin frame. It whistled through the air, catching the Moor in the right temple. His skull cracked, a wet sound not unlike a boot heel crushing an egg. Khadim cartwheeled off the old physician's body; he landed in a twisted heap by the door just as a handful of eunuchs and soldiers entered, drawn in by the commotion. Mustapha stood at the forefront, his bruised face pale.

'Most Excellent One!' he said. 'What . . . ?'

'Stay back!' Rashid dropped the bent water pipe and fell to his knees beside Harun al-Gid's body. The old physician lay in a widening pool of blood, barely clinging to life. His eyes fluttered open at Rashid's touch. 'My dear old friend,' the Caliph whispered, tears rimming his eyes. He smoothed Harun's brow with a trembling hand. 'I am so sorry this happened. May Allah preserve you and keep you. Tell me what I should do.'

Gritting his teeth, the old man turned his gaze on those who clustered in the doorway. Condemnation blazed in his eyes. Condemnation and disgust. 'N-Not . . . trust . . . t-them!' he gasped.

'I won't, my old friend,' Rashid replied. He glanced up at the throng of murmuring functionaries, his own antipathy mirroring that of the dying physician. 'I won't. I will remember all that you've said.' Very slowly, Harun al-Gid raised a gnarled hand. The Caliph clasped it, heedless of the smeared blood. At the contact a racking sigh left the old man's body; the muscles of his face grew slack as the life seeped out of him. Rashid al-Hasan bent over and kissed his forehead. 'I will do what is right for Egypt.'

After a few moments, the Caliph straightened; he rose to his feet, bloody and dishevelled, and turned to face the men who milled in the doorway, his wrath like a living thing between them. The servants and lesser eunuchs dared not meet his gaze – they stared at their dead comrade, at the floor, at their feet – while Mustapha looked askance at the young Caliph, gauging all possible responses to questions he had yet to ask. The soldiers, whose turban-wrapped helmets sported thick nasals and inlays of gold, and whose gilded mail gleamed beneath white khalats, watched him warily, though with grudging respect.

'Will you kill *me* now?' Rashid sneered. He staggered over the physician's body and scooped up the Moor's fallen knife, fixing his eye on Mustapha; for the first time in a long while, the old eunuch appeared at a loss for words. 'Come, you gutless conniver. Kill me. Do it!' The young man threw his arms wide. 'You're my jailers, are you not? Why not end your tedium and put me down like the dog you believe me to be?' None of them moved. 'No?' The Caliph spat. 'By Allah, I should have the lot of you hanged!'

Rashid's tirade against them might have continued had the vizier's voice not cracked above their heads like a whip: 'What the devil is going on?' Visibly relieved, the eunuchs and guards gave ground, splitting ranks to allow him entry. Jalal stormed into the Caliph's chamber in a swirl of fine white linen. Gold glittered on his fingers and crusted his turban. 'Are you deaf? I said what—'

'Yes, join us, Jalal,' the Caliph said. 'Perhaps you can provide your minions with enough spleen to see their assassination through! Or is it only my friends and my visitors that you're plotting to kill?'

The vizier's narrowed eyes flickered from the Moor's body to the discarded pipe to the corpse of Harun al-Gid, and finally came to rest on the knife in the Prince of the Faithful's hand; the pieces fell into place like the tiles of a violent mosaic. Jalal stepped closer to the young man, his lips thinned to a hard line. 'The physician paid you an unanticipated visit and Khadim mistook him for someone who meant you harm? Allah's mercies upon them! This was assuredly a tragic accident, Most Excellent One. Had we known you were expecting him—'

'I wasn't expecting him, Jalal, but you already know that! Harun told me you forbade him from seeing me!' The Caliph paced back and forth like a caged lion, his gait unsteady despite the fury surging in his veins. 'Why, Jalal? So you could keep me in a drugged stupor with no one the wiser? What foul schemes have you hatched in my name, I wonder?'

'Great One, please.' The vizier held his hands palms-up in a pleading gesture as he drifted close. 'We are loyal to you and zealous – perhaps overly so – for your safety, but we are not the evil men you imagine us to be. Have you forgotten it was Harun himself who first suggested the opium? He administered it to quiet your mind so you might rest, not to keep you docile and pliant. If you wish it no more, then there will be no more.

'And what of poor Harun – may Allah's mercy rest upon his soul! Through their husbands, it was his own daughters who begged me to release him from service, as he had grown too old in their estimation to be at your beck and call. I thought I'd done the proper thing in returning him to his family so he might pass his final years in their company. But he must have misunderstood my intent if he told you I *forbade* him from seeing you, even as Khadim misunderstood Harun's intent. Herein lay the true tragedy, Most Excellent One: both men saw danger where none existed, and both men died because of it.'

Rashid stood still as the vizier came up beside him; the young man said nothing, his brow furrowed as he stared at the body of the slain physician. Jalal's reasoning made extraordinary sense, and on any other day the young Caliph would have accepted it with little conscious thought. On this day, however, his yet raw and festering anger – coupled with Harun's dying admonition to trust no one – stripped away the veil of complacency. Stripped it away and trampled it underfoot.

'Come, Great One,' the vizier murmured. 'Let us put things right . . .'

Faster than Jalal would have thought possible, the Caliph rounded on him. With a violent shove he forced the vizier back against the bedside table; Rashid grabbed his khalat, catching him before he could stumble and fall. 'Do you take me for a fool, Jalal? Do you think I'm weak? Your man's death was no tragic accident! He died for the crime of murder, and I condemn his body to a criminal's fate!' Sweat beaded the Caliph's forehead and his limbs quaked with the first signs of opium sickness; even still, however, his eyes burned with a resolute fire. 'Things have changed, Jalal. From this day hence, you and those who follow you serve at my pleasure. I will choose from among them those whom I wish to stay at my side. The rest I will dismiss. There will be no exceptions. I alone will choose my chief eunuch, my physician, the captain of my guard.' Rashid raised the knife, holding its razored edge against the side of the vizier's neck. 'Do we understand one another?'

Jalal did not flinch. 'Of course, Most Excellent One.'

'Good.' The Caliph nodded. He lowered the blade and methodically wiped it clean on the shoulder of Jalal's pristine khalat. 'It is a new day, Jalal. For now, you may remain as my vizier, since I value your experience. But heed this, and heed it well: let even the slenderest rumour reach me that you've renewed whatever schemes you may have had against me and I swear before Allah that I will have you gutted and your carcass hung from the Zuwayla Gate.'

Both men looked up from the stain of transferred blood spreading across the snowy linen; their eyes met – ice versus fire, immutable opposites. 'I would expect nothing less,' Jalal replied, sketching a slight bow.

Rashid released him. The Caliph turned away and staggered towards the open doors leading to his garden. 'See Harun's body receives a proper funeral and that his daughters are justly compensated for their loss. Throw the other one to the dogs,' he said. 'This is Friday, is it not? I will attend noon prayer at the Grey Mosque, Jalal.'

'Yes, Most Excellent One. I will have a bath drawn, and a light meal, should you desire it.' The vizier clapped his hands, sending the servants scurrying. He motioned for Mustapha to follow him, and for the guards to bring the bodies.

Alone, the Prince of the Faithful stepped out into the too-bright sunlight of his courtyard.

8

'How?' Jalal hissed to Mustapha as the pair of them returned to the antechamber. The vizier stripped off his stained khalat and flung it aside. 'How did that meddlesome old fool get to him?'

'Not through us, as Allah is my witness!'

'Well, he did not simply sprout wings and fly over the courtyard wall!'

Mustapha was emphatic. 'Nor did he come through that door, Excellency! There are a dozen Jandariyah on station in the hallway leading to it; two more guard the door itself! It is impossible, Excellency, to think an old man could slip past so many eyes without being seen!'

'Then how did he do it?'

'Are you certain the Jandariyah are loyal? Could not someone have convinced them to turn against you?'

Jalal's slitted eyes glared at nothing as he weighed the old eunuch's concerns. That betrayal might come from the ranks of those guarding the Caliph was not something he could dismiss lightly. The Jandariyah were mercenaries, after all. Could Harun al-Gid, who lived comfortably on a physician's stipend, have bribed his way into the apartments? Inevitably, Jalal shook his head. 'No. Perhaps he could have bought off one of them, but not all of them. Their captain, Turanshah, understands I've tied his fate – and the fate of his Syrians – to my own. Harun must have found another way in.' The vizier turned. 'Retrace his steps through the palace. Find out where he was, whom he talked to, why he was here. Others must have seen him.'

'As you wish, Excellency.' The old eunuch sidled closer. 'What about . . .' He opened his hand, revealing a small glass phial. Jalal knew the purplish liquid inside was not opium.

'Did you not hear our noble Prince?' Jalal looked back down the hallway to the Caliph's chambers, where servants bustled in with pails of steaming water and out with wads of blood-soaked linen. Contempt twisted his features. 'It is a new day. Al-Hasan is on guard against subtlety. He expects craft and guile; thus, we must be brazen and forthright. How could such a strong young man fall victim to fever? No, his demise will no doubt come at the end of a sword.' A burst of murderous inspiration brought a cold smile to his lips. 'Perhaps the sword of a new-found ally?'

9

Parysatis sagged against the hidden door, sobbing, her eyes squeezed shut and her fists pressed to her ears in a vain attempt to block out the memory of al-Gid's screams. *Why? Why didn't I help him? All I had to do was shout a warning!* Instead, she froze. The shock of seeing a knife-wielding man creeping up on the old physician had left her bereft of voice. By the time she regained her wits, all she could do was look on in horror as her ally – her saviour – took a dagger in the back. *Why didn't I help him?* Sick with guilt, Parysatis let her body slide to the ground.

I dragged him into this! I dragged him into this and sent him to his death! And for what? Does the Caliph know any more now than he did before? Did al-Gid have a chance to warn him? Parysatis wanted to believe al-Gid had triumphed in death, and yet she had seen nothing on which to hang her belief. True, the Caliph was furious and he had acted more decisively than she could have imagined, but since he neither killed his vizier outright nor summoned troops to drag him away, what else could Parysatis conclude but the obvious: al-Gid had died in vain. *Why didn't I help him?*

Wiping her eyes, Parysatis raised her head and stared at the door's handle. She could help him now. She could still make this right. This stone portal was the only barrier between her and the Prince of the Faithful. If she rushed out and confessed everything, if she flung herself on the Caliph's mercy, it would bring meaning to al-Gid's sacrifice. Of course, she would likely vanish in the upheaval, but what of it? Her life was of little consequence. Parysatis clambered to her feet. Her lips quivered with nervous resolve. She would do this, as much to honour al-Gid as to protect the Caliph. Closing her eyes, she reached for the rusted iron handle of the door . . .

A sound behind her – the soft *crunch* of a slipper on loose scree – spun Parysatis around. She shrank back against the stone, trembling fists knotted as her imagination filled the passage with the vizier's murderous followers. She held her breath, waiting, her heart hammering in her chest . . . and then her body slumped with relief as Yasmina's slender face drifted into the light.

'Mistress,' the young Egyptian hissed. 'Why do you tarry?'

Tears rimmed Parysatis' eyes. 'They killed him, Yasmina.'

The girl stiffened. 'Who?'

'Al-Gid.' Parysatis hid her face in her hands. 'I l-let him die.'

'Mother of bitches!' Yasmina pushed past her mistress and strained to peer through the spy holes. The courtyard was empty now; she saw but a lone slave inside, on his knees and scrubbing blood off the floor. She cursed again. 'Was he killed outright, mistress?'

'W-What?' Parysatis looked up.

'Did they kill him outright or did they question him first? Quickly, mistress!'

'None questioned him that I saw.'

The girl nodded and took Parysatis by the hand. 'Thank Allah for small blessings. Come.'

'Blessings?' Parysatis snapped, wrenching free of her grasp. 'I should have you whipped for saying such a thing! How is his murder a blessing?'

Yasmina's dark eyes grew hard. 'Don't be a fool, mistress. A quick death meant al-Gid didn't have an opportunity to be tortured, to betray you to the vizier.'

'He would never betray me!'

'No?' The girl arched her fine eyebrows. 'Have you ever seen a man tortured, mistress? He would betray his own mother if it meant an end to the pain. I am not as well schooled as some, but this I know: right now, the vizier is burning to know how al-Gid got past his guards. I would wager my life that he has already dispersed his people into the palace with orders to learn all they can of the physician's comings and goings. How long, do you think, before they find out he was last in the harem?'

Blood drained from Parysatis' face. 'Merciful Allah!'

'Let us pray so,' Yasmina replied, extending her hand. 'Come, we must hurry. The longer we dawdle, the more likely it is someone will poke their head inside the hammam to check on you. What would you rather they find: an empty bed or a woman who is delirious with fever?'

Shaken, Parysatis nodded and took the younger woman's hand. 'No, you're right. I . . . I'm sorry for getting you caught up in all this.'

Yasmina's lips curved into a faint smile. 'Don't be sorry, mistress, be swift. Come.' Hand in hand, the two women sprinted the distance from the courtyard door to the hammam, heedless of stealth. Parysatis clutched at her aching side as they neared the end, gasping for breath while the young Egyptian appeared barely winded.

Yasmina stepped out into the bath first. Her eyes sought the main entrance. Parysatis followed her gaze. The resourceful girl had propped a shard of pottery against the bottom of the door and there it remained, undisturbed. 'Good,' the Egyptian said. 'Hurry, mistress!'

As she crossed the hammam, movement caught Parysatis' attention. She spotted the African eunuch, awake now and sitting upright. He glared at the women, cursing through his gag; his hands twisted at their silken bindings. 'What are we going to do with him, Yasmina? We can't drag him off.'

'No,' Yasmina replied. The tone of her voice was abrupt and vicious. 'We can't.' Without breaking stride, she hiked up the hem of her gown to reveal a makeshift sheath strapped to one long brown thigh; from it, Yasmina drew a thin-bladed dagger.

Parysatis' eyes bulged. 'What . . . What are you doing?'

The Egyptian girl did not answer, and before Parysatis could intervene she had reached the struggling eunuch, planted a petite foot on his chest, and in one quick motion laid open his throat. Bright blood spurted over the turquoise tiles.

Parysatis turned away, eyes squeezed shut and a hand clamped to her mouth as she fought the urge to be sick. She listened, horrified, to the African's final throes: the wet gurgle as he tried to draw breath; the muffled grunting; the drumming of his heels. Mercifully, he did not linger, and in a dozen heartbeats the sounds ceased altogether.

The metallic stench of blood filled the dusty air of the hammam.

Parysatis opened her eyes to find Yasmina standing in front of her. The girl rested a consoling hand on her forearm. 'I did what was necessary, mistress,' she said, her gaze frank and utterly without remorse. 'Alive, he was a witness. Dead, he affords you deniability.'

'Merciful Allah!' Parysatis whispered. Her guilt outweighed her horror and both left her dizzy, her face pale, her red eyes swollen. 'Where did you learn such things?'

Yasmina's answer came tinged with macabre pride: 'I had an extraordinary teacher.' Gently, the girl bound Parysatis' wrists with the dead eunuch's sash. 'When they come, you must appear distraught. You remember very little. You heard the struggle, and when you tried to rise the physician tied you up. The last thing you saw was al-Gid pressing a leaf and vanishing into the far wall. You've lain here in a stupor ever since. Do you understand?'

Parysatis nodded. She felt numb as Yasmina guided her into bed, an empty vessel drained of emotion. 'What of you?'

'Don't worry about me, mistress. If this hammam is like the others, it will have a slaves' entrance. I'll be gone before the hounds arrive.'

'Gone where?'

Yasmina swiped her hair off her forehead. 'With or without your permission, I go to find the Gazelle. This is beyond us now, mistress. *She* is the only person I can think of who will know what we can do, whom we can trust.'

'I should just confess my part in this and beg for mercy,' Parysatis replied, her voice thick with despair.

'That would solve nothing, mistress.' Yasmina frowned. 'And I would rather kill you myself – though it would break my heart to do so – than see you suffer at the hands of the vizier's torturers. No, mistress. Now is not the time to act the martyr. Lie back and remember the part you're playing. When I return, *inshallah*, it will be with good news.'

'Do not place too much faith in your Gazelle, Yasmina. She is only a woman, after all.'

'So was Scheherazade, mistress, and she wrapped a sultan around her finger. I'll be back soon. Be strong.' Yasmina planted a quick kiss on Parysatis' forehead before darting away. In a moment, all traces of the Egyptian's passing had faded.

Shivering, Parysatis shrank down into her pillows and stared at the domed ceiling far above, its white patina awash in golden sun-light. The stink of blood filled her nostrils, and the young woman soon discovered the illness she meant to feign had become real.

10

The mosque of al-Aqmar stood at the head of the Bayn al-Qasrayn, that broad marble-paved square separating the East and West Palaces. Dubbed the Grey Mosque for the colour of its stonework, its façade displayed an array of elaborate decoration, from soaring keel arches and ribbed niches to stone rosettes and bands of Qur'anic verse chiselled deep into pale stucco. A single minaret rose from the heart of the mosque, adding its own slender bulk to a jagged skyline of domes and spires that caught the hazy midmorning sun and reflected it down into the crowded streets.

In the cool shadow of the mosque's entry arch, Assad paused to remove his sandals. He glanced back into the Bayn al-Qasrayn. Hundreds jammed the broad square, a colourful sea of turbans and veils, tarboushes and headscarves. Native Cairenes and provincial Egyptians eager for a glimpse of their beloved Caliph mixed with foreigners of every stripe; Moslems mingled with Nazarenes who mingled with Jews. Slaves darted through the throng; porters staggered past under heavy loads. Merchants hurried to conclude their business before the markets closed for the morning, while courtiers and men of influence held forth beneath parasols of striped linen. Soldiers peppered the crowd: grim Turks, hawkish Circassians, and Sudanese mercenaries; all of them bristling with swagger and steel.

Though he trusted his disguise, Assad was in no mood to take chances. Slowly, he swept his back trail for signs of suspicious interest, of pursuit. He found neither. Indeed, in the press and shuffle of market day – with all its myriad sights, smells, and sounds – who would think to glance twice at a crippled holy man leaning on his ivory-headed walking stick? Satisfied, Assad nodded to himself.

'*As-salaam alaikum*, brother,' said a man's voice from deeper inside the mosque.

The Assassin turned, falling effortlessly into character. '*Alaikum as-salaam.*'

'Are you lost, my friend?'

'Lost? Not if this is the mosque of al-Aqmar, praise be to Allah.' Assad hobbled closer, dragging one foot as he leaned on his 'walking stick' – his salawar in a makeshift sheath constructed from elongated laths of old black-daubed teak bound in leather and copper wire; only the pommel of the blade protruded, a knob of sculpted ivory hidden by his hand. Faint tremors of hatred whitened his knuckles. At his back, a crescendo of sound caused him to glance once more into the square. 'Where I am from, we conduct our Friday market with much less . . . fanfare.'

The clean-shaven man who faced Assad smiled, though the gesture did not extend to his eyes; these were deep-set and agleam with innate distrust. Though plainly dressed in a linen khalat and a tulip-shaped turban, Assad reckoned him a palace chamberlain – one of the vizier's eunuchs sent ahead to keep an eye on the mosque prior to the Caliph's arrival. Obviously, part of his task was to keep the undesirables at bay. He made no move to step out of Assad's path. 'And where do you hail from, my friend?'

'Teyma, in the Hejaz.'

'A harsh land, the Hejaz. What brings you to Cairo?'

Though the eunuch's tone was pleasant and his manner one of affable curiosity, Assad recognized a subtle interrogation was taking place. The Assassin played along; to do otherwise would have raised alarm in the eunuch's mind. 'A pilgrimage,' he said, patting the cool stone wall beside him. 'My mentor, ere he passed on, always sang the praises of the Grey Mosque. He was here as a boy, when Caliph al-Amir first laid its foundations, and was one of the first congregants through this very arch. I have come in honour of his memory to make my submission to God. *Allahu akbar.*'

'*Allahu akbar*,' the eunuch echoed. He looked Assad up and down, seeing exactly what he was supposed to see: a backwater mystic from the heart of Arabia, scarred, crippled, and perfectly harmless. Slowly, the eunuch's eyes lost their suspicious gleam; he stepped aside. 'I suggest a spot under yonder colonnade, my friend. You'll find it is coolest in its shade.'

'My thanks,' Assad replied, shuffling past.

Arches dominated the open courtyard of the Grey Mosque: keel arches held aloft by ancient columns of smooth marble, the whole braced and interconnected by timber tie-beams. Lamps of smoky glass and bronze hung from these, unlit during the day. The scent of perfumed oils drifted in the air. The mosque was far from deserted. Already, men sought refuge from the heat, sitting alone or in pairs; some engaged in quiet conversation, while others simply closed their eyes and dozed. In one corner, beneath a narrow window, a wiry old man sat cross-legged in a patch of light, his grey-bearded lips moving as he read from his Qur'an.

Assad chose a spot opposite the niche in the eastern wall indicating the direction of Mecca; his position also kept the main entrance in his field of vision. With exaggerated care, he laid his disguised salawar on the ground and spread out his prayer rug. Assad exhaled and knelt. He cleared his mind as he performed the first of many prostrations. Whispering the Shahada, his body rocking back and forth, he appeared to lose himself in a fog of religious ecstasy. He became a holy man.

And while Ibn al-Teymani, a rustic Sufi from the Hejaz, guided Assad's physical actions, it was the *Emir* of the Knife who maintained his sense of predatory alertness, patient and calculating . . .

11

Away from the tumult of the Bayn al-Qasrayn, deep in the maze of narrow alleys stitching the Soldiers' Quarter, a carpet-seller from Aleppo ducked under a crumbling archway. Two confederates followed close on his heels; all three men moved at speed, their dusty robes swirling as they descended a flight of shallow steps. The alley ended in a mudbrick cul-de-sac, where an old wooden gate led to a hidden courtyard long bereft of a gardener's care. Weeds grew knee-high around an old lotus pool, its basin bone-dry and cracked from the merciless heat; ruptured paving stones allowed a tangled mimosa to take root in the scabby earth.

With his companions in tow, the carpet-seller made no attempt at stealth as he crossed the courtyard and stopped next to a jagged fissure in the wall. As the man favoured keeping his head on his shoulders, he dared not step through unannounced. '*Askari!*' he panted, one half of the prearranged code.

From inside, a voice answered with the other half: '*al-Din!*' Nodding, the man who claimed to be a seller of carpets from Aleppo squeezed through the cleft and into another garden, this one green and pleasant, with shady sycamores around a small pool. Incongruously, a black-clad soldier waited next to the fissure with a naked scimitar cradled in his hands. Other fedayeen loitered nearby.

'You're late.'

'Is he already here?' The carpet-seller, Gamal, brushed dust from his embroidered burnous. He wished for a clean cloth to blot the tears streaming from his left eye, red and swollen with infection.

'By Allah, he's been here for the past hour.'

'What's his mood?'

The armed man shrugged. 'He has but one mood, brother.'

Cursing under his breath, Gamal left his companions to slake their thirst in the garden pool and entered the house alone. Constructed of stone slathered in a layer of cool white stucco, the place had rooms on multiple levels with arched galleries and broad casement windows – mashrafiyyas; its layout was intended to foster a constant flow of air. Pots of herbs and flowering plants added their soft fragrance to the breeze. Save for a handful of fedayeen, the house was all but deserted, its owner and his family unfortunate casualties of the clandestine war between Massaif and Alamut.

The house's highest point was in the women's quarters; in the harem reception room, where the master's wife received her female visitors, a delicate mashrafiyya set with panels of stained glass overlooked the street. Here, Gamal found the man he had kept waiting.

Garbed in a girdled khalat of sombre hue, Badr al-Mulahid reclined on a divan of yellow brocade, his legs crossed at the ankles

– Death in quiet repose. He passed the time by dragging a whetstone along the edges of his Frankish dirk; those long rasping strokes punctuated the silence.

Gamal licked his cracked lips with the tip of his tongue. His eye ached. 'Forgive my tardiness, *ya sidi.*'

The Heretic didn't look up; stone and steel grated. 'Well?'

'So far, nothing.' The carpet-seller – in truth a captain of Massaif – twisted the heavy ring he wore as part of his disguise. 'We spread the offer to the beggars at every gate. If they can't lay their hands on the bitch, no one can.'

'What of the *Emir* of the Knife?'

'He's going to be a hard one to run to ground, especially as the only thing we have to go on is a scarred face and the description of his knife. I look for those ignorant wretches to attempt a deception on us – like murdering some poor pox-ridden peasant and tucking an Afghan knife in his belt – hoping we will be stupid enough to hand over the money with no questions asked.'

'If they try it, kill them.' The Heretic raised his dirk and studied its twin cutting edges. 'Cairo does not have enough beggars to bring low the *Emir* of the Knife. When he gets wind of the bounty, though, perhaps he will be encouraged to act before he is truly ready – and thus reveal himself. I will strike once your men have identified him.'

'The woman . . . does she remain our chief priority?'

The Heretic's pale eyes transfixed him. 'Both are equally important. But, yes, we must take the woman first, and soon. Her death will answer the original commission Ibn Sharr laid upon us, to obliterate Alamut's influence in Cairo, and in the same stroke we rob the Emir of a valuable ally.'

Before Gamal could respond, another of the fedayeen entered. 'There's movement, *ya sidi!*' Nodding, Badr al-Mulahid uncoiled from the divan like a steel spring. He sheathed his dirk and moved to the latticed window; Gamal followed in his wake.

The window overlooked the Street of Perfume Makers, nearly deserted as the noon hour approached. Across the way and to their left stood the House of the Gazelle; from this vantage Gamal could just make out the entryway. A figure stood at the mouth of the alley. Though his aspect seemed ragged and unkempt, he nevertheless moved like a man who knew how to handle himself. 'Another of her customers, *ya sidi?*'

The Heretic said nothing; he watched the man through slitted eyes. There was something familiar about him, something he recognized, although he could not put his finger on it. The figure peered out into the street – Badr could sense his suspicion – then he turned and swept his gaze across neighbouring rooftops, his head cocked to one side to compensate for having but a single eye.

The gesture triggered recollection, the memory of a place. *The Mad Caliph's mosque!* 'I know you.'

'*Ya sidi?*' Other fedayeen clustered in the doorway, eager killers ready to strike a blow for Massaif; to die, if need be.

The Heretic lifted his chin, scowling down his nose at the figure as he faded back from the mouth of the alley. 'I have seen that one before. He was one of al-Hajj's creatures.'

Gamal swore. 'Can it be coincidence?'

'Does it matter? Take four men and follow him, but keep out of sight. Perhaps he will lead us to the Gazelle's hiding place.' *And,* the Heretic thought, *where we find the Gazelle, no doubt we will find the* Emir *of the Knife as well.* 'Go!'

'At once, *ya sidi!*'

The Heretic resumed his scrutiny of the street, a shiver of anticipation creeping up his spine. His quarry just came one step closer.

12

While the Caliph's quarters buzzed like a hive of angry bees kicked on to its side by an indelicate keeper, the rest of the palace continued to function at its normal pace. Chamberlains and stewards went about their daily duties, unhurried and unaware of the goings-on of the mighty; courtiers and honoured guests arrived by way of a dozen gates, ready to clog the Golden Hall in hopes of getting a moment of the vizier's time – some to forward their ambitions, others to beg for an indulgence. Through it all, servants like Yasmina moved unseen.

Her usual avenue of escape, the Emerald Gate in the northeast corner of the palace complex, she found blocked by the arrival of fresh troops, a company of Jandariyah no doubt summoned from their barracks in the West Palace by the vizier himself. At their head strode a powerfully built man clad in gilded steel and linen, the hilt of his great sabre jutting from a girdle of rich red silk. He was the captain of the Syrian mercenaries, a wolfish cavalier who'd earned his reputation fighting the Nazarenes. Wisely, Yasmina veered away from the Emerald Gate; though it took longer than expected, she found a way out in the kitchens, through an unguarded door lead-ing to the herb gardens; once clear of the palace walls she set off for the Street of Perfume Makers at a dead run.

Yasmina knew Cairo's streets better than the Prophet knew salvation; in her ninth year, after the bloody flux took her parents and brothers, these streets had kept her sheltered, fed, and clothed. She found a mentor among the scavengers and the rag-pickers, a wizened old drunk called Flea who taught her how to harvest the refuse of the wealthy, how to turn broken pottery and cast-off metal into a few copper coins. By twelve, under Flea's auspices, she had graduated to slitting purses and burgling homes.

That was how Zaynab found her: a feral, half-naked child living on scraps and stealing for a man too lazy to steal for himself. She recognized in Yasmina a peculiar adroitness, a velocity of thought which outstripped that of the dregs she associated with. But for all her gifts, the girl had no craft save luck . . . and luck had a way of petering out. Unless Zaynab intervened, it would only be a matter of months until Yasmina lost a hand or worse to the cadis who dis-pensed justice from the cool shadows of al-Azhar Mosque.

So intervene she did. Plucked from Flea's grasp, Yasmina found safety in the House of the Gazelle; she found a mistress who encouraged her to learn, who challenged her to excel, and who gave her the gift of independence. Under Zaynab's tutelage the feral child once destined to die a thief before her fifteenth year disappeared, replaced by a young Egyptian woman who blossomed into one of the Gazelle's most effective spies.

Yasmina darted through the tangle of narrow streets east of the palace, where ragged tenements stood cheek by jowl with the domed mausoleums of long-dead princes; crossing a tiny square dominated by a public fountain of brilliant blue tile, she plunged down a short alley and emerged on the Street of Perfume Makers, not far from the House of the Gazelle. Already, she knew something was amiss.

The street was too quiet.

Where she should have seen dozens of servants scurrying off to the different markets and countless porters returning loaded with purchases, white-shirted messengers flying in all directions bearing missives and responses, and beggars drawn by the promise of charity, Yasmina saw hardly any movement at all. She slowed her pace, her heart gripped by a sudden frost. *What's happened? Could she have left the city for some reason? Would she have left without telling me?*

Further up the street, a porter lounged against the wall of a neighbouring house. Yasmina heard the incessant barking of a small dog, a scolding voice. A hot breath of wind stirred up zephyrs of dust. Walking now, she came abreast of the alley leading to the entrance to the Gazelle's house and stopped. She heard nothing, saw no movement; yet the sensation of scrutiny was palpable. Yasmina looked over her shoulder. Her narrowed eyes swept from one end of the street to the other before she slowly edged into the alley.

Framed in arabesqued stone, the Gazelle's familiar red door stood open and from within came the coppery-sweet smell of day-old blood. The smell of death. A rising tide of panic threatened to choke the young woman; she fumbled with the hem of her gown, drawing her knife with a trembling hand. *Where is she?*

She craned her neck. 'M-Mistress?'

In answer, a figure lunged from the shadow of the entry hall. Yasmina's reaction was instinctive: her knife sliced empty air as she danced back into the alley and dropped to a fighter's crouch. Raising her free hand to protect her head, she curled her fingers into raking talons. Muscles tensed as she made ready to gut the man who emerged from the doorway.

It was a one-eyed beggar.

'Musa?'

He cocked his head to the side. 'Yasmina? What are you doing here?'

Tension drained from her body. She staggered forward and embraced him. 'I came to see Zaynab. Where is she, Musa? What's happened?'

'There's been some trouble, girl,' he said. 'Mistress is fine, but she's been forced into hiding.'

'What kind of trouble?'

Musa shook his head. 'It's not safe to linger here. Not right now. Come with me. We can talk on the way back to the palace.'

'No!' Yasmina said. 'I must see Zaynab, Musa! It cannot wait!'

The one-eyed man scratched his wiry beard; exhaling, he glanced in both directions – out to the street and back down the alley. The hiss of air between his teeth turned to a soft clicking sound. 'It's not safe. She's not expecting you . . .'

'Please, Musa! I promise you, the news I bear she's going to want to hear!' Tears welled at the corners of Yasmina's eyes. Embarrassed, she swiped at them with the heel of her hand. 'Damn you! I have to see her!'

'Fine, girl. Fine. But we must move fast. It's a long slog to the River Quarter from here—'

Yasmina bristled. 'I can keep up.'

'Come, then. Let's see if you can still outrun old Musa!' The one-eyed beggar gave the street a last glance, then he turned and set off down the alley. Yasmina matched his pace, staying close on his heels.

Neither of them saw Gamal or his four Syrians break from hiding across the Street of Perfume Makers and plunge into the alley after them.

13

Sound roused Parysatis from her stupor; she stirred, tasting bile, and twisted her wrists against the sweat-drenched sash that bound them. Men were coming for her. Soldiers. She heard the clash of their harness and the tramp of their boots, shrieks of alarm and a babble of voices. The Chief Eunuch's strident call for silence cut through the din; the resulting calm plucked at Parysatis' nerves. She squeezed her eyes shut and fought the urge to scream, to call the hunters to her.

You remember very little, she reminded herself. *You remember very little. A leaf on the far wall; al-Gid* – her breath caught in her throat – *al-Gid vanishing. That's all you remember. That's all* . . .

'I do not know how that's possible, Excellency,' she heard Lu'lu say, his voice rising in pitch. 'A trusted man of mine never left the physician's side. I swear, as Allah is my—'

A voice she recognized as the vizier's cut him off. 'Then your man has played you for a fool! Move!'

Parysatis flinched as the doors to the bath banged open, sending the pot shard Yasmina had propped against them skittering across the tiles. Talons of ice shredded her stomach as men pounded into the room, their mail shirts rustling. Sweat and tears stung her eyes. 'Fan out!' she heard the vizier growl. 'Search every inch!'

The young woman dared not move, dared not call out for help. *You remember very little. Draw no attention to yourself; let them find you.* Seen through swollen eyes, half closed, figures moved at the periphery of her vision – Jalal, she reckoned, and the Chief Eunuch. They edged closer. Spotting the African's corpse on the floor, Lu'lu gasped, his face paling; pudgy hands covered his nose and mouth as though in prayer. Jalal glanced over at him. 'Your trusted man, I take it?'

The eunuch nodded. 'Allah preserve him.'

'And the girl?'

'One of the lesser concubines,' Lu'lu said, golden rings flashing as he made a dismissive gesture. 'She was ill upon waking, which is why we fetched that old villain, al-Gid. He wanted her brought here so he might bleed her. Is she . . . ?'

Scowling, the vizier approached her bedside, careful not to get blood or vomit on his silk-slippered feet. She felt the bed shift as he sat on its edge. 'She lives. Why did he bring her here to bleed her?'

'Tile cleans easier than silk carpets, Excellency.'

'No, you fool!' the vizier snapped. 'Why this hammam? What significance did it hold for him? Why did he choose it?'

Lu'lu shook his head, unsure of how to answer.

Parysatis saw an opportunity in the eunuch's hesitation. Twisting her bound wrists, she groaned piteously, muttering like a sleeper on the verge of wakefulness. It had the desired effect. Jalal leaned closer; his fingers loosened the knots in the silk sash.

'What did you say, child?'

'W-Wall . . .' she repeated, eyes fluttering open. 'V-Vanished . . . in t-the . . . wall.' With feigned effort, she crooked a finger towards the west wall. 'T-There . . .'

'She must be out of her mind with fever, Excellency,' Lu'lu said. 'How can a man vanish into a solid wall?'

'How, indeed. Our physician was something of a magician in that respect.' Jalal rose and walked towards the area Parysatis had indicated. He gestured to the soldiers. 'Search along this wall for hollow spaces, for latches disguised as ornaments, anything out of the ordinary!' A few of them drew their daggers and used the pommels to tap the walls; others twisted and tugged every protuberance – to no avail.

As the search continued, the Chief Eunuch came to sit by Parysatis' side. He took her hand in his and stroked it, his face a mask of concern. *A mask only worn for the occasion.* 'Did that monster harm you, my flower?' Parysatis shook her head. Lu'lu leaned closer; rank breath mixed with the cloying scent of perfume. 'If you were party to this, you would do well to confess now and throw yourself on the vizier's mercy, for you will get none from us!'

Parysatis shrank away from him. 'C-Confess, lord? I h-had no part . . . n-no part in your man's murder. I . . . I am sorry . . .'

'Why did you wish to speak to al-Gid alone, then?' The Chief Eunuch pitched his voice above a whisper. Jalal overheard him; the vizier turned, his brows drawn into a suspicious glower. He stepped closer.

'She spoke to him alone? When?'

'When he first arrived, Excellency,' Lu'lu said. His continued petting of her hand became an unbearable mockery. 'Drove us all out at her request.'

The vizier's cruel eyes fixed on Parysatis. 'Is that so?'

She hesitated. Her dictum to draw no attention to herself was failing, and miserably. *A misstep, a wrong word, and you will join al-Gid in the grave.* She blinked back tears. *Tell him something he will believe . . .*

'Well?'

'I . . . I f-feared . . . poison, Excellency,' she said, tugging her hand from the eunuch's grasp. She gave him a look of mock condemnation. 'The Caliph's aunts often conspire with the eunuchs of the harem to remove those girls whom they dislike. I am Persian, Excellency. They fear what might happen if I become the principal wife. I have neither allies nor friends—'

'Lies!' the Chief Eunuch spat, lunging to his feet.

The vizier ignored him. 'You told al-Gid this?'

Parysatis rubbed her eyes. 'I . . . I begged him for an antidote. He gave me a bitter draught from a small glass vial and . . . and after that, I remember very little.'

'But you remember seeing him vanish?'

She nodded.

Lu'lu snorted. 'Do you countenance such obvious deceits, Excellency? Poison? Harem conspiracies? A vanishing physician? Why not put the irons to her and—'

'Excellency!' one of the soldiers sang out. The vizier turned to see an older Syrian with a beard the colour of iron drop to his knees, his fingers brushing dust from a faint crack at the juncture of wall and floor. 'We've found something!'

Jalal hurried over to the wall; Lu'lu, after giving Parysatis the darkest of looks, scuttled after him. Free of their scrutiny, the young woman willed her aching body to relax. She closed her eyes and listened at length as the Caliph's enemies – were they not her enemies now, as well? – stumbled over the hidden catch. Stone grated as the door's counterweight engaged.

Its opening provoked a chorus of sharply drawn breaths, and an excited babble. 'Merciful Allah!' she heard the vizier hiss. 'She was right. That wily old fool *did* vanish into the wall. I suspect this will provide the answer to another conundrum as well.' Jalal dispatched the grey-bearded Syrian into the passage. 'Follow it. Find out where it ends.' The fellow nodded, drew a knife, and crept into the passage like a man entering a lion's den. The vizier ordered the rest of the soldiers out of the hammam. 'Post a guard. No one enters without my permission. Is that understood, Lu'lu? No one!'

'Of course, Excellency.' The Chief Eunuch glanced over his shoulder. 'And what of *her*?'

A shiver cascaded down the young woman's spine as she felt the vizier's eyes on her, contemplating her fate. She was at his mercy. A mere word, a gesture, and she would cease to exist. Parysatis dared not move.

'Yes, what of her?' Jalal said. 'Al-Gid could easily have sliced her delicate throat, and yet he did not. Why, I wonder? Clean her up, Lu'lu. Make sure no harm comes to her. I will return later, when she and I can continue our conversation.' The vizier turned back to the now-exposed passage.

'As you wish, Excellency.' Parysatis detected a note of triumph in the Chief Eunuch's voice; returning to her side, Lu'lu stared down at her and smiled, thin and cruel. 'Oh, my dear flower,' he said with a sadist's glee. 'You should have confessed to us when you had the chance.'

14

Through the winding streets of the River Quarter, southwest of Cairo's twin palaces, Gamal and his Syrians dogged their prey. With every step, he developed a grudging respect for the one-eyed beggar: on at least three occasions, if Gamal had been alone or working in tandem with but a single companion, the cunning dog would have given him the slip. Nor was the girl he travelled with any less astute; indeed, she seemed predisposed to suspicion and fixed a wary eye on their back trail. Her vigilance forced Gamal to change tactics. He and his men kept their distance, using impromptu markets and foot traffic for cover. They moved along parallel paths where they could and leapfrogged down alleys in order to keep up.

But keep up they did.

At the intersection of two streets, one leading to the Nile Gate, Gamal watched their quarry duck through the keel-arched doors of a sprawling caravanserai. Four storeys high, its façade studded with mashrafiyya windows, the building was a relic of a time when the canal beyond Cairo's walls – now little more than a reed-choked ditch – brought goods from the Nile into the city. Whatever purpose the caravanserai served today, Gamal knew it was well guarded: mailed Berbers in etched steel helmets stood to either side of the gate; others patrolled the roof.

Covertly, he signalled his men to fan out, to watch from the corners of the building in case this was another of the one-eyed beggar's ruses. Gamal himself took up a position across the street, under a frayed awning and out of the ferocious sun. He noticed a curious thing, then. Beggars. Dozens of them, coming and going under the cursory glances of the Berbers at the caravanserai's gate.

A water-seller in a ragged blue galabiyya trudged down the street, the brass cups tied to his bloated goatskin bag clinking like cymbals. Gamal motioned him over. 'The Prophet's blessing upon you,' the water-seller said, his wares sloshing as hurried into the thin shade. Gamal passed him a copper coin, a Damascene fals; after a moment, the seller handed him a cup of water.

'I am lost, my friend,' Gamal said, thickening his Syrian accent. He nodded at the caravanserai. 'Tell me: is that the house of al-Suhaymi?'

The seller chuckled and shook his head. 'Al-Suhaymi? No. That's the palace of Ali abu'l-Qasim.'

'Abu'l-Qasim, eh? And who is he to have such a magnificent palace? A great merchant? A cavalier? A friend of the Caliph?' Gamal drained his cup and handed it back to the man.

'A king,' the water-seller replied.

'You jest!'

'Allah smite me if I lie! Abu'l-Qasim is a king among thieves, men say.'

'Cairo is a wondrous place indeed,' Gamal said, grinning, 'if even the thieves have a king. But indulge me, my learned friend: is there a woman who dwells within?'

'I would know this? I am a seller of water, stranger, not a pander.'

Gamal dipped two fingers into his sash and drew out first one golden dinar, then another. 'Of course you're no pander, my friend. But I can see you are an observant man, and this woman . . . she is lithe as a gazelle and her beauty has no equal. Perhaps you have seen her?'

The water-seller licked his lips. His eyes flickered from the coins to Gamal's face, seeking some hint of deception; he glanced around, suddenly unsure of himself. Two dinars would keep his family fed for a month. What was the harm . . . ? Again, his tongue darted out. 'Such . . . Such words could be spoken of Abu'l-Qasim's daughter, Zaynab. Though she makes her home nearer the palace, I have heard she visits her father on occasion.'

Gamal added a third coin. 'And is now such an occasion?'

The water-seller nodded. 'So I have heard.'

Smiling, Gamal pressed the coins into his calloused palm, then produced a fourth. 'For your silence. *Alaikum as-salaam.*' With that, Gamal left the water-seller in the thin shade of the awning and crossed the street to where one of his fedayeen loitered, crouching with his back to a rough mudbrick wall.

'They are still inside?'

'Of course they are.' Gamal glanced back to see the water-seller shoulder his sloshing burden and hurry off, no doubt bound for the fly-infested hovel his family called home. 'Go, fetch Badr. Tell him we've found the Gazelle's hiding place.'

15

Zaynab read the scrap of paper a third time before passing it to Farouk. 'I can make nothing of this,' she said. 'It says something about a death in the palace . . . is that "this morning", perhaps?'

'Who is it from?' The Persian held the missive, torn from a sheet of fine Samarkand paper, up to the light and studied the cramped handwriting. Whoever penned it was either barely literate or in a tremendous rush.

'A courtier from Alexandria who owes me – well, my father, actually – a substantial amount of money. He repays it by keeping me apprised.'

'Lady, you would do well to school your informants in the art of decent penmanship. *Bismillah!* A death, but he doesn't say whose? If this is his idea of "apprised", then I'd say this poor courtier from Alexandria is not a worthwhile investment.'

Zaynab snorted. With the last remnants of intelligence her people had managed to gather, she had repaired to the roof of her father's caravanserai, to a comfortable divan under a loggia of stone and wood. Farouk joined her there after he had made his morning's enquiries. He, too, had come up dry. The Persian had adopted the dress of a native Cairene: a long white galabiyya and a small turban wrapped around a red tarboush – nothing ostentatious and no outward signs of affluence. Though Zaynab had only spoken to him twice before now, she sensed a kindred spirit beneath his garrulous and disarming façade; a fellow purveyor of information. She took the scrap of paper from him and held it up again, her brows knitted.

The loggia faced north to better catch the breeze. Diamond-shaped holes pierced its roof and walls, allowing shafts of light in to brighten the interior. 'My courtier is actually a fine investment, brimming with such innate suspicions as you would expect of a native Egyptian, but this passing of notes is not the most efficient way of handling him. He prefers a quiet word spoken in an intimate embrace.'

'Obviously, because he cannot make letters with even the facility of a child.'

Zaynab shook her head and smiled. Away in the hazy distance, over the roof-tops of the River Quarter, the domes and spires of the twin palaces glittered in the broiling sun, the minaret of the Grey Mosque all but lost among them. 'It is almost noon,' she said. 'Do you think Assad will be successful?'

Farouk exhaled. 'I have not known him long, nor do I know him well, but if any man can slip through the vizier's defences it is Assad. I have heard stories about that man that would make the Prophet tremble.'

'I'm more interested in the truth than in a collection of fanciful tales.' Zaynab shifted on her divan, suddenly uncomfortable. 'Have you ever asked him how he acquired his name; if it were true he fought a djinni?'

'I have never given it much thought. I assumed there was some truth to it, like the stories in *The Thousand Nights and One Night*, but that it was something far less fanciful. Still, I imagine it's easier for men to believe the unbelievable than for them to believe God could create such a perfect killer.'

'I think God has nothing to do with it. His knife . . .' Zaynab shivered despite the sun's warmth.

'His knife is merely a tool, lady,' Farouk said. 'Albeit a powerful one. Without it, Assad is no less dangerous. Imagine a lion: cold and predatory, a man-killer possessed of speed and strength. Now imagine that lion acquiring a man's intellect, a saint's patience, and a conqueror's drive. Can you imagine it, lady? Good. Then, I ask you, what mummery could make it any more frightening?' Farouk looked at her for a heartbeat. 'What did he tell you?'

A faint smile touched Zaynab's lips. 'Am I that transparent? Oh, Assad spun a fine, mundane tale about slain emissaries, a madman, and a duel to the death. Not a djinni or afreet in sight.'

'But . . . you do not believe him?'

'I laid a hand on the hilt of that knife,' Zaynab said, shuddering at the memory. 'The blessed Qur'an tells us, in no uncertain terms, that we share the earth with beings created from smokeless fire, with djinn and women-stealing afreets and ghûls that slink through the wastes. Thus, it must be so. But, this was something else . . . something ancient and foul.' She shook her head. 'I cannot explain it.'

The Persian shrugged. 'Then simply accept it and give thanks to Allah for making the *Emir* of the Knife our ally and not our enemy.'

'I do, my friend. I do.' Zaynab glanced up at the sound of footsteps coming from the flight of wide, worn stairs that ascended from the caravanserai's fourth-floor gallery to the roof; she peered through the loggia wall and saw Musa approaching, with another figure, small and quick, close on his heels. The Gazelle rose to greet him.

'Did you have any trouble delivering the message to Massoud?' she asked as he rounded the corner of the loggia.

'None, mistress,' he replied. 'All is prepared. What's more, I went by your house to check things over and found this ragged scrap of bones loitering outside your door . . .'

Musa grinned and stepped aside; the girl in his shadow hesitated before hurtling forward, all but tackling the older woman in her eagerness to embrace her. Zaynab rocked back. Her face lit up in genuine delight, and she laughed aloud. 'Yasmina!'

'Mistress! I heard there's been trouble! Are you all right? Why have you been forced into hiding?'

Zaynab kissed the top of the Egyptian girl's head. 'Trouble? Pish! Merely the price of a woman doing business among men. Sometimes, one must lie low. But, what goes?' She disengaged from Yasmina's grip and held her at arm's length. 'How is Parysatis? Have you been causing her trouble again?' A scowl darkened Yasmina's brow; she glanced warily at Farouk, trying through slitted eyes to pigeonhole him as friend or foe. The sight of such a sober expression on the young woman's face banished Zaynab's levity. She stepped closer. 'It's all right. This is Farouk. He's a friend. What has happened, Yasmina?'

The young woman shook her head. 'Things are not at all well in the palace, mistress. Parysatis has stepped in a vipers' nest; aye, stepped in it with both feet.'

Zaynab motioned to one of the guards. 'Bring us food and drink.' Then, draping an arm around Yasmina's brown shoulder, she guided the girl into the cooler shade of the loggia. She bid Musa follow, motioning for the one-eyed man to sit. Zaynab took note of Farouk's questioning glance. 'Yasmina serves as my eyes and ears in the Caliph's harem,' she said with no small measure of pride in her voice. 'And I trust her word without reservation. Her mistress, Parysatis, is a lesser concubine with a surfeit of curiosity for the outside world.' Further conversation paused as a servant bustled up bearing a tray of honeyed dates, bread and cheese, and four cups of rose-water sharab. After he left, Zaynab turned to Yasmina. 'Now, start from the beginning.'

The young woman exhaled, collected her thoughts. 'It began

with the two Nazarenes who arrived last night – "Templars", Parysatis called them – and the message they brought from their King in Jerusalem.'

'Assad was right. They *are* emissaries,' Farouk said, and then leaned forward. 'Do you know why they are here?'

Yasmina nodded. 'To warn the vizier. An army from Damascus is marching on Cairo. The Nazarenes have decided to cast their lot with us, rather than the Sultan's dogs. These Templars and their King have become the vizier's allies. They are sending an army of their own to aid him.'

The pronouncement stunned Farouk to silence.

Musa scratched and tugged at his beard in consternation. 'Two armies? Impossible! News like that would set the streets afire!'

Zaynab answered for Yasmina. 'Not if the vizier is suppressing the information – which would be sensible, if only to delay the inevitable chaos. Likely he's sequestered the Templars in some out-of-the-way corner of the palace and ordered his own people to spread rumours that they're nothing but renegades.'

Farouk stood. He wanted badly to pace, but the cramped interior of the loggia precluded it. '*Bismillah!*' He took a step in one direction, then the other, and finally sat down again. 'This changes everything! We must get word to Assad before he makes contact with the Caliph. The young man is liable to be in on the deception with his vizier. If Assad reveals himself . . .'

'Does the Caliph know?' Zaynab asked Yasmina. 'Does he know any of this?'

'No, mistress. After Parysatis found out she tried to warn the Caliph, but she discovered the vizier has been keeping him drugged. That vile old bastard plans to poison the Caliph and have himself declared Sultan.'

Farouk nodded, tugging at his lower lip with his thumb and forefinger. 'Another reason to suppress news of an imminent invasion: there's nothing like the threat of war to rally support for a ruler. The vizier will not be able to put the Caliph quietly aside if the people are clamouring for him. I'm surprised his enemies didn't do away with him last night.'

'They tried,' Yasmina said. 'Parysatis thwarted the attempt by replacing their poisoned wine with water. Then, this morning, we found an ally in the old physician, al-Gid—'

'Harun al-Gid,' Zaynab said suddenly. 'Yes, I know his daughters. He is a good man.'

Yasmina's face was grim. 'He *was* a good man. Parysatis showed him a secret way into the Caliph's apartments, but before al-Gid could do much more than rouse him, one of the vizier's lackeys knifed him cold.'

Zaynab cursed.

Farouk leaned back, eyes closing as he pinched the bridge of his nose. 'A vipers' nest, indeed, and soon the nest will be surrounded by an army of vipers. This cannot end well.'

Musa looked from one to the other. 'So, what do we do?'

In the distance, the ancient muezzin atop al-Azhar Mosque sang the first notes of the adhan, calling the faithful to the noon prayer. Across the city, others picked it up. Farouk smiled. 'Prayer might make a fine start.'

'Mistress,' Yasmina said. 'Parysatis is alone in the palace, and she's fallen prey to despair. I've covered her tracks as best I can but she needs your help.'

'And she'll have it.' Zaynab clasped the young Egyptian's hand.

Farouk's smile faded. 'Have you a plan, lady?'

Zaynab did not say anything immediately, but her face lost any hint of feminine softness and her eyes glinted like dagger-tips. 'It is only by the grace of Allah that the vizier's influence doesn't yet reach far beyond the palace walls. The bulk of Cairenes still profess loyalty to the Caliph, and Jalal knows it. Thus his need for secrecy. What would happen, I wonder, if knowledge of his perfidy became the talk of the bazaars? Would it ruin his bid for the sultanate?'

'Or would it instead spark riots and unrest?' Farouk's brows beetled. 'Loyal though they may be, the folk of Cairo are not known for their restraint, lady. By feeding the rumourmongers and the gossips, we could be doing more harm than good.'

'Darkness abhors light, my good Persian. Yasmina has risked much to bring us this ember; now it is our duty to nurture it and keep it alive, to coax it into a roaring fire. But you are right. We must do this gently. Musa, can you find my father?'

The one-eyed man nodded. 'He made mention of joining Assad after noon prayers.'

'Finding them together would be providence indeed. Go to the Grey Mosque and await them. Tell them all you've heard, Musa.'

'And what of us?' Farouk asked.

The Gazelle's fingers intertwined with Yasmina's; she met the Persian's level gaze with one of her own: rigid and unyielding. 'You and I will see Yasmina back to the palace, and then I have a meeting with an amir of the Circassian Mamelukes to prepare for,' she said. 'I dare say he can rally enough of the White Slaves of the River to threaten the vizier's hired soldiers, if not crush them outright. And if he needs more of a reason, then, as Allah is my witness, I will give him one!'

16

The echoing call of the adhan brought a swarm of congregants to the Grey Mosque. Assad watched them from the corner of his eye: men of a dozen nations bound by faith, men of influence drawn to Cairo for reasons of their own design. The Assassin spotted a delegation of black-clad Maghribis, envoys of the Almohades of Andalusia, walking arm in arm with dispossessed Seljuk princes in fine silks and gold; he saw Turkish atabegs and Bedouin shaykhs; stern sharifs of Mecca and brooding mullahs from the Persian hinterland; Sudanese captains and Egyptian admirals; scholars and judges; merchants and commoners. Men who would be at one another's throats on any other day, in any other place, put aside their disagreements in order to make their submission to Allah.

The faithful fell into formation like veteran soldiers, kneeling on their rugs, their serried lines stretching across the courtyard. The eldest among them, those poor of sight and hard of hearing, sat in front and faced the mihrab, the niche indicating the direction of Mecca; beside the mihrab, a pulpit of gilded and arabesqued wood towered over the congregants. From its height, the prayer leader – today a venerable cleric from Upper Egypt – would deliver the sermon.

Assad expected the Prince of the Faithful to arrive under a banner of spectacle. Instead, the Assassin witnessed only a slight flurry of activity as servants laid cushions and intricate rugs to one side of the pulpit, in the shade of the colonnade; even before they had finished, a knot of grandees filed in – eunuchs in muted silks who haemorrhaged jewels from throats and wrists – followed by a man whose hawkish and demanding manner fit well with what Assad knew of the vizier. Bringing up the tail of the cortège was the Fatimid Caliph Rashid al-Hasan li-Din Allah.

Assad studied Alamut's potential ally with a critical eye, seeking outward signs of the sort of decay that might prove him unfit to rule. The Caliph's physical appearance did not foster hope. Too thin by far, al-Hasan's sallow complexion and sunken eyes stood in stark contrast to the resplendence of his dress: a khalat of crisp white linen, pearl-sewn and girdled in cloth of silver, and a snowy turban sporting a brilliant spray of peacock feathers held in place with an emerald brooch. Slight tremors ran through the young man's body, and sweat beaded his brow; still, despite his obvious ill health the Prince of the Faithful showed signs of life; he muttered something to his vizier, shook off the hand seeking to guide him by the elbow, and made his own way to the cushions his servants prepared for him.

With an upraised hand, Rashid al-Hasan acknowledged the men who gathered to pray. He allowed his gaze to drift from face to face; those he recognized received a cursory nod by way of greeting, while others were satisfied with simply being in the Caliph's notice. After a moment, Assad felt the young man's eyes on him.

In any other setting, the demands of protocol meant men of all ranks must abase themselves, to show their respect for the descendant of the Prophet through an endless parade of bowing and scraping. In the mosque, however, all men were equal before God, thus there was no affront when a rustic holy man of the Hejaz caught the Prince of the Faithful's eye and held it, nor was there disrespect in the slow inclination of the Sufi's head. Rashid returned the gesture; his brows knit as though the sight of Ibn al-Teymani inspired . . . what? Was it consternation or fascination? Did he see through the Sufi to discover the Assassin beneath? Assad doubted that, but he had little chance to deliberate it further. As one, the congregation followed the prayer leader's example and clambered to their feet.

The venerable cleric from Upper Egypt, raising his hands to either side of his face, called out: '*Allahu akbar* . . .'

17

To Gamal's eye, the streets surrounding the caravanserai of Ali abu'l-Qasim were nigh deserted; even the Berber guards had withdrawn to the interior courtyard, no doubt to make their submission to God alongside their fellows. All that remained of the robust ebb and flow of foot traffic from the Nile Gate to the Qasaba was a handful of rag-pickers, miserable men reduced to abject poverty, using the lull brought on by the demands of Moslem piety to root through the middens and rubbish heaps of a rival's territory. Gamal's lip curled in a sneer of contempt.

This same absence of traffic which aided the rag-pickers forced Gamal's fedayeen to remain still and inconspicuous so as not to draw attention to themselves. Even he had trouble spotting them. One stood just inside the shadowed mouth of an alley; another crouched down beside a jumble of old wicker panniers; the remaining two loitered on the far side of the caravanserai, using the terrain to their advantage just as Badr had taught them.

Gamal himself lurked in a low-roofed alley across the street from the caravanserai, sheltered from view by a latticework door; its twin at the far end stood open, creating an alley between the two buildings that stank of animal dung and ancient brick. He leaned his shoulder against the alley wall and dabbed at his watery eye with the sleeve of his burnous, wincing at the discomfort. *Cursed sand!* Like the heat and the oppressive stench, there was no respite from the powdery grit. It swirled on the slightest breeze and invaded every crack, crevice, fold, and wrinkle; sand clogged his nostrils, flayed his throat, and abraded his eyes. More than anything, it made him long for the fountains and gardens of his native Damascus. He—

Gamal froze. He felt a presence behind him; heard a whisper in his ear that was both colder and sharper than the knife blade laid suddenly across the back of his neck. 'Have you forgotten our master's teachings, Gamal?' the Heretic purred. 'Death comes on black wings for those who give in to discomforts of the flesh.'

'I . . . I've not forgotten, *ya sidi*,' Gamal replied, his voice grim. 'It was careless of me to lower my guard. I deserve the death which awaits me.' Closing his eyes, Gamal tilted his head forward. It would have taken nothing, a simple motion on the Heretic's part, to rip the killing steel across Gamal's neck, to slice through muscle and bone and sever his spinal cord. But the blow never came.

'Give thanks to Shaitan that I need you alive.' Badr al-Mulahid sheathed his dirk. 'What have you found?'

Gamal exhaled. 'We followed them to this place,' he said. 'I made enquiries. A man called Ali abu'l-Qasim dwells within. It seems the Gazelle is his daughter.'

'You're certain?'

'I've not laid eyes on her, but the man I questioned was fairly adamant. He called her "Zaynab".'

The name provoked a rare response in the Heretic: a smile, though humourless and thin.

'The name means something to you, *ya sidi*?'

'It means you've done well. Keep your men in place and out of sight while I work out a stratagem by which we might gain entry; failing that, we need a way to flush the Gazelle from her bolt-hole. I am done with waiting.'

Gamal leaned forward, peering through the latticed door. 'Perhaps a fire?'

The Heretic weighed the idea of a conflagration, but then dismissed it with a terse shake of his head. 'Leaves too much to chance. Without a proper cordon in place she could use the chaos to slip our grasp, and that cannot be borne.'

'A diversion, then? Some odd goings-on in the street for the guards to focus on? While they're distracted, our fedayeen could enter through the back or cross from an adjacent roof.'

Again, Badr al-Mulahid rejected the idea. 'No. If the *Emir* of the Knife also hides within he will see through our ruse and we will become the hunted. In close confines and on unfamiliar ground, it can be easier for one man to kill many than for many to kill one. No, we need a way to lure the Gazelle . . .' Badr al-Mulahid trailed off in mid-sentence. He glanced sidelong at Gamal, then over his shoulder; his eyes narrowed to slits.

'*Ya sidi?*'

A sudden zephyr of air through the alley brought a familiar stench to Gamal's nostrils, and one not easily forgotten: rank sweat and rotting garlic. The smell of the Mad Caliph's mosque and the beggars who dwelled within. Though ham-handed, their attempts at stealth – betrayed by the crunch of a heel on sand and the faint wheeze of pleuritic lungs – meant he doubted they had come as allies. Had the fools got it in their minds to try and rob him? *Ignorant wretches! Do they think I carry a whore's weight in silver on my person?* Gamal squelched the urge to whirl round and curse the beggars for their impudence. Instead, he followed the Heretic's lead and remained motionless . . .

Then, with a barely perceptible nod, Badr al-Mulahid wheeled; steel flashed in the gloom of the alley as he drew his dirk. Three men sought to take them unawares: three beggars, scabrous and filthy, their weapons makeshift cudgels and knotted strangle cords. The speed of the Heretic's movement caught them by surprise, but it came too late to alter their plans.

In the tight confines of the alley, the three beggars rushed in to die.

Faster than the eye could follow, the Heretic sidestepped, one calloused hand catching a cudgel in mid-descent. Its wielder – a lean, hatchet-faced Arab with a matted beard – gawped as Badr wrenched the weapon from his grasp and struck him a back-handed blow across the face. Bone crunched, and the man dropped like a felled tree.

A second beggar skidded on his heels, stumbling to avoid the body of his fallen comrade. The fellow opened his mouth; his lungs wheezed as prelude to a bellowed warning. The Heretic gave him no chance to voice it. Lunging like a swordsman, Badr drove the end of his purloined cudgel into the beggar's mouth with savage force, snapping his head back. Blood spewed from broken teeth.

Beside them, Gamal grappled with the third beggar, a sinewy Ethiopian who tried to loop a strangle cord around his neck. The fellow was slippery, his limbs covered with sweat and a thin film of oil. Cursing, Gamal rammed him up against the alley wall; four times he elbowed the African in the belly before the man doubled over, gasping for breath. Gamal took advantage of his adversary's weakness. He stripped the cord from the beggar's hands, reversed it, and drew it round his thin neck. The Ethiopian's eyes bulged. He thrashed and kicked as Gamal tightened the garrotte.

'I want that one alive,' the Heretic growled.

Gamal nodded; he throttled the Ethiopian to the brink of unconsciousness before easing back, allowing him to gulp a lung-ful of air. For good measure, the Heretic slit the throats of the two he'd cudgelled. Wiping his blade clean on a torn galabiyya, he turned to their unfortunate captive.

'I will ask you only once: why are you here?'

The Ethiopian had no fight left in him; he rolled his eyes up, indicating Gamal. 'Him,' he croaked. 'S-Seller of carpets.'

'What about him?' the Heretic said.

'S-She ... She w-wants him ... alive ... d-doubled his offer ...'

'She? The Gazelle, you mean?'

The Ethiopian nodded.

'Wily bitch,' Gamal grunted, perturbed at being a marked man. 'Al-Hajj's informants must have come running to her.'

'No matter. This display of proud spite has given us the perfect avenue to reach her. Finish him, then give me your robe.'

The Ethiopian opened his mouth to plead for his life, but before he could utter so much as a syllable Gamal planted a knee in his spine and cinched the strangle cord tight, sawing the knots deep into the flesh of his throat. This time, there would be no reprieve. While the beggar died, the Heretic stepped out where Gamal's men could see him; he raised his hand and gave the signal to regroup.

The Ethiopian kicked his last; Gamal shoved the corpse away and straightened. After a moment's respite he shrugged out of his linen burnous. 'What do you have in mind, *ya sidi?*'

'She seeks the seller of carpets alive, does she not?' Badr al-Mulahid replied, stripping off his khalat and passing it to Gamal. The Heretic's eyes lost none of their murderous fire. 'Then that's what she will get, the gods' mercy upon her!'

18

From the pulpit of the Grey Mosque, the venerable cleric from Upper Egypt preached of Hell's fires and damnation; he preached of past Fatimid glories and the need for unification against the Infidel invaders from across the sea. He preached of salvation through holy war. By and large, Assad reckoned his exhortations fell on deaf ears. He read scepticism on the faces of those men around him. Men who believed the sun had set on the Caliphate of Egypt; men who believed the wars in Syria and the Lebanon had little to do with them. True, the fire to reclaim holy Jerusalem from the Nazarenes yet smouldered in their breasts, but the flames were not what they used to be and it would take more than impassioned rhetoric from an old cleric to renew the call for jihad.

More surprising than their collective apathy, however, was the Caliph's reaction to it. Assad watched him with all the subtlety his art would allow; he watched a shadow of confusion flit across young Rashid's pale features, followed by bewilderment and even a flash of anger – like a man who discovers the cherished truths of his childhood are nothing more than convenient lies. *He wants to believe*, Assad thought, *and he wants others to believe as well.* He recalled Daoud's judgement of the young Master of Alamut – *brimming with dreams and ideals not yet tarnished by disappointment or grown faint with age* – and wondered: could he say the same of Rashid al-Hasan? Was the Caliph an idealist, hobbled by a pragmatic and ambitious vizier, or a dilettante who is appalled today and jaded tomorrow? Assad had no answer either way.

The service ended with fresh prostrations and an invocation in the Caliph's name; aided by his son, the elderly cleric hobbled down from the pulpit and made his way to where Rashid sat, to make his obeisance to the descendant of the Prophet. Others pressed close, too, though more to pay their respects to the vizier than to the Prince of the Faithful. The rest trickled out into the Bayn al-Qasrayn.

Assad kept his place as the crowd around the Caliph slowly thinned. The grandees chattered among themselves while the vizier stood to one side, exchanging low words with a black-clad mullah. He needed to make his move and soon, before the opportunity escaped him. He was on uncertain ground, now: he had never targeted a man for *conversation* before . . .

Unexpectedly, the Prince of the Faithful got to his feet. Consternation rippled through the bedizened eunuchs as Rashid stepped through their ranks to survey the mosque's corners and colonnades as though seeking something. His sunken eyes lit on the false Sufi, Ibn al-Teymani; with a resolute nod, the young man started across the courtyard, his servants scrambling in his wake.

Jalal cut short his audience with the mullah. He moved to intercept the young Caliph, gesturing back towards the entrance. 'The palace beckons, Great One.'

'The palace can wait a moment,' Assad heard the young man reply. As he neared, Assad bowed low at the waist.

'Peace be upon you, O Prince of the Faithful,' he said.

'May I sit and partake of your shade?'

The vizier rushed up, glaring at what he took to be a crippled holy man. 'Great One, I—'

The Caliph silenced him with a look that could curdle milk. 'Did I not tell you last night that I wished to talk with a Sufi?'

'You did, Great One.'

'Then have done and go wait with the others! I will speak with this man alone.'

'As you wish, Great One,' Jalal replied, offering a deep salaam – no doubt to hide the murder dancing in his eyes – as a gesture of reconciliation. He backed away. The Caliph returned his attention to Ibn al-Teymani. 'May I?'

'I would be honoured, my lord.' Assad allowed a look of open curiosity to cross his face even as he thanked Allah for this stroke of good fortune. 'How can I be of service?'

Pearl-sewn linen rustled as the Caliph sank down on a cushion one of his quick-thinking servants had put in place. It was plain the young man was exhausted; one hand twitched uncontrollably and the muscles of his jaw clenched and unclenched; sweat soaked the collar of his khalat. All were telltale signs of a man emerging from an opium haze. 'I seek the benefit of your wisdom. How are you called, my friend?'

'Ibn al-Teymani, my lord,' Assad replied. 'Of the Hejaz.'

'Does the path you follow place much stock in dreams, Ibn al-Teymani of the Hejaz?'

'All men who seek the benefit of wisdom should listen to their dreams, my lord,' Assad said, slipping deeper into his role as a holy man. 'Who is to say our dreams do not bring us closer to Allah?'

Rashid leaned forward, his brow furrowed. 'Have you any facility at their interpretation? At reading the dreams of others?'

Assad pursed his lips. 'I have not practised the interpretation of dreams in many years, O Caliph, but there was a time when it was my consuming passion.'

'Indulge me then, Ibn al-Teymani of the Hejaz. Will you listen to my dream and render without fear your learned opinion?'

'I am not so learned as the sages of Cairo, my lord,' Assad said, bowing. 'But if the simple wisdom of the Hejaz can bring you solace, then who am I to refuse you? Speak, O Caliph, and I shall listen.'

'It is a strange dream,' Rashid said after a moment, his voice low. 'I am sitting in the Golden Hall of my forefathers watching a grand gala unfold. Around me are courtiers and scholars, men of rank who share my admiration for the fine dancers leaping and twirling to the music of the flute and the tambourine. Other musicians fill the air with silvery birdsong. It is a fine evening, and I am content.

'Suddenly, a man staggers through the dancers, a Circassian – one of my Mamelukes – and he is wounded unto death. There is a sense of urgency about him as he fights his way through the crowd and up to my seat. He is frantic to tell me something. But when he opens his mouth to speak, all that comes forth are gouts of black blood. Afterwards, darkness falls and there is naught but chaos and screaming.'

'This Circassian, was he an enemy?'

'He was, though I had long acknowledged him as a friend,' Rashid said, casting a sidelong glance back at the knot of grandees who awaited him. 'He was slain almost at my feet, and I later learned he was embroiled in a plot to assassinate me.'

'Do you believe this to be true?' Assad's eyes narrowed at the familiarity of the scene the Caliph described. He had heard a similar tale yestereve, from the lips of the old merchant Umar.

'I do not know,' the Caliph replied. 'As Allah is my witness, I do not know if Othman was coming to speak to me or to kill me. But speak to me about what, I cannot say.'

Assad's eyes flickered from the Caliph to his fuming vizier. 'Who sits with you in this dream, my lord? Are the men at your side known to you?'

'Indeed they are,' Rashid replied, stroking his jaw. 'Chamberlains and hangers-on, the familiar faces of my court. Men I would expect to join me in such entertainment.'

'Does this Circassian single any of them out? A glance, an importuning look, anything?'

'I . . . I do not recall.'

Assad nodded. 'When next this dream occurs, my lord, endeavour to study how these fellows react. If your instincts prove true, then the dying Circassian is obviously a harbinger of violence – as betokened by the blood pouring from his mouth. And if in life he was the victim of another's ambition, then perhaps his dream-self can identify the culprit without the need for words. Regardless, tread with care, my lord. There is something afoot. We have an old saying in the Hejaz: render blind trust only unto Allah and the Prophet; all others must earn your trust anew every day.'

'Wise advice,' Rashid said, grief clouding his eyes. 'And you are the second man to counsel me thus today. I shall not waste such precious guidance.'

'I hope my predecessor was a man of great erudition, so I might be counted as an equal in his presence,' Assad said. Perhaps the boy had sense, after all. He had seen enough to recognize a rift between Caliph and vizier – large enough that he doubted Rashid would mourn Jalal's murder. But a long road yet existed between sanctioning the deeds of one Assassin and embracing an alliance with

Alamut. *Will he be amenable to the Hidden Master's offer, I wonder?*

The Caliph glanced over his shoulder. 'I've kept them waiting long enough.' He staggered to his feet; a servant scurried up, followed by the vizier. Jalal's face had a stern cast to it, but he wisely kept his tongue between his teeth. 'I thank you, Ibn al-Teymani of the Hejaz, for the generosity of your time. Ask anything of me in return, and if it is within my power I will grant it.'

'There is one thing, my lord,' Assad said, his thoughts racing. Mindful of his disguise, the Assassin followed Rashid's lead and hobbled to his feet, the pommel of his hidden salawar couched in his palm. Contact sent fresh jags of rage twisting through the muscles of his forearm, bombarding him with images of violence and slaughter. *It wants blood.* Assad's nostrils flared. 'I . . . I would beg an hour of your time to tell you of my master. You and he share many of the same traits, my lord, and perhaps the tale of his life and travels would be a balm to you.'

The vizier made to speak, to answer on the Caliph's behalf, but Rashid cut him off. He nodded to the false Sufi. 'Granted, and easily so. Come to the palace tonight, my friend, after the evening prayer, and dine with me so that I might learn of your master and his travels. Jalal?'

Through gritted teeth, the vizier said: 'As you wish, Great One. I will arrange for an escort to meet him tonight at the Emerald Gate, after the evening prayer.'

'Excellent. I look forward to further discourse, my friend.'

Assad sighed inwardly and salaamed. 'As do I. May the many blessings of Allah be always upon you, O Prince of the Faithful.'

With a smile and a nod of thanks, the Caliph withdrew from the Grey Mosque, his harried cortège flogged along by the growing wrath of the vizier. Assad watched Jalal through slitted eyes. 'Enjoy your last day under heaven,' he muttered.

For Assad knew in his marrow that, by the end of the night, Jalal al-Aziz ibn al-Rahman would be a man marked for death.

19

Musa stepped into the street outside the caravanserai of Abu'l-Qasim and shivered despite the midday heat. His empty eye-socket ached and his head swirled like the Nile at full flood, brimming over with schemes others had entrusted to him. Him! A simple beggar, by Allah! Still, he had no choice; he was in it now, neck-deep in this business of caliphs and killers. He would do what he could and leave the balance in God's hands.

And when this is over, he thought as he hurried up the street towards the Qasaba, *when this is over I'm going back to the Mad Caliph's mosque and to minding my own affairs, as Allah is my witness!*

Distracted, Musa did not see Gamal and a pair of fedayeen drift into the street behind him.

20

'There's no call for you to endanger yourself, lady,' Farouk said, again, as Zaynab made ready to leave the caravanserai. 'If your girl needs an escort to the palace, then I will gladly do it.'

Trailed by a maidservant, he and the Gazelle emerged on to the third-floor gallery where Yasmina awaited them; the Egyptian's black hair was damp from a quick plunge in her mistress's bathing pool. Clad now in a gown of pale blue cotton, she sat on a divan and polished off a handful of dates, her eyes restless.

Zaynab stopped a moment to bind her hair beneath a grey silk scarf, fringed in gold. 'My mind is made up, Farouk,' she said, selecting a plain veil – a hijab – from among those her maidservant held out for display. 'Yasmina will guide me into the palace, where I might speak with Parysatis about these matters. It's imperative she knows she's not alone in this. I will linger at the palace to pay court to my contacts, then go straight to my rendezvous at the Inn of the Three Apples. I think I can find the Caliph's staunchest allies among the White Slaves of the River. Besides, with all that's going on there's no time for caution, my friend.'

Yasmina stood as they approached, and wiped her mouth with the back of her hand. 'By what route should we go, mistress?'

'What is the most direct route?' Zaynab replied. Frowning, she ran her hand through the young woman's hair, shaking it free of knots. Yasmina flinched away.

'Most direct of all would be the Road of Eagles.'

'Then that's our road.' Zaynab took note of Farouk's confusion. She said: 'For a small donative, the guards at the Nile Gate will grant you access to the parapet atop the city walls; for a larger fee, they will guide you along the parapet to a different gate – the Road of Eagles, it's called.'

The Persian shook his head. 'A sieve would form a better perimeter around Cairo! Why bother with these trappings of intrigue if, in the end, the army of Damascus will simply buy their way in?'

'Perhaps our toils will make the price too steep,' Zaynab said. 'And we can always pray God has mercy upon us.'

'Pray or not, it makes no difference.' Farouk's voice dripped resignation. 'God does not listen . . .'

But before Zaynab could respond, one of her father's white-turbaned Berbers hurried up the stairs and across the gallery. The man's henna-stained beard bristled; he wore a jazerant, a mail shirt sewn between two layers of cloth, the inner layer padded, the outer layer richly embroidered in gold and silver thread. His sheathed sabre rattled on its tooled leather baldric as he came to a halt and salaamed.

'Yes?'

'Two beggars have come, lady,' the Berber said. 'They say they've brought you a prisoner. A seller of carpets.'

Zaynab glanced sharply at the man and then went to the railing and looked down in the courtyard. A pair of ragged beggars waited alongside another Berber; on his knees in front of them was a man whose hands were bound – a clean-shaven fellow with close-cropped hair who wore a soiled and torn burnous. Pale eyes glared up at her.

In return, the Gazelle graced him with her most predatory smile. 'Take him down to the old hammam,' she said. 'I'll be along shortly.'

The Berber nodded and withdrew.

Farouk raised an eyebrow. 'Have we time for this, lady?'

'For this?' The Gazelle's eyes were cold and savage. 'For this, we make time!'

'Who is that man, mistress?' Yasmina asked.

'One of those who have been hunting me.' Zaynab turned to the young Egyptian, one hand cupping her cheek. 'I must beg your patience, child. I know you're anxious to return to Parysatis, but this man has information we need. *Inshallah*, he must be made to talk.'

Yasmina watched the men below drag the prisoner away; her face hardened like a concrete mask, losing all hint of youth. 'I have learned a great many things in the palace, mistress,' she said. 'Perhaps one of them might serve to loosen his tongue.'

21

As Ibn al-Teymani, Assad rested his weight on his walking stick as he hobbled from the cool shade of the Grey Mosque. He did not plunge into the chaos of the broad square outside the mosque, the Bayn al-Qasrayn; rather, he skirted it and entered a narrow lane which ran along the mosque's eastern side. Façades of stucco and carved stone thrust into the street, creating an undulating path for traffic to follow. Higher up, awnings and latticed windows from opposing buildings nearly touched, casting pools of shadow on the pavement below. Down the way, a merchant sold melons and pomegranates from the back of a push-cart.

A sharp left brought the would-be holy man into an alley which ran behind the mosque. Here it was darker still; a thin runnel of sewage gave the heavy air a nigh-unbearable stench. The false Sufi picked his way carefully. Ahead and to his right, he caught sight of a familiar face, age-seamed and russet-bearded, poking around the corner of a recessed doorway: Ali abu'l-Qasim.

'*Y'Allah!*' the King of Thieves muttered. He leaned against a tightly shuttered door, cutting slices from a pomegranate and eating them with his dagger. Sweet juice dribbled into his beard; a few drops spattered a sack at his feet. 'I was beginning to think you might have fallen afoul of the vizier.'

Assad grunted. 'Bastard's as blind as he is ambitious.'

'It went well, then?'

'Well enough.' The Assassin stripped off his cloak and dropped it on the ground; next, he kicked off his sandals and removed his belt before retrieving the sack from Abu'l-Qasim. From it, he took his trousers and his boots, his khalat and his turban, his sash and his empty sheath.

Abu'l-Qasim bore witness to a curious transformation as Assad reversed the physical changes he had adopted as Ibn al-Teymani. He straightened his leg, massaged the kinks from the muscles of his thigh; he cracked the vertebrae of his upper back and neck, stiff from adopting a stoop-shouldered pose, and drew himself up to his full height. Within moments, the crippled holy man of the Hejaz was gone and in his wake stood a penniless freebooter, scarred and cruel. The older man shook his head in wonderment. 'Did you have an opportunity to present your master's offer?'

Assad dressed as he relayed to the King of Thieves the news of his invitation to dine at the palace. 'Rashid al-Hasan has more spine than I gave him credit for. Neither is he the passive puppet of your daughter's description. Whatever put a fire in his belly may also have caused a rift between

Caliph and vizier, perhaps something wide enough to exploit.'

'The Emerald Gate, after evening prayer,' Abu'l-Qasim said, giving a low whistle. 'By the Prophet! You had far better luck than I.'

'What did you find?'

'Nothing.' Abu'l-Qasim spat a pomegranate seed across the alley. 'I found nothing, as Allah is my witness! The man you marked must have been a djinni, for he has truly vanished like smoke on a desert wind. No flesh-stitcher I know, and I know them all, has bound such a wound in the past day.'

Assad gathered up the remains of Ibn al-Teymani and thrust them into the empty bag. Last of all, he slipped his salawar free of the walking stick. Tendrils of rage and despair crawled up his arm. Gritting his teeth, Assad eyed the blade for any damage, then returned it to its accustomed sheath and settled it into his sash. 'It seems the Gazelle's attackers will remain a mystery a while longer,' he said, nodding towards the opposite end of the alley. 'I'm famished. Come.'

'What of this?' Abu'l-Qasim gestured to the bag holding the detritus of Assad's disguise, to the hollow walking stick.

'It has served its purpose. Besides, one cannot dine with the Prince of the Faithful looking like a vagabond. But the stick . . .' Assad looked around until he found a long horizontal crevice running along the base of the alley wall – one easily enlarged by gouging his booted toe into the mudbrick. Whole chunks crumbled and flaked away. Kneeling, Assad tucked the walking stick into the crevice and replaced the shattered bits of brick. 'I will return for it tonight.'

Nodding, Abu'l-Qasim shied his half-eaten pomegranate down the alley and sheathed his knife. He wiped his hands down the front of his khalat. 'I wonder what Zaynab and your Persian have discovered, eh?'

'Allah alone knows.'

22

The stifling heat of midday did not reach into the heart of the King of Thieves' sanctuary; here, beneath six generations of stone, brick, and stucco, the vaults of the old hammam remained cool and moist. Farouk shivered, his nose wrinkling at the stink of pigeon droppings and mildew. High above, a chink in the stone allowed a shaft of sunlight in, and gave egress to the birds nesting in the rafters. In hurried whispers, Zaynab recounted how men had been asking after her, and how Assad had trumped their offer of a bounty by proposing one of his own. Ever greedy, Cairo's beggars moved fast.

Their prisoner sat in that diamond of pale light, in a straight-backed chair with his hands bound at his back. Farouk watched him closely. He had a clean-shaven face as hard and angular as a bronze mask but he was no eunuch, and the dark gold of his close-cropped hair hinted at origins other than Aleppo. *Frankish blood*, Farouk decided. But it was the prisoner's manner – cold and collected – that gave the Persian pause. *He has no fear. Another man would be begging for his life. Why not this man?*

A pair of Abu'l-Qasim's Berbers stood near; with them, the two beggars who had brought the man to Zaynab. Both were barefoot and clad in ill-fitting rags. They bowed gracelessly at the Gazelle's approach.

'You have my thanks, my friends,' she said, and gestured to one of the Berbers. 'Follow him and he will take you back to the court-yard. Partake of some wine, some food, and I will be up shortly so that we might settle our accounts.' The men murmured their assent; as they left, their eyes slid to the prisoner. One of the beggars grinned, no doubt finding macabre humour in the poor fellow's plight.

Zaynab turned to the prisoner. 'I am pressed for time, so let us cut to the chase: who sent you? Give me a name, my old friend – for you said we are old friends, did you not? Give me the name of the man you serve, give me his location, and your end will be swift and painless.'

Nothing. The man simply looked at them each in turn.

'Fetch irons and a brazier of coals,' Yasmina offered. She matched his blank stare with one of her own. 'Start with the left eye. By the time you move to the right, you will have all the answers you require, mistress.'

'Obstinate fool!' Zaynab snapped. 'Do you understand the boon I'm offering? You will not leave this place alive! Answer truthfully and I will have my man dispatch you with all the mercy you would have denied me! But, play games and I swear – as Allah is my witness – *she* will make sure you linger for days! What say you, now?'

Still, the prisoner made no response; he stared at her, pale eyes lit from within by the fires of fanaticism. *Pale eyes . . . eyes . . . of course! His eyes!* Farouk leaned closer to Zaynab. 'Notice his eyes, lady,' he said.

'What about them?'

'You said your informant made special mention of them, that one was infected. Look at him. This man's eyes are healthy. Those beggars are playing you for a fool, lady. He cannot possibly be our Aleppan seller of carpets.'

Zaynab frowned. 'Then who . . . ?'

'You have a keen sense for detail, Persian,' the prisoner said, lips curling into a sneer. 'Your Emir should be commended. Where is he? Where is the *Emir* of the Knife? I would speak with him.'

Farouk cast an uneasy glance at Zaynab. 'How do you know I am not the Emir?'

'Like recognizes like, Persian. You are no killer, nor are these two.' He nodded to Zaynab and her Berber guard. 'The girl, though . . .' His hot stare travelled up and down Yasmina's body, bringing a flush of colour to her cheeks. Zaynab stepped in front of the prisoner.

'Which means you are a killer, I take it?'

'Ask al-Hajj. Ask the Angel of Death, for you will see him soon enough, my little Gazelle.' His patronizing smile widened.

'You will see him before me, you murdering son of a bitch!' Zaynab whirled and snatched a curved dagger from the Berber's sash; she lunged at the bound man. Farouk, however, caught her before she could strike him down.

'Calm yourself, by Allah! The dog is baiting you! Think! Even if he is the one who killed your companions, will slaying him out of hand get us any closer to the answers we crave?' Unable to argue, Zaynab wrenched free of his grasp and turned away. Farouk looked at the prisoner. 'That's the question, dog! Who are you and whom do you serve?'

'Dog, is it? I am surprised you have not pieced the answer to that together yet, brother. Let me help you. Who else besides Alamut employs men skilled enough to hunt their prey with such stealth and cunning? Who else would slay the followers of a feckless boy but the followers of one who seeks to supplant his leadership? Who else, brother . . . ?'

Farouk face grew pale; he cursed.

'Yes,' the prisoner gloated. 'You see it now, don't you? You merely needed a nudge in the proper direction.'

'Cursed swine!' Farouk hissed, tearing the knife from Zaynab's fist. 'I'll take care of this one! Send your father's men to kill the other two, the ones claiming to be beggars! Quickly, before it's too late!'

Zaynab stumbled back, her hand on Yasmina's shoulder. She glanced from man to man. 'Why? Who are they . . . ?'

'Renegade al-Hashishiyya!' Farouk tightened his grip on the knife. 'Assassins from Mount Massaif in Syria, and if my guess is right this pale-eyed Frank is one of their emirs! The one they call the Heretic! Allah, I should have known!'

'Indeed, you should have,' the Heretic said, his smile vanishing.

In that instant, Farouk realized their peril; he realized it even as he heard Yasmina loose a shrill cry of warning – for the girl saw the same danger as he: behind the prisoner's back, the bonds they thought secure dropped away . . . and a heartbeat later, the old hammam exploded into chaos.

The Heretic was in motion before Yasmina's shout reached its crescendo. Unexpectedly, he threw himself backwards, toppling his chair and rolling to his feet, dirk in hand. Farouk cursed under his breath. *It was in his boot!* The Persian retreated, putting himself between the Heretic and Zaynab; steel rasped and flickered as the Berber guard, not lacking in courage, drew his sabre and launched himself at their one-time prisoner.

Quick as a snake, the Heretic ducked under a wild swing that had it landed would have split him in half; his dirk flashed low, its keen edge parting the fabric of the Berber's trouser leg and continuing into the flesh behind his knee. The soldier bellowed in pain, staggered, and tried to rake the hilt of his sabre across the Assassin's unprotected eyes.

Again, the Heretic sidestepped; his riposte was no less savage. He slammed the pommel of his dirk into the Berber's face, driving the nasal of his helmet into the bridge of his nose. Cartilage snapped; blinded by tears and spurting blood, the Berber's head snapped back to expose his jugular.

The Heretic ended his life with a flick of his wrist.

Even as the soldier toppled, his throat a red ruin, Farouk whirled and shoved Zaynab away. 'Run!' he screamed. 'Run, damn you! Find Assad! Go!'

Yasmina caught Zaynab's arm and dragged her to the door. This roused the Gazelle from her daze; she dug in her heels. 'No, the other two are out there! This way!' Hand in hand, the two women sprinted deeper into the maze of rooms that made up the ancient hammam.

Alone, Farouk blocked the Heretic's way, the Berber's curved knife in his fist. Badr made an impatient gesture.

'Step aside, Persian. You and I, we have no quarrel today.'

'Oh, but we do,' Farouk said; though not a man of action, neither a fighter nor a killer, he resolved to stand his ground so Zaynab and the girl would have a chance to escape. Live or die, he left his fate in the hands of God. 'You have the murder of my master's servants to atone for, by Allah. Bind yourself over to our judgement and I will see your end is fairly wrought.'

'Now who plays games?' The Heretic's nostrils flared. 'Though you do not ask my mercy, you will receive it, brother, for I need a man who can bear a message to the *Emir* of the Knife.'

'Mercy? O infidel of Massaif, what would you know of that word? Your kind has perverted the teachings of Ibn al-Sabbah; you've sullied the path to Paradise with your base ambitions and porous loyalties!'

'And what of your kind, Persian? Alamut has become a nest of close-minded antiquarians who live only for past glories! Faugh! The world is larger than Baghdad or Cairo or Damascus! We, at least, fight for our place in it! Go back to your mountain-top, brother! Bear witness, for this is a duel you cannot win!' Badr made to move around him but moved back when Farouk lashed out with his dagger, missing him by a hair's breadth.

'Win or not, there is no way forward save through me!'

'Then more the fool are you, Persian!' The Heretic advanced slowly this time, on the balls of his feet, his dirk weaving silvery glyphs in the dim light of the hammam. He lunged once; then he lunged again, feinting high and slashing low, driving Farouk back.

The Persian blinked sweat from his eyes. '*Allahu akbar!*' he panted.

Badr al-Mulahid chose that moment, that instant of minor distraction, to drive home his advantage. A pantherish leap carried him inside Farouk's guard and into a deadly embrace; before the Persian had a chance to react, before he could block or shift ground or bring his own dagger into play, the Heretic's Frankish dirk slammed into his chest, left of centre.

The Persian's world exploded in white-hot agony. He gasped, and as he stood at the precipice, awaiting the inevitable fall into darkness, the last thing Farouk of Palmyra heard was the silky whisper of his killer: 'Your god is not great, brother, but mine are.'

23

South of the Bayn al-Qasrayn, the Qasaba branched off into indi-vidual markets – souks – each under their own roofs and canopies: perfume and spices, slaves and silk; smiths sweated over their forges, those of copper hammered utensils or cast finials; those of gold and silver collaborated with jewellers to create works of art while their ironmongering brethren forged the swords that would protect them. Adding to the roaring din, the men who made sheaths, boots, and books all haggled with tanners' agents over the price of the finest calfskin. Myriad odours clashed in the smoke-heavy air – incense, urine, oil, pepper, and sweat – creating a stinging haze that made it impossible to draw a deep breath.

At a stall outside the spice market, where sunlight slashed through an awning of scarlet linen, Assad wolfed greasy chunks of mutton off a wooden skewer, barely tasting the stringy meat as he washed it down with draughts of too-sweet khamr. Abu'l-Qasim stood a short way off, his back to Assad as he argued with a muhtasib, one of the market chiefs responsible for enforcing public decency in the souks. From what little he overheard, Assad reckoned some of the King of Thieves' followers had been a bit too brazen in the pursuit of their profession. The muhtasib, an overbearing man in a silk kaftan and bulbous turban, demanded an end to it, lest his constituents force him to involve the Ahdath in the matter.

Assad tossed the empty skewer down and wiped grease from his chin with the back of his hand; nodding his thanks to the merchant, he walked over to stand beside Abu'l-Qasim. The muhtasib eyed him as one would a feral dog.

'You understand my dilemma, then?' the man said, his gaze shifting back to the King of Thieves.

Abu'l-Qasim leaned closer. 'Have I not said I would take care of it personally? Do you hold my word in such low esteem, friend?'

The muhtasib grumbled. 'No, but neither do I trust the word of those curs in your employ!'

'Leave them to me. As Allah is my witness, they will bedevil you no more.'

Finally, with a curt nod, the market chief salaamed and vanished into the heart of his tiny demesne. Abu'l-Qasim shook his head.

'Men like that make honest commerce seem unclean.'

Assad hooked a thumb in his sash; he looked sidelong at Abu'l-Qasim. 'So, these merchants give a portion of what they earn to the urban militia so their shops and stalls will be protected. But you also tithe a portion of your earnings to the militia so they will turn a blind eye to your business of thievery. Thus, the officers who command the militia are well compensated for doing nothing for the merchants or *against* you?'

'Aye.'

Assad grunted. 'And men call you the King of Thieves? The title should go to whoever thought up this scheme.'

'This arrangement goes back a generation and more. It benefits us all, in the end: the militia have coin in their purses, provided their officers are generous; the merchants recoup their losses by selling their wares at inflated prices to the militia, and my thieves go about their business unmolested.'

'Perhaps,' Assad said, stroking his jaw. Ahead, he caught a glimpse of a familiar face weaving through the crowd. The Assassin gestured. 'Isn't that your man, Musa?'

Abu'l-Qasim followed Assad's gaze, his brows knitting in concern. 'Merciful Allah! Can the dolt not follow simple orders? I told him not to stray too far from Zaynab's side. He had best be bringing me news of staggering importance.'

Assad, though, made no reply. Still more than a dozen yards away, he studied the beggar's approach, taking note of his speed and lack of concern for keeping a low profile. Impatiently, the man skirted a knot of folk who had stopped to watch a mountebank's capering monkey and nearly tripped over a darting child. Assad saw Musa hurl a curse after the boy; then, from long-ingrained habit, looked past him and searched the beggar's back trail.

Suddenly: 'Fool!' the Assassin hissed, turning so Musa could not see his features. 'He's being followed!'

'Followed? Impossible! He—'

'Over his right shoulder. Three men twenty paces behind, moving too quickly to be browsing merchants' wares. Every few steps, the one in the lead looks ahead to make sure Musa hasn't stopped or veered off. He's subtle, but there's no doubting it. They're shadowing him.'

'*Y'Allah!* What do you wish to do? Avoid him? Let them pass by?'

Assad's eyes narrowed to slits. 'I will take care of them. Greet Musa as you would normally and draw him off, down a quiet street and into an alley. They will no doubt follow. Once you're in the alley, duck out of sight however you may and do not tarry about – make straight for your caravanserai. I will join you there once I've dealt with them. Understood?'

Abu'l-Qasim nodded. Like a stranger, Assad stepped around him and walked away, back towards the bustling spice market. There, amid heaps of saffron, baskets of cloves and seeds, and bundles of paper-thin cinnamon bark, he felt sure he could observe the men following Musa with little chance of detection.

Musa caught sight of Abu'l-Qasim and rushed to him, more animated than Assad had yet seen him. The man waved his hands about as he spoke to the King of Thieves, who reined him in with an embrace; whatever passed between them was lost to the din of the crowd. Musa's three shadows stopped as well, ostensibly to watch the mountebank's monkey dance to the music of a reed flute. All three were Arabs: dark-skinned, bearded, and so nondescript in dress and manner that their lack of individuality raised suspicions in the back of Assad's mind. *Like soldiers trying to be anything but.* One had an infected eye, which was all that set him apart from the other two.

Now, Abu'l-Qasim turned and walked arm in arm with Musa, back towards the Bayn al-Qasrayn, two old friends locked in earnest conversation. Strolling past the entrance to the spice market, the pair turned left off the Qasaba. Their shadows followed with predictable diligence.

After a moment, so too did Assad.

24

Thin grey light filtered into the heart of the old hammam, illuminating basins of age-worn marble and heaps of shattered terracotta: ruined pipes and vessels; a generation of accumulated rubbish. The place must have been grand in its heyday, when its fixtures were of silver and gold and cut crystal, but that day had long passed. Now, it bore the aspect of a tomb.

Zaynab's slippered feet pattered on cracked faience tiles. She and Yasmina kept to the pools of shadow, their eyes ever cast behind them, seeking signs of pursuit as they made for the brightest source of natural light: a fissure in the wall of the bath.

'Where does it lead?' Yasmina hissed.

'Out. To the street.' This Zaynab knew well. She had played in these warrens as a child, spying on her brother Qasim as he learned their father's trade, and she had watched him come and go by way of this fissure – sometimes empty-handed, other times loaded down with spoils, for he was truly the Prince of Thieves. None of her father's followers had used the cleft in years, though, not since Qasim's death in a raid on a Nile barge; now, a grate of thick bronze bars secured with chains and an iron lock kept inter-lopers at bay. Beyond, weeds grew in the joints of sandstone steps leading to the surface. To safety.

Yasmina reached the grate first. She dropped to her knees and wriggled between the bars, struggling to force her lean hips past the pitted bronze. For a moment she hung suspended, half in and half out until her flailing feet found purchase; then, cursing at the patches of abraded skin left behind, she kicked free.

Yasmina turned to give Zaynab a helping hand. 'Hurry,' she hissed.

But the look on the Gazelle's face as she gauged the span between the bars stole the breath from Yasmina's lungs. 'I cannot squeeze through this,' Zaynab said.

'You must try, mistress! Let me help you!'

Zaynab shook her head. 'No, you cannot draw a camel through the eye of a needle. Go ahead. I will find another way out.'

'I can't leave you!'

'You must, Yasmina. I'll be fine, I promise you. Get back to the palace and bid Parysatis meet me tonight, at the Inn of the Three Apples. You know it?' The girl nodded. 'Good. The White Slaves of the River are her best hope for protecting the Caliph. With her knowledge of the palace's secret ways and their fighters, the vizier cannot stand against them for long. Tell her this! Make her understand she must come to the inn! She must speak to the Circassian amir, Massoud!'

'She will, mistress. I will make sure of it. What about you? What will you do about him?'

Zaynab made a rude noise, her bravado more forced than real. 'I can elude the Frank for hours down here. Long enough for more soldiers to arrive and send him on his way to Hell.'

'Keep this, just in case.' Yasmina passed her knife through the bars.

Zaynab received the blade with a smile of thanks; she took the young Egyptian's hand and kissed it. 'Remember all I've taught you!' she said, her voice brimming with ferocious urgency. 'Remember all you've seen! I will meet you tonight, if it is Allah's will, but if I cannot make it to the inn then you must speak for me! Do you understand?'

Yasmina nodded, resting her forehead against the bars; she felt Zaynab squeeze her hand in reassurance before letting it loose.

'Good. Now you must go. Hurry, dear Yasmina!'

The girl's composure slipped; her lips trembled, and she blinked back tears. 'Mistress, I . . .'

'No!' Zaynab replied, swallowing her own anguish. 'No grim

thoughts. Go! I will find a way, I promise you!' Yasmina nodded again, wiping away her tears; her face became once more a mask of iron. Slowly, she backed away. 'Go! Hurry!' And, with a final nod, the young Egyptian vanished up the stairs. For an instant, sunlight etched her shadow in the stone and then that, too, was gone.

Zaynab stood there a moment longer before turning her back on the barred cleft, her eyes hardening to cold points. She had lied to Yasmina. There was no place to hide down here, no bolt-holes where her enemy could not find her. Farouk – poor Farouk! – must have fallen defending them from that cursed madman, that renegade Assassin. That no soldiers had come looking for her yet meant the other two would-be beggars must have disposed of their escort without raising an alarm. Zaynab al-Ghazala was alone; she had no way out and little hope of rescue.

Even still, the Gazelle was not without her wiles.

Swiftly, she retraced her steps a short distance and ducked beneath a crumbling brick archway. The chamber she entered had once been a fountain room, its walls turquoise tile set with faded calligraphic plaques, its marble floor cracked and littered with detritus. Ribbons of dusty light filtered from sculptured perforations in the roof. Sound, too, drifted in from the streets above: faint voices; ghostly laughter.

Zaynab nodded. *Not perfect, but it would do.* If she could distract him, she reckoned on having one chance to strike. *If* she could distract him . . .

She moved to the far wall, to the fountain's edge; with her free hand, she loosened her robes and drew open her undergarments, revealing the curve of her breasts and a long expanse of skin above her navel. Stripping off her scarf, Zaynab leaned back, her shoulders against the wall, her face framed by tousled chestnut hair. She held her knife low against her thigh, out of sight. And she waited.

Exhaling, Zaynab closed her eyes and prayed for Yasmina, prayed that Allah might grant her peace and long life; so too did she pray for her father and her long-dead brother, for loyal Musa and Farouk, and even for the grim *Emir* of the Knife. For if she failed, it was on his shoulders that she placed the onus of her vengeance.

The rustle of cloth signalled an end to her brief vigil. She opened her eyes, her throat tightening. The Heretic stood in the archway, half-cloaked in shadow, one hand – his knife hand – hidden from view. Pale eyes shimmered in the gloom.

'Where's the girl?'

'I sent her to rouse the guard,' Zaynab replied, feeling his gaze drawn to the glimpses of flesh.

'Pity,' the Heretic said. 'You've led us on a fine chase. I should make you pay for that, but my mercy outweighs my frustration. Your death will be swift.' He made to step closer but paused, his brow furrowing.

It was her reaction that startled him. The Gazelle did not dissolve into tears, nor did she beg for her life or try to flee. Instead, with a mysterious smile, she straightened and sketched a languorous curtsey; the gesture revealed even more skin.

'I thank you for your compassion, but would it not be infinitely crueller to leave me alive? Witness: by killing al-Hajj and leaving me alive you will have destroyed any trust Alamut had in me – how could they know it was not I who betrayed him? I will be an outcast. Doubly so if, with a well-placed word, you let slip my role as a spy for al-Hashishiyya. I will be hounded from Cairo, most likely to end my days as a two-copper whore in the stews of Alexandria. If that be my fate, then death becomes a welcome boon.' Zaynab swayed closer, stopping at arm's length from the Heretic; she tilted her head to one side and swept her hair back to expose the graceful curve of her neck. She watched him from the corner of her eye. 'But you are an Emir of Massaif and I trust you will do what's best.'

The Heretic closed the gap between them. To her credit, Zaynab did not flinch when, with his free hand, he ran his fingers from her earlobe to her collar bone, stroking her silky skin as one caresses a lover. 'Your argument has some merit,' he murmured. 'But if I allow you to live, how long before you run back to the *Emir* of the Knife? How long before you come up with a plan to ingratiate yourself with your dog-shit Hidden Master? No, I would trust you no more than you trust me.'

'You overestimate my ambition, O Emir.'

'I think not.'

'Hmm,' the Gazelle purred. 'Perhaps you are right.' And in that instant, Zaynab al-Ghazala struck. Her knife lashed out; even as she heard it rip through the Heretic's loose kaftan, she winced as a weight thumped into her left side, driving the air from her lungs. Something moist and hot spread down her ribs. Zaynab sprang back; she stumbled against the wall, staring down in mute fascination at the blood soaking through her robes from where the Heretic's dirk had pierced her side.

She glared at him with eyes cold as hoarfrost. Badr al-Mulahid was doubled over, his hand pressed to his side; slowly, his gaze never leaving hers, he straightened and brought his fingers away. Only a thin laceration scored his flank.

'Close, but it was not the will of the gods,' the Heretic said.

Zaynab's legs gave way. She slid down the wall, gasping as the first tendrils of pain lanced through the haze of disbelief. Tears blurred her vision. 'A heretic you truly are,' she said, coughing blood. 'In Allah's name I curse you, dog of Massaif! With my dying breath, I curse you! Cairo will be your doom!'

'Perhaps.' Badr shrugged. 'Perhaps not. Who knows what the gods of this dark land have in store? I admire your spirit, lady, so I will keep my word to you. Your end will be swift.'

'Come, then.' Zaynab al-Ghazala tilted her head back. Tears sluiced down her cheeks as she closed her eyes. 'End it, damn your black soul! End it, and may Allah—'

The Heretic's steel flashed in the gloom.

25

Gamal cursed under his breath as the one-eyed beggar, arm in arm with an older man he'd met, left the teeming Qasaba behind. Side streets meant a change in tactics. He slowed their pace, allowed their interval to widen, and prayed to Allah for relief from the sweat stinging his swollen eye. Though he would have preferred to stay behind and cover the caravanserai, the Heretic had set him a different task: 'Follow whoever leaves and mark well their destination.' He did as ordered. But who was the old man and where were the two of them headed? To meet the *Emir* of the Knife, perhaps? Unless the old man was the fabled Emir . . . ?

Gamal shook his head. *Don't be a fool! Focus, and be vigilant!*

Heading west, flights of shallow stairs – never more than a dozen – carried the cobbled street down into a hollow older than the city itself. Plaster flaked from stone foundations to reveal ancient writing, pictures scored by the hands of long-dead Egyptians. Here were the mausoleums of Cairo's earliest settlers: squat buildings with crenellated façades and keel-arch doors, some with inlaid plaques detailing the lineage of those buried within and others carved with extracts of verse older than the Prophet. Yet, while the dead lay in their crypts, the living made their homes among them, for most of the mausoleums exhibited signs of life, from the sounds of squealing children and muttered voices to freshly washed laundry hanging from lines strung between the tombs. The din of the Qasaba was but a faint echo.

Ahead, Gamal's quarry ducked into an alley. He resisted the urge to run after them, to keep them in sight at all costs. Patience. That was the quality of the hunter and Gamal reckoned himself one of the best. He reached the alley, rounded the corner . . . and stopped.

The way ahead was empty.

'Mother of bitches!' He frowned, looked about. Willow trees overhung the alley from a rooftop garden; the narrow way ran a short distance before dead-ending against a wall of dull grey stone. Graffiti scrawled in charcoal declared it to be Fumm al-Gahannam – the Mouth of Hell. Gamal shivered; he dropped his hand to the hilt of his knife as he moved deeper into the alley. Narrow fissures, some hung with wooden doors, led off into the heart of this city of the dead. He shivered again and cursed. 'Only in Egypt would the living sleep among their ancestors.'

'Mayhap they entered one of these mausoleums?' one of his fedayeen murmured, making the sign of the horns to ward off evil.

'Mayhap,' Gamal replied. 'Fan out. Find them.'

'They are no longer your concern,' a voice behind them said.

Gamal and his two companions whirled, curved blades hissing from sheaths at their waists. A solitary figure stood at the mouth of the alley: a tall man, scarred of face and clad in a ragged white turban and a green khalat. The hilt of a knife jutted from the sash about his lean waist, and to this Gamal's eyes were drawn.

It was an Afghan salawar, long and straight, its ivory pommel carved with the leering face of a djinni.

Gamal's breath caught in his throat.

The *Emir* of the Knife.

26

Fear.

Assad's nostrils flared. He could smell it: cold, palpable fear, seeping from the pores of the three men he confronted in that blind alley. But more than fear, the unmistakable scent of hashish permeated their clothing, and this, as much as their uniform appearance and Syrian accents, confirmed his suspicions about the identity of Alamut's unseen enemy in Cairo.

'Where is he?' Assad stalked towards them.

The man with the infected eye raised his hands, a gesture of capitulation. 'What? N-No, effendi. We . . . We are merely lost. Can you—'

'Where is your master, dog of Massaif?'

The fellow paused, and then gave a short bark of laughter. 'I see your reputation is well founded.' He hawked and spat on the cobblestones at his feet. 'My master? My master is making an end of your precious Gazelle just as we will make an end of you, swine!' With a flick of his chin he set his companions into motion; both fedayeen crouched and edged sidewise, their knives low and ready.

For all Gamal's bravado, their fear redoubled as Assad's hand fell upon the hilt of his salawar, loosening it in its sheath. Venomous hatred coiled like a living thing through his body; muscles ridged and corded, straining against the onslaught of emotion. He seized on to this feral rage, embraced it; he kindled it into a savage light that blazed in the depths of his dark eyes. 'And how is your master called?'

'That . . .' the fellow replied, pausing, 'is no longer *your* concern!'

The pause was the signal for the fedayeen to make their move. They attacked in unison, fast and well rehearsed from long association; curved daggers flickered as they surged in from left and right. While a lesser man, a man not versed in Massaif's tactics, would doubtless have fallen prey to their concerted assault, this time they faced the *Emir* of the Knife. He read their intent before ever they took a step.

Assad surprised them by darting right; with tigerish grace, he ducked the clumsy blow of a dagger and swept his own blade from its sheath. Watered steel flashed and glittered. The Syrian's outraged bellow turned to a wet choking scream as Assad's salawar ripped him from hip to sternum. The man reeled away, trailing blood and viscera.

Assad wheeled and twisted; the momentum of his attack kept his blade aloft as the second attacker lunged, teeth bared in a grimace of hate. His dagger sliced empty air, and before he could recover his balance Assad delivered a devastating riposte. He hammered his crimson-spattered steel into the Syrian's neck with murderous fury.

He struck the ground a corpse, head half severed.

Assad straightened, his reddened blade levelled at the final Syrian, the captain of Massaif called Gamal, as though daring him to move. 'Once more, dog,' Assad growled, 'how is your master called?'

Gamal did not answer; his face paled, and sweat beaded his brow. Still, he dropped to a crouch, the grip on his dagger shifting as he edged away from Assad. His infected eye was nearly swollen shut; the other had a martyr's gleam. He would take his secrets to the grave, one way or another . . .

Seeing his foe's resolve, Assad gave a low laugh, merciless and as hard as stone. An instant later he sprang; Gamal had no time to react as Assad's salawar snapped out with uncanny precision. The Syrian's dagger clattered to the cobblestones and with it four of his fingers, amputated at the knuckles.

Gamal screamed and clutched the mangled hand to his breast, his eyes wide with terror. Assad had seen such looks before. *Something* passed between blade and victim; something that wormed into his body and stripped away the last vestiges of his courage. Unmanned, Gamal tumbled to his knees. The *Emir* of the Knife towered over him, his salawar inches from his face and dripping blood.

'Will you make me ask you a third time?'

27

The King of Thieves heard a man scream, the sound muffled by distance; he glanced over his shoulder, looking for signs of pursuit, and saw nothing. Indeed, he doubted any of Musa's shadows had escaped the labyrinthine alleys of the Rub al-Maiyit, the Abode of the Dead – not with Assad dogging their steps; only by long association with the poor folk living there did Abu'l-Qasim know a speedy path through the mausoleums. Now, he and Musa headed southwest along shaded residential streets, making for the Nile Gate and home.

He returned his attention to Musa. The one-eyed beggar was babbling on like a man in the grip of a fever. 'Slow down,' Abu'l-Qasim said, frowning. 'What is this about an army from Damascus?'

'Word has come from the palace, effendi, from one of Zaynab's moles who overheard the vizier bargaining with emissaries of Jerusalem! The army of Damascus marches on Cairo, and a second army – one from Jerusalem – is marching to the vizier's aid!'

'*Y'Allah!* That cannot be right! Are you certain that was what she said?'

'It is, effendi! What's more, Farouk believes the vizier will try and supplant the Caliph ere the news reaches the souks. The mistress's mole thwarted an attempt to poison him last night, and this morning old Harun al-Gid the physician was slain trying to rouse the Caliph!'

At that, Abu'l-Qasim's lips thinned to a hard line. He recalled Assad's assertion that something had put a fire in the Caliph's belly, and that whatever it was had caused a rift between him and his vizier. The murder of the Caliph's childhood physician seemed the likely candidate. 'Harun al-Gid, eh? Have his daughters been told?'

Musa shrugged. 'I cannot say, effendi. The mistress believes if we spread the word of the vizier's treachery, his attempt to seize power will fail. And she believes the Circassian Mamelukes, the White Slaves of the River, can help.'

The King of Thieves chuckled. 'If there's anything those peacocks are good for, it's a palace coup.' Both men fell silent.

The news Musa bore was almost too much to digest. On one hand, imminent war meant an increase in spoils. Abu'l-Qasim's followers would grow fat looting the bodies of slain cavaliers, both from Damascus and from Cairo, and no doubt there would be an increase in slave revenue when captured Nazarenes made it to the blocks. On the other hand, a prolonged war could easily wipe him out – especially if Allah turned away from His faithful Moslems and allowed the Nazarenes to sack Cairo. And given the state of the city's defences, its factional fighting, and its history of intemperance, God's disfavour was not outside the realm of possibility.

The narrow street they followed debouched near the Nile Gate, and Abu'l-Qasim gave a relieved sigh upon seeing the familiar bulk of his caravanserai. An instant later, however, his relief turned to alarm. Something was amiss. A knot of ragged men milled about outside, staring up at the tall keel-arched doors with their elaborate bronze arabesques.

'They're shut,' Abu'l-Qasim muttered, blinking as though he did not believe what he saw. 'In Allah's name, what goes?'

Not in a dozen years had the King of Thieves allowed the gates of his caravanserai to close. Indeed, he preached often how open access fostered a spirit of brotherhood; Cairo's thieves embraced him as much for his disdain of formality as for his good sense and charity. Thus the men gathered before his door looked to him for answers as he shouldered through their ranks. Abu'l-Qasim rapped on the heavy portal with his balled fist. 'Open these doors, by God!'

A helmeted head poked over the edge of the roof, one of his Berber guards. He heard voices bellowing the news of Abu'l-Qasim's return down into the courtyard; within moments, one door trundled open – but no more than half a yard. 'My lord! Quickly, come inside!'

'What?'

'Please! Hurry!'

Scowling, Abu'l-Qasim and Musa slipped through the barely open gate. Inside, the whole of his household stood near: his stewards, the master of his spies, the slaves and eunuchs of his bedchamber and his bath, and his two dozen Berbers. Their faces were pale and drawn; some openly wept. The captain of his Berbers stepped forward, a lean, red-bearded giant whose gentle eyes belied his profession. He ducked his turbaned head, bowing.

'What's going on here?' Abu'l-Qasim barked. 'What the devil has happened to make you close off my house? Answer me!'

'We . . . Someone infiltrated the caravanserai, my lord. We closed the doors to prevent their escape, but I fear we were too late.' He gestured to where four white-shrouded bodies lay under the court-yard colonnade. Splotches of red stained their linen sheets.

'Infiltrated, you say? How did this happen?' Abu'l-Qasim glared as he and the captain walked towards the corpses. 'What were they after?'

'Two beggars showed up, my lord,' the captain replied, 'and they had with them a captive, a rug-seller from Aleppo who had been spreading word of a bounty on your daughter's head. She ordered him taken down to the old bath for questioning. It wasn't until later that we realized something was amiss.' He indicated the first and second bodies. 'Salim we found on the stairs leading to the bath. Nabil was inside, along with your Persian guest.' The captain tugged back the cloth covering the third body. Farouk's sightless eyes stared up at the rafters of the colonnade, his mouth open slightly. 'As for what they were after . . .' the captain trailed off, gesturing to the fourth body.

From this distance, one could not fail but notice its feminine outline.

Ali abu'l-Qasim felt his heart shudder; the air in his lungs became heavy, like water. He sank down beside the shrouded body. 'No,' he whispered. Almost of its own volition, his quaking hand reached for the blood-stained mantle. 'No! Not again! Not her, too!' The linen slipped back, revealing a mass of chestnut hair followed by Zaynab's waxen and lifeless face. She lay with her head canted to the right, staring at her father through half-open eyes. A piteous sob tore through Abu'l-Qasim's breast and he seemed to crumple in on himself, his eyes clouding. 'There is no god but Allah, and Muhammad is His prophet . . .'

The captain glanced back at Musa. 'S-Salim must have been guiding the beggars back to the courtyard when they killed him.

The others . . . the others died in the bath. None of them suffered.'

Musa, tears rimming his good eye, shook his head. 'W-What of the girl?'

The Berber frowned. 'We came across no others.'

'What . . . What girl?' Abu'l-Qasim said, hollow and hoarse – an empty vessel.

'Yasmina. She was with the mistress and the Persian.'

'Your daughter we found near the old thieves' entrance,' the captain said. 'Perhaps the girl was able to escape through the bars.'

'And her killers?'

'No sign of any of them, my lord. We . . . We're not certain how they escaped.'

Abu'l-Qasim leaned over, kissed Zaynab's cool forehead and smoothed her hair. *She's the very image of her mother.* For a long while he stayed bent over her, touching her cheeks, her hair. But when at last he sat upright, all could see a fire had kindled in his eyes, searing away the clouds of grief and filling him with murderous resolve. 'I want the man who did this, and I want him brought to me alive!'

'No,' a voice answered. The members of the household parted as Assad stalked through their midst. How long he had stood in the caravanserai's doorway none could say. 'No, Abu'l-Qasim. The enemy who did this is beyond your reckoning. Your people cannot hope to best him, much less to take him alive.'

Livid, Abu'l-Qasim staggered to his feet. 'You know who did this? You know? Tell me, or as Allah is my witness, I will tear your black heart from your breast!'

Assad shook his head. 'Mourn your daughter, but leave the man who did this to me.'

'To you? *Y'Allah!* It's your kind who got my daughter into this in the first place! Leave him to you? Why? Has he wronged you? Has he spilled the blood of your kin? By what right—'

'You know by what right!' Assad reached the line of corpses. 'Open your eyes, damn you! This man walked into your home, killed with impunity, and walked out again unseen! What do you think a handful of beggars and footpads can do against one such as that?'

Abu'l-Qasim's face purpled. 'Give me his name and I will show you!'

'Are you so eager to die? To see your people slaughtered?'

'His name! Tell me his name, you spawn of a jackal!'

Assad exhaled. 'He is an Emir of Massaif, of the Syrian al-Hashishiyya, called the Heretic. He and his swine are holed up somewhere in the Foreign Quarter. I counsel patience, and after my business with the Caliph is concluded I will bring you this man's head.'

'Patience? Faugh!'

Assad knelt and drew the sheet back over Farouk; he squeezed the Persian's shoulder in farewell. His eyes slid next to Zaynab's corpse; the light that had animated her face, that had made her the object of every man's desire, was gone. An unfamiliar weight shackled Assad's limbs – was it sadness? – as he reached out to cover her up again. The Hidden Master would hear of both their sacrifices.

Assad knelt a moment longer, then he stood. When he turned to face Abu'l-Qasim, the Assassin bore the pitiless expression of a man inured to death. 'Do what you will, but mark this well: if you go after the Heretic you will die, my friend, and soon.'

The King of Thieves sighed, returning his gaze to his daughter's body. The fires of resolve blazing in his eyes were already beginning to dim. 'Not soon enough.'

28

Shadows were lengthening across the Bayn al-Qasrayn by the time Yasmina returned to the East Palace. She had taken a circuitous route from the caravanserai, doubling back on herself, ducking through courtyards and making sudden turns, all to thwart the pale-eyed killer she knew had to be following her. She never saw him; indeed, she never noticed anyone gracing her with so much as a second glance. Still, she remained vigilant.

Three-quarters of an hour later, after two turns around the wide square dividing the East and West Palaces, Yasmina slipped through the Emerald Gate of the East Palace amid a gaggle of servants returning from the markets. Her lank hair and grimy feet were unremarkable among her new-found companions and aroused not the slightest suspicion in the mailed and brooding guards. She passed unnoticed. Beyond the gate, a lush fountain court – its flagstones washed by silvery sprays of water and shaded by the spreading boughs of a plane tree – provided a place of respite. Swallows darted in and out, chasing insects through the late afternoon sky. Yasmina paused here for a drink and to sluice the dust from her feet and legs before continuing into the heart of the palace. The halls and corridors were oppressively silent.

At the gold-chased doors to the harem, the ebony-skinned eunuchs who stood their posts with bared steel knew her by sight; one gave her a kind smile and levered the heavy door open. Inside, the silence continued unabated; the parrots in their silvered cages, the sleek cats, the tiny dogs on their golden leashes all kept quiet, not daring to shatter the pregnant calm for fear of never regaining it. A few of the women were out. Some played shatranj in the colonnaded court, under the bored gazes of eunuchs; others lounged around the lotus pool, dabbling their fingers and toes in the cool water. They spoke in soft voices. The business with the slain physician was already old news, and Yasmina could only guess what obsessions occupied their evening hours, what vicious rumours they were spinning and at whose expense.

Neither eunuchs nor women bothered to look her way as she twitched aside the curtain and entered Parysatis' alcove. The room's morning brightness had long since fled, leaving the air heavy with gloom and despair. Parysatis was still abed; someone had changed her linens and fetched a fresh gown. A pitcher of water stood at her elbow.

The Egyptian crept to her bedside. 'Mistress?'

Parysatis stirred; her face was ghostly in the dim light. 'I'm not asleep, Yasmina.'

'I have news! We—'

'No, Yasmina,' the Persian woman said, shaking her head. She fought back a flood of tears. 'I . . . I want nothing more to do with the intrigues of the palace. What men do to one another, whom they choose to betray or whom they choose to promote, is none of my affair. Women have no place meddling in such business.'

'But, mistress—!'

'I said no, Yasmina! No!'

'No?' The young woman's eyes flared. 'You would abandon your Caliph; leave him at the mercy of his enemies? I thought his suffering moved you to tears?'

'I cannot help him!' the Persian sobbed.

'Cannot, or will not? Don't tell me a little spilled blood has washed away your resolve?'

Parysatis rolled away, her voice thin and cold. 'I thank you for your service, Yasmina, but I . . . I no longer require it. Return to your Gazelle. I do not doubt she will have a place for you in her household . . . or that you will be all the happier for it.'

'Damn you!' Yasmina stared, blinking back hot tears. 'She doesn't have a household any more! Her enemies have taken it from her even as they seek to deprive her of her life! Yet she risks everything to send you aid! To help you, because yours is the cause of truth!'

'Truth?' Parysatis said bitterly. 'What truth? Mine is the cause of death!'

'Stop being naive!' Yasmina snapped. 'Do you hold yourself above Allah?'

'It was not Allah who sent al-Gid to his doom, it was me! My meddling! And soon Lu'lu will drag me before the vizier where I'll be made to answer their questions! Do you understand, now?'

'And of this you're certain? Does not Allah write our fates at birth? I've heard men say all the good and evil in life is preordained. If that's true, then the physician died because such was the will of Allah, not because of anything you did.' The young Egyptian's voice softened. 'Come, mistress, do you truly want al-Gid's death to have been in vain? What of the Gazelle? Do you want her sacrifices on your behalf to mean nothing? Is it your wish for the vizier's treachery to go unpunished?'

Parysatis sat up; she cradled her face between trembling hands. 'Even if I wanted to, I can't be party to this, not after this morning! Allah may have written al-Gid's doom long ago, but He made me the instrument of that doom, and I cannot bear it! Nor can I bear the carnage that must come to pass if we go forward! Men will die – innocent men – and I don't have the courage to be a catalyst for that!'

'These men you think to save by giving in to your fear will die, mistress, regardless of what choices you make. Such is the way of the world. As for your courage, I say do what you must to find it again, and quickly! You have this one chance to help the Caliph retain the throne of his ancestors – a throne that goes back to the Prophet himself. You have been chosen for this task, mistress! You and no other!'

Parysatis closed her eyes. *Merciful Allah, is that true? Am I the Caliph's only hope?* Fear roiled in the forefront of her mind, dark and primordial; it threatened to extinguish the ember of rage that flared beneath. But that rage brightened as she recalled the dismissive look on Jalal's face; he thinks he can dispose of the Caliph and no one will care. *The dog believes himself beyond reproach . . .*

'Say you're right, Yasmina,' Parysatis said, opening her eyes. 'Say Jalal must be made to pay . . . but how? We are two women against a vizier. How else can this end save with our deaths?'

The young Egyptian gave her a wan smile. 'First, we become more than two women. The Gazelle has arranged a meeting with a man of influence, a staunch supporter of the Caliph. His name is Massoud and he is the amir of the Circassian Mamelukes, the White Slaves of the River. If you speak to him of the vizier's treachery, I promise you he and his men will do all they can to preserve the Caliph's life and his throne.'

'But I must speak to him?' Parysatis chewed her lip. 'You're certain?'

'Yes, mistress. The Gazelle has already arranged a time and place. All that remains is for me to guide you to him.'

'How? Especially after this morning, I doubt Lu'lu will be inclined to simply stand aside and let me walk out.' Parysatis shivered. 'I'm told he waits for the vizier to return, to oversee my torture . . .'

'Let *how* we escape be my concern,' Yasmina said, rising and going to Parysatis' tall armoire. 'First, we must make you present-able. There's little chance of you escaping at all if you're wandering about the harem in your night-clothes.'

29

Jalal al-Aziz ibn al-Rahman studied the assembled commanders of Cairo's military: a disparate group of slaves and mercenaries who clustered around their leaders as tribal fighters might cleave to their chieftain. The vizier sat on a divan, beneath delicate lamps of glass and gold filigree, on a portico that overlooked one of the palace's innumerable gardens. Through the dusty leaves of ancient sycamores, the gilded dome of the Caliph's residence gleamed in the setting sun.

To his left, the black-turbaned men of the Sudan hovered around their prince, Wahshi, a giant of a man who slouched in an ivory chair and sneered at his brother commanders. Before him, the mailed Syrians of the Jandariyah followed the example of their captain, Turanshah, and stood at rigid attention to await the pleasure of the vizier. And to Jalal's right, as wary as caged beasts, stood the disgraced White Slaves of the River. Their ranks were a mix of Turks and Circassians, men gaudily dressed in silks and brocades, silver-stitched leather and gilded mail, who deferred to their amir, Gokbori.

Gokbori was a Turk, a barrel-chested man with the heavy arms and shoulders of a brawler. Barely one generation separated him from the barbaric steppe of his homeland, north of the Black Sea, and though he affected touches of civilization – such as keeping his greying beard waxed – the savage ways of his people still endured. Tufts of hair sliced from the scalps of his enemies hung from his golden belt, and he toyed with a string of worry beads carved from human knuckle bones. His dark eyes gleamed with mistrust.

Of the three, only the Jandariyah knew the truth about the approaching armies. Turanshah was solid as bedrock; his Syrians were well led and not given to factional fighting or to dangerous fits of rioting – both hallmarks of Cairo's other regiments. Thus, to spare the city from potential unrest, Jalal revealed only part of the tale to Cairo's other commanders: the approach of an army from Damascus. He painted it as merely another of Shirkuh's footloose escapades, one spurred on by the maunderings of an exiled vizier whose day had long passed. *Let them learn of our alliance with the Nazarenes when it's too late to refuse their aid.*

Jalal smiled, a gesture both thin and humourless. 'Your orders are simple,' he said to Gokbori. 'You and your Mamelukes are to defend Atfih from that pig, Shirkuh.'

'Atfih? Let him have it, Excellency,' Gokbori said, frowning. 'We could seal Cairo against Shirkuh in the two days and more it would take to reach Atfih.' The Turk's silver boot heels clacked against the green marble flagstones of the portico as he paced back and forth. 'If we divide our forces like this, we risk defeat twice over.'

'I want Atfih defended,' Jalal said coldly.

Gokbori bristled. 'And what does the Caliph want? Is it his wish or yours that we waste our lives in vain?'

'You dare question me?' Jalal shot to his feet, white robes rustling like an afreet's wings. He towered over the squat Turk. 'The White Slaves of the River will muster tonight, outside the Soldiers' Gate! You will leave quietly or your families will pay the price! That is the will of the Caliph!'

Gokbori glanced sidewise in hopes of gleaning support from his brother commanders. But neither man rose to the Mamelukes' defence. Turanshah's face remained an unreadable mask; Wahshi, however, revelled in his rival's misfortune. He winked, lips peeling back over yellowed teeth.

Jalal took a step closer. 'Do you understand your task, or must I explain it again to your successor?'

Gokbori sniffed in disdain, though he knew the vizier's threat was not a hollow one, nor could he ignore his orders; slaves, even precious Mamelukes, fell beneath the executioner's blade for less. 'Aye, by Allah!' he said finally. 'Aye. We leave tonight for Atfih.'

The vizier nodded. 'Wahshi, double your patrols in the city. I am placing the urban militia under your command as well. Use them to seal the gates after evening prayer. Shirkuh will likely try and send infiltrators in to spread rumours and lies. Have your men watch for agitators and the like. Turanshah, do what you must to make the palace secure.' From the corner of his eye, Jalal saw Mustapha signal to him. The vizier ended the audience with a sharp nod. 'To your posts. I have other business to deal with.'

Gokbori salaamed with a stiff formality that bordered upon mockery and, with his retinue in tow, ambled for the door, moving with the wide, rolling gait of a born horseman; Wahshi stood, bowed, and motioned for a slave to gather up his chair. The men of the Sudan laughed and chatted as they followed their Turkish comrades. The Jandariyah officers were the last to leave, silently filing out after their captain.

Jalal, his forehead creased in thought, turned to Mustapha; the old eunuch nodded.

'Your guest is here.'

'Did anyone see him arrive?'

Mustapha shook his head. 'I had a pair of my most trusted eunuchs escort him here by way of the Daylam Garden, through the House of Memory. It is little used these days.'

'You are ever the soul of discretion, my old darling.'

'Are you certain this is the proper path, Excellency?' Mustapha said. Concern furrowed the old eunuch's brow. 'There is little delicacy in the course of action you are proposing.'

Jalal clasped his hands behind his back and gazed out over the garden, watching as a flock of pigeons alighted at the apex of the distant dome – smudges of grey against a fiery gold background. A warm breeze rustled sycamore leaves. 'The time for delicacy has passed, Mustapha. It is decisive action or nothing.'

'This is certainly decisive.' The eunuch turned and clapped his hands; the vizier's door wardens levered open the gold-arabesqued portals to allow a single man entry. Mustapha salaamed. 'Sir Godfrey de Vézelay, Excellency.'

'Peace be upon you, Templar,' Jalal said.

'Lord Saracen,' Godfrey replied, offering his host a slight bow. The Templar had put aside the trappings of war for the evening. Under the white mantle of his Order, emblazoned with a red cross, he wore a belted tunic of unbleached linen and trousers; a silver crucifix hung from a chain about his neck. 'I was surprised to receive your invitation, though I am curious why it did not include my brother-knight, Hugh. Are you hatching some heathen plot to divide us?' Godfrey looked around him, obviously smitten by the sight of so much easy wealth. No doubt his blunt mind was already designing schemes for getting hold of it.

'I will not dissemble with you, my friend,' Jalal said. He gestured for the Templar to take a seat on the divan as Mustapha served them wine. 'A problem has arisen that threatens to undermine our alliance.'

Godfrey's eyes narrowed. 'What sort of problem?'

'The most delicate sort.' Jalal selected a goblet at random from Mustapha's tray, sipped it, then put it back and took the other. 'It concerns the Caliph. It seems he is no longer amenable to your lord's offer. Indeed, he is pressuring me to seize you and your companion and have the both of you executed.'

'What?' the Templar roared. 'God's teeth! We had your assurances, dog!'

'And you *still do*,' Jalal said hurriedly. 'You still do. The Caliph's reticence, his hostility, is something we must deal with, which is why I invited you here. I would ask a tremendous boon of you – of you, personally, Sir Godfrey. A boon that if properly executed will no doubt enrich us both.'

That piqued the Templar's interest. Godfrey cocked his head to one side. 'Enrich us both, you say? How so?'

Jalal shook his head. 'Not so quickly, my friend. First, swear on your oath to God and the Temple that nothing I say will ever pass your lips, by accident or design, upon pain of damnation.'

Godfrey smoothed his moustache with one scarred knuckle. The vizier could see his mind at work, weighing intangibles and things unseen as a moneylender in the souk weighs copper against gold. Of the two Franks, Godfrey possessed the loosest moral fibre; Jalal reckoned him the worst kind of Infidel: a warmonger who only paid lip service to the tenets of his Order, to the pronouncements of his Nazarene lord, and to his own oath. Still, his eyes betrayed all. Where the acquisition of wealth was paramount, Godfrey de Vézelay's eyes declaimed the depths of his fidelity. Finally, the Templar nodded. 'You have my word, Lord Saracen. Upon my oath to God and the Temple.'

After a moment, Jalal nodded in return. 'I accept your oath. Our problem, you see, is one of religion. The Caliph is refusing to join with Nazarenes against his fellow Moslems, not considering that these selfsame Moslems condemn his Fatimid ancestry at every opportunity, and they have pledged loyalty to the Caliph of Baghdad. He does not see the folly in that sort of blind faith. An enemy is an enemy, regardless of the direction in which they pray.'

'Then put him aside and find a more agreeable Caliph,' Godfrey said with accustomed bluntness.

Jalal smiled. 'Indeed, we see eye to eye on this, you and I. And in the same breath know that this is the boon I would ask of you.'

The Templar's head snapped around. 'Christ and the Saints, man! What are you saying? You want me to—?'

'Nay,' Jalal said, raising his hand in a gesture of warning. 'Speak it not aloud, my friend. You know precisely *what* I am saying. We agree there is a delicate task at hand and, in all honesty, whom else can I trust? Certainly not another Moslem, for we hold the Caliph inviolate. A Jew, perhaps? Maybe a Maronite beggar from Fustat? No, my friend. I need a man I can rely on – as much for his skill as for his discretion. You, Sir Godfrey.'

'I'm no martyr, Lord Saracen,' Godfrey put in. 'Nor am I in the mood to be torn apart by a Cairene mob.'

The vizier shook his head. 'Nor am I. But hearken: what if I tell you I have a way to smuggle you into his presence with no one the wiser? That my men will be slow to respond to any sounds of a struggle, giving you time to withdraw unseen? And more to the point: what if I tell you I have a ready scapegoat in mind should word escape prematurely? Your name, your Order, will never be associated with this deed.'

The Templar swirled the wine in his goblet, staring into its depths as he grappled with the implications of what the vizier was saying. 'I see now why you didn't include Sir Hugh in this conclave,' Godfrey said, glancing at Jalal through narrowed eyes.

'No doubt he is a very fine man, and worthy of renown, but he lacks your sense of self-preservation. You understand as well as I that it is only the outcome that matters, not the way in which it is achieved.' Jalal leaned back, his legs thrust out before him. In the distance he could hear the first strains of the adhan drifting over the city. The time for evening prayer was at hand.

'You do not rush to your knees like the others,' Godfrey noticed, draining his goblet.

'Allah understands the needs of those who rule and accords us leeway.'

The Templar stroked his beard. Already, the vizier could see the scales of acquiescence tipping in his favour as Godfrey balanced the iron weight of greed against the feather of risk. The Frank's eyes gleamed. 'If I do this thing, what am I to receive in return? You spoke of enrichment . . . ?'

Jalal spread his hands, encompassing the whole of the palace – perhaps the whole of Egypt. 'What is your heart's desire? Gold?

Jewels? Horses? Slaves? Name your reward, my friend, and you shall have it. But, this task – it must be done soon.'

'How soon?'

'Tonight.'

Godfrey pursed his lips, and then gave a slight sidewise nod, acknowledging the vizier's need for alacrity. 'He will be alone?'

'No. He will have a guest with him. A holy man. And make sure you dispose of him, too, Sir Godfrey.'

The Templar frowned. 'I'm no fool to leave alive a witness.'

'Oh, he is more than that.' The vizier of Egypt grinned at his own cleverness. 'We must have his corpse to put on display if the folk of Cairo are to believe their beloved Caliph met his doom at the hands of a murderous Sufi.'

The Fourth Surah

Knife's Edge

1

'Careful!' Yasmina snapped at the two harem guards, each of whom carried one end of the rolled-up rug from Parysatis' alcove. 'It's Persian,' she added quickly.

The guards, both eunuchs, grinned at the fastidious young Egyptian. 'Where you want it?' one asked in thickly accented Arabic.

'That old storage room across the way.' Yasmina gestured across the courtyard. 'I'll leave it there tonight so it won't sour the air in my mistress's room. Tomorrow, I'll fetch the laundry slaves to give it a good cleaning.'

The eunuchs, Ethiopian giants in white silk and mail vests, shrugged to one another as they shouldered their burden and set off towards the storage room, muscles bulging through smooth layers of fat. Dusk had faded in swift progression to star-flecked night, leaving the courtyard deserted; most of the women had retired to the hammam for an evening bath, while certain favourites dined with the Caliph's aunts in their more intimate fountain court – no doubt to apprise the old bitches of the day's goings-on and to entertain them with fresh scandals. Yasmina heard faint peals of laughter coming from both venues.

Larger than Parysatis' alcove, the L-shaped storage room held an array of items, from linens in need of mending and extra cushions to sun-faded parasols and the pieces of an old pavilion.

The space served as a receptacle for things no longer used but still not quite ready for the rubbish heap. Its most striking feature, however, was the beautifully scalloped niche at the top of the 'L'.

Yasmina winced as the two eunuchs hauled the rug inside and dropped it heavily against the back wall. The girl gave each a gold coin as they filed past, nodding and whispering her thanks; she paused outside the door to the storage room. Watching from the corner of her eye, she exhaled in relief as the two eunuchs returned to their posts without as much as a backward glance. They rounded a far corner . . .

Yasmina darted back inside the storage room. Crouching, she quickly untied the cords binding the rug and unrolled it as best she could in the room's tight confines. With a final shove, Parysatis tumbled into view, dishevelled and breathing heavily as she writhed against the rug's clinging folds.

'*Y'Allah!*' the Persian gasped.

Yasmina caught her hand. 'Not so loud.'

Parysatis was clad in plain garb: billowy pantaloons and an embroidered shirt of Damietta cotton beneath a long blue mantle. Her hair she had bound up in a turban, now askew, and she wore a scarf to veil her features. With luck she might pass for a boy or a slender eunuch. 'A devilish idea,' she muttered, climbing unsteadily to her feet. She shook dust from her mantle and straightened her turban. 'You say it's been done before?'

'By an ancient queen of Egypt. She hid in a carpet to escape the madness of her brother, the king. Once free, her lover, who was a prince of djinn, bore her far away, beyond Samarkand, some say.'

'I pity her if she travelled that distance wrapped in a carpet.' Parysatis made her way to the rear of the storage room, to where the scalloped niche gleamed in the faint light. This was the first such door she had found, over a year ago, its catch discovered by accident when she stumbled against it. The passage itself had several branches, including the one she had taken to reach the Golden Hall the night before. No doubt one of them would eventually lead to the Mad Caliph's sanctuary, his fabled and blasphemous False Kaaba. She turned to Yasmina. 'Are you certain you can find us a path out of the palace?'

The young Egyptian nodded. 'The same one I used earlier – through the kitchens and out of a small gate in the herb garden wall. From there, we head almost due north into the Soldiers' Quarter. The Gazelle will meet us at the Inn of the Three Apples, and together the two of you will speak with Amir Massoud.'

The confidence in Yasmina's voice reinforced Parysatis' own. She triggered the door's hidden catch – a carved rosette worn smooth from use – and watched the portal swing inward on hinges she had greased herself. 'Lead the way, and pray no one realizes I am gone.'

Yasmina did just that.

2

Assad squatted on his haunches at the mouth of a narrow alley running between two tall tenements, one quiet, and the other alive with the lights, sounds, and smells of an extended family gathering for their evening meal. Children played ball in the street by the light of iron cressets; their fathers, uncles, and elder brothers sat on cushions and carpets around the doors to the caravanserai, talking of the day's events while the sharp tang of hashish drifted on the night air. Though unseen, he heard the women murmuring as they shared the duties of the kitchen. None of them – men, women, or children – had the slightest inkling of the doom riding ever closer.

Two armies! Merciful Allah! That was what Musa had told him before he left the caravanserai; that was the news Zaynab's spies had brought out of the palace. The two Templars were here to broker a deal: Jerusalem would add its forces to Cairo's against the Sultan of Damascus, who had sent an army at the behest of the deposed vizier, Dirgham; like a fish lunging for a baited hook, Jalal went for it without hesitation. Why? And what did Jerusalem hope to gain? A foothold in Egypt? No doubt Amalric meant to double-cross Jalal even while the vizier sought to play Moslem against Frank and barter for himself a more dominant position. Assad marvelled at the vizier's appalling arrogance. Despite defences more porous than wet linen and an army prone to self-destructive fits, Jalal still reckoned he had leverage over Damascus and Jerusalem; in a way, he did. The vizier had the wealth of the Nile to draw upon.

Assad shook his head, still disbelieving. *Allah!* He doubted the vizier's death would change anything now. But such was not for Assad to decide. His task had not changed: protect the Caliph, secure his throne, and cement an alliance between Cairo and Alamut. To make that happen, he would kill the vizier – and anyone else who got in his way. *I only pray I'm not too late.*

Assad stood. Down the street, the row of buildings ended. He could see a patch of open ground ringed with tall palm trees, a parade field, and then the glimmer of pale stone that marked the Emerald Gate, in the northeast corner of the Great East Palace. It was time to go and meet his escort.

Once again a Sufi, Assad was clad in better fashion than he had been at the Grey Mosque: a black cloak of light-weight wool over a silk-girdled kaftan, its grey cotton embroidered at the shoulders and hemmed in black thread. He wore a small green turban indica-tive of his status as a haji, one who has made the pilgrimage to Mecca. Sandals and his salawar in its shell of a walking stick, recovered from the alley behind the Grey Mosque, finished his dis-guise. With each step, Assad's shoulders grew more rounded; his limp worsened, so that by the time he reached the edge of the parade field his transformation from Assassin to crippled holy man was complete.

Skirting the parade field, Assad discovered a curious thing taking place. Soldiers gathered in small groups under the cloak of darkness: Turks in full harness, bearing cavalry spears and bow cases, with a few Circassians scattered among them – the White

Slaves of the River; Assad read something sinister in the way they crouched together, heads bowed in heated conversation as if waiting for . . . *for what? For an order to muster or a reason to riot?* Assad could catch no hint either way.

As he neared the Emerald Gate, a tall Ethiopian in bright silks stepped from the deeper shadow and bowed low, seeming unconcerned about the growing number of soldiers beyond the palace precincts. '*As-salaam alaikum,*' he said in a voice at once deep and lilting. 'You are Ibn al-Teymani of the Hejaz?'

'*Alaikum as-salaam.* Indeed, I am he.'

'My master bids you follow,' the huge African intoned. Moving with stately grace, he led Assad through the Emerald Gate, past the company of Jandariyah detailed to guard it, and across the verdant garden that gave the gate its name.

Entering the palace proper was like plunging into a world of unparalleled splendour, breathtaking even to Assad, whose eyes had beheld the treasure vaults of the Hidden Master beneath the foundations of Alamut. Thick carpets muffled their footfalls as Assad trailed his escort down broad corridors; between scalloped niches, richly coloured tapestries seemed to drink in the light of countless glass and gilt lamps. Soaring keel arches opened on salons, on courtyards bordered by fretted arcades supported by columns of marble and porphyry and gold. At every hand he saw paired sentinels: tall Syrians, soldiers of the mercenary Jandariyah, who stood their posts as motionless as the statues of Old Egypt.

At last, his escort brought him to a pair of gold-arabesqued doors set into a sculptured stone arch, flanked by the ever-present Syrians. *They truly have him surrounded.* Here the Ethiopian bowed and handed Assad over to an ageing eunuch. This old man studied the crippled Sufi from under arched eyebrows, no doubt taking stock of his myriad scars.

'A dangerous place, the Hejaz,' the eunuch said after a moment, 'when even its holy men bear the aspect of veteran warriors.'

As Ibn al-Teymani, Assad gave a wry smile, as though the notion was not something new to him. 'Even those who do not partake directly in war can be scarred by it, my friend. These I bear are the work of a rival tribe, of a Bedouin who thought it best to air his grievances with the edge of his sabre. But Allah, in His infinite wisdom, ordained my survival and I repay Him by following the path of His mystery.'

'And the Bedouin?'

Ibn al-Teymani shrugged. '*Inshallah*, we will meet again. Or not.'

The eunuch chuckled. A gesture from him caused the guards to lever open the heavy doors, revealing a narrow vestibule leading to yet another arch. Armour clashed and clattered as the dozen Jandariyah lining the way snapped to attention. 'Are there any dishes which disagree with you, effendi?'

'Only those forbidden by the Qur'an.'

The eunuch nodded, lips pursed. 'Of course. Come, then. We must not keep the Prince of the Faithful waiting.'

The inner doors led to the Caliph's apartments: a score of rooms glittering with gold, precious wood, and silken finery. Despite this display of opulence, the apartments had the air of a prison about them, guarded from without by the vizier's corps of mercenaries and from within by his eunuchs; the Caliph's smallest movements came under the direct scrutiny of men who did not have his best interests at heart. Men who were loyal to another. In all, it seemed a very different existence from that which the Hidden Master of al-Hashishiyya enjoyed, from his uncontested sovereignty to the wild freedom of Alamut. *How would they fare as allies?*

Assad followed the old eunuch through the antechamber and down a long hallway echoing with the soft strains of flute, sitar, and tambourine, to a sitting room whose broad doors opened on to the Caliph's private fountain court; wreathed in perfumed smoke, Rashid al-Hasan reclined on silk cushions and dictated correspondence to a scribe while musicians played in the background.

The young man looked up and flashed a wan smile. 'Peace be upon you, Ibn al-Teymani of the Hejaz.' The Caliph was dressed informally in a galabiyya and trousers of the purest white, a sash of golden brocade, and a turban-wrapped tarboush. His condition had improved since the mosque; although hollow, his face had a touch of colour and his dark-circled eyes were lucid and glittering with intelligence.

Assad bowed. 'And upon you be peace, my lord.'

'Sit, my friend. Sit.' The Prince of the Faithful gestured to the cushions beside him. 'Mustapha, have food and wine brought, and then leave us until you're called for. The rest of you: that will be all.' Scribe and musicians filed from the sitting room, followed by the old eunuch.

Careful of his disguise, Assad lowered himself on to a cushion, the ivory head of his walking stick close at hand. There was much to discuss with the young Caliph, but broaching the subject of Jalal's perfidy meant Assad would need to reveal himself, to shed the identity of Ibn al-Teymani. Instinct told him to take it slowly. *Earn his trust first.*

'My lord, I . . .' the false Sufi trailed off, frowning. After a moment, Ibn al-Teymani smiled and shook his head apologetically. 'I am pleased to see you.'

'And I you. What troubles you, my friend?'

'Forgive me, O Caliph. It is just . . . well, I saw a curious sight as I arrived this evening and I cannot quite banish it from my mind.'

'What was it?'

'A mustering of the White Slaves of the River, my lord. A goodly number of them were loitering outside the Emerald Gate, all armed and clad for war. I am sure their purposes were lawful and beyond reproach, but the scene reminded me of the rumours I had heard of past troubles . . .'

'Curious, indeed.' Rashid scowled; suddenly, he clapped his hands. The old eunuch, Mustapha, returned before the echo faded.

'Where is my vizier, Mustapha?'

The eunuch pursed his lips. 'He is . . . dining with the cadis of al-Azhar Mosque. Shall I fetch him for you, Most Excellent One?'

'No. But send word I would see him ere he retires for the night.

Tell him I am curious why my Mamelukes are mustering outside the Emerald Gate. Go.' Rashid al-Hasan leaned back. 'Your wisdom intrigues me, Ibn al-Teymani. You claim simplicity, but I perceive you to be far more astute than you let on. Before we speak of your master, and I do wish to hear of his travels and travails, let me put a question to you: how does Cairo fare in the eyes of an outsider?'

Assad looked askance at the Caliph, assuming the pose of a man weighing his words, afraid he might say too much. 'Cairo is the Mother of the World, my lord. Who am I to judge its manners and mores?'

Rashid opened his mouth to respond, but the arrival of food and drink prompted him to silence. Quickly, slaves laid out platters of roasted fowl in rich sauces and dishes of vegetables drizzled with olive oil; hard and soft cheeses, loaves of fresh bread spread with ghee and honey, candied figs, dates, and Syrian raisins. One eunuch lingered, tasting each dish in turn and then sipping from two moisture-beaded pitchers of khamr. The Caliph dismissed him after he showed no signs of ill effect.

'A wretched commentary,' Rashid said, his hand shaking as he drained his first goblet of wine, 'wretched, indeed, when I cannot enjoy a simple meal without fear of poison. But, come, my friend. Back to the question at hand. Surely you must have an opinion of Cairo, for good or ill? I bid you speak candidly and give no thought to offending me. The truth, even a truth that's difficult to hear, is always best in the eyes of Allah.'

'My master might disagree.' Assad grunted; despite his best efforts, a piece of his scrupulously maintained façade sloughed away. His eyes hardened and his face lost a measure of its perceived softness as Ibn al-Teymani grew sombre. 'The truth is a curious thing, my lord. Difficult or no, those in power rarely wish to hear it pronounced. Most prefer the lie, which is like clay on a potter's wheel. It is malleable, easily kneaded into any shape for any situation. Truth, though, is hard as granite and equally inflexible. Hearken, my lord. Here is the truth, and may Allah bear witness to the veracity of my words: despite its many splendours, Cairo bears the mark of a horrible affliction.'

Rashid nodded, lines of concern etching his opium-ravaged face. 'How is this affliction called?'

'*Ambition*, my lord. Naked, unchecked ambition. Why else do your amirs give their men free rein to riot in the streets, if not to further their own ambitions? Why, too, do your eunuchs enrich themselves at the expense of your honour, if not to further their own ambitions? Yet, as terrible as their transgressions are, no one man has done more to the detriment of Cairo than Jalal al-Aziz ibn al-Rahman, your vizier. His ambition is to supplant you, my lord, and rule over Cairo as Nur ad-Din rules over Damascus – as Sultan. Already, he's done more damage than you can imagine.'

Assad braced for a tirade, steeling himself to weather the rigorous denials of the Prince of the Faithful, thus bolstering his claim that the truth was never something a ruler wanted to hear. But what Assad did not expect was Rashid's silence, his measured acceptance of the accusations. The young man leaned back, his food untouched; a shadow of pain crossed his face.

'I take it you're not surprised to hear this?'

'No,' Rashid said, exhaling. 'I'm not. I learned early in life that such ambition goes hand in glove with the mantle of vizier – a necessary evil, if you will. I cannot say I approve, but I find myself too weak, too bereft of support here in the palace, to do anything about it. No, my friend, what shames me is hearing this from a man of the Hejaz. I had no idea my plight as a useless figurehead was such common knowledge.'

'It's not so common as you think,' Assad replied. 'Jalal covers his tracks quite well. Fortunately, my master trained me to recognize such tracks wherever I see them. He also trained me to . . . *remove* the man responsible for making them.'

Rashid jerked as though stung. 'What do you mean?'

'I mean . . .' Assad sat straighter, flexing his leg; he rolled his shoulders and cracked the tendons in his neck. The timbre of his voice changed, and his eyes grew cold and merciless. 'I mean my master is of the belief – and it is one I share, as well – that you and all of Cairo would be best served if Jalal al-Aziz ibn al-Rahman met an untimely end. Tonight.'

The Caliph blinked. 'Impossible! How . . . ?'

'My master has sent you a weapon, my lord. A weapon and an offer of friendship. He stands ready to forgive the grievances that have divided your two houses since long before either of you were born. He wants to see you reclaim what Jalal has taken.'

'Why? Who are you? Who is your master?'

'Have you not guessed? My master is a young shaykh of storied lineage who dwells on a mountain-top by the shores of the Caspian Sea . . .'

3

In the shadow-clotted alleys of the Rub al-Maiyit – the Abode of the Dead – the Heretic crouched and studied the fly-blown corpses of Gamal and his brother-fedayeen. The thin light of the rising moon revealed that Gamal had been tortured, the fingers of one hand hacked off, before a thrust to the heart ended his life; though milky-eyed and waxen, his features yet bore the stamp of abject terror. The Heretic looked up from the bodies and stared at the silent mausoleums, at the faceless alley wall. Whoever Gamal and his men followed from the caravanserai had lured them into a trap; one Gamal either could not or would not bluff his way out of.

'What have you done, you fool? What did you tell him?'

Cloth rustled at the Heretic's back; he shivered as a distinct chill rippled through the warm night air. He glanced over his shoulder. Around him, veteran fedayeen – men who had proven themselves hard as iron many times over – grew suddenly anxious, tense, and afraid. As well they should.

Ibn Sharr had come.

Swathed in black from toe to crown, all that could be seen of the sorcerer's face as he emerged into a shaft of pale moonlight were his eyes, dark and hypnotic, agleam with mysterious fervour. Badr al-Mulahid rose to his feet and bowed.

'You take an unnecessary risk in coming here, my lord.'

'Sometimes,' Ibn Sharr replied, 'it is not enough to examine a newly made corpse. One must also examine the place in which it was made.' He raised his head and inhaled, snuffling the air like a hound scenting blood. 'The *Emir* of the Knife did this?'

The Heretic's gaze shifted to the bodies. 'I'm certain of it. And, before I martyred the Gazelle, I overheard one of her confederates speak the Emir's name. It is "Assad".'

'"The Lion". How appropriate.' Ibn Sharr gathered his robes around him and crouched next to Gamal's body. 'What witnesses were there to this slaughter?'

'None that we have found.'

Ibn Sharr nodded. Dipping a hand into his robes, he brought forth a small, flat box of polished ebony, its hinged lid inlaid with silver filigree. The sorcerer opened it with exaggerated care. Inside, a fine grey dust gleamed like powdered moonlight. Muttering an invocation under his breath, Ibn Sharr took a pinch of dust and sprinkled it over Gamal's bloodless lips. '*Itkallim!*' he said. '*Itkallim!*' He rocked back on his heels and waited, eyes flaring bright in the darkness.

Nothing happened.

'Useless,' the sorcerer said, half to himself. Swiftly, Ibn Sharr repeated the ritual, first over the disembowelled corpse and then over the one with the gaping wound to his neck; each time, nothing materialized. Ibn Sharr grew agitated. 'All of them, useless!'

'What is it, my lord?'

Ibn Sharr's eyes narrowed as he snapped the lid of the box shut and returned it to his robes. 'Perhaps our enemy is craftier than even I imagined.'

'How so?' The Heretic looked closer, trying to discern what he must have missed.

'A soul is like the flame of a candle, Badr. Though you extinguish it, a tiny ember – the sharara – remains within the body. This, in time, will burn itself out. But until then, one well-versed in the necromantic arts can agitate this spiritual cinder, fan it temporarily to life; the dust should have induced the sharara to reveal the last thing the dead man witnessed.'

'Are we too late, you think?' The Heretic glanced from body to body. 'Could this dying spark not have dissipated already?'

'Perhaps for one, mayhap even two, but for all three? No, we have underestimated the *Emir* of the Knife. Whatever else he may be, it is clear to me that he has sufficient knowledge to undertake the destruction of the sharara, lest I use it to see through Gamal's eyes at the moment of his death.'

'Could it be true, then, what they say about him? That he is a slayer of djinn? Would not such a man know something of sorcery?'

Ibn Sharr said nothing for a moment, his eyes ablaze. Suddenly, in a swirl of fabric, he stood and spun about. 'Bring them! I require further study before I can discern the nature of his art.'

The Heretic gestured to his men, who between them unfurled a length of heavy canvas – sailcloth, likely scavenged from the wreck of a Nile felucca. 'I will find this Assad, my lord, as I found Alamut's other dogs.'

'Be cautious, Badr,' Ibn Sharr said. 'This quarry is more dangerous than all of the others combined. Never forget: as you search for him, so too is he searching for you, and no doubt he now knows more than merely your name.'

4

Parysatis tasted freedom. Moving unnoticed through the raucous kitchen and into the low-walled herb garden – where the night air itself seemed spiced with thyme, coriander, and dill – she shivered in delicious anticipation at what lay beyond. Finally, she would breech the walls that had been her prison for the last two years! She would be free! Yet a sense of gravity tempered her elation. If discovered plotting against the vizier she would likely trade her sumptuous prison for a shallow grave.

Yasmina nodded, motioning her forward. No guards patrolled the tiny garden, its rough stone walls easily the height of a tall man; past the old bronze-barred gate was a neighbourhood known as Barqiyya, a district of changing houses and moneylenders' villas interspersed with tall caravanserais and taller warehouses. Yasmina unlatched the gate, ushered her through, and closed it again in their wake.

So simple! Parysatis glanced up at the star-flecked sky; she felt heat radiating from the paving stones, heard faint music and voices emanating from buildings across the broad street. Shafts of light angled through latticed windows to stain the night with pools of ruby and citron. *So beautifully simple!* Parysatis laughed aloud.

Yasmina frowned at her. 'Hurry, mistress. Soldiers patrol this street. It's not safe to tarry.'

Hand in hand, the pair fled north. Yasmina guided them with unerring instinct through nameless alleys that twined between tenements of dun-coloured brick, where the jewel-soft lights of Barqiyya gave way to the more lurid illumination of the Soldiers' Quarter. Here, by the greasy orange glow of iron cressets, Parysatis saw Fatimid soldiers and foreign mercenaries meet in drunken congress, bellowing songs of past glories in a dozen tongues. Her elation faded to fear. She averted her eyes from the pimps and ragged street thugs, harafisha, who whistled at her from open doorways. Prostitutes leaned out of second-storey windows and called after her, mistaking her for a would-be client; naked from the waist up, the whores' veiled faces made mockery of the laws of decency.

The Inn of the Three Apples stood at the heart of the quarter, in a converted mercantile warehouse some three storeys high. The apples that gave it its name, cast from copper, were set into the stone above a tall entry arch whose vaulted passage gave on to a courtyard brimming with low tables, cushions, and bolsters. Clouds of incense and hashish stung tears from Parysatis' eyes as she glanced around. On tables, women clad as scantily as street whores danced to the discordant music of a sitar and a hide drum. The men watching their gyrations ran the gamut: young and old, labourers and merchants, caravan guards and out-of-work mercenaries; among them were scattered a dozen or so grim-looking Turks and an equal number of Circassians, who wore distinctive green sashes over their white robes.

Yasmina paused a moment, scanning the courtyard like a huntress seeking her prey. She spotted the proprietor, the old soldier men called Ahmed the Cripple, sitting away to their left. 'He can tell us if the Gazelle has arrived yet,' she said, leaning close to Parysatis' ear.

Ahmed, a Turk whose bristling moustaches had gone silver with age, massaged the stump of his left leg as he confirmed what Parysatis secretly feared: he had not seen the Gazelle. 'Amir Massoud awaits her, though none but Great and Glorious God can say for how much longer.'

'Where is he?'

'Up the stairs. First door to the left.'

Yasmina nodded to Parysatis; the Persian caught a glimmer of pain in the young woman's eyes, as if the Gazelle's absence struck her as a physical blow. 'Come, mistress. We . . . We must speak with Massoud on her behalf.'

'Are you sure? Should we not wait for her?'

'She may not come.' Yasmina's voice was flat and emotionless. 'And we can't afford to squander this opportunity by dawdling.'

'Lead on, then.' Parysatis exhaled as she followed Yasmina, composing herself for the task at hand: convincing a man she did not know that the Caliph needed his aid. She imagined how their conversation would unfold: he would ask for proof; she would answer with what she had heard from the vizier's own lips. And he would likely curse her as a gossip and a teller of tales . . . but she had to try, regardless. The Caliph's life depended upon it. Upon her.

Even before they reached the head of the stairs Parysatis heard raised voices.

'Who, brother?' one man said, his accent the hard gutturals of a Turk. 'Who will protect our wives and sons from that whoreson Wahshi and his silk-swaddled master?'

A step creaked under Parysatis' heel; the voices ceased. At the same instant, a Circassian Mameluke in a turban-wrapped helmet, his mail shirt girdled with a green sash, stepped from the gloom at the head of the stairs and lifted his hand in warning. His other hand held a naked sabre.

'State your business!'

Yasmina answered. 'We must see Amir Massoud! The Gazelle sent us. She bid us speak to him.'

Before the Mameluke could respond, the door over his left shoulder opened to reveal a smouldering visage, dark-eyed and fierce. The man who stared out at them was also a Circassian: long of jaw with an aquiline nose and a high forehead; he was clean-shaven but for a goatee and drooping moustaches weighted at the ends with scrimshaw beads. He wore a gold-chased steel cap beneath his black turban and a mail jazerant, its outer layer of fine black linen embroidered with gold thread; a girdle of green silk and leather supported a sabre and curved knife. His inscrutable gaze sent chills down Parysatis' spine.

'I am Massoud. What of the Gazelle? Where is she? Speak, quickly!'

'I saw her last at the caravanserai of her father,' Yasmina said. 'A man had come to do her harm, but she was confident her father's soldiers would do away with him. She said to meet her here tonight.'

The Circassian digested this in silence for a moment. 'It is not like her to be late. Sayeed,' he said, gesturing to his officer in the hall. 'Go to Abu'l-Qasim's caravanserai and make an enquiry. Be discreet, but bring me news of her.' The officer bowed and withdrew; Massoud opened the door wide, motioning for Parysatis and Yasmina to enter. From the glint in his eyes he would brook no refusal.

The room was sparse, with only a table, a short stool, and a divan. The walls were pale stucco, whorled with soot from the guttering oil lamp. In one dim corner, a glowering Turk in full mail paced, his fingers toying with a strand of worry beads. Yasmina turned to the Circassian amir. 'We must speak alone.'

'For all that he's a Turk, you can trust this one. Gokbori, you'll keep your tongue between your teeth, won't you?'

'Aye,' the Turk growled.

Massoud closed the door and turned. 'Now, what is so important that you would risk a beating or worse to slip from the palace?'

'The Caliph's life,' Yasmina replied. The Turk ceased his pacing; Massoud's manner grew guarded. He stared at them through slitted eyes.

'How so?'

The young woman would have spoken further, but a soft touch on her upper arm stilled her. Parysatis stepped forward; she closed her eyes and dug deep, seeking an untapped vein of courage. *Do not let al-Gid's death be in vain!* She squared her shoulders, nostrils flaring at the memory of Jalal's mocking face. When she opened her eyes again they were alight with the flames of vengeance. 'First, are the White Slaves of the River creatures of the vizier, or are you true men?'

'The vizier?' Gokbori growled. 'Faugh! Do not insult us, woman! Not a day passes without a prayer to Allah for the gift of a moment alone with that misbegotten spawn of a dozen fathers!'

Massoud nodded, tugging on his beaded moustache. 'What he says is true. The Caliph has always been our master. We would see him safe and in control, as it was in the days of his forefathers.'

'The time for that grows perilously short, then. Jalal has betrayed the Caliph. He plots to supplant him and make himself Sultan, and he must do it soon, for an army approaches—'

'Yes. From Damascus,' Massoud interrupted. 'If that is your news, lady, then I fear you have wasted your time and mine, for we are well aware of his ambitions. Within the hour, we ride south for Atfih, where we plan to meet Shirkuh's swine as they come streaming out of the desert.'

Parysatis shook her head. 'A fool's errand. Jalal knows Atfih will not hold. What's more, he expects you and your Mamelukes will desert to Shirkuh. But even if you don't, even if you remain loyal to Cairo, Jalal believes the Damascenes will annihilate you. Regardless of the outcome, you will no longer be a thorn in his side.'

'Allah!' Gokbori lurched forward, slamming his fist down on the table's top and causing the lamp to jump and waver. 'I knew it! But how could you know this, woman? Are *you* a creature of the vizier? Sent to tempt us into folly?' Beside him, Massoud scowled.

Parysatis experienced a surge of anger. 'Now who hurls insults? I know this because I overheard him plotting! But this is not the worst of it. Surely you're aware of the two Templars who arrived last night? They are envoys from Amalric of Jerusalem. Jalal has allied himself with the Nazarenes against Damascus. As we speak, their army is on the road to Cairo.'

Gokbori spun away, cursing. 'A second army? The dog made no mention of a second army!'

Massoud stroked his jaw; he stared hard at Parysatis, unsure whether to believe her or not. 'This is ill news indeed,' he said finally. 'If it's true. I know the vizier to be a black-hearted rogue, but I don't think even he is capable of this sort of betrayal. Have you any proof?'

'Beyond my word, you mean?'

'A woman's word is wind,' Gokbori muttered.

Parysatis gestured. 'Look around you! Do not the vizier's Syrian mercenaries, the Jandariyah, control all the main avenues into the palace? And do not his Sudanese mercenaries have the run of the streets? Jalal has disposed of any who could disrupt his plan, leaving only the Caliph between himself and the Seat of Divine

Reason. What more proof do you need?' Parysatis' eyes glistened in the pale lamplight as she clutched Massoud's arm. 'Whether you believe me or not, Rashid al-Hasan needs your help. You are the White Slaves of the River, charged with the Caliph's safety. Please! He needs you!'

Gokbori's prayer beads ticked together as he ran the strand between calloused fingers, unmoved by the woman's impassioned plea. Massoud stepped back; arms folded across his chest, he studied Parysatis with burning intensity as he weighed her arguments in his mind; he dissected and flayed each word in search of even the slightest hint of fabrication. Finally, he cocked an eyebrow at Gokbori. 'My gut tells me she speaks true. We said we were the Caliph's men, brother. It's time we proved it.'

'*Y'Allah!*' the Turk replied. 'It's not your gut they'll slice out if it turns out she's just an adept liar in the vizier's employ. You're too trusting.'

'And so? Does that make the vizier any less of a jackal? He's all but condemned us to death and promised our wives and daughters to the Sudanese! What do we have left to lose? I say we roll the dice.'

After a moment's hesitation, the Turk shrugged. 'When you put it like that, I'd rather spit in the Devil's eye and die tonight than dance on the end of the vizier's string!'

'It's settled, then,' Massoud said. 'My men are scattered. I have maybe sixty I can call upon at a moment's notice. Not enough by far to challenge Jalal's Syrians.'

Gokbori made a rude sound. 'Faugh! I have men enough to handle the cursed Syrians, though we'll be hard pressed if they call for help from the Sudanese.'

'So what do we do?'

Parysatis blinked at the sudden reversal. 'Must . . . Must this be an all-out assault?'

Massoud turned to her. 'Have you another way?'

'The Jandariyah have reinforced the main gates, but they are not as diligent at some of the lesser gates. If we can show you a way in, as well as a series of passages that would allow you to move unseen, could you not then spirit the Caliph from the vizier's grasp? Once he is safe, Rashid al-Hasan could appeal to the folk of Cairo, perhaps even to the rank and file of the Sudanese mercenaries, and convince them it would be in the city's best interests to remove the vizier.'

'Possibly,' Massoud said, one forefinger tapping the hilt of his sabre, 'but if we could get in unseen, there's a chance we might be able to take control of the whole of the East Palace, perhaps even capture Jalal. And if we seize him the rest of his cabal will crumble. Tell me about these passages, lady . . .'

And for the better part of an hour, Massoud questioned Parysatis about the way into the palace. She walked him through it step by step: first through the herb garden and the kitchens, and thence to the secret passages. Her revelation that the Mad Caliph's tunnels were more than just fanciful tales elicited sulphurous curses from Gokbori. 'And Jalal – he is unaware of their existence?'

'No, he knows they exist,' Parysatis replied. 'But he only knows the location of the one running from the unused women's bath to the Caliph's garden. Of course, this is the one we will need to use if we are to reach the Prince of the Faithful.'

'It's guarded?'

Parysatis nodded. 'But not heavily so.'

'Still, we should expect stiff resistance over it,' Massoud said.

The Circassian dispatched runners to the urban militia's barracks on al-Hujar Street to fetch those men he trusted, his fellow Circassians, while Gokbori himself prepared to depart for the parade field outside the Emerald Gate. Their plan was simple enough: they would meet in the neighbourhood of Barqiyya and enter the palace together. Massoud and the Circassians would protect the Caliph and seize control of the Golden Hall while Gokbori and the more numerous Turks would handle the assault against the vizier's Syrian mercenaries.

'Secure those gates, brother,' Massoud said as they parted company. 'Keep the Sudanese out and Jalal in. If it is Allah's will, by dawn the Caliph will be in control of Cairo once more.'

'*Inshallah*, brother,' the Turk replied. '*Inshallah*.'

Through this exchange, Parysatis noticed Yasmina sitting in the corner on the room's only stool. Lines of worry etched the girl's forehead; every time the door creaked open she leaned forward in anticipation, praying for the sight of the Gazelle's familiar face rather than yet another green-girdled messenger. Parysatis went to her side.

'Something's wrong,' the Egyptian whispered. 'Something must have happened after I left her.'

Parysatis draped an arm around the girl's trembling shoulders. 'I'm sure it's nothing. She—'

Behind them, the door opened again. Parysatis felt Yasmina stiffen; she turned and followed the Egyptian's frightened gaze. Standing in the door was Sayeed, the officer Massoud had sent out to find the Gazelle; his face was shroud-pale.

The Circassian amir took note of the man's expression and frowned. 'Well?'

'T-The Gazelle, amir,' the officer stammered. 'S-she . . . she's dead!'

'What?' Massoud recoiled as if struck, his sheathed sabre rattling against the table's legs as he steadied himself against its edge. 'What do you mean she's dead? That's impossible! When? How . . . ?'

'Sometime after the noon prayer, amir. Murdered by an intruder, I was told.'

In the corner, Parysatis gasped; she turned to comfort Yasmina. The girl's lips had become bloodless, and she clenched her hands into fists, whitened knuckles audibly cracking as she fought to stave off her anguish. All to no avail. Yasmina screamed: a bestial cry that was equal parts grief and rage. She came off the stool and shook herself free of Parysatis' arm. Before the older woman could stop her, the Egyptian barged out of the door, shoving the officer, Sayeed, aside in her haste.

'Yasmina! Wait!' Parysatis made to follow, but Massoud caught her arm before she crossed the threshold of the door. 'Yasmina!' She struggled in the amir's grip, her face a mask of desperation. 'Let go of me!'

'Give the girl into Allah's keeping,' the grim-eyed Circassian said.

'She's liable to do something foolish! The Gazelle was—'

'The Gazelle can no longer vouch for you, can she?' Massoud's free hand fell to the well-worn hilt of his sabre. 'Perhaps her murder is as it seems, a tragic coincidence, or perhaps it isn't. Regardless, there's too much at stake. You're not leaving my side until I can be certain this is not part of some elaborate ruse. Allah will keep your girl safe, if that be His will. Come, it's time we were away.'

Parysatis sagged in his grasp, the fight gone out of her. Maybe this was for the best. Grief-stricken or not, wherever Yasmina was headed must surely be safer than the palace.

5

Jalal's footsteps rang against cold marble. The vizier walked the floor, a minuscule speck of life beneath the soaring dome of the Golden Hall of al-Mu'izz li-Din Allah, in the shadow of the Seat of Divine Reason. With each pass, he allowed his eyes to drift up to the Caliph's throne. *My throne! By sunrise, that foolish boy will be dead and I will be Sultan! Sultan Jalal al-Aziz ibn al-Rahman of Cairo!* Jalal stopped. His chest expanded as a sense of euphoria flowed through his limbs. He could feel it, the breath of much-anticipated victory, like a Nile breeze against his fevered skin; its proximity wrapped him in its seductive embrace, granting him the confidence to step forward and set his foot on the lowest course of the dais upon which was raised the hallowed throne.

This was how Mustapha found him, beginning his inexorable climb from vizier to Sultan. 'Excellency,' the old eunuch said, bowing.

'Things are in place?'

Mustapha nodded. 'They are, Excellency. All our players, those both willing and not, have taken their marks. The Caliph sits with his guest, Turanshah has withdrawn his Jandariyah from their posts, and as we speak a few of my trusted brothers are listening for the sounds of a struggle. Now, it is merely a matter of patience.'

'Patience!' Jalal said. He stared up at the white-brocaded throne, its gold fittings and ivory trim gleaming in the light of countless lamps. *So close!* 'Yes, virtuous patience. We've come far together, have we not?'

'We have, Excellency.'

Jalal pried his gaze from the throne and turned to face the old eunuch. 'And what price for your years of loyalty? What reward would you ask of me?'

Mustapha smiled, lines of age and weariness crinkling his eyes. 'To serve you has been reward enough, Excellency. But I would not refuse your generosity if it took the form of a small palace of my own and perhaps slaves to see to my needs, so I might pass my remaining years in comfort.'

'That's all?' Jalal raised an eyebrow. 'A small palace and a handful of slaves? Surely you desire something more?'

The old eunuch shrugged. 'Anything more I leave to your discretion, Excellency. Or should I say, Sultan?'

Jalal flashed a shark-toothed smile. 'You are as wise as you are cunning, my old darling. But let us not get too far ahead of ourselves. Return to your post and keep me informed. I want to know when the deed is done.' The vizier returned his attention to the Seat of Divine Reason, as cold and gleaming as a distant star.

Mustapha bowed and withdrew.

'Sultan,' Jalal hissed; the word echoed about the Golden Hall, becoming a roar of approbation as the vizier raised himself the next step up on the dais . . .

6

'Al-Hashishiyya!' Caliph Rashid al-Hasan recoiled from the false Sufi, from the man who called himself Ibn al-Teymani of the Hejaz. Blood drained from the young man's features. 'You're . . . You're an Assassin!'

Assad laid his disguised salawar across his knees. 'I am, but I mean you no harm, my lord. I come in peace, with offers of aid and friendship from my lord, the Hidden Master of Alamut.'

At first, the Caliph did not respond. All he knew of al-Hashishiyya came from the lurid stories his father's ministers had told; tales of wild-eyed dagger-men, fanatics who sprang upon their unwitting victims and sliced them to ribbons even as they themselves paid the ultimate price. From their near-legendary fortress of Alamut, agents of al-Hashishiyya sowed terror across the Moslem world, exacting tribute from princes and kings and silencing any opposition with the threat of sudden, gruesome death.

Now an emissary of that reviled sect sat beside him, presenting a strange contrast to the tales Rashid had heard. This man, this Assassin, had nothing of the fanatic about him; his eyes were as clear and reasonable as those of a trusted jurist, his manner no less calm. Still, as his disguise sloughed away, the Caliph sensed an undercurrent of violence in him, a savage and pitiless nature held in check by the slender bonds of civility. *I come in peace*, he had said, *with offers of aid and friendship*. And, by Allah, Rashid al-Hasan believed him.

'I do not understand,' the Caliph said. 'Why would your master wish to aid me? The Fatimids broke with al-Hashishiyya in my grandfather's day.'

'Must that always be the case? For his part, the Hidden Master would prefer to see the animosity between Cairo and Alamut come to an end. Too long have our true enemies united while we have done nothing but revel in our division, fighting a war for succession that no longer holds any meaning. My master believes enough is enough, my lord. You and he are akin in age, and he fancies your goals are not too dissimilar from his own: to cast down your Sunni rival in Baghdad, to drive the Turks back beyond the Black Sea, and to reclaim Jerusalem from the Infidel. Is he wrong in this, my lord?'

'No,' Rashid al-Hasan said; his brows knitted in a contemplative frown. 'No, he is not wrong. I would see those selfsame objectives come to fruition, as well. But . . . how? My vizier—'

'Your vizier', Assad put in, with heat, 'has betrayed your trust, my lord! Do you remember a man called Dirgham?'

The Caliph scowled. 'He was Jalal's predecessor, but he is dead these past three years. Killed as he attempted a palace coup.'

'Dead? No, my lord. That's another of Jalal's lies. Dirgham has been living in exile at Damascus. As we speak, he marches on Cairo with the full support of Sultan Nur ad-Din . . . and with the support of his army. Worse yet, Jalal plots against him – and against you – with the infidel King of Jerusalem, who has dispatched an army of his own. It is only a matter of days until both forces reach Cairo.'

'Allah!' Rashid al-Hasan muttered, rubbing his forehead. 'Are you certain?'

'I am,' Assad said. 'It was overheard coming from the vizier's own lips by a woman of your harem. She relayed it to another of my master's servants, and it came thence to me. What's more, I believe the man killed in your presence this morning may have been trying to warn you.'

'Harun al-Gid.' The young man looked up, pain and anger clouding his eyes. 'Yes, he told me I must not trust my vizier. This is ill news, my friend. How can I fight one army, let alone two? Must I throw myself on Damascus' mercy to keep the Frankish dogs at bay?'

'Let me remove your most immediate threat, my lord. Give me your blessing and I will dispose of Jalal this very night, along with those army commanders and chamberlains not expressly loyal to you. Once your position is secure then, perhaps, Allah will reveal to you the proper course of action. I need only your approval to set things in motion.'

'My approval?' The Caliph laughed, a grim sound bereft of humour. 'Why not? Dirgham has allied himself with Damascus and Jalal with Jerusalem. Why should I not ally myself with the killers of Alamut? Go, then. You have my—'

Assad raised his hand, a curt gesture that prompted the younger man to silence. The Assassin frowned; he cocked his head, listening . . . and heard the distinct rasp of stone on stone, followed by the rustle of cloth and the thump of boot heels on the springy turf of the courtyard. 'Your palace has too many ears, my lord.' The muscles of Assad's sword-arm ridged and corded as he grasped the pommel of his salawar.

'By Allah!' A sudden gust of anger played across the young Caliph's face. 'I weary of this! You there, out in the courtyard! Stop this slinking about and come forward this instant! Do you hear me? I said—'

In answer, an apparition loomed from the darkness. Rashid al-Hasan had the impression of swirling white fabric, of piercing eyes hidden by a cowl, and of steel flashing in a scarred fist. Assad, however, saw something else, something sewn on to the white cloth that wrenched from him a sulphurous oath.

The blood-red cross of the Order of the Temple.

'Keep still, Saracen!' The intruder's voice grated as he strode forward, sword rising in anticipation of a killing blow. 'God wills it!'

God wills it! Assad remembered that same cry drifting through the scarlet streets of Ascalon, after its gates had buckled and given way. *God wills it!* He remembered a Templar, his surcoat stained with soot and blood, crowing those words in triumph as he clutched a Moslem infant by its heels and dashed the child's head against a wall. *God wills it!*

Vengeance blazed in the depths of Assad's eyes. He lashed out with one sandalled heel to strike the low table, sending it skittering across the floor and into the Templar's path. Dishes slid off;

porcelain shattered against the marble tiles, spraying bits of untouched food about the room. The intruder backpedalled as Assad sprang to his feet and bared the edge of his salawar. 'Infidel!' he growled. 'Will your god hear you in Hell?'

'A Saracen with spleen? Ha! Your head first, then!' The Templar, Godfrey de Vézelay, gave a wild laugh and kicked the table aside. He came on in silence, his heavier sword slashing lazy patterns through the air. Though he and Assad were alike in height, the breadth of the Frank's muscular shoulders and his longer reach gave him a natural advantage – and he knew it. Godfrey's thin lips curled in a sneer of supreme arrogance as broadsword met salawar.

Steel crashed and slithered . . . and faster than the eye could follow, Assad's riposte drew a scarlet line across the Templar's cheek. Wild-eyed, Godfrey leapt back, fingers pressed to the stinging wound. They came away smeared with blood.

The Assassin flashed a cruel smile. 'Allah wills it, dog!'

Howling with rage, the Templar hurled himself at Assad in a whirlwind of steel. Hatred backed every blow, hatred and a lust for slaughter that transcended the meeting of mere enemies. Neither man spoke; the only sounds were the scuff and stamp of their feet on the tiles, the crunch of broken porcelain, the hiss of breath between clenched teeth, and the ringing clash of blades.

Stroke followed stroke; in the close confines of the sitting room, the Templar seemed less a swordsman than a blacksmith, hammering out a staccato rhythm on the iron anvil of Assad's guard. The heavy Frankish broadsword should have snapped the Assassin's Afghan blade at the hilt. Yet the salawar's ancient Damascus steel showed barely a notch while the broadsword was fast losing its edges, its cutting surfaces growing ragged from constant punishment.

The timbre of the fight changed suddenly. The thunderous crash of steel faded; now, the Templar's blade only split empty air as Assad ducked and sidestepped, keeping his body in motion and nullifying the Templar's twin advantages of strength and reach through sheer predatory quickness. Assad feinted, lunged, and forced his Frankish enemy back to the courtyard door.

'By God,' the Templar panted, 'you're no holy man!' His cowl fell back, revealing a pock-marked visage and black hair heavy with sweat; blood dripped from his lacerated cheek to redden the breast of his surcoat. His gaze flickered to the young Caliph, on his knees and scrabbling through the riot of cushions in search of a weapon. Two long strides separated them.

Assad made no reply; he saw the Frank's muscles tense, saw desperation gleaming in his eyes. The man sought an opening to make his move – a moment of distraction, anything. Assad obliged him. He shifted his feet, feigning to slip on a patch of greasy tile . . .

And with a roar like a wounded tiger, Godfrey de Vézelay, knight of the Holy Order of the Temple, sprang for the Caliph; he flung his left arm wide, intent on sweeping his seeming off-balance foe aside. But, even as he surged forward, unable to check his momentum, the *Emir* of the Knife was in motion. Assad ducked that wide-flung arm and drove his salawar into the Templar's chest, just forward of his armpit. The Frank grunted as rich red gore spurted down the blade and over the Assassin's hand.

'For Ascalon!' Assad hissed, his teeth clenching against the surge of raw, incandescent hate that flowed into his body.

Godfrey staggered and swayed. His sword clattered from nerveless fingers; a heartbeat later, he fell to his knees amid the trampled ruins of the Caliph's dinner. The Templar rolled his eyes heavenwards, his face taking on a deathly pallor. 'God,' he pleaded, bubbles of blood breaking on his thin lips. 'God . . .'

With a contemptuous shove, Assad wrenched his blade free. The Assassin staggered; panting, he knelt and wiped his salawar clean on the fallen Templar's surcoat. A moment later he glanced up to see the Caliph, on his feet now and inching towards him.

Wide-eyed, Rashid al-Hasan's gaze fixed on the Frankish corpse. 'Merciful Allah,' he muttered, swallowing thickly. 'A . . . A Templar . . . in Cairo? In my palace?'

'One of the two who arrived yesterday. Emissaries of Amalric of Jerusalem.'

The young man wiped his brow. 'I am in your debt, Ibn al-Teymani of the Hejaz – if that is truly your name.'

Assad straightened. 'My enemies know me as the *Emir* of the Knife, my lord.' The Caliph started, evidently well aware of the reputation associated with that appellation. 'But you may call me Assad, if it pleases you.'

'What now . . . Assad?'

The Assassin padded to the sitting room's arched doorway and glanced down the long corridor, back towards the antechamber. They were alone and ominously so – thus far, the clamour of violence had drawn no one's attention, not the eunuchs or the chamberlains, not the stewards or even the guards. 'If that old snake, Mustapha, heard the clap of your hand earlier, how is it he did not hear the racket this Infidel made?'

'Shall I summon him?'

'No,' Assad replied, turning. His eyes narrowed with suspicion. 'It must be a part of the vizier's game. How long they plan to ignore sounds of a struggle I cannot say, but I imagine it won't be much longer. We need to find a safe place for you, my lord. Somewhere beyond Jalal's reach.'

Rashid al-Hasan exhaled. 'Does such a place even exist?'

'Outside these walls,' Assad said, softly yet in earnest, 'men of every stripe revere you as Caliph, my lord. They praise you as the Prince of the Faithful, and consider your voice to be the voice of the Prophet. If I can get you out from under the vizier's thumb, then I have little doubt the multitudes of Cairo will protect you from harm – at least long enough to allow me to finish my sworn task. And after I've disposed of Jalal and his faction, his ministers and his sycophants, these selfsame multitudes will make short work of anyone who hasn't sworn allegiance to you. First, though, we must quit the palace.' Assad stepped into the courtyard, pausing to give his eyes a moment to adjust to the darkness. The sickle moon lent the night a faint sheen of silver. 'Keep an eye on that corridor, my lord.'

'Wait,' the Caliph called after him. 'There's no way out through there. The only other door leads to my bedchamber.'

'That may be, but the Nazarene got in somehow and I doubt he planned to linger once the deed was done. Nor can I see a dozen Jandariyah, plus assorted menials, being trusted to keep the truth of your murder a secret. No, my lord, his escape is somewhere in this courtyard. Bide a moment.'

Bent nearly double, Assad loped along the perimeter of the wall, looking for some sign of where the Templar had entered the courtyard. He spotted the latticed entrance to the Caliph's bedchamber, faintly illuminated by a lamp burning within, and a tinkling fountain of cold marble. The wall itself was blank save for a single scalloped niche, like the mihrab of a mosque. He slowed to a walk as he came abreast of this niche. Assad discerned no ropes. Perhaps the Templar planned to climb one of the potted poplars? But, no. They were flimsy and decorative, and none of them reached the level of the wall's summit. *How, then? How . . . ?*

'Is it done?'

Assad whirled, stifling a curse. Beside him, stone grated on stone as the interior of the niche, partially blocked by one of the ornamental trees, swung inward. He took a step back, inverting his salawar so that it ran unseen along his forearm.

'Is it done?' The speaker repeated the question, harsher this time. He was expecting the Templar; similar in height and breadth, cast in silhouette by the distant lamp, Assad and the dead Nazarene could have been one in the same.

'Aye.' Assad mimicked as best he could the Templar's guttural voice. 'Done.'

'Praise be to Allah!' To the Assassin's surprise, a shaven-headed eunuch clad in the robes of a high chamberlain stepped out and gestured impatiently at him. 'Come, we must get you back to your chambers ere anyone grows suspicious. Make haste, lord kni—'

The eunuch apprehended his mistake even as Assad struck. Before he drew another breath, the Assassin ripped the edge of his salawar across the eunuch's throat; quickly, he bore the thrashing chamberlain to the ground and held him still while his life's blood gushed over dry grass and soil. No others followed him, and the eunuch's twitching legs kept the secret door ajar.

'What the Devil . . . ?' he muttered, peering into the dark passageway beyond the cunningly hidden entrance.

Assad did not waste time with idle speculation over who built the passage or why, nor did he let where it might lead to trouble him. It was enough that it existed, and that it would carry them away from what the vizier meant as a death trap.

With a grim smile, he went to fetch the Caliph.

7

An army moved through the streets of Cairo.

Hundreds of shuffling feet raised a pall of dust invisible against the night sky. Steel rustled and clashed; moonlight reflected off helmets and mail hauberks like the play of distant lightning on a hot summer evening. The rattle of war-harness set dogs to barking; their masters, roused from slumber by the sudden clamour, threw open shuttered windows. They were poised to bellow curses when the source of the disturbance revealed itself.

Parysatis heard windows banging shut as she advanced with Massoud and his Circassians through the neighbourhood of Barqiyya. She wrung her hands at the noise and dust raised by the movement of so many men. Surely someone would hear them and sound an alarm? Yet Massoud appeared indifferent as he walked beside her, silent but making no pretence at stealth.

She understood his lack of concern when they came across the first body. The corpse of a thickly muscled Sudanese soldier sprawled face-up in the middle of the street, a pair of arrows standing out from his bull neck. Already, the spilled blood attracted a swarm of flies. Beyond were more bodies, the remains of an ambushed patrol. Parysatis stepped around the arrow-riddled corpses and tried not to stare at their slack faces, grey and frozen in death.

'Gokbori sent his scouts out ahead of us,' Massoud whispered. 'His Turks have eyes like owls in the dark.'

She nodded and said nothing, still numb from the news of the Gazelle's murder, from Yasmina's flight from the Inn of the Three Apples. She glanced at the armed men flanking her. *Merciful Allah, I pray we're doing the right thing.* Yet, whether they were in the right or not, it was too late to second-guess their decision; it was far too late to seek other alternatives. By shedding blood in opposition to the vizier they had sealed their fates. Now, a new terror crept into the pit of her stomach, edging aside her fear of detection: *What if we fail? What then?* Parysatis shuddered. She had no answer.

The domes and minarets of the East Palace gleamed against the star-flecked heavens. Ahead, the alley they followed debouched into a wider avenue that ran alongside the palace. She could barely make out the low wall of the herb garden with its old bronze gate, a lamp burning in a niche beside it.

Parysatis stiffened at the sight of a pair of Jandariyah loitering outside the gate. 'T-There were no guards posted when we left!' she said, clutching Massoud's arm. 'You m-must believe me!'

The Circassian amir turned to her. 'I believe you. Now, keep quiet and play along,' he hissed, motioning one of his men forward – a red-bearded soldier clad in silk and steel. 'Throw her over your shoulder and follow my lead.' The fellow nodded; Parysatis gasped as he did his amir's bidding: none too gently, he caught her up and flung her over his mailed shoulder like a sack of grain.

The man swaggered in Massoud's wake. Parysatis faced the narrow alley they had just quit; though she could not see ahead of them, the sound of Massoud muttering under his breath reached her: 'That's it. That's it. We're two fellow soldiers on an errand to the palace.' She felt tense knots of muscle in the Circassian's shoulder despite his best efforts to appear nonchalant.

After a few more steps, a harsh challenge sent chills down her spine.

'Who goes?'

'Returning a bit of property, brother,' she heard Massoud say, his tone jovial. 'This one here belongs to the palace, or so she says. I expect she's lying, but by Allah, she's comely enough to be a harem flower . . . though, if you ask me, she could do with a proper bit of fertilizing.'

The soldiers laughed along with Massoud. 'Put her down, then, and let's get a look at her.'

The Circassian slung Parysatis unceremoniously off his shoulder. She squeaked in alarm, but somehow managed to keep her footing. Calloused hands spun her around to face the two Jandariyah: Syrians in spired helmets and gilded mail, their white khalats embroidered in silver and black thread. They leaned on tall spears, their shields propped against the stone wall. Her cheeks flushed at their brazen scrutiny.

Massoud stepped past the soldiers and peered through the bars of the gate. 'Allah, but this is a lonely post. What did you do to deserve it?'

'Got the short shrift,' one of the Jandariyah replied; the other leered at Parysatis and licked his lips. Lust gleamed in his eyes. 'Why, you can barely tell there's a woman under there. You'd best leave her with us. We'll take—'

Massoud struck without warning. He snatched the spire of the Jandariyah's helmet, wrenching the soldier's head back. A cry of alarm turned to a bloody gurgle as the amir's dagger tore open his throat. The remaining Jandariyah spun. Yet, before Massoud or the red-bearded Circassian could raise a hand against him, Parysatis heard a soft hiss followed by a meaty *thunk*. The Syrian's head snapped back and he pitched against the wall, his spear clattering from his hands; slowly, to the accompaniment of metal scraping stone, he slid to the ground. An arrow stood out from his left eye socket.

At close range, driven by the powerful Turkish bow, it had pierced not only the flesh and bone of the Jandariyah's skull, but the steel of his helmet as well.

Stunned, Parysatis glanced across the avenue. Gokbori stepped into the wan moonlight. The Turkish amir grinned like a madman as he tossed his bow to another and drew his curved sabre. Massoud nodded his thanks. The Circassian knelt and wiped his dagger on the dead soldier's khalat before returning it to its sheath. Quickly, he stripped a knife from the corpse's sash, stood, and held it out for Parysatis to take.

The Persian woman stared at the curved blade, with its delicate inlay of silver leaves; her hand flinched from its worn ebony grip as she finally accepted it from him. 'I . . . I am no fighter, my lord.'

'I know,' Massoud said, 'but if things go badly for us, do not let them take you alive. Do you understand?'

Parysatis did. All too well.

Satisfied, Massoud turned away. The amir's sword rang from its sheath. He held it aloft for his men to see, silver light gleaming from its edge. 'White Slaves of the River! With me! *Allahu akbar!* For the Caliph! For Cairo!'

Hundreds of swords thrust at the sky; their owners, be they Circassian or Turk, added their voices to his: '*Allahu akbar!*'

And Parysatis, standing forgotten in Massoud's shadow, cradled a dead man's knife in her hands. 'For Rashid al-Hasan,' she whispered.

8

Yasmina had only dim recollections of her flight from the inn: tear-streaked memories of a voice calling her name; of faces blurred by grief; and of the blood-warm darkness beyond, its embrace alive with whispers of self-recrimination.

It's your fault! You left her to die!

Her body moved of its own accord down the narrow alleys of the Soldiers' Quarter, running ever southwards; instinct guided her around obstacles, from an ox-cart loaded with stone blocks to knots of grim-eyed Sudanese mercenaries. She skirted squares where lamplight and mocking laughter seeped out from behind the closed doors of pleasure houses.

You left her to die!

Yasmina increased her pace. Her lungs worked like a forge's bellows, drawing in the dusty air in great racking gasps; she ran on, heedless of what lay in her path, as though her guilt were a living thing that gave chase. It hounded her through the Glassblowers' Bazaar and across the Qasaba, where the evening market was in full swing. And amid the din of merchants and tradesmen, she heard the echo of Zaynab's voice.

Why did you leave me to die?

The young woman's endurance gave out. She stumbled and pitched off to one side, old wicker crunching as she collided with a small pyramid of empty cages and dovecotes outside a fowler's shop. She lay there a moment and listened to the pounding of her heart, the ground beneath her still hot from the baking sun. Sweat stung her eyes and mingled with the tears cascading down her cheeks.

The fowler, a wiry-muscled Egyptian in a filthy galabiyya and turban, came barging into the street, shaking his fists and gesticulating wildly; he screeched at Yasmina in a voice not unlike that of the birds he trapped in the reeds and marshes of the Nile. The girl ignored him. She shoved aside a mud-crusted dovecote and scrabbled to her feet, one hand braced against the shop's mudbrick wall, her eyes fixed on a point down the street, on her destination.

The caravanserai of Ali abu'l-Qasim.

Why had she come here? The caravanserai was as dark and lifeless as the House of the Gazelle; no lights gleamed from its upper windows, nor did any spill out through the tall doors, closed now and likely barred. All of Abu'l-Qasim's followers must have travelled with the funeral cortège to al-Karafa cemetery, beyond the Zuwayla Gate. Still, the girl staggered on, knowing only that the caravanserai was the last place she had seen Zaynab, the last place she had known happiness.

The fowler's curses fading behind her, Yasmina allowed grief to guide her footsteps. She avoided the tall doors of the caravanserai, where men of all sorts had gathered to await the return of the King of Thieves. Instead, she slipped unseen into an alley between neighbouring buildings where, hidden by broken stone and cast-off debris, she came to the flight of crude sandstone steps leading down into darkness, to the bronze-barred fissure in the wall of the old underground bath.

Yasmina descended slowly. Moonlight gave a faint sheen of silver to each step; the air wafting up from the fissure was moist and cool, though tainted with the coppery stench of blood.

Zaynab's blood.

Yasmina sobbed. Tremors racked her body as she stopped short of the bottom step. Here she sat, staring at the faint glimmer of bronze as though it were a gate to the underworld, as though Zaynab's soul waited beyond. *You're dead because of me, because I left you alone!* Her fingers groped in the darkness beside her, searching. *I won't leave you alone again! I promise!* She came up with a thin wedge of sandstone, its edge flaked and serrated. *I promise!*

Yasmina blinked back tears and bared her left arm to the elbow. She understood what she had to do; she understood why. *I won't leave you alone again!* Gripping the stone in her right hand, the young woman scraped its edge across the soft flesh of her wrist, teeth clenched against the pain. It would take some time, but she was certain she could rip a gash large enough to empty her arteries. What's more, the agony of it would serve as an act of atonement, penance for abandoning Zaynab when she needed her most.

Her features set in a mask of grim resolve, Yasmina prepared herself. She bore down on the stone, ready to grind and saw and rip, ready to gouge her flesh until hot blood slicked her fingertips. She was ready to follow Zaynab into the afterlife. Yasmina sucked her lower lip between her teeth. She was ready. By God, she was ready . . .

A sound, though, caused the girl to fumble and nearly drop the instrument of her sacrifice. In the alley above, voices grew near: one voice was raspy and wet; the other she recognized. It belonged to the one-eyed beggar, Musa. 'What do you want, wretch?'

At first, the other's reply was indistinct, then: '. . . true you're seeking our poor Gazelle's murderer in the Foreign Quarter? That he is a tall man, clean-shaven but not a eunuch. Perhaps a Frank?'

'It's true,' Musa murmured. 'What of it?'

'Perhaps I know where this killer is . . .'

Yasmina stiffened; mention of the Gazelle's Frankish slayer caused all thoughts of suicide to fade away. Rage boiled out from the dark places in her soul, filling the void Zaynab's death had left behind and turning her heart to stone. By all reckoning, vengeance trumped penance; she could die any time, but she had perhaps one chance to strike back, one chance to avenge the woman who had been as a mother to her.

Hate twisted Yasmina's lips as she strained to overhear.

9

The funeral cortège had returned to the caravanserai of Ali abu'l-Qasim in dolorous silence, each mourner wrapped in his own thoughts. The procession was a polyglot: dour Berbers troubled by the deaths of their companions; merchants and tradesmen who hailed from the same neighbourhood as Abu'l-Qasim; old thieves clad like desert shaykhs who recalled Zaynab as a precocious girl; and beggars who wept for their lost patroness. In the midst of it all, half a dozen slaves bore Abu'l-Qasim's palanquin on their shoulders. The curtains were drawn, and none could see the King of Thieves' grieving visage, least of all Musa, who brought up the rear of the cortège.

The one-eyed man wiped his face, knuckling at the dull ache

which blossomed behind his empty socket. A crushing despair informed his every gesture and made each step more ponderous than the last. Zaynab was dead, and though he had seen the body Musa could barely fathom it. *Dead and buried.*

Three women, the wives of a neighbour, had done for Abu'l-Qasim what no man might: they had washed the Gazelle's body, braiding her hair and shrouding her in clean linen, making her ready for prayer and burial, the whole completed before sunset in accordance with the long traditions of Islam. That only a small stone with rough-cut letters marked her resting place seemed insufficient to Musa, an insult. She deserved better.

The one-eyed man sighed. Already, the head of the procession stood at the doors to the caravanserai. Hinges creaked as Abu'l-Qasim's Berbers levered them open, and then stepped aside to allow the cortège entry to the courtyard. Stewards kindled lamps and would soon fetch food and wine for the mourners, but Musa had little in the way of an appetite. No, he decided to pay his respects to Abu'l-Qasim and then slip away, maybe head north to the Mad Caliph's mosque and pass the night among his people, among the beggars. He—

Musa flinched as, from his blind side, a small hand tugged at his sleeve. He cocked his head and saw a boy standing there, an unkempt urchin clad in little more than rags yet who smelled strongly of perfumes, rich and cloying. He stared in rude fascination at Musa's empty socket. 'What is it, little brother?'

The boy answered in pidgin Arabic: 'What happen your eye?'

'It was burned out,' Musa growled, 'after I asked a man with one eye a foolish question. Now, what do you want – and think before you speak, boy, lest I fetch hot coals and an iron.'

The urchin stared, half in disbelief and half in fear. He took a step back before replying: 'Djuha want talk to you.'

'Djuha, eh?' The name brought a grimace to Musa's lips. The man was a pander of the worst sort, a dealer in perversions and aberrations so foul as to render him a pariah to even the most hedonistic of Cairo's denizens. Therefore he found his custom where he could, mostly in the Foreign Quarter among the dregs and flotsam of a dozen lands. The one-eyed man spat. 'What the devil does that swine want with me?'

The boy shrugged. 'You come?'

'Where is he?'

The urchin jerked his chin over his shoulder.

Musa looked past the boy and spotted a figure across the street, cloaked in shadow. There was no mistaking the tall and emaciated silhouette. Djuha was Bedouin, an outlaw from the Prophet's own clan, the Banu Hashim, who had fled to Egypt to escape punishment for his myriad crimes; yet, there was no escaping Allah's wrath. As Musa heard it, the man was dying with agonizing slowness, the victim of divine retribution in the form of leprosy.

'You come?' the boy repeated.

'Why should I?'

'He say it important.' The urchin nodded to the caravanserai. 'About her.'

Musa's eye narrowed. *What could he know about the mistress?* 'Tell him to cross the street and await me in that alley.'

With a nod, the boy darted off. Musa watched carefully as the urchin delivered his message; he saw Djuha glance up and nod. Draping a rotting hand around the boy's shoulder, the leper stepped into the street. Robes of striped silk and wool hung from his wasted frame. He used a fold of linen from his head-scarf to mask his disease-ravaged features. Passers-by who had come to pay their respects to Abu'l-Qasim flinched away from Djuha, making signs to ward off evil as he vanished into the alley.

Moments later, Musa followed.

Perfume barely masked the stench of corruption that clung to Djuha. It filled the alley, a smell like a slaughtered carcass left too long in the sun. The leper waited with the urchin at his side, stroking the boy's hair and warbling in a wet, raspy voice. Djuha's words were too low for Musa to hear, but his tone sent a wave of revulsion washing over the one-eyed man. How he wanted to draw his knife and strike down the abomination! But for Zaynab's sake

Musa exercised restraint, if not civility. 'What do you want, wretch?'

Djuha glanced up, his bloodshot eyes unblinking. 'Nothing, beggar, save only to be of service. Is it true you're seeking our poor Gazelle's murderer in the Foreign Quarter? That he is a tall man, clean-shaven but not a eunuch. Perhaps a Frank?'

'It's true. What of it?'

'Perhaps I know where this killer is . . .'

Musa started forward. '*Perhaps?* What is *perhaps?* Either you know or you don't!'

'I believe I have seen this Frank you seek.'

'*Perhaps* you've seen him or you have seen him for certain?'

Djuha straightened. 'Your tone offends me, beggar.'

'My . . .' Musa's jaws clenched; veins in his neck stood out as, with titanic effort, he brought his sudden burst of fury under control. 'My . . . apologies. It has been a day of great sadness. Where . . . Where did you see this man?'

'Deep in the Foreign Quarter. Come, I will show you.'

Musa hesitated. He glanced back at the alley mouth, wondering if he should first pass word on to Abu'l-Qasim. *But what if this proves to be nothing? What then?* The one-eyed man scratched his unkempt beard in indecision.

'You need not fear me,' Djuha said. 'And if by chance it is not the man you seek, there is no harm done.'

Musa exhaled, unable to refute the leper's logic. 'I will follow you, but heed what I say: if this is but some dark jest on your part, as Allah is my witness, I will finish what the Almighty has started!'

Djuha, his red-rimmed eyes impassive, bowed in acknowledgement before setting off, cooing to the urchin who bore the weight – and stench – of his arm's embrace. Musa followed, though he kept his distance from the pair.

None saw the shadowy form emerge from cunningly hidden stairs leading down into darkness, to the bronze-barred cleft in the wall of the old underground bath.

10

Pale and shaking, Mustapha moved with exaggerated care through the wreck of the Caliph's sitting room. He stepped as gingerly over the crushed fruit and spilled khamr as he did over the smears of blood, the sight of which caused the churning in his stomach to treble. Nor was he alone. A gaggle of eunuchs watched him from the shelter of the doorway, their faces like waxen masks of revulsion.

'What deviltry is this?' Mustapha muttered; reluctantly, the old eunuch leaned over to take a closer look at the Templar's corpse, nose wrinkling at the stench of blood and bowel. He shook his head. *How? How could he have failed?* But Mustapha already knew the answer. It had to be that cursed Sufi, Ibn al-Teymani. The man was obviously more than he seemed. But what was he, an agent of Jalal's enemies? More to the point, where was he? Mustapha straightened as another eunuch approached the sitting room from the fountain court.

'Well?' Mustapha snapped.

'I . . . I found Babek,' the fellow stammered; fear left him breathless. 'He's over by the niche. S-Someone cut his throat.'

'What of the Caliph and his guest?'

The eunuch shook his head. 'No sign of either of them.'

Mustapha cursed. *They must have discovered the passage!* Whirling, he retraced his steps from the sitting room. The old eunuch snatched one of his waiting chamberlains up by the collar of his robes. 'You! Take a dozen Jandariyah to the harem and re-inforce the guard at the doors to the old hammam. Let no one exit that room alive!' Mustapha shoved him away.

'Hearkening and obeying, *ya sidi!*' The chamberlain salaamed and turned. But before he had taken more than a handful of steps, a wild-eyed Egyptian servant collided with him, sending the chamberlain sprawling as he barrelled on down the corridor.

'Allah's mercies!' the servant bawled. 'Allah's mercies, we are undone!' He skidded to a halt and flopped down on his belly, grimy hands clutching at the hem of Mustapha's galabiyya. 'Allah preserve us!'

The old eunuch twitched out of the servant's grasp and scowled. 'What is it? What goes, damn you?'

'We are undone, I tell you! *Doomed!* They have risen against our master, against the vizier. Allah! They are coming.'

'Who? Stop yammering, dog, and sit up! What are you talking about?'

'The Mamelukes! The White Slaves of the River are inside the palace, looting and killing!'

Instantly Mustapha's mind linked the two events; could it be coincidence that the Caliph was spirited away even as the White Slaves of the River went into open insurrection? *Of course not. This must be Gokbori's doing!* The old eunuch ground his teeth in frustration, feeling the fool for misjudging the miserable Turk; plainly he was far more cunning than even Jalal imagined.

The servant's news caused chaos to take root among Mustapha's followers; a frenzy of terror erupted at the notion of rampaging Turks and Circassians loose inside the palace – Turks and Circassians who viewed eunuchs as spoils of war. A dozen voices babbled at once, a deluge of questions accompanied by high-pitched wailing and praying. Their incontinence impinged upon Mustapha's well-ordered thoughts. 'Fools!' he roared, stamping his foot for emphasis. 'Be silent. You speak as though we are defeated already. Have you forgotten the Jandariyah? What are a few armed slaves against the cream of Syrian soldiery?' The old eunuch thrust a gnarled finger at the chamberlain. 'You! You have your instructions. Now go! The rest of you, dispose of these bodies and put our master's sitting room back in order. Move, lest I hand you over to the Mamelukes myself!' The threat had the desired effect. Slowly, the eunuchs mastered their fear and went about their assigned tasks.

Mustapha reached down and caught the cowering Egyptian servant by one long-lobed ear, hauling him to his feet with a savage twist. 'And you, Inciter of Riots, you will come with me. No doubt our blessed vizier will want to hear your tale for himself!'

11

Single file, Rashid al-Hasan followed Assad through the darkness, its caress stifling and impenetrable save in those places where spy slits afforded a wedge of light and a breath of air. The pair crept with care, easing around the twists and turns of the narrow passage as it followed the centuries-old foundations of the East Palace; Assad paused often to listen for sounds of pursuit, or for any indication that the vizier's confederates waited ahead.

'Who would have thought the legends were true?' the Caliph whispered, peering through one of the slits.

'Legends?'

'As a boy, my nurses would tell me stories of al-Hakim, whom men named the Mad Caliph. They say he used to creep between the walls of the palace to spy on his slaves, and that he would sneak out from time to time to steal the bits and baubles others left lying about – a cup, a sandal, a pendant – the pettiest of thievery.' Rashid stepped back, the faint light of a distant torch glistening on his sweat-dampened forehead. 'If ever I misplaced a toy, my nurses would tell me the Mad Caliph had taken it.'

Assad grunted. He walked a few paces up the passage and stared out into the darkness. 'Did he not also kidnap and murder his own wives?'

The Caliph's melancholy smile faded. 'So they say.'

'Do you know where we are, my lord?'

Again, the younger man leaned closer, this time pressing one eye to the slit. 'We're looking into the outer court. That far door, yonder, leads to the Golden Hall and to my own apartments. That's curious.'

'What?' Assad glanced over his shoulder. He frowned, as though suddenly bedevilled by something unseen.

'I have never known it to be unguarded. But I suspect fewer witnesses mean fewer tongues Jalal must trust not to wag.' The Caliph made a noise, somewhere between a chuckle and a sob. 'Ever the practical man, my vizier. How could I have been so—'

'My lord,' Assad hissed; he cocked his head to one side and motioned the Caliph closer. 'Do you hear that?'

Rashid held his breath and listened. After a moment, he *did* hear something: a faint ringing, distant, like the sound of dozens of hammers striking an anvil, along with muffled shouts and screams. 'What is it . . . ?'

'Hurry,' Assad replied. The Assassin moved through the wedge of light and plunged into the darkness beyond, trusting the Caliph to follow. The sounds grew more strident as the pair traversed a long and lightless stretch of the passage, their hands brushing the jagged brickwork to either side. Cut into the foundations of walls dividing palace courtyards and squares, the tunnel made a sharp left, continued on straight for a few dozen paces, and then cut back to the right.

Rashid struggled to keep up. Through the sweat stinging his eyes, he could see the light was fast rising; a smoky glow the colour of blood suffused the darkness ahead. He lost sight of Assad as he rounded the far corner. Gasping for breath, blood pounding in his ears, the Caliph lengthened his stride. He, too, came round the corner . . .

. . . and skidded to a halt, reeling from the sounds of steel and fury that pierced the thick walls. The clamour was as nothing he had ever experienced; it reached through the spy holes like a living thing to snatch the breath from his lungs.

'Merciful Allah!'

A battle raged in the courtyard beyond the tight confines of the passage, not a score of paces from where the Caliph stood. Harsh voices echoed amid the crash of sword upon sword, upon shield, upon mailed flesh; terrible shrieks erupted from the slashed and riven throats of men who had but seconds to live. Above it all, Rashid al-Hasan heard someone bellowing in the hard, guttural tongue of the Turk, a war-cry that jolted his body like a physical blow.

'*Allahu akbar!* For the Caliph! For Cairo!'

Stumbling to one of the spy slits, the young Caliph pressed his palms flat against the rough brick and put an eye to the narrow aperture. In the flickering chaos, he caught a glimpse of bloody silks and gold as iron-shod Turks hewed through the Jandariyah, breaking with savage efficiency the backbone of the vizier's small army. Curved swords flashed in the light of countless torches; spears thrust and shattered, and archers loosed their arrows haphazardly into the throng of defenders.

'*Allahu akbar!* For the Caliph! For Cairo!'

'The White Slaves of the River,' Rashid heard Assad murmur at his back. 'We have to get clear of these tunnels and find their leader. This could be our best opportunity, my lord. Come. We should not tarry.'

'Wait, Assad! Wait! What's going on? I cannot see!'

'See? What is there to see? You need only listen to hear the tale unfold. Your vizier's maltreatment of your Mamelukes forced their hand; they've found a way into the palace, and the Jandariyah are too few, too scattered, to stop them. Yonder Syrians are men whose traditions and discipline preclude them from ever turning their backs on Jalal; they are bound by oaths as hard as iron chains. Nor will they seek quarter; they prefer slaughter to enslavement. Listen and you'll hear the veterans among them shouting for their comrades to fight on, to fight harder.'

Rashid did, hearing Syrian voices tinged with desperation. He craned his neck and tried to locate the loudest of them, but found his view blocked. A man reeled from the fray, staggering towards the courtyard wall – Syrian or Turk, the Caliph could not say; gory hands clutched at the lacerated flesh of his face. He pitched forward suddenly like a puppet unstrung, the weight of his mailed body shattering potted azaleas. Only then did Rashid see the white-fletched arrow standing out from the dead man's cervical spine. Blood splashed the emerald leaves of the azaleas; its stench mingled with the heavy air of the passage.

'Listen, my lord,' Assad said slowly. 'Listen and you can hear the sound of a Turkish mace staving in a shield or a helmet, splintering the bones beneath. In a fight like this your enemy is so close you can smell the garlic on his breath; you look into his eyes and he looks into yours, and you pray the fool stumbles or loses his grip. You pray for speed, accuracy, and the blessings of Allah. You know he's doing the same, so you pray that Allah hears your pleas first. And you kill him, if that be the will of God, before he kills you. Steel rings on steel, and spilled blood makes your footing treacherous. Go down in such a press of mailed bodies, my lord, and you'll never rise again.'

Drawn by the curious timbre of the Assassin's voice, Rashid al-Hasan turned his hollow-eyed gaze away from the spy hole. Assad crouched with his back against the far wall, his naked salawar upright between his knees, fists wrapped around the hilt. Flickering torchlight bathed the scarred half of his face in blood; the other half remained cloaked in shadow. The young Caliph swallowed hard at the grim emotion swirling in those cold black eyes. 'What . . . What will happen next?'

'What do you think will happen?' Assad gave a sharp jerk of his chin, indicating the courtyard beyond. 'Listen. Already, you can hear it. The Syrians are falling back. Make no mistake, my lord: they do not flee. There is no shame in their withdrawal. And those who survive will fall back again and again, to interior gates never meant to contain an armed host, even to the very doors of the Golden Hall. Each time, at each courtyard, at each redoubt, they will stoke their courage back to fighting pitch. They will convince themselves that *here*, that *now* is where they will stop these sons of Turkish whores! This far, and no further! But all the courage under heaven will avail them nothing. Their allies are too few, their enemies too many. Death becomes a certainty, less a matter of *when* than of *how* . . .'

The Caliph frowned, though not from perturbation. The Assassin's demeanour confused him. 'You pity those men.'

'Pity? No. They deserve no man's pity. But I understand them, my lord. I understand them, for I was at Ascalon.'

'And so?' Rashid shook his head, unsure of what Assad meant. Ascalon was a Frankish port on the Levantine coast; one that, in his father's day, had been under Moslem control.

Assad said nothing for a long moment. When he finally spoke, his voice was flat and emotionless. 'I was but a common soldier, my lord, about the age that you are now, when the infidel King of Jerusalem – Amalric's elder brother – decided to take Ascalon, to deprive Egypt of its last port in the Levant near enough to mount an expedition on his lands. Not long past midsummer that year, a Frankish fleet from Sidon blockaded our harbour, though the siege only began in earnest when the machines of Jerusalem's god-forsaken champions, the Templars, commenced their vile work; day and night, they flung stones and incendiaries at the walls. We endured this for five months and more. But, at sunset on the one-hundred-and-sixty-eighth day, the Infidel breached the Great Gate of Ascalon, and throughout the night wave after wave of Nazarenes hurled themselves against it. We could not hold.

'Some eight thousand souls died during the siege, from injury and illness; we lost countless more at the breach. The rest, untold thousands, were slaughtered in the streets, fighting the Nazarenes from house to house. We set the price high, and the Infidel paid for each cubit of Ascalon's soil with a pound of flesh. I know not how many others escaped, for at the end the Templars offered no quarter and took no prisoners. So, yes, my lord. I understand those soldiers who fight on though their cause may be lost – and what-ever pity I have left to me I reserve not for those fated to die, but for those destined to live. The men who survive this will never know another night's peace. Nor will another day pass without them asking of themselves: "What more could I have done?"'

The Caliph returned his gaze to the courtyard and saw it again through the prism of Assad's words. Chaos gave way to clarity. He saw grim Syrian faces splashed with blood, their own and their enemies', withdrawing through an archway to the Caliph's left, a route that would take them nearer to the Golden Hall; opposite them, howling Turks fought with passion, this assault the last gambit of desperate men forced to the edge of reason. *What more could I have done?*

'This folly is my own doing,' Rashid al-Hasan said quietly, pushing away from the slit and turning to face Assad. 'Mine and Jalal's. Two armies bear down on us, if what you say is true, and yet here we stand fighting among ourselves. Is there not any way we can salvage this? Would not the Jandariyah accept quarter if I held them blameless?'

'You would pardon them, even though they're the vizier's allies?'

'Is the sword to blame for its master's ambition?'

Assad rose from his crouch and shrugged. 'Then follow me, my lord, and quickly. We must find who commands the Turks and force him to rein in their slaughter, if he is truly loyal.'

'And if he's not?'

Resolve flared in the *Emir* of the Knife's eyes; he skinned his lips back over his teeth, a snarl of barely contained fury. 'Perhaps his successor will be?'

12

Hugh of Caesarea awoke to the sound of voices. Saracen voices, tinged with anger and muffled by the heavy cedar door of his chambers near the Saffron Gate and the House of Memory. Surrounded by Eastern opulence – by vessels of alabaster and gold, clouds of rich incense, tapestries woven of Cathayan silk, and rugs of costly make – the Frankish knight sprawled like a sybarite on a pillow-strewn divan, his muscular frame clad only in the long tunic his Arab steward called a galabiyya. His mail hauberk and leggings hung from a wooden tree in the far corner, away from the door; his white surcoat, sewn with the blood-red cross of the Temple, lay folded atop it. His broadsword, however, rested near his sinewy hand, its worn wood-and-leather sheath incongruous amid the many splendours around him.

The knight of Caesarea opened his bleary eyes and stared in annoyance at the door to his chambers. Idly, he wondered if the guards had perhaps caught de Vézelay, ever one to feel the thorns of lustfulness, sneaking into the Saracen harem. But the Frank bolted upright when one of the angry voices turned to a choking scream.

'God's teeth!'

A weight thudded against his door, followed by the sounds of steel rasping on steel, fierce howls, and the scuff of feet. Rising, Hugh unsheathed his broadsword and went to the door. It shuddered again, and then a desperate Arab voice called upon their heathen god for succour. The Frank cursed, throwing the door wide . . .

. . . and beheld a scene wrought of confusion. His servants and his guards, Syrians in white turbans and gold-edged mail, were down, blood from their hacked limbs and severed necks pouring over the polished tile of the corridor. Their slayers were men likewise armoured, though in mail more functional than decorative; Hugh had the impression of swarthy faces and bristling beards beneath iron caps fringed in grey fur. *Turks!*

The one nearest him, crouching over the body of his Arab steward, howled like a wolf and leapt, his gory sabre whistling for the Frank's throat. Easily, Hugh caught the blow on the edge of his uplifted broadsword. His riposte smashed through the Turk's helmet and split the skull beneath. Kicking his blade free of the corpse, he wheeled to face half a dozen others.

'Godfrey!' he bellowed. De Vézelay's room lay across from his, the door yet closed. 'By God, man! Rouse yourself! We're betrayed!' Together, fighting side by side, the pair of Templars could hold the hallway against a horde of would-be slayers. But

Hugh could spare no more concern for his companion. Fired with bloodlust, the Turks came on in a ragged wave of steel and fury.

The blond lord of Caesarea met them breast to breast. '*Sanctum Sepulcrum!*' he roared, his broadsword licking out to shear through a Turkish neck. The heathen's head rode a geyser of blood as his body tumbled to the ground, tangling the feet of those in his wake.

The Frank did not pause; it was not his nature to fight on the defensive. He hurled himself into their midst, his sword a-flicker in the dim lamplight, its blade slithering on mail and crashing down upon hastily raised sabres. Blood spattered the walls. Men bellowed in pain and rage as the battle-cry of the Order of the Temple drifted over the mêlée.

'God wills it!'

The end, though, was inevitable. Turkish mail and Turkish shields bore the brunt of the Frank's blows; with no such advantage of his own, Hugh's limbs soon grew bloody from the slash and bite of sabres. A spear darted through the press and gored a furrow in his thigh even as a dying Turk at his feet raised himself on one elbow and plunged a dagger into the Frankish knight's groin. Hugh staggered and fell to one knee.

'Godfrey!' he cried out, coughing on blood. He batted aside another sabre thrust and gutted the man with a backhand swipe. The hot, metallic stench of spilled gore filled his nostrils. 'God damn you, Godfrey!'

Hugh looked up as a heathen Turk ran at him, his sabre held in both hands like a spear. The knight tried to stand, to meet the onslaught on his feet, but the Turk was on him before he could get his legs under him. His sword clattered from his weakened grip. Hugh of Caesarea, soldier of the Holy Sepulchre, bared his teeth in defiance. 'God damn you!'

'*Allahu akbar!*' the Turk exulted, driving the point of his sabre in under the Templar's left eye and up into his skull.

13

Down brick-lined tunnels lit by slashes of distant torchlight, Parysatis guided Massoud and his grim-faced Circassians to the secret door in the women's quarters. She was breathing hard, a combination of fear and exertion, by the time she stepped out into the cluttered storeroom. The amir was hard on her heels; one by one, a dozen of Massoud's soldiers followed, filling the air in the small space with the rank odours of sweat and perfume, wood smoke and sour wine, oiled iron and old leather. The remaining men waited in the tunnel. In the distance, Parysatis heard cries of alarm, terrified weeping, and Lu'lu's high-pitched voice calling for calm.

'Damn Gokbori's heathen zeal!' Massoud said. 'He goes too swiftly through the palace. We must make haste, too, before the vizier decides simply to knife the Caliph and blame it on the White Slaves of the River.' He sidled to the door and risked a quick glance. Parysatis knew what he would see: a long fountain court-yard tiled in coloured marble and sparsely lit with lamps of enamelled glass and gold filigree. Likely no women milled about; the threat of strife would drive them nearer to the Chief Eunuch's quarters, to that portion of the harem complex reserved for the Caliph's family and favoured concubines, in the vain hope that such proximity would mean safety. Massoud spat; he gestured for her to come closer and pointed away to the left. 'Look, but carefully.'

Parysatis nodded and leaned across the threshold, just far enough out to see in the direction Massoud had indicated. Near the end of the courtyard, she spotted one of the vizier's silk-clad chamberlains waiting with a detachment of Jandariyah; the soldiers stood with hands on sword hilt and spear shaft, all eyes focused on an ornate set of double doors as though expecting something ferocious to emerge. Gold flashed as the eunuch chamberlain twiddled his fingers. *Is he nervous or impatient?*

'Those are the doors to the old hammam, are they not?'

Parysatis caught his unspoken implication; she managed a nod, her tongue suddenly too dry and thick for speech. *Whom were they waiting for?* She clutched the cold hilt of her knife all the more tightly to her breast. *Are we too late?*

The amir's naked sabre flashed in the gloom. He relayed orders back through his men. 'Twenty of you with me. The rest will secure the courtyard. If the Syrians resist, kill them.' To Parysatis, he said: 'Stay back until we've dealt with them.' And with that, Massoud plunged from the storeroom, his men fanning out at his back. Parysatis slipped out among them and took shelter in the colonnade ringing the courtyard.

The Circassians made no pretence at silence. Mail jazerants and hauberks clashed; with each step boots scraped and harness clattered, and, overlaying it all, the sinister rasp of swords sweeping from their sheaths. The Jandariyah heard it and wheeled about, cursing as they bared their own blades.

Massoud strode to the fore, his sabre levelled at the Syrians. 'If you be loyal to the Caliph,' he roared, 'then lay down your weapons and stand aside!'

The officer of the Jandariyah, his gold-chased helmet twinkling in the lamplight, displayed preternatural calm as he inclined his head, making a show of deferring to the vizier's eunuch. Parysatis stood on the tips of her toes, her view partially blocked by a forest of mailed shoulders and turban-wrapped heads. She saw as best she could the chamberlain backing away, milk-faced, his eyes bulging at the sight of so many green-girdled Circassians, each one burning with a desperate desire to regain the Caliph's favour. He came up against the ornate doors of the old hammam; then, yelping like a whipped dog, the eunuch hurriedly stumbled through and slammed them shut in his wake.

The Syrian officer shook his head; steel rasped as he drew his sword and turned back to face Massoud. 'Brother, we are loyal to Turanshah. We stand down by his order, and by his order alone.'

'A pity, then, to throw your lives away over nothing.'

The Jandariyah shrugged. 'It's all one in the eyes of Allah.'

'I've heard no truer words spoken. Your master will know you died well.' The twenty set to follow Massoud into the disused bath massed at his back; the others looked poised to trample the Syrians under heel, swords glittering and ready. Massoud saluted the Jandariyah officer as an equal. 'Peace be upon you.'

'And upon you be peace.' The Syrian drew a knife with his free hand; resigned to their fates, his dozen fighters set their spears and kissed the rims of their shields, the iron etched with sayings of the Prophet.

Icy worms crawled down Parysatis' spine. The young woman edged around the column, her eyes never leaving the back of Massoud's head as she steeled herself to make for the doors as soon as the first blow fell. *And what would she do about the eunuch?* Her gaze dropped to the knife clutched in her fists. She could do this. She *had* to do this. The Caliph—

A piercing shriek from inside the old hammam sent Parysatis' heart leaping into her throat. Nor was she alone. That terrible disembodied cry caught Circassian and Syrian alike off guard; veteran soldiers glanced about, uneasy now, their bloody resolve scuttled by a sudden burst of superstitious dread. What was the eerie screech, a harbinger of victory or an omen of doom? Massoud and his Syrian nemesis eyed one another over bared blades, unwilling to look away in case this was but the other's ruse. But both men wheeled and cursed in unison as something heavy crunched against the ancient cedar doors, shattering hinges and panels and dislodging inlaid gold and silver arabesques.

'Allah!'

Impact flung the doors wide; from her vantage, Parysatis caught a brief flash of gold, a swirl of torn silk amid the dust and splintered wood. She stared in disbelief as the vizier's chamberlain cartwheeled through the air and landed in a heap, his head twisted at an impossible angle.

Silence gripped the courtyard as a man stalked through the wreck of the hammam doors, a long, straight blade in his fist. Clad in a blood-spattered grey kaftan, this tall newcomer paused at the threshold and raked the soldiers of both factions with a glare that promised death to those who crossed him. A short beard did nothing to hide the sinister scar running from his left eye to his jaw. With a slow nod, the man stepped aside and allowed another to pass, a pale figure, dark of hair and dressed in stained white linen.

Parysatis' breath caught in her throat; around the courtyard, others cried out in recognition.

Caliph Rashid al-Hasan had come.

Parysatis could not pry her eyes off the Prince of the Faithful as he looked from soldier to soldier, from man to man. Few met his gaze. 'What goes on here?' he said. 'Why do you make ready to fight? Are these men not your brother Moslems, your allies? Why this base animosity when we are all threatened by foreign armies? What goes?'

'They are traitors, O Caliph!' Massoud said suddenly. Parysatis heard the clatter of steel as the Circassian amir fell to his knees. 'Followers of that dog, Jalal!'

'Liar!' The officer of the Jandariyah stepped forward and knelt, as well. 'We serve our captain, Turanshah, who serves you, my lord. We take our orders from him, not from the vizier.'

Parysatis saw the Caliph arch an eyebrow at his silent companion; the taller man merely shrugged. Rashid returned his attention to the Syrian. 'And what are your orders?'

'To . . To apprehend any who come through those doors.'

'Will you apprehend me, then? I came through those doors. Will you take me prisoner in my own palace?' The officer fidgeted, looking uncomfortable. He made to answer, but the Caliph stopped him with a raised hand. 'No. You need not dissemble. Whether you were privy to it or not, this eunuch brought you here to kill me at the behest of my wayward vizier.' Rashid raised his voice so the Circassians might hear. 'But I hold you men blameless! You, too, are victims of Jalal's unchecked ambitions!' A rustle of disbelief went through the soldiers.

The officer prostrated himself. 'My lord, I—'

'No,' the Caliph said. 'Do not speak yet, for I would ask a boon of you.'

'Anything, my lord!'

'Return to your captain and tell him what I have said. Tell him I hold him blameless, and that I extend my hand in pardon to the Jandariyah. Tell him it would grieve me beyond words to see you and your brothers annihilated by my loyal Mamelukes, especially since in days to come Cairo will have grave need of men such as you. He has only to leave the vizier's side. Tell Turanshah this. Leave no word of it out.'

'I hearken and obey, O Caliph.'

Rashid nodded. 'Then go, and may Allah grant your captain wisdom.'

The officer of the Jandariyah salaamed; as one, he and his men backed out of the Caliph's presence, wary eyes cast on the Circassians in case this proved merely an elaborate ruse. However, no one raised a hand against them as they hurried from the court-yard, their retreat through the heart of the harem provoking fresh cries of terror from the women and barks of outrage from their eunuch custodians.

Once the Jandariyah were out of sight, the Prince of the Faithful turned his attention to the waiting soldiers and their kneeling amir.

'How are you called, my friend?'

'Massoud, O Glorious One. Amir of the Circassian regiment of the White Slaves of the River.'

'A bit less than glorious now, I think.' Rashid smiled, plucking at his dust-and-sweat-stained robes. 'Rise, Massoud. Tell me, how did you come to be here?'

Coming smoothly to his feet, the amir sheathed his sabre and maintained a respectful distance from the Prince of the Faithful, eyes downcast. Still, despite his submissive stance, Parysatis could see satisfaction flicker across Massoud's visage. It bolstered his esteem to have his name spoken by a blood descendant of Fatimah, favoured daughter of the Prophet. 'We heard you were in peril, Exalted One.'

The Caliph grunted in surprise. 'Did you?' The younger man glanced at his silent companion, a knowing look passing between them. 'From whom? Was it a woman of my harem?'

Massoud turned slightly, lines of confusion etched into his brow; his eyes raked the colonnade until they came to where Parysatis stood, half in the shadow of a fluted marble column. Knowledge of what surely must come next left a cold knot in her belly and set her limbs to trembling. 'Indeed, my lord,' she heard the Circassian amir say, gesturing in her direction, 'Lady Parysatis came and fetched us to your side.'

Parysatis quailed as every eye in the courtyard fixed upon her, Rashid al-Hasan's among them. The Caliph's visage reflected an odd sense of curiosity. He nodded and motioned for her to come forward.

'Lady Parysatis?'

Reluctantly, the Persian woman left the comparative shelter of the colonnade. The soldiers split their ranks to let her through. She kept her eyes averted, suddenly conscious of her lack of a proper veil. How inappropriate she must seem: a Caliph's concubine flouncing about in a young man's trousers and consorting with slave-soldiers like some two-copper whore in the shadow of the Bab al-Askar. Her cheeks prickled with colour at the idea of the Caliph seeing her in such a sorry state.

Reaching Massoud's side, she made to prostrate herself, to show her obeisance to the Prince of the Faithful as custom demanded. But, as she started to kneel, Rashid al-Hasan arrested her movement by reaching out and taking her hand. She gasped at the unexpected contact.

'Wait,' the Caliph said. 'I know you. You're the daughter of Ishaq ibn Khusraw – may Allah's mercy rest upon his soul – who was the staunchest of my father's Persian allies.'

Parysatis raised her eyes in wonder, meeting his gaze for an instant before remembering her place. She bowed her head. 'I . . . I am, Exalted One. His daughter and only child.'

'And Massoud and his men are here because of you?'

She nodded.

'As are the Turks, I'll warrant,' the mysterious man at the Caliph's side said, his cold eyes narrowed to slits. A flick of his chin encompassed the palace. 'All of this is your doing?'

'A-After a fashion, perhaps.' Parysatis felt the hot blush of her cheeks treble. 'Last n-night I . . . I overheard the vizier plotting against your life, Exalted One. He planned to seize power and ally himself with the Nazarenes against Damascus. I . . . I did not know what else to do, so I slipped into your chambers and tried to warn you. Mustapha, the vizier's eunuch, had already drugged your wine and prepared a second draught laced with poison, one you were to drink upon waking. I could not rouse you, so instead I emptied the draught and replaced it with water.'

'That was you?'

'Yes, Exalted One. Then, this morning, I confided everything to Harun al-Gid, who agreed to warn you. I showed him the secret way into your chambers.' Parysatis squeezed her eyes shut as tears welled unbidden. 'I . . . I saw . . . I was in t-the passage when . . .'

The Caliph stiffened. 'You saw al-Gid murdered?'

'And I could do nothing,' she sobbed. 'I would have given in to despair had my handmaiden not saved me. She knew Massoud's name as a man who was loyal to you, Exalted One, and who might be in a position to help. So, this evening we used the hidden passages to escape the harem and brought the amir news of your plight. Please forgive me, Exalted One! I did not know where else to turn . . .'

Smiling, Rashid al-Hasan clasped her hand in both of his. 'There is nothing to forgive, dear Parysatis. Indeed, that you saved my life means I am in your debt. If we survive this night, ask anything of me and if it is within my power it shall be yours.'

She returned his smile, nodding through a fresh round of tears. The sensation of a great weight being lifted from her shoulders left Parysatis deliciously exhausted. She relished the moment, revelling in the touch of the Caliph's hand on hers, in the play of distant torchlight in his smoky eyes, until the grim voice of Rashid's companion broke the silence.

'Time grows thin, my lord.'

Rashid al-Hasan blinked like a man waking from pleasant slumber, his smile fading as he gathered himself up. He released Parysatis' hand. 'You are right, Assad. We've tarried too long.' He turned slightly, his face growing sombre. 'Who leads the Turks, good Massoud?'

'My brother amir, Exalted One. Gokbori.'

'We must find him and exhort him to curb his followers' murderous zeal. The Jandariyah will accept no leniency from me if they feel their backs are to the wall.'

Massoud nodded, looking askance at his Circassians. 'It will be safer if I send a few of my men to seek Gokbori out and fetch him here to you, my lord.'

'My friend, the time to be safe has long passed. Now is the time for action.'

'He's right,' said the man the Caliph called Assad. 'Let him bring this Gokbori to you.'

Anger flared in Rashid al-Hasan's eyes. 'By God, man, I will not cower in the women's quarters while others risk their lives for me! That's how we arrived at this juncture in the first place. I must save myself, if it be Allah's will.'

Assad shook his head. 'My lord—'

'No! We're wasting precious time!'

Parysatis took a hesitant step forward. In a quiet voice, she said: 'I . . . I could guide you to him along the hidden ways, Exalted One. They riddle the palace walls, and though the path might take you as near to your enemies as I am to you, none will ever see you.'

Rashid's anger evaporated. 'An excellent idea! What say you, my counsellors?'

Massoud raised an eyebrow at the scarred and dour stranger, Assad, who gave the barest hint of a shrug in return.

'It's settled, then. We are in your care, lady. Show us these secret paths, and quickly.'

Parysatis' heart soared as the Prince of the Faithful clasped her hand again and motioned for her to lead the way.

14

Yasmina cleaved to the shadows like a creature born of Night. She made barely a sound as she trailed Musa and the leper, Djuha, down refuse-strewn alleys that reeked of despair and across dim courts hedged in by walls of age-gnawed mudbrick, each step taking them deeper into the labyrinthine heart of the Foreign Quarter. With practised care, Djuha led them around the places where men gathered for their evening's sport, the wine shops and pleasure houses with their guttering cressets and copper censers and drunken laughter. Places where one with his affliction would not be welcome.

Yet Allah must have been smiling upon Yasmina, for at every turn – when habit caused Musa to glance behind them for any sign of pursuit – chance obstructions hid her from the beggar's glowering eye. She kept just within earshot and just out of sight.

'How much further?' Yasmina heard the one-eyed beggar snap. They paused near the juncture of two narrow streets; beneath veneers of flaking plaster, the ancient buildings on either hand still bore blackened scars of a long-forgotten conflagration, an inferno that likely gutted the whole neighbourhood. Not a stone's throw away, the Egyptian girl crouched in the lee of a jutting façade, in a well of gloom cast by crude mashrafiyyas hanging precariously over her head. From these, faint voices chattered in a tongue Yasmina found incomprehensible while strains of alien music drifted on the still air. 'How much further, damn you?'

The rotting pander, who purred a constant litany of endearments to the filthy urchin serving as his crutch, was slow to answer. 'Not far now.' Even at a distance the sight of Djuha fawning over the boy, stroking his hair and caressing his cheek, sent waves of disgust shuddering through Yasmina; it must have been worse for Musa, who cursed under his breath as each obscene delay forced his hand closer to the hilt of his knife.

'So you've said before! Merciful Allah, if this is your idea of a jest . . .'

'Don't be a fool, beggar,' she heard Djuha wheeze. 'We might have taken a more direct approach, but all that would accomplish is to alert your mistress's killer that we are watching. No, we must instead come upon him crab-wise, to a spot where we might survey his lair from relative safety – which is, I presume, what you want.'

'You're not even certain it truly is her killer.'

'The man I saw matched his description down to the slightest detail. Surely that must account for something?'

'Perhaps,' the beggar growled, his voice fading as they continued on down the street. Quietly, Yasmina emerged from her hiding place and followed. 'When did you see this man?'

'I have glimpsed him on occasion over many months, coming and going from his lair. I saw him last this evening, after sunset, returning from some errand. He had six other men with him, and between them they looked to be carrying – Allah smite me if I lie! – they looked to be carrying corpses.'

'Corpses?'

'Aye. Three of them. They—'

Musa had stopped abruptly. The leper paused as well, his head cocked to one side. 'What goes, beggar?'

Yasmina froze, certain that Musa had got wind of her. Perhaps he had heard something, or simply felt the intensity of her gaze. Regardless, she steeled herself, her mind already spooling convenient lies for questions he had yet to ask. But, rather than whirl about and confront her, the one-eyed beggar simply stood in the middle of the street, nodding from side to side and tugging his beard as though trying to work something out on his own. Yasmina took advantage of this pause, quickly sidestepping into the shelter of an open doorway.

'Three, you say? Allah! This cannot be coincidence!' Musa's hand shot out, iron fingers digging into the leper's arm without regard to his affliction. Djuha hissed and tried to pull free, but the one-eyed beggar dragged him closer. 'Forget stealth, man! Get me to this lair, and swiftly!'

Djuha tore his arm from Musa's grasp and staggered against the cowering urchin. 'Do not touch me!' The leper glared at Musa. Slowly, he regained his balance, his composure, and gestured for the beggar to follow. 'Come, then. It is not far.'

Nor was it. The winding street emptied into a ragged square, a hollow where moonlight picked out sparse detail in a faint wash of silver: the tall weeds and shattered chunks of masonry; the drifts of refuse like sand dunes piled against the foundations of a pair of ramshackle tenements. These jutted from the earth, misshapen fingers of crumbling brick and age-blackened timber, with crude keel arches and windows hacked into the walls almost as an after-thought. Both looked abandoned to Yasmina. Abandoned and ominous.

Djuha slunk to the right-hand side of the street and dared go no further. 'This place is called the Maydan al-Iskander, after an old Greek king. Do you see it?' he hissed, pointing. 'There, between those two buildings . . .'

Yasmina sidled closer, cognizant of her every footfall, and tried to follow the leper's gesture. A few hundred yards to the east – beyond the tangled streets – lay Cairo's walls and the crenellated towers of the Bab al-Rum, the Foreign Gate. Its relative proximity afforded her little in the way of solace.

Musa leaned out. 'I don't . . . Wait! What is that?'

From her vantage Yasmina saw it too, though just barely: a long black cleft in the ground between the two tenements, still showing raw earth and fresh growths of weeds around its edges.

'A cellar entrance, perhaps,' Djuha said.

'That's where they took the bodies?'

'It is, and that's where I have seen the one you seek – coming and going into the earth like a djinni.'

Musa raised a hand as though to grab on to the leper, then thought better of it. 'I would ask a favour, Djuha. Return to Abu'l-Qasim's caravanserai by the quickest road possible. Tell him what we – what you – found here! By Allah! Bid him gather his Berbers and come with all haste!'

Cloth rustled. Djuha shook his diseased head. 'No, no. I have done all I set out to do, beggar. Now I must see to my own business as you must see to yours.'

'God damn you, man! Forget your cursed business! Abu'l-Qasim will make this worth your while!'

Yasmina, though, had heard enough. Even before Djuha could answer, she left the relative shelter of the open doorway and glided in the direction of the two men, her movements as silent and deadly as an emir of al-Hashishiyya. She was within arm's reach before either man noticed her.

'Leper,' she said, in a voice harder than stone. Both men whirled; the urchin squeaked, clutching at Djuha's legs. Musa had his knife half drawn before he recognized the slender figure.

'Yasmina? What the devil . . . ?'

She ignored him. 'You, leper. This man you say you saw so often – what manner of weapon did he carry?'

'What goes?' Djuha glared at the one-eyed beggar, who shrugged and eased his blade back into its sheath. 'Who is she?'

'One of Mistress Zaynab's companions.'

Yasmina stopped in front of the Bedouin, her head barely reaching the level of his sternum. 'Answer me, damn you!'

Djuha frowned. 'He . . . He sported a knife – long and straight with a Frankish hilt. Why do you ask?'

Yasmina nodded. 'Leave us,' she said to the leper. Turning to Musa she said, 'He is the man we seek.'

Musa glanced at the leper, indicating with a sharp jerk of his chin that he should take the urchin and go. Djuha, his eyes burning slits of suspicion, draped an arm around his boy and did as he was told.

'You were right to trust him,' Yasmina said, returning her

attention to the square that lay before them. 'Wait here. I'm going in to flush our quarry out.'

'I'll decide what we will and won't do, girl! You shouldn't even be abroad this time of night. It's—'

Yasmina turned to face the beggar. 'We failed her, Musa. You and I. Her father. We let him take her from us. It's time to settle accounts.'

'Don't be a fool, girl.' Musa exhaled. His voice was heavy, pained; the voice of a man forced to confront a harsh reality. 'We didn't fail her. She fell victim to her own ridiculous pride. Issuing a counter-challenge? She should have known her enemies would try and use that against her! No, girl. By not thinking her actions through properly – as her father damn well taught her – Zaynab failed us, not the other way around. We can talk about this later. You wait here and keep an eye out. I'm going back to fetch Abu'l Qasim—'

Yasmina cracked the back of her slim hand across the beggar's jaw. 'Hold your tongue!'

The blow filled Musa's vision with dancing motes of light. Anger suffused his pox-scarred visage as he shook his head to clear it and wiped at the trickle of blood starting from his split lip. 'Damn you!' Musa snatched her up by the scruff of the neck. 'You're just as foolish as she was! I don't know what will come to pass, if Abu'l-Qasim will send his Berbers to deal with the killer or if he will come himself, but I do know this: you're going back to the palace where you damn well belong! This is a matter for men, not a scrap of a girl like you!' Musa shook her for emphasis.

Yasmina's eyes were aglow with the lambent flames of madness, her lips curled in a rictus of hate as she tore free of the beggar's grasp. The speed of her movement caught Musa wholly off guard. Before he could so much as raise a hand in his own defence, Yasmina's fingers closed on the knife at his waist. The blade sang free, flashed in the gloom, and then sank hilt-deep into Musa's abdomen.

The one-eyed beggar howled. He stumbled back, hands clawing

at Yasmina's arm as she sawed the blade upwards. Blood spurted over her fingers; it soaked the fabric of her gown as she wrenched the knife free.

Musa staggered and fell, curling his body around the gaping wound in his belly. Hands slick with blood clawed furrows in the hard-packed filth of the street. He glared up at her, tears streaming from his good eye, and tried to curse, to scream, to pray, but waves of white-hot agony allowed for a single gasping plea: 'W-Why . . . ?'

'Why?' Yasmina hissed. The youthful Egyptian Zaynab had saved from a life of misery was no more; in her place stood a grim and haunted figure, unrecognizable under a patina of gore. Musa flinched as she knelt by his side. 'Why? Do you see the blood on your hands, Musa – on my hands? It's not yours or mine . . . it is Zaynab's! You called me a fool for thinking we'd failed her, but I know whereof I speak. *We let her die!* And as she suffered, so must we . . . and so must he!' She jerked her chin towards the cleft in the square. 'It is Allah's will.'

'You . . . You s-stupid little bitch!' Musa gasped. 'He'll k-kill you!'

'Not before I kill him. It is Allah's will.' And with that, Yasmina rose and stepped over the beggar's writhing form. She stalked towards the cleft between the tenements. A ribbon of blood drooled from the knife clenched in her fist.

She was a killer. Yasmina wanted that pale-eyed Frank to remember his words. *She* was a killer . . .

15

All but invisible in the stygian murk cloaking the foot of the nearest tenement, the black-clad Syrian tasked with guarding the stairs heard a bellow of agony erupt from one of the nearby alleys. Such cries were commonplace amid the dregs of the Foreign Quarter, where a knife in the back remained the preferred method of settling disputes. Still, the Syrian glanced up out of curiosity and saw a young Egyptian woman step from the alley-mouth and enter the moon-lit square.

His hot stare missed nothing, in particular the moist stain moulding the fabric of her gown to the swell of her breasts. He drank in her midnight hair, her narrow waist, her long brown legs; the knife clutched in her right hand he dismissed as a curious affectation, nothing more. Fresh blood spiced the night air.

Closer she came, on an unerring path for the head of the stairs. The Syrian's lips peeled back in a predatory smile; he dropped his hand to his crotch, feeling the too-familiar stirrings of lust. She—

Iron fingers dug into the Syrian's shoulder; he winced, pain and apprehension dispelling whatever salacious thoughts he entertained. Only one man could move with such utter stealth, unseen and unheard even by a soldier of al-Hashishiyya. The sentry swallowed hard; he glanced to his right and quickly averted his eyes as he received the full measure of the Heretic's eerie gaze.

'She's mine,' Badr al-Mulahid hissed.

16

Yasmina reached the cleft and peered over its edge. Moonlight lent a pale lustre to the flight of rough-hewn steps leading down into the earth. Apprehension constricted the muscles of her chest. *What if the stairs go nowhere? What if that wretched Djuha was lying all along? What if . . .*

But her fears evaporated when a whisper of air – faint and hot – caused fabric to rustle at the bottom of the cleft. For an instant, an oily yellow glow limned the ragged outline of a doorway hacked into the wall. The air stilled again; a curtain of heavy cloth settled back into place to await the next phantom exhalation.

Yasmina's lips curled in a predatory sneer. She tightened her grip on the blood-stained knife as she hurried down the stairs, left arm thrust out to the side for support. Her fingers brushed deep furrows scored into the sandstone wall, crumbling and uneven, abraded by time and the elements. Curiosity drew her gaze to these carvings. After a moment's study she apprehended a monstrous figure in the moonlight: a falcon-headed devil hewn of stone and shadow. It emerged from the rock with axe upraised, in defiance of the Prophet's admonition against graven images. Yasmina flinched away from it. Here was a thing of Old Egypt, a relic of the Time of Ignorance; she had seen its like before, smaller and more careworn, hacked deep into the ancient columns the Gazelle scavenged for the courtyard of her home. Abu'l-Saqr, she had called it, Father of the Falcon. Shivering, the young woman averted her eyes and made her way down to the curtain-hung fissure.

Another breath of air sent fingers of light escaping into the cleft, and with it the mingled smells of dust and old resins, natron and cerecloth, hashish and dried blood. The soles of Yasmina's bare feet rasped on stone as she shifted her weight. In one hand she clutched her knife, blade angled up and ready to strike; in the other she gripped the edge of the heavy curtain.

The young woman paused. She exhaled, her every nerve tingling. Death lay beyond the curtain. Death and Vengeance: the pair entwined like desperate lovers awaiting the release only consummation could bring. Yasmina's slim brown fingers grew white-knuckle-tight around the haft of Musa's knife. Death and Vengeance waited for her. *It is Allah's will. Strike quickly. Don't hesitate.* Anything less would give the pale-eyed Heretic a chance to gain the upper hand. *To hesitate is to fail.*

To hesitate is to fail. This awareness steeled her to action. Yasmina ripped the curtain aside . . .

. . . and swore under her breath as she beheld, not the covey of killers she had expected, but rather a deserted anteroom, its pitted sandstone walls lit by a pair of small clay lamps. Cobwebs fluttered in the corners; the stones underfoot were dusty and irregular, cracked with age and marred by dark splotches of what may have been dried blood. Yasmina took a hesitant step over the threshold, her eyes searching from side to side. A dozen paces ahead a yawning doorway led deeper into the silent edifice.

No, she realized, her head cocked to the left, *not silent*. Sound reached her, faint yet unmistakable: a singsong voice chanting in a tongue she could not understand, accompanied by the sharp pulse of a drum – a rhythmic throb that sent chills down her spine. It reminded Yasmina of the beating of her own heart.

The Egyptian crossed the anteroom on cat's feet, pausing in the open doorway beneath a lintel carved with the likeness of a winged dung beetle. Of the chamber beyond, Yasmina could make out precious few details. A forest of thick columns stretched off into darkness, their immense stone trunks covered in a veneer of symbols; vertical registers of deeply etched glyphs surrounded images of men in tall headdresses and falcon-headed devils. The otherworldly figures flickered and danced in the feeble lamplight.

How the Heretic and his men could live underground like this, amid the djinn and the ghûls, was a mystery to Yasmina – and not a mystery she cared to plumb. It was unnatural, but Allah had set this task before her and she gave thanks for the gift of opportunity. Lips set in a grim slash, the young Egyptian padded through the doorway and bore left, creeping between columns, skirting the rare pools of light as she let the murmur of the drum guide her.

For an instant Yasmina's eyes flickered to the ceiling. Despite the oppressive gloom, she could yet see traces of pigment glittering on stone architraves and roofing slabs, swirling constellations of silver and copper oxide blending to form a picture of the ancient firmament, the heavens frozen in time. The girl's pace faltered. She was accustomed to the spectacle of extravagance, to the jewelled gardens and gilded arcades of the Fatimid palace, but nothing in the short span of Yasmina's years had prepared her for the awesome antiquity of this place. Its witchery was breathtaking, its mystique infectious. How many such crypts – how many statues and colossi, obelisks and columns – lay beneath the streets of Cairo, buried and forgotten? Who had built them and for what purpose? What—

The eerie harmony of voice and drum reached a shuddering climax, which gave way to heavy, pregnant silence. Its ominous weight smothered the questions smouldering in the forefront of Yasmina's mind. Mouthing a litany of curses, she shook off her lethargy and resumed her path through the stone forest, her attention fixed firmly on the task at hand.

At the end of the great hall an elaborate post-and-lintel doorway opened on a smaller chamber, one lit by a blood-red glow that streamed out around the edges of another curtained entry. By this feral light Yasmina observed deep alcoves carved into the walls, each one sheltering a statue in a flowing headdress, arms rigid at its sides, a stone serpent perched upon its brow and an angular beard jutting from its chin. Cobwebs hung from broad shoulders like ghostly mantles. Whether images of gods or men Yasmina could not say, only that their flawless features were as cold and aloof as those of the Caliph himself.

The girl crept nearer to the curtained doorway, her eyes sweeping from side to side. She wrinkled her nose at the stench in the air. The miasma of blood, offal, salt, and incense reminded her of the slaughterhouses south of the Zuwayla Gate. *Fitting*, she thought, *a fitting place to confront my mistress's killer.*

The knife in Yasmina's fist lent her a measure of bravado matched only by her thirst for vengeance. She bared her teeth, lips peeling back in a vicious smile.

I will see that pale-eyed bastard dead!

Closer, she came; on the balls of her feet now.

I will cut his black heart out and offer it up to the gods of this forbidden place!

Edging to the right, twisting her torso, she reached with her left hand for the rough hide curtain.

I will . . .

A low moan turned her marrow to ice. It came from the

chamber beyond, a bestial sound, like the death-rattle of an animal trapped on a huntsman's spear. Yasmina froze; the moan resolved into a single word, distant and sepulchral as though the very act of articulation had sapped the speaker of his will: 'W-Why . . . ?'

Another voice answered, one that did not belong to the Heretic. 'I have need of answers. Do you remember your name?'

Yasmina heard nothing for a moment, then a racking croak that barely resembled human speech: 'I . . . I was Gamal. Why have you called me forth? Release me . . .'

'In due time. What happened to you?'

'I . . . I . . .'

'What happened to you, Gamal?' the questioner pressed. 'Do you remember?'

'I . . . I was slain!' Something elicited such a groan of agony from the man called Gamal that even Yasmina felt a momentary twinge of compassion. He was on the verge of death, surely; delirious, his words made little sense. 'The pain . . . you cannot begin to fathom the pain of its touch! It hungers! Even n-now, I feel it . . . I feel its hatred!'

The questioner's voice quivered with excitement. '*It?* What is *it*? Do you mean his knife? Is the Emir's knife a thing of power?'

Gamal hissed. 'Old, it is . . . forged of strife and agony . . . quenched in blood! Its hate . . .'

'Does it have a name, Gamal?'

'A . . . name . . . ?'

'The blade! Has the blade a name?' The questioner's voice grew sharp. 'Speak, Gamal! I command you!'

'No! Do not . . . Do not make me . . . !'

'Speak! What is its name?'

Yasmina heard a piteous gurgling that trailed off into muffled pleas for succour, as though the very name the questioner sought caused Gamal unbearable anguish. While she did not pretend to understand what was going on, the exchange nevertheless stoked Yasmina's curiosity. She shifted her knife to her left hand, leaned the right side of her body against the door jamb, and with two fingers gingerly nudged the curtain aside until she could peer within.

She beheld a room bathed in the ruddy glow of bronze lamps, its walls carved in the same peculiar style as the columns of the great hall with glyphs and animal-headed djinn. To one side, on a low table jumbled with papyrus scrolls and scribe's implements, coils of yellowish smoke rose from a bronze chafing dish to drift in the unnaturally chill air. A man knelt at the centre of the room, a hide drum at his side. He was turbaned and clad in rich black brocade with a face as sharp as a hawk's and a beard peppered with grey. Terrible wrath blazed in his eyes as he stared hard at a supine figure before him.

'Its name, Gamal!'

The figure stretched out upon the ground writhed, or seemed to. In truth, Yasmina had trouble discerning even the slightest detail about him, save that to look at him made her skin crawl. *Something* obscured his features from view; something gauzy and vaporous – a milky-white mist that shifted and stretched, opaque tendrils straining upwards like tongues of flame only to peel away and vanish amid a haze of incense. Surely this was but a trick of the light . . . ?

'Give me its name!'

Whatever else was afoot, the wet, mewling voice that came from the prostrate figure was no illusion; its desperation raised goose-flesh on Yasmina's skin. 'The b-blade . . . it called itself . . . Matraqat al-Kafer! The Hammer of the Infidel!'

Yasmina saw the black-clad man's eyes narrow. He rocked back as though Gamal's words had dealt him a physical blow. 'The Hammer? May the gods bear witness: I will cast you down into a lake of fire if you think to lie to me! I ask you once more—'

Gamal wailed: 'The . . . The Hammer it was, *ya sidi*! Matraqat al-Kafer! M-My soul upon it!'

The questioner said nothing for a long moment, his brow furrowed as though lost in thought. Finally, he nodded to himself. 'You have served me well, Gamal. I release you.' He made a complex gesture in the smoky air above Gamal's head. 'Begone! I command thee!' No sooner had he spoken those words than the mist cloaking Gamal's form began to break down, to lose its cohesiveness. Curling ribbons of vapour drifted away. Some of it evaporated; the rest sank to the floor, soaking into the bare stone like water into a sponge.

The mist's dissipation gave the Egyptian her first clear look at the recumbent figure. Yasmina recoiled from the sight of it, blood draining from her dark features as she bit back a horrified scream. The figure, the man called Gamal, the man who had pleaded and begged with the black-clad questioner but a moment ago, was already a corpse, naked and swollen, its skin purple with putrefaction . . .

She stumbled back from the curtain. Her skin crawled; she tasted the sting of bile on her tongue. *How could it be? What deviltry—?*

And in that instant, terror stripped away every last vestige of her resolve, leaving a glacial abscess in the pit of her stomach. The room spun. Fear assaulted her from all sides – fear of the inhuman statues and the bestial carvings, fear of the cloying darkness and the memory of the caravanserai. Tendrils of dread slithered up her spine and threatened to choke off her air. The knife in her hand forgotten, Yasmina turned to run even as a familiar voice shattered the grim and terrible silence.

'Why do you flee, girl? I thought you were a killer.'

She ground to a halt. The Heretic stood in the open doorway, his body blocking her path to the hall of columns. Pale eyes gleamed in the ruddy half-light; a cruel smile played upon his thin lips as he raised both hands, fingers splayed to show he carried no weapon. He took a step closer.

'Have you come to seek instruction from your betters?'

The Heretic's sudden appearance did not add to Yasmina's fear; indeed, the sight of him served to anchor her, to remind her of why she was here, to silence the voices yammering in her skull. His derisive tone sparked her anger, causing it to flare anew. Yasmina's lips curled into a perfect sneer of contempt as she shifted her knife from her left hand to her right. 'I've come for you. Allah desires your death. I am to be the instrument of—'

'If Allah wishes me dead, let Allah Himself come and see the deed done,' the Heretic snapped. 'And if revenge is what brings you here, then you are more of a fool than I imagined!'

'So says the dead man!' Yasmina spat.

The Heretic's smile widened. 'Am I a dead man? By your own hand, I expect. And for what? What wrong have I done to you to earn your wrath, girl? Where have I transgressed?'

'Dog!' Though Yasmina knew better than to rise to his baiting, she could not keep her choler in check. Her body grew taut; the tendons in her neck stood out like steel cords as rage suffused her cheeks. 'Zaynab's murder!'

'I did not murder your precious Gazelle.'

'Liar!'

'Believe what you will.' The Heretic shrugged. 'But I promise you this: I did not *murder* her. The hard truth is the Gazelle died years ago. She died when she pledged herself to the pretender of Alamut and joined his degraded cult. Her soul departed that night, no doubt bound for the fires of eternal damnation. Indeed, if I am guilty of anything it is of putting an end to the shame of her soulless existence. You should thank me—'

But it was not gratitude that sent Yasmina lunging for the Heretic's throat. Few men could have duplicated the feral grace of her attack, raw and driven by wrath; fewer still could have avoided it. Yet, in that instant of vengeful consummation, when her enemy's riven corpse should have flopped to the ground, Yasmina's knife sliced nothing but empty air.

Few men, it seemed, were as the Heretic.

The Assassin sidestepped the blow; with a casual flick of his hand, he sent Yasmina tumbling against the glyph-etched door post. She recovered quickly and glared over her shoulder at the Heretic, oblivious to the blood oozing from the corner of her mouth where his knuckles had raked her in passing.

'You fight like an urchin,' he said. 'Did the Gazelle teach you this as well?'

Yasmina spat and pushed away from the door jamb, using it as added leverage as she swept her blade out and up in a backhand blow.

This time, the Heretic did not deign to move.

A gasp burst from Yasmina's lips as he caught the blow, his fingers clamping like a vice around her right wrist. The Heretic gave the limb a savage twist, turning her gasp into a hiss of pain as bones spiralled near to breaking. Yasmina's fingers loosened of their own volition and her knife clattered to the floor. The Heretic's other hand found her throat.

The girl's eyes widened; she clawed at his forearm, plucking ineffectually at the corded muscle and sinew. The pale-eyed killer's smile faded as he tightened his grip on her neck. The room spun. Yasmina fought to take a breath, twisting, writhing as congested blood pounded in her ears.

With little effort, the Heretic lifted her clear of the floor, pulling her closer until their faces all but touched. His tongue clicked against his teeth. 'As I thought – a fool!' And with that, Badr al-Mulahid twisted and flung Yasmina from him as a child would fling a rag doll. Bursts of light flared before her eyes; pain rippled down her spine as she struck a statue hard enough to rock it back on its pedestal. The girl crumpled into a heap at its feet, dazed and gagging on the dusty air.

Her senses returned little by little, hearing first; dimly, she discerned the voice of the black-robed questioner. 'What is this, Badr? What goes?'

'My lord,' the Heretic replied, 'I've caught a night-skulker. A girl who would play at being a killer.'

Yasmina pried her eyes open and looked around, coughing, her vision blurred. She could see the Heretic had his back to her; in the curtained doorway was the grim figure of the questioner – *of the sorcerer*, she reminded herself – his hypnotic gaze fixed upon her with withering intensity. She glanced away, praying he did not notice . . .

. . . and saw a glimmer of steel just out of arm's reach. Her knife. Though beaten and bruised, defiance rose up through a veil of pain. Defiance and hope. She might still have her revenge. Her muscles flexed and tightened.

'Is she one of Alamut's?'

'Not this one,' the Heretic said. 'Her allegiance is to the Gazelle. She seeks recompense . . . or a martyr's death.'

The sorcerer's voice held a note of interest. 'Does she? Bring her to me.'

But Yasmina was in motion before the Heretic could turn and do his master's bidding. She scuttled forward, reaching for the leather-wrapped hilt of her knife, for its strength and surety. Her fingers brushed the pommel even as the Assassin whirled and planted the toe of his boot in her belly. The blow sent her sprawling; she wheezed and huffed, struggling once more to draw a breath. Eyes brimming with hate, Yasmina glared at the Heretic as he kicked the blade away – and with it went her final chance at vengeance.

'On your feet, little fool!' He snatched her up by her hair and dragged her, bloodied and dishevelled, to kneel before the black-clad sorcerer. 'Shall I send her the way of her mistress?'

'Not yet. Look at me, child,' the sorcerer said. With difficulty, Yasmina raised her eyes to meet his; shadowed beneath a craggy brow, black irises flecked with gold caught her gaze and held it with unseen shackles. She could not look away. It was as if she stared into an abyss, into the cold fires of Hell. 'Do you believe,' he said, 'that the eyes can provide a measure of a person's soul?'

Slowly, Yasmina nodded.

'Your eyes betray you. You have done murder this day. A man—'

'A eunuch,' the girl blurted out, eyes widening in surprise over her outburst.

'Ah, a eunuch. He stood in your way, did he not? An obstacle on the path to your goal?'

Again, she nodded.

'And you did what you deemed necessary. You murdered him in cold blood. Why, then, would you begrudge me the same? On my order, Badr removed an obstacle standing in the path to my goal. He did as you did. You and he are the same, child.'

'No!'

'Why not?'

'I . . . I . . .' Yasmina's jaw clenched and unclenched; tears welled up in the corners of her unblinking eyes to run in rivulets down her flushed cheeks. 'I . . . I'm not . . . I'm not like *him*!'

'So you say. And yet, have you not trespassed into my domain in search of prey, interfering with that which is beyond your ken for the sake of murderous vengeance? How are you and he not alike?'

It was the Heretic who answered, and in a tone that was thick with indignation. 'She is as a thing of the street, my lord. She lacks skill . . .'

'Oh, she has skill,' the older man said. 'She lacks training. Training and purpose.'

Badr al-Mulahid frowned. 'Would you initiate one such as this?'

'No!' Yasmina spat. 'I would never become one—'

The sorcerer silenced her with a look. '*Never* is a span of time beyond your comprehension, child. And neither do you have a say in your fate. You belong to me now. As surely as if I had given you life.' He sighed, nodding to the Heretic. 'Her will is strong. Perhaps too strong to make her into an effective tool. Still, there is something about her . . .'

'What is your wish, my lord? Shall I give her a cold knife and a shallow grave?'

'No.' Ibn Sharr held Yasmina's gaze a moment longer before straightening and walking past. This simple gesture snapped the mesmeric hold over her; the young woman's shoulders slumped; her limbs trembled as she cast about, suddenly fearful. From the corner of her eye she saw other figures clustered in the open doorway, figures clad in black. 'No,' the sorcerer said again. 'You and I must speak, Badr. I have learned much from poor Gamal. Give the girl to the fedayeen. Let them break her will, if they can. It has been too long since they enjoyed the pleasures of a virgin of Paradise.'

Yasmina apprehended his meaning. Wild-eyed, she fought to free herself from the Heretic's grip, to rise and find a means of escape. All to no avail. The pale-eyed killer scooped her up and hurled her into the arms of the black-clad figures waiting in the doorway – men whose glassy eyes and leering faces promised unspeakable degradation. Yasmina thrashed and struggled as their grimy hands ripped her gown from her shoulders.

She screamed, and the mockery of its echo resounded through the hall of columns, through this sanctuary of long-forgotten gods.

17

Beyond the Maydan al-Iskander, in the streets of the Foreign Quarter, Musa heard the faint reverberation of Yasmina's scream. The sound roused him. He stirred, his good eye fluttering open. He lay on his side, his body resting in a slurry of grit and gore. His limbs were cold, leaden, and crusted with blood. Its heavy metallic reek mixed with the stench of bowel rising from his perforated belly. Musa shifted his legs, and even that slight movement caused hooks of white-hot agony to tear through his abdomen.

'Allah . . .' he croaked, grinding his fist fruitlessly into the earth. With his other hand he clutched at the wound, a slick coil of intestine pressing into his palm as he rolled to his knees. 'Allah . . . have . . . mercy!' Musa's breath came in ragged gasps. He stayed doubled over for a time, his head bent nearly to the dirt as he fought the urge to retch. He was certain the motion itself would kill him.

A single mote of purpose burned through the pain, burned like an ember through a tissue of gauze: *I must tell Assad! He must learn of the Maydan al-Iskander!* And to tell him, Musa reckoned, he had to first reach the caravanserai. He had to move. He had to walk.

His jaw clenched against the pain, Musa pushed one foot under him . . . then the other . . . and he took one staggering step before he fell back to his knees with an agonized moan.

A deeper night clouded the edges of the beggar's vision, and hot blood washed over his hand. 'Allah!' He coughed. Strings of spittle hung from his lips. 'Will . . . Will you m-make me c-crawl?'

'No,' a familiar voice rasped.

Musa raised his head. He blinked, tears and cold sweat washing down his cheeks, and saw Djuha's veiled face floating through a crimson haze of agony. 'L-Leper? Is t-that you?'

'Be at ease, beggar,' Djuha said, stroking the dishevelled hair of his pet urchin. 'And give thanks to God for the gift of my boundless curiosity. I watched from up the street. Why would one of Mistress Zaynab's companions do this to you?'

'I . . . I don't k-know . . . Help me . . .'

Djuha gestured to several nebulous figures standing outside Musa's periphery; not children, yet smaller than full-grown men, they were enswathed in dark burnouses, and they hid their features behind heavy veils of their own. They drifted closer to Musa. 'Bear him up, but gently. We must return him to his master.'

'T-The . . . The g-girl . . . Where?'

'Hush, my friend,' the leper replied, glancing once towards the Maydan al-Iskander. 'She is beyond your concern. Save your strength. Come, my nightingales. Come, my beautiful houris. Lift him gently.'

Musa groaned as a dozen bandaged-wrapped hands, some little more than fingerless paws, raised him to his feet. He sagged in their grasp, gnashing his teeth against the endless waves of pain; it was though the talons of some unkind beast tore at his innards. Mercifully, he sank into unconsciousness.

And like a cortège of ghosts, Djuha's women bore Musa through the stinking alleys of the Foreign Quarter.

18

The Golden Hall of al-Mu'izz li-Din Allah echoed with the sounds of men readying themselves for battle. Jandariyah officers in gold-chased steel growled words of encouragement to their troopers, some of whom were already streaked with blood and breathing heavily. Other soldiers limped through the Hall's massive doors, leaning upon their spears or upon one another, some aided by terrified eunuchs pressed into service by the palace surgeons. These men, their fine robes now smirched with gore, circulated among the fallen, stitching and binding their wounds as best they could. And above it all – above the rustle of mail hauberks and the rattle of harness and the clatter of sword and shield – the vizier's voice cracked like thunder.

'What do you mean he's dead?' At the base of the dais, in the shadow of the Seat of Divine Reason, Jalal paced back and forth like a caged tiger. Mustapha weathered his master's tirade with all the patience his long years afforded him. 'How do a crippled Sufi and a drug-addled half-wit get the better of a cursed Templar?'

'He was no Sufi,' the eunuch replied softly.

'By Allah, of course he was. I saw the wretch with my own eyes!'

Mustapha shook his head. 'The man was no Sufi, Excellency. I would swear to it.'

'Then who was he?'

'I have given this much thought, and though I cannot say for certain who he was, I suspect he was an agent of Gokbori's. The timing of it is simply too precise. The Turk must have been planning this for at least a fortnight!'

'And yet no word came to you?' Jalal said, his eyes narrowing. 'You, with your countless eyes and ears; you whom I trust to bring me knowledge of what goes on in the city beyond these walls? No word came to you?'

'None, Excellency.' The old eunuch bowed. 'Whoever planned this did so with masterful subtlety.'

Jalal's arm shot out, catching the eunuch unaware; his fingers dug cruelly into the soft flesh of Mustapha's jaw. 'This is the second time you have failed me,' the vizier hissed. 'I had that foolish boy under my thumb and your incompetence allowed him to escape!'

'I . . . I sent s-soldiers to . . . to block his . . . his exit from the old hammam, Excellency!'

'And so? I should throttle you right here!'

Mustapha's bruised lips writhed. 'M-Mercy!'

The crack of boot heels on marble caused Jalal to cut short his threat of bodily harm. He flung the old eunuch to the ground and turned as the Syrian captain, Turanshah, approached. The grim lord of the Jandariyah seemed the personification of War, clad as he was in a full hauberk of black mail edged in gold, mail leggings, and an etched steel helmet inlaid with gold and onyx. One scarred hand rested lightly on his sabre, its hilt jutting from a silken girdle the colour of blood. 'Excellency.' Turanshah inclined his head. Hard black eyes flickered down to the eunuch and then back again, his lip curling in obvious distaste.

'What news?'

'The White Slaves of the River have seized control of the palace gates, Excellency. The outer courts have fallen to them, and even now they are forcing their way inward, driving my Jandariyah ever closer to the doors of this Hall.'

'How did they get in?'

'It does not matter how, vizier,' Turanshah replied. 'All that matters is they are in, and they are wreaking havoc. I do not know how much longer my men can hold them at bay. You should entertain the possibility of surrender, Excellency, before our position erodes any further.'

'Should I?' Jalal resumed his pacing. 'What of the Sudanese mercenaries? Can we not get word to Wahshi and his dogs, order them to break through the Mamelukes and make their way into the palace?'

'How?' Turanshah replied, anger flashing through his normally reserved manner. 'Did I not speak clearly, vizier? The slaves control the gates, and they will defend them to the last – against the Jandariyah or against the Sudanese, it makes little difference! And why should they not? Your foolish threats against their families have forged them into a brigade of martyrs!'

'Hold your tongue, Syrian, lest I have it torn out!' The vizier rounded on his mailed captain. 'What has become of the Jandariyah's famed loyalty? Have you lost your nerve, man?'

'The Jandariyah are as loyal as they are courageous, and none more so than I, but only a fool throws his life away for a hopeless cause! Gokbori has us surrounded! This' – Turanshah raised his hand, indicating the soaring dome of alabaster and gold – 'will likely be where we make our final stand! The Sudanese might seize the initiative and drive off the Mamelukes, true, but it will only be long after we are dead. Your bid for power has failed, vizier. But we are not without options.' The Syrian turned and motioned for one of his men – an officer, by the gold inlay adorning his helmet – to come closer. The man stopped at a respectful distance and saluted. 'Ghuri, tell the vizier the words of the Caliph.'

Jalal started forward. 'You saw the Caliph? Where?'

'The harem, Excellency.' The officer, Ghuri, bowed. 'We were sent to apprehend him but our task was interrupted by a strong force of Circassian Mamelukes, led by their amir, Massoud. They took charge of the Caliph.'

'But al-Hasan spoke to you?'

Ghuri nodded. 'He said he hoped to pardon the Jandariyah, Excellency. He said it would grieve him beyond words to see my brothers and me annihilated by his Turks, and that in the days to come Cairo would have a grave need for soldiers.'

'A fine offer for you, Turanshah, but where does that leave me?' Jalal gave a short bark of laughter. 'Alone with my eunuchs and my dreams?'

The Syrian dismissed Ghuri, returning his salute; he watched the captain rejoin his men, and then turned to face the vizier. 'You are a cunning man, Excellency. Feign remorse, prey upon the young Caliph's need to show mercy, and live to fight another day.'

Jalal exhaled, a drawn-out suspiration that came as much from the depths of his soul as it did from his lungs. His plans – his meticulous and carefully laid plans – were spooling off into the ether like string unrolling from a spindle. Where had he gone wrong? Whom had he misjudged? More importantly, what could he do to stop this reversal?

Scowling, the vizier met Turanshah's expectant gaze and waved him away. 'Allah! Let me weigh your counsel in peace!'

'Time is of the essence, Excellency,' the Syrian said, sketching a brief bow. 'For each moment you tarry means more casualties – and I can ill afford to lose more men.'

Jalal turned to face the dais, the Seat of Divine Reason gleaming like a prize beyond his grasp. He felt Mustapha's presence at his side. 'I will never be Sultan of Cairo now,' Jalal said, his voice a mingling of anguish and anger. 'Nor will I remain its vizier if, indeed, al-Hasan permits me to live. What is left to me, my old darling? Humiliation and a lingering death at the hands of my enemies?'

Mustapha said nothing for a long while. Jalal glanced sidelong at him; the old eunuch seemed lost in thought, his brows drawn, and one wrinkled hand massaging the loose flesh of his neck. The weight of years bore down upon his shoulders like a porter's burden. When he spoke, however, his words carried silken promise. 'You said before that all of this is naught but a shatranj match, Excellency. If that is true, do we not now stand upon the brink of *Shah Mat*?'

Jalal frowned. 'How? The board does not lie. I have lost my pawns, my elephants, my rukhs; my horsemen are too distant to be of use, and all I have by my side is a single wazir. My shah stands bare before my enemy.'

'And still, Shah Mat is possible,' Mustapha said. 'If a man possesses a sultan's audacity. It is said Nur ad-Din won his first match against his father, the atabeg Zangi, by employing a manoeuvre known as al-Jambiya, the Curved Dagger. He lured his opponent close and . . .'

'And took him at unawares,' Jalal whispered. The Curved Dagger was a thorny mansuba, one predicated upon recklessness and a flagrant disregard for the safety of one's own shah. It was a move of last resort. 'If I do as you suggest I won't live to enjoy my triumph.'

'Neither will al-Hasan. This way, at least, you control your own fate.'

'What of you?'

Mustapha sighed. His eyes, too, flickered to the throne of the Fatimid Caliphs. 'I am old, Excellency. I have lived a full life, and one that has earned me the trust of men far greater than I. Beginning anew holds no attraction for me. Let me be the wazir at your side, my shah, as I have ever been. Let me be the lure.'

Slowly, Jalal nodded. 'As you wish, my old friend. Gather what we need while I prepare the way forward.' He glanced at the captain of the Jandariyah and caught the Syrian's eye for a significant moment. '*Inshallah*, our enemies will be caught off guard.'

'And God willing,' Mustapha said, more to himself than to Jalal, 'our end will be quick.'

19

Assad trailed Rashid al-Hasan and the woman, Parysatis, through endless narrow passages, each one as featureless as the last: nondescript brick, yellow and crumbling with age, inlaid with spy holes at regular intervals, and lit by slashes of lamplight from the world beyond; ramps and rough-hewn steps following the track of the palace's ancient foundations. Despite a maddening similarity, Parysatis navigated every twist and turn with confidence, pausing at junctures only briefly to get her bearings. Always, she led them in the direction of Turkish voices. At his back, Assad heard the scrape of boots and the clank of mail and harness as Massoud and three-score Circassians followed in his wake.

They found Gokbori a quarter of an hour later, in the vaulted corridor that ran between the doors of the Golden Hall and the Gate of al-Mansuriyya – the main entrance to the Great East Palace – trumpeting orders in the harsh tongue of the steppe. Massoud emerged first; a grim smile touched his visage as he hailed his brother-commander.

'Have you left any for my Circassians, Turk?'

'Mayhap they can handle any stragglers!'

Gokbori stood at the centre of an eerie battlefield, one lit by the buttery glow of gold-filigreed lamps. He grinned at the logjam of corpses that marked the site of the fiercest fighting. The Turkish assault had been a whirlwind of steel and fury – though Moslem, Gokbori and his kin remained sons of the distant steppe, barbarians who hungered for the glory of battle. The Syrians, it seemed, had obliged them.

The broad corridor stank of slaughter. Delicate tapestries hung awry, splashes of crimson marring the lustrous marble walls. Underfoot, the carpets of far Samarkand were awash in the ghastly fluids that leaked from riven flesh. Assad stepped over the wrack of war, over discarded shields and splintered spears, over corpses hacked asunder. Arrows jutted from mailed breasts. A headless body sat upright against the far wall, as though the man had simply had enough and decided to rest for a while. All around, the wounded twitched and moaned and called out for succour.

For all its savagery, the sight of the Turks' handiwork paled beside Assad's memory of Ascalon. Not so for the Caliph. The Assassin saw horror reflected in the eyes of the young Prince of the Faithful; Parysatis clung to his arm, blinking back tears at the terrible vista of the corridor.

'Merciful Allah!' the Caliph said. 'This was done in my name?'

Assad nodded. 'For the good of Cairo.'

'Good? What good? These men—'

'These men were soldiers, my lord. Honour them for their sacrifice, but do not pity them their fate.'

'Yes,' Rashid al-Hasan replied, swallowing hard. 'Yes. You are right. But we must help the wounded. Parysatis . . . ?'

The young woman gathered herself together. 'I will . . . I will fetch water, bandages . . . I will do what I can, Exalted One.'

'Massoud, detail men to help her.'

Gokbori heard Rashid al-Hasan's voice and hurried over; as the White Slaves of the River fanned out, the Turkish amir knelt in the broth of carnage and made his obeisance to the Caliph. 'Rejoice, Great One! Through Allah's good graces, we now control all nine of the palace gates, and we have driven the vizier's dogs back to the Golden Hall. We will put an end to them once we find something heavy enough to smash through those doors—'

'No,' al-Hasan said. He was pale and trying his best not to focus for too long on any particular detail of the slaughter. 'No. Rise, Gokbori, and call off your men.'

Gokbori clambered to his feet, a scowl darkening his features as he acknowledged his master's order with a bow. 'Have we offended you, O Caliph?'

'No, amir. On the contrary, you and your men have done me an immeasurable service, but I have offered to pardon the remaining Jandariyah, and I cannot have you slaughtering them out of hand. See to the wounded . . . to the wounded of both sides.'

'As you wish, Great One.' Gokbori turned and motioned for his adjutants.

'You have heralds?' Assad said suddenly.

The Turk glanced at the Caliph, noting the sobriety of his expression upon hearing this man speak. Though he did not recognize him Gokbori afforded the man the same respect. 'Aye, I have heralds.'

'Send them to the gates. Have them proclaim the vizier's death at the hands of Caliph Rashid al-Hasan. No doubt word of your uprising has reached the Sudanese by now. This way, if they believe their patron is no more, they might think twice about attacking the gates.'

'And if they demand proof?'

'Tell them they will soon see all the proof they need.' Assad turned to the Caliph. 'My lord, it would perhaps be prudent if you summoned the captain of the Sudanese mercenaries to the palace, to have him renew his oaths and pledges in your august presence.'

'Is that not premature?'

'No.' Assad gestured; his hand dropped to the hilt of his salawar, muscle and sinew twisting in a vice of hatred. Off in the distance, the gold-and-ivory arabesqued doors of the Golden Hall were trundling open. 'Whether in slaughter or surrender, it ends now.'

Silence fell upon the assembled men. Even the wounded ceased their struggles for a span. Bow strings creaked as, with exaggerated slowness, a man of the Jandariyah sidled into view.

'God grant them wisdom,' Rashid al-Hasan muttered, 'for I have no stomach for further bloodshed.'

Assad glanced sidelong at the young Caliph. In Palmyra, he had expressed concern to Daoud ar-Rasul, concern that the young Prince of the Faithful was likely a degenerate of the basest sort. Thus far, Rashid al-Hasan had proven him wrong – which would doubtless amuse Daoud to no end. The Caliph must have sensed his scrutiny, though, for he turned slightly and met the Assassin's stare, his own eyes betraying his hope for a speedy resolution. 'My master was right about you, my lord,' Assad said.

Rashid smiled, lines of fatigue etching his face. 'You and I must speak in private once all of this is said and done. I would know more of your master, and of his offer of friendship.'

'As you wish, my lord.' At the end of the corridor, the officer – Assad recognized the golden decoration adorning his helmet – edging through the door raised his hands aloft . . . and in one he clutched a length of white silk. Assad grunted. 'It seems wisdom has prevailed.'

Beside him, the Caliph exhaled.

In short order, an embassy of twelve Jandariyah officers marched in two files through the doors of the Golden Hall of al-Mu'izz li-Din Allah, led by the proud figure of their captain, Turanshah. Though battered and blood-stained, they nevertheless walked with their heads held high, their spears inverted, and their sheathed swords held upright before them. The White Slaves of the River watched in silence.

Massoud and Gokbori flanked the Caliph, their hands on their sword hilts; Assad moved to one side, an implacable shadow, his scarred face immobile and unreadable. A spear-length from the Prince of the Faithful, Turanshah stopped. The Syrian bowed three times, and then knelt and placed his sheathed sabre on the floor at Rashid al-Hasan's feet. 'I began this day with a thousand men under my command,' Turanshah said. 'Now I have fewer than five hundred. Forgive them, O Prince of the Faithful. Forgive them and put the onus of your anger on me.'

Rashid al-Hasan sighed. 'But it was not you alone who betrayed me, was it, captain? It was you and all your men. Before Allah and the Prophet, would I not be well within my rights to have every last man under your command put to death?'

On his knees, Turanshah bent his neck. 'Such is your right, O Prince.'

The Caliph raised his voice. 'And so it is. But it is also my right to pardon any who have wronged me. This, then, is my decree: the Jandariyah are no more. I order your standards and battle flags to be desecrated and burned, so too your symbols and insignia. Rise, captain. I will spare you and your men, for Cairo has need of skilled troops and skilled commanders; thanks to Jalal's treachery we will soon face not one army but two. If it is Allah's will, you will redeem your honour on the battlefield. Now, where is my vizier?'

'He awaits you inside, Glorious One.'

'Does he?' Despite a veneer of exhaustion, resolve flared in Rashid al-Hasan's dark eyes. 'Well, let us not keep him waiting.'

Preceded by Turkish archers and surrounded by a bodyguard of mailed Mamelukes, Caliph Rashid al-Hasan entered the Golden Hall of his ancestors with little pomp or ceremony. The remaining Jandariyah, who had already divested themselves of their weapons, stood quietly by, tending to their wounded and awaiting their captain. Knots of eunuchs and courtiers milled about; supplicants who had sided with the vizier and had sought safety in his presence when the uprising began now tried to distance themselves from him. They cried out when they saw the young Caliph enter, wishing Allah's blessings upon him or begging that he remember a kindness once paid, a compliment once given. For his part, Rashid al-Hasan ignored them.

He fixed his attention solely upon Jalal.

In gleaming white raiment, the vizier waited in his customary place of honour to the right of the dais. He nodded in greeting, his face a blank mask that betrayed nothing. His creature, Mustapha, stood near with his hands folded, his manner that of an intermediary who waited patiently to reconcile two warring factions. The old eunuch bowed low as the Caliph approached.

'Great One, we—'

'Be silent, wretch,' the Caliph said, his voice brimming with venom. He stepped closer to Jalal, the Mamelukes shifting to envelope all three men. 'There is no explanation you can give, no lie you can spool, that will gull me into thinking you any less guilty of treason.'

'Then let us tell the truth,' Jalal replied. 'I am guilty, as you say. But not of treason. My crime is one of caring too much for the welfare of Cairo.'

Rashid raised an eyebrow. 'Your hypocrisy is staggering, matched only by your arrogance! You care so much for Cairo's welfare, and for the welfare of its people, that you would enter into a blasphemous alliance with the Nazarenes? That you would provoke violence in order to advance your own fortunes?'

'If it meant a chance for stability in the future, then yes on both counts! The Caliphate – *your* Caliphate – has become a laughing stock! Cairo needs and deserves a strong Sultan . . . not a boy who would play at being a ruler!'

The Caliph's nostrils flared. 'I swore today what would happen if you further tested my patience, and so it will be! I condemn you to death, Jalal al-Aziz! And, once my executioners have wrung every last ounce of agony from you, you will be gutted and your miserable carcass hung from Zuwayla Gate!'

At this, Jalal only laughed. 'You fool! Amalric is coming, no matter what you do to me. And the Infidel will be here sooner than you think. What will you do without me to bargain on your behalf? What will you do when the hosts of Jerusalem appear at your gates?'

'Look to our steel and place our faith in Allah!'

'Faugh!' Jalal swaggered towards where Massoud and Gokbori stood, giving Assad an evil look as he passed. 'Without me, Amalric will crush your paltry army and Cairo will become a city of Nazarenes. Is that what you want, Turk? And you, you Circassian dog . . . do you want to see your families on the slave block or worse?' Jalal gestured to the captain of the Jandariyah, who stood with his officers. 'And what of you, my feckless Turanshah . . . do you want to see the streets flow ankle-deep in blood? Such is what will come to pass if you follow this misguided boy! I bid you seize him, throw him in the deepest dungeon, and perhaps I can be persuaded to intervene on your behalf . . . before you are compelled to kiss the rings of your new Nazarene masters!'

'Silence!' Rashid al-Hasan strode towards his deposed vizier, balled fists rigid at his sides. 'Now you will listen to me, swine. I—'

A blood-curdling cry split the air; Mustapha, forgotten in the exchange between Caliph and vizier, sprang forward, intent on driving the dagger in his aged fist into Rashid al-Hasan's back. But the old eunuch moved too slowly; startled, the Prince of the Faithful whirled even as Amir Massoud stepped into the dagger's path. The slender blade ripped through the black linen covering his jazerant before snapping on his mailed breast. He flung the eunuch back with a shout, and a trio of Circassian sabres licked and darted, accompanied by the slaughterhouse sound of cloven flesh. A heartbeat later, Mustapha's headless corpse crashed to the ground, bright blood washing over the pristine white tiles.

In that same instant, from the corner of his eye, Assad caught a flicker of steel as Jalal drew a blade from inside the sleeve of his khalat. No one else noticed this small movement – not the Caliph, whose back was to him; not Massoud, who staggered and clutched his bruised chest; not the Turk, Gokbori, who turned to issue orders to the White Slaves of the River. The old eunuch's death had been nothing more than a diversion, a sacrifice . . .

And Assad alone saw the gleam of triumph in the vizier's eyes.

Too long had he held himself in check; now, with the mission entrusted to him by the Hidden Master a hair's breadth away from ruin, the *Emir* of the Knife did his lord's bidding. Assad leapt sidewise. Ancient steel sang. Driven by an age-old rage, it cleft the golden air of the Hall; the triumph in Jalal's eyes turned first to disbelief, then to fear as the edge of the Assassin's salawar took his hand off at the wrist.

Limb and blade clattered to the floor in a rain of blood.

Assad did not hesitate. Faster than the vizier could react, he plunged the tip of his salawar into Jalal's chest, impaling him with such ferocity that the reddened blade stood out a hand-span from between his shoulder blades.

Jalal looked down, confused, and then raised his head to meet Assad's scarred visage. A familiar grimace twisted the vizier's face, the sudden realization that *something* had entered him, something dark and implacable, something that filled his skull with a thousand cries of agony and rage. His mouth opened in a silent scream and, like a marionette unstrung, Jalal's legs buckled. Assad bore him to the ground amid shouts of alarm. 'Allah!' The Caliph spun back around, wide-eyed, his Mamelukes pressing close to him.

The fingers of Jalal's remaining hand knotted desperately in the breast of Assad's khalat. 'W-Who . . . W-Who are . . . you?'

'My master is a young shaykh of storied lineage,' Assad growled, 'who dwells on a mountain-top by the shores of the Caspian Sea . . .'

Jalal's eyes widened in recognition. 'Al-Hashi—'

But, as he tried to gasp out the name, Assad wrenched his salawar free with a savage twist. And Jalal al-Aziz ibn al-Rahman –

the man who would be Sultan – died in a choking rush of blood.

Assad wiped his blade clean on the leg of Jalal's trousers and stood, turning to face the Caliph. The young man stared at the body of the one who had been his vizier – and his sworn enemy – as though unable to grasp the reality of his death. 'Cairo is yours, my lord.'

The Caliph blinked. 'We . . . We must prepare,' he said. 'Spread the word to my people, to the people of Cairo. Tell them we must prepare for the city's defence, for the defence of Egypt.'

'*Allahu akbar!*' Assad said, raising his voice for all to hear. 'Long live the Prince of the Faithful!' Instantly, the cry was taken up by the White Slaves of the River, by Turk and Circassian. The suspect courtiers responded with thunderous acclaim; even the defeated Jandariyah spoke up, adding their voices to the din. '*Allahu akbar! Long live the Prince of the Faithful! Long live Rashid al-Hasan!*'

The Fifth Surah

Son of Wickedness

1

In the grey half-light that presaged the dawn, the gardens of the Great East Palace were cool green oases, the very air alive with birdsong. The *Emir* of the Knife sprawled on a divan, on a portico overlooking one such garden – the slain vizier's favourite, he had learned. The Assassin studied a delicate shatranj board and its myriad pieces: one side in ebony, the other in ivory. A faint breeze set the portico's sheer linen drapes to billowing, spicing the air with the scent of oranges and flowering jasmine.

Assad had forsaken his bloody kaftan and sandals; now he wore a tunic and belted trousers of grey linen beneath a rich black khalat, its sleeves adorned with bands of Kufic script embroidered in gold. Boots of soft leather cased his feet, while a black silk sash and a turban sat neatly folded upon a settee. His sheathed salawar lay across his knees.

Assad lifted the ivory shah off the game board and stared at it. Exquisitely carved, its silver trim and pearl and opal inlays sparkled as it caught the rising light. 'The Caliph,' Assad muttered. He placed the piece at the centre of the board. *I've cut his strings; he stands now on his own two feet, free and unfettered. But for how long?* Mercy was Rashid al-Hasan's weakness; an hour ago, he forbade his Mamelukes from decimating the ranks of the palace chamberlains and courtiers – Jalal's cronies who supported him in all things. 'Too many have died already,' the Caliph told them, and

319

no argument Assad could make would change his mind. The courtiers praised his mercy and swore their allegiance, true, but how long would it take their praise to turn to scorn? *This mercy, will it be his strength or his downfall, I wonder? And will it matter?*

The Assassin caught up the two ebony horsemen, turbaned cavaliers on rearing mounts. Frowning, Assad placed one at each edge of the board, to the left and the right of the gleaming white shah. An army at Bilbeis and another at Atfih, with Cairo between them, like an ingot of brittle steel caught between hammer and anvil. *Is the Caliph cunning enough to play one against the other?*

There was another threat, too; one the Prince of the Faithful was wholly unaware of: the dogs of Massaif. Assad lifted an ebony pawn from the board and placed it in the shadow of the ivory shah. *Are they in league with Shirkuh or Amalric, or do they have their own agenda?* More often than not, the Syrian al-Hashishiyya held their knives for sale; they were consummate infiltrators, capable of spreading terror and fading into the night, distracting city leaders from the true threat of an invading army. Hiring them was the kind of stratagem Assad expected of Amalric. *And is it mere coincidence that their emir, the one called the Heretic, is of Frankish blood?*

Assad stared at the board. Daoud ar-Rasul's admonition to him echoed in his skull: 'Use your formidable skills to strengthen the Caliph's position and dispose of any who would do him harm.'

Dispose of any who would do him harm. Assad massaged his forehead, stretched, and sank back into the divan. Where should he begin? Should he let Shirkuh and Amalric fight over Cairo, and then put the victor down as he came to claim his prize? Or should he visit each camp the night before the battle and spike their heads to a tent-pole? And what of the Heretic? No doubt he meant the Caliph harm, as well. And then there were the countless lieutenants and underlings in each man's entourage, all of whom would gladly do what their masters could not. *Dispose of any who would do him harm*, Daoud had said. *Dispose of any . . .*

'An easy order to give, my old friend,' Assad murmured, closing his eyes. 'But I am only one man . . .'

2

Dawn spread across the Nile Valley, the sun's rays lending a tinge of gold to the mist overhanging the stubbled fields around the fortress-city of Atfih. Groves of date palms and dense thickets of sycamore fringed the fields, and hard by stood clusters of drab shanties where geese cackled in wicker cages and chickens scratched the dusty ground. Thin plumes of smoke rose from outdoor ovens as village women ground barley into flour and kneaded out flat loaves of bread; sleepy-eyed children went about their chores. Already, the fellahin were up and about – men burned dark by the sun and clad in dirty white head scarves and galabiyyas – field workers and brick-makers, carpenters and potters, all bound for field, forge, or kiln.

As the day brightened, villagers paused in their labours and glanced up from the ground, shading their eyes to stare at the crenellated battlements of Atfih. An errant breeze stirred the banners above the citadel. But the cloth that rippled and snapped and caught the morning light was not the familiar gold and yellow of the Fatimid Caliphate. It was black, a square of silky night emblazoned with silver script: the standard of the Lord of Damascus. The banner of Shirkuh.

At this, the villagers merely shrugged and returned their attention to the hard soil at their feet. New master or old, in war or in peace, all things were equal in the eyes of Allah.

3

The officer tasked with rousing the new master of Atfih from slumber shared in the fatalism of the common man. He understood that Allah apportioned all things in equal measure, for good or ill, as He saw fit. 'And there is no God but He,' the officer, Yusuf ibn Ayyub, said. He was a slender Kurd with a neatly trimmed beard and melancholy eyes. This morning a hint of a smile graced his thin lips, for he had the opportunity to be the bearer of glad tidings. News had come during the night. News from Cairo.

Yusuf's path carried him away from the citadel of Atfih and into the tangle of streets by the main gate. Shirkuh, who was both his commander and his uncle, refused to claim the citadel for his quarters, as was his right. Instead, he bedded down among his beloved troops, savage Turkomans who were eager to prove themselves not only against the Infidel, but against the Moslem enemies of Nur ad-Din as well. Yusuf admired them. They were unparalleled horsemen, masters of bow, lance, and sword, and they loved their Kurdish leader as much for his fury in battle as for his raucous nature.

The caravanserai Shirkuh took for his quarters gave evidence of this nature. Broken crockery littered the courtyard amid a sprawl of snoring bodies: Turkoman atabegs and hetmen side by side with a few curious officers of the local garrison drawn in by the promise of koumiss, a strong drink of fermented mare's milk not explicitly prohibited in the Qur'an. Yusuf shook his head, ashamed by the way his uncle parsed the Prophet's words, teasing and tugging them out of shape in order to justify a beloved vice.

He found Shirkuh inside, upright and perched on the edge of a bench, his head cradled in his hands. Though long past his prime, Shirkuh ibn Shadhi was still a powerfully built man, the knots and cords of muscle lacing his hard frame sheathed in a layer of fat. He glanced up at Yusuf's approach, his right eye dark and bleary; his left eye was as white and sightless as a boiled egg.

'By God, is it dawn already?'

'The second hour after,' Yusuf replied. 'I bring news, uncle.'

Saying nothing, Shirkuh got to his feet and staggered over to a basin of water. He thrust his face into it, shaking his head, blowing and burbling before wringing the excess from his beard on to his stained robe. 'Where is our would-be vizier?' he said, turning back to face his nephew, oblivious to the water streaming down his chin. 'Have you seen Dirgham this morning?'

Yusuf frowned. 'He's made a nice lair for himself in the citadel, where the merchants of Atfih can more easily fawn over him. He embraces his role as liberator too readily, uncle. You took Atfih without striking a blow, and yet Dirgham accepts the accolades that by rights should be yours.'

Shirkuh grunted, pushing away from the basin and going to the door. He squinted out into the courtyard. 'Let him. Egypt is a country without *men*, Yusuf. The ease with which we took Atfih is proof of that. Let Dirgham dream his petty dreams of restoring himself to the vizierate. Let the fool bask in the adoration of dogs. I have other plans. We will rest here a day or two, and then march north to Cairo.' Shirkuh turned. 'You said you had news?'

Yusuf's smile returned. 'A pigeon alighted upon the citadel at first light, uncle. A pigeon from Cairo.'

'And so?'

'It bore a message for the commander of Atfih's garrison.' Yusuf paused, savouring the look of anticipation on his uncle's face.

'By God, boy! What was the message?'

'Jalal al-Aziz is dead. Slain in an uprising . . . one sparked by the Caliph himself! Imagine the chaos, uncle! Their vizier is dead and an untested boy sits upon the throne. The Cairenes will likely capitulate faster than did the folk of Atfih. I wager they will open the gates for you themselves!'

Shirkuh's face went blank for a moment, and then suddenly he roared with laughter. 'By the Prophet's beard, your news sits well with me, nephew! Does Dirgham know?'

Yusuf shook his head. 'I decided it best that you learned of it first.'

'Don't tell him – let it be a surprise!' The Kurdish general whirled and stepped out of the door, into the courtyard. 'On your feet, you fatherless curs!' he bellowed. 'Get them up, Yusuf. Roust out the trumpeters and have them sound assembly. I've changed my mind, by God! We march on Cairo today!'

4

The stink of Ascalon choked him. The stench of charred flesh and hot blood, pulverized rock and piss-soaked earth, wood smoke and corpses left to rot under the merciless sun. These were the smells of a city in its death throes.

A city whose murderers stood just beyond its gates, waiting to defile its body.

Beneath a yellowing sliver of moon, the young soldier walked the ragged battlements of Ascalon, not far from the crumbling Jaffa Gate. A breeze from the sea did little to relieve the heat, and the reek rising from the city's heart made each breath searing agony. The soldier licked his cracked lips with a tongue swollen from thirst; hunger gnawed at his belly.

Beside him walked the son of a muezzin, a deep-voiced boy of fifteen who dreamed of martyrdom against the Infidel. 'God damn them!' Clad in rusting mail and wearing his slain father's ill-fitting helmet, the boy stopped and peered over the ragged battlements at the Nazarene camp. 'May Allah smite them with a plague of flies! With boils! With—'

'You think Allah hears you?' the young soldier said, leaning against the still-hot stones of the battlement. Exhaustion and privation had loosened his tongue. 'You think He cares what happens to you? To any of us?'

'Have you sided with the Infidel now?' the muezzin's son snapped.

The soldier shook his head. 'The truth has no side, you idiot. Look around you. We stand on the floor of Hell. God has abandoned us.'

'"Allah is the master of His affairs",' the boy replied, quoting the exalted Book. 'If we suffer here, then we suffer because it is His will. Who can know the mind of God?'

'Then we suffer for no reason.'

'That it is the will of Allah is reason enough!' Mail rattled as the muezzin's son stalked off, leaving the soldier to stand alone.

'Enough for you, perhaps,' he muttered, listening to the sounds that rose from the city below: the screams of the wounded as crushed limbs

were amputated; the sobbing prayers of women who sought their sons and husbands in the rubble; the cries of children orphaned by the plague. 'But not for me. Not for me.'

'Do you believe what you say,' a voice said from the darkness behind him, 'or do you simply parrot what others have told you?'

The young soldier wheeled, his hand going to the worn hilt of his sword – a fine Turkish sabre that had once belonged to his father. Unlike his mail hauberk, looted from the body of a dead Infidel, the sword was well tended. 'Who's there?'

The man who emerged from the shadow had the woollen cloak of a Sufi wrapped around his thin shoulders; his beard was sparse and grey, and from beneath a tattered green turban a tangle of silver hair fell to his shoulders. His eyes were sharp but not unkind.

'You should not be up here, old father,' the soldier said. He relaxed his guard but his hand remained perched on his sabre's pommel.

'Answer my question. Do you believe what you say?'

The young soldier exhaled; he glanced through an embrasure at the lights of the Nazarene camp below and spat. 'I would not say such things if I did not believe them.'

'You are not like these others, are you?'

The soldier's eyes narrowed. 'What do you mean?'

'You appreciate the artistry of it. Of this. The artistry of death. Nay, boy, do not look at me so. I have seen this appreciation enough in my life to recognize it for what it is, though it has never plagued me as it must plague you.'

The young soldier turned fully towards the embrasure. On the plains below the walls the hellish machines of the Templars swarmed with workers; lanterns and torches bobbed as Genoese engineers inspected ropes and capstans, gears and winches, preparing for the infidel king of Jerusalem's order to resume the bombardment. Above their heads, the black-and-white standard of the Temple fluttered. 'I cannot control this, these machines. They kill without rhyme or reason. But in the breach, facing the blades of my enemy, I am in control. When the spears shiver and the swords clash, my fate resides here' – *he raised his right fist –* *'and not in the lap of some uncaring God.'*

'I have seen you at the walls, boy,' the old Sufi said. 'Where you go, men die. But it is not enough for you, is it?'

The soldier looked away from the Nazarene camp, turning around to face the torn and bloody heart of Ascalon. The near-constant bombardment from the Templar machines had toppled minarets and cracked open domes; once-pleasant gardens yet smouldered, embers gleaming like the eyes of ghûls amid the wreckage. 'What honour is there in death when it serves no higher purpose?'

'My master believes in the same things. Oh, he could make much of you, my boy. From you he could forge a weapon that would strike fear into the enemies of Islam, both within and without. He could give you such a purpose as you have never dreamed of.'

'Who is your master?'

The Sufi leaned closer. 'He is a shaykh of storied lineage who dwells on a mountain-top by the shores of the Caspian Sea, and he would very much like you to live, my young lion.'

5

'Assad?'

The Assassin's eyes snapped open, his hand falling to the pommel of his salawar. The tang of hatred flowing from the ivory hilt brought with it a sense of crystalline awareness. He reclined still on the divan, on the dead vizier's favourite portico. Outside, night had fallen.

'Assad? Are you here?' He recognized the voice. It belonged to the Circassian amir, Massoud. An instant later, the man's silhouette loomed in the open archway of the portico.

'Aye,' Assad replied, forcing his hand to let go of the blade. 'I'm here.' He swung his long legs off the divan and stretched, rolling his shoulders and cracking the tendons in his neck. He reached for his sash and turban. 'What goes? Is there something wrong with the Caliph?'

'No, the Prince of the Faithful is resting, finally. The Lady Parysatis watches over him, and the White Slaves of the River guard his chambers, as well they should.' Pale light flared as a slave shuffled in front of Massoud, carrying an oil lamp of blown glass and gold to a low table by the divan – a table strewn with pieces from a shatranj board. The slave sat the lamp down, but the Circassian waved him away before he could gather up the fallen game pieces. 'Leave us.'

'If all is well, then why are you here?'

'I bring a message.'

'From?'

Massoud tugged at a scrimshaw bead woven into the end of his moustache. 'Ali abu'l-Qasim. You know him?'

'The self-appointed King of Thieves,' Assad said, a faint smile touching his lips. 'Yes, I know him.'

'One of his Berbers waited most of the day to get into the palace, and he was only allowed through al-Mansuriyya Gate because my name was invoked. When I went to investigate, he told me he carried a message from Abu'l-Qasim for the Sufi, Ibn al-Teymani.'

'Where is this message?'

Massoud fished a square of paper from inside the breast of his jazerant and handed it to Assad. It bore a seal of red wax, pressed with the face of a dirham minted in the name of the Caliph. 'Did you know Abu'l-Qasim's daughter, Zaynab, whom men called the Gazelle?'

Assad broke the seal on the paper; he paused before unfolding it. 'I knew her only in passing, but well enough to know she thought highly of you.'

'And I of her, despite her father's unsavoury reputation.'

'Her . . . *calling*, it did not give you pause?'

Massoud's gaze softened. 'I am a slave, the bastard son of a Circassian outlaw and oath-breaker. Who am I to cast aspersions? No, I would have taken Zaynab as my wife if only she had

permitted me. As Allah is my witness, I will miss that dear woman.'
He paused. 'She was . . .'

'Enchanting.' Assad finished for him, brows knitted in a deep
frown as he remembered the silvery sound of her laughter – heard
once, but impossible to forget. 'She was enchanting.'

A bitter smile twisted Massoud's thin lips. 'Exactly so.' He
turned and made to quit the portico for the quiet of the garden
beyond, nodding to Assad. 'I pray I am not the bearer of bad
tidings.'

'Massoud,' Assad said. The Circassian paused, glancing over his
shoulder. 'Zaynab al-Ghazala's murder will not go unanswered.
You have my word on this.'

Massoud studied Assad's scarred face. 'Who are you? Not a
Sufi, surely. I have never known a holy man with your skill. Nor
have I known a Sufi to hate the Nazarenes with a zealot's passion
or to promise retribution for a slain courtesan. So who are you,
Assad ibn al-Teymani of the Hejaz, if indeed you are a true son of
the Hejaz . . . ?'

'It is enough that I am a friend.'

His gaze inscrutable, Massoud stared at Assad for a moment
longer before simply shrugging and stepping out into the garden.

By the light of the oil lamp, Assad read Abu'l-Qasim's message.
The script was formal, a scribe's hand, and the missive itself was
predictably terse and without embroidery: *More blood has spilled.
Return to the caravanserai with all possible haste.*

Assad's eyes narrowed to slits of cold black fire. He read it once
more, then reached out and touched a corner of the paper to the
flickering flame in the oil lamp. Its edge blackened, charred, and
crumbled to ash. He let the burning note fall to the stone flags
and finished dressing.

Massoud tarried in the garden, leaning against the bole of a
willow tree and staring off into the star-flecked heavens. He turned
at the sound of Assad's approach.

'I have business I must attend to outside the palace,' Assad said,
settling his long Afghan blade into the sash about his waist. He

clapped Massoud on the shoulder as he passed. 'Can I expect trouble at the gates?'

'I will ensure the guards know your name, and know not to restrict your comings and goings. For now, use al-Yazuri Gate; it is closest and my own men command it this night. Is there aught else I can do?'

Assad stopped and turned back to the Circassian. Dappled moonlight filtered through the willow boughs, shadow and silver light playing across the hard planes of the *Emir* of the Knife's visage. There was no compassion in his dark eyes, no sense of warmth or human empathy. 'Guard the Caliph as though your life depends upon it.'

6

From al-Yazuri Gate, which opened on the neighbourhood of Barqiyya, Assad made his way south and west, crossing the nigh-deserted Qasaba even as the final adhan of the evening drifted out from the minarets of al-Azhar Mosque. The sonorous call to prayer echoed from quarter to quarter; it whispered down wide streets and noisome alleys. It rang across empty rooftops and off shuttered windows, through souks and stalls where on any other evening merchants would have clamoured for the night's last custom. As Assad reached the road leading to the Nile Gate, the final stanza of the adhan faded and Cairo fell silent once again, a city afraid to move, afraid to breathe – afraid the slightest misstep would spark a holocaust of bloodshed and retribution among its factions. Cairo, Assad reckoned, had grown afraid of itself.

Sullen light, like the glow of banked embers, seeped from a handful of windows in the upper storeys of the caravanserai of Abu'l-Qasim. Its tall doors were open despite the sense of imminent doom gripping the city, and to the right and left mail-clad Berbers stood sentinel. Others walked the roofline: hawk-eyed mercenaries whose skill with the bow was second only to that of the Turk. Their vigilance gave Assad the impression Ali abu'l-Qasim was bracing for an attack. *More blood has spilled,* the message had said. *But how much more?*

The Assassin approached the door wardens, ignoring the spears they levelled at his breast. 'Fetch your master,' he snapped. 'Tell him his guest has returned.' The guards relayed his message and without delay he was ushered into the courtyard, where the pillow-strewn carpets and divans were devoid of their usual complement of beggars – though Assad counted a score of armed Berbers, marking time like men awaiting orders to move. Abu'l-Qasim's blue-turbaned spymaster hustled out from an interior room and greeted Assad with a flurry of hand-wringing and exhortations to Allah. He was a squint-eyed son of the Banu Zuwayla, local Arabs who had lived in the shadow of the Muqattam Hills long before the first Fatimids had arrived.

'Come quickly,' he said, as breathless as a sprinter. 'You were expected much earlier in the day! Hurry, effendi, I beg of you! *Inshallah!* Perhaps there is still time!'

'What goes?'

'Hurry! *La ilaha illa'llah, Muhammadun rasul Allah!*'

The Arab retraced his steps, nigh dragging Assad through the carpeted halls to a closed door near stairs leading to the upper floors. He rapped once, then he pushed the door open, revealing a small, bright chamber – a sitting room with reed mats and carpets, lit by three copper stands wrought to resemble the trunks of trees, their branches holding half a dozen glass-paned lamps apiece. The room stank of blood and sweat.

A man lay on an old divan, writhing in agony as a grey-bearded doctor carefully peeled pads and bandages of blood-soaked linen away from his abdomen, replacing them with fresh ones from a stack at his side. Abu'l-Qasim stood behind the doctor, the *tick* of ivory worry beads through his fingers marking the injured man's final hours like a metronome. The King of Thieves turned as Assad entered, a look of relief spreading across his weathered face.

'By God, man, I thought you had forsaken us!'

'I only received your message a short time gone. Did the killer return?' Assad moved closer to get a better look at the wounded man, at the ragged laceration in his belly, and found he recognized the fellow's blood-streaked visage.

'Musa? What the devil happened, Abu'l-Qasim?'

'My guards found him like this before dawn this morning, on the street outside the caravanserai. He would not say much beyond that he had to speak to you. Though I fear you've come too late.'

'Give us a moment.' Nodding, Abu'l-Qasim helped the old doctor to his feet and guided him to the door. Assad knelt by Musa's side and grasped the beggar's gory hand. 'Musa. Who did this to you?'

Musa's one good eye fluttered open. 'A-Assassin?' he whispered.

'I'm here. Who did this?'

'The girl – the girl, but no matter – listen, Assassin! I found it. I found – found the Heretic's lair. I found it!' Musa shivered. The words came with tremendous effort; his narrow face was pale as a winding sheet, and a froth of blood and spittle matted his beard. 'F-Found . . . it!' The beggar grabbed a handful of Assad's khalat, using it to pull himself closer. 'F-Found – found him in the – in the F-Foreign . . .'

'In the Foreign Quarter? Yes?' Assad said. 'But where?'

Musa nodded. His breath was coming in ragged gasps now. The resolve that had kept him alive throughout the day was rapidly fading. He muttered something. Assad leaned closer. 'M-Maydan . . . al-Iskander! D-Do you . . . Do you k-know it?'

'I do.' Assad remembered the place from his childhood: a square in the heart of the Foreign Quarter where his mother once washed linens for the wife of a Greek merchant.

The beggar drew a racking breath. 'B-Beneath . . . look beneath . . .'

Assad frowned. 'Beneath?'

'L-Look . . . *beneath*!' A spasm racked Musa's tortured frame; he exhaled, bubbles of blood breaking on his lip, and abruptly the hard pain-etched lines scoring his face softened as he gave in to Death's embrace. Assad eased Musa's body back down on the divan and stood. Abu'l-Qasim rejoined him.

'May Allah bless and preserve him. He was a good man.' Abu'l-Qasim glanced sidelong at the silent Emir. 'What were his last words?'

'None of your concern. Bury him, Abu'l-Qasim. Mourn him, mourn your daughter, and live out the rest of your days as you will. I thank you for your hospitality, but our business is done.' Assad turned for the door. Bristling with menace, the King of Thieves stepped into his path.

'No, our business is far from done. What did Musa say? Did he tell you who killed him? Was it this Heretic? It was, wasn't it? By Almighty God! I will have the swine's head!'

'I said' – Assad's eyes narrowed to slits – 'it is not your concern.'

'Where is he? You said earlier he was in the Foreign Quarter! Where?' Recklessly, Abu'l-Qasim touched his hand to the pommel of his curved knife. 'I will not ask you again! A word from me and my Berbers will—'

The *Emir* of the Knife moved like the flicker of summer lightning. Without warning, he drove one iron fist into Abu'l-Qasim's belly. Air *whuffed* from the Arab's lungs; wide-eyed, the older man staggered and fell against the wall. Steel rasped on leather. Before the King of Thieves could recover, before he could draw his own dagger, the cold touch of Assad's salawar at his throat wrenched a gasp from his bearded lips. Sudden terror robbed Abu'l-Qasim of his voice. His limbs froze; it was all he could do to meet the Assassin's gaze, dark eyes smouldering with volcanic fury.

'Another word from you and you'll take your next breath in Hell. I have been patient with you, Abu'l-Qasim, out of respect for your daughter. But my patience has its limits. For the last time: forget the Heretic. I say my master's claim on him far outstrips the claim of any grieving father. He has spilled the blood of al-Hashishiyya, and for that – for that alone – he will pay.' Assad bore down on the blade until a thin ribbon of blood welled up beneath its edge. 'And if you cross me one more time, if you interfere in my business, by my oath to Alamut, the next time we meet will be your last day above the earth. Do you understand?'

'Y-Yes,' Ali abu'l-Qasim managed, his tongue cleaving to his palate. He sagged, shaking visibly as Assad withdrew the blade from his throat. The older man's legs gave way and he sank to the floor with a desolate sob, head cradled in his hands. Abu'l-Qasim was as brave as any three men, but the kiss of age-haunted steel unmanned him. *He understands, now, that there are things worse than death.*

Nodding, Assad sheathed his salawar and turned again for the door. 'I bid you farewell and long life, O Malik al-Harami.'

7

Seven men. Seven devils, their foul breath hot against her skin. Seven twisted faces blurred by the rank sweat dripping into her eyes. Features engorged with lust, they grunted and howled like beasts as they violated her in every way. Again and again she felt their calloused hands clawing at her breasts; they slapped her, their nails tearing and ripping as they wrenched her thighs apart. Again and again they drove into her, filling her with white-hot agony, pounding her bruised pelvis until the last dram of their molten seed spilled across her belly . . .

'What is your name?'

The sorcerer's voice cut through a haze of pain. Yasmina lay on her side, naked and shivering on the cold stone floor. One eye fluttered open; the other was matted shut with blood. She saw the hem of a man's dark robe enter the periphery of her vision. 'Please,' she whimpered. 'N-No more . . .'

'Then answer me without fail. What is your name, child?'

'Yas . . . Yasmina.'

'Sit up, Yasmina,' he said.

The girl raised herself up on one elbow, stopping as sharp jags of pain flared in her hips and lower back. She sobbed: 'I c-can't.'

'You must. If you cannot sit, you cannot stand; if you cannot stand, you cannot walk – and if you cannot walk, what use are you to me? I may as well call my men back and let them resume their sport.'

'No,' Yasmina said. 'P-Please, no more.' She bit her lip against the agony and slowly levered herself into a kneeling position, like a supplicant, her weight supported on her arms. Her thighs were slick with blood. Pale and sweating, she glared at the sorcerer through the black veil of her hair.

The man nodded. 'Good. Have you become accustomed to your new life, Yasmina?'

'W-What?'

'This . . . your new life. Do you find it agreeable?'

Yasmina cringed, squeezing her eyes tight against a fresh flood of tears. 'No . . .'

'A shame.' The sorcerer *tsked*. 'They *will* return, those men, and they will not leave until they have slaked their lusts. What will you do, child, when the act of rape grows too commonplace for them? What will you do when they decide to explore new and more inventive ways to sate themselves – to practise on you such obscene perversions as to make the fabled whores of Babylon hide their faces in humiliation?'

'Allah, n-no!' Yasmina sobbed. 'P-Please . . .'

'Oh, your Moslem god has abandoned you, child. Would you be here if he had not? No, in this matter I am your only hope.'

'You?'

'I can pluck you from this darkness, dear Yasmina. O, the things I can show you! My tutelage can save you from those who would use you merely for their pleasure and cast you aside. I can make you strong, child, in body and in mind; I can show you a world you never dreamed existed.' The sorcerer's voice dropped to a mesmeric whisper. 'But only if I deem you worthy.'

A scintilla of hope glimmered in Yasmina's eye. 'D-Do you . . . Am I w-worthy?'

The sorcerer stopped pacing; crouching near the girl, he stared at her in silence for a time, brow furrowed as the fingers of one hand smoothed his beard. He presented the picture of stern contemplation. 'Perhaps,' he said at length. 'But you must continue to prove your worth to me. You must renounce your old life with its flawed ways and embrace the path of Massaif. You must pledge yourself to my service.' His voice turned blade-sharp. 'And should you prove insincere, the wrath I shall visit upon you will make your last few hours seem as a pleasant diversion.' Ibn Sharr stood.

'I . . . I will serve you,' she said. 'I give you my word.'

'She lies.'

Yasmina flinched as the Heretic's voice cracked whip-like from the darkness behind her.

'She thinks herself clever, master. She tells you what she believes you want to hear only to spare herself further humiliation. But, deep inside her heart, she harbours animosity. One day, she will use it to betray you.' The Heretic emerged from the gloom and moved to stand alongside his sorcerous master, pale eyes narrowing in cold scepticism. He carried a bundle of rough cloth in his hands. 'Do not trust her.'

'Ever the cynic, Badr. You know better than any man how difficult it is to earn my trust,' Ibn Sharr said, 'and what ills befall those who break it. She understands what manner of chastisement my displeasure will bring. Is that not so, Yasmina?'

The young Egyptian nodded. 'It is . . . master.'

'See, Badr? Already she has learned her place, if not her purpose.' Ibn Sharr raised an eyebrow to his sullen lieutenant and spoke a word in a tongue unfamiliar to Yasmina: '*Sacrifise*.'

At this, the Heretic nodded, a slow smile spreading across his face. 'Fitting.'

'Indeed. Now, give her a tunic. She will accompany me upriver to find the place the ancients called Ta-Djeser. Do your fedayeen understand the importance of what must follow?'

'They do, master.' Badr al-Mulahid pitched the bundle he carried on to the floor near Yasmina, gesturing for her to take it. She was skittish. Expecting some gesture of cruelty, the girl kept a cautious eye on both men as she reached for the wad of cloth. It was a galabiyya of homespun linen, patched and worn, its colour faded from a vibrant blue to a curious shade of grey. Carefully, she shook it out and drew it over her head.

'Take as much time as you require on this hunt, Badr,' Ibn Sharr said. 'No mistakes! The Hammer is an uncommon prize. Imagine the power we will command with a relic of such staggering antiquity at our disposal!'

'We stand ready, master. The *Emir* of the Knife will not escape us.'

'See that he does not, my loyal Heretic!' Ibn Sharr motioned to the girl, and then turned for the door. 'Make her ready to travel. I leave within the hour. We—'

Ibn Sharr staggered, his head swivelling to the entrance to the underground temple. He closed his eyes; his nostrils flared as something akin to a shudder of pain rustled down his spine. The Heretic rushed to his side. The sorcerer steadied himself, laid a heavy hand on his lieutenant's shoulder. 'By the grace of the gods below,' Ibn Sharr hissed, 'I can feel its presence. Rouse your fedayeen, Badr! The *Emir* of the Knife is here!'

8

The Maydan al-Iskander. It was smaller than Assad recalled; the slow creep of decay blurred its edges, where hovels of mudbrick and palm-thatch clung like barnacles to the hull of a wrecked galley. Assad came upon it from the west, down a warren of narrow alleys that ran through the worm-eaten heart of the Foreign Quarter. He stopped on its fringes.

Once, the Maydan had been an open-air market, a place where merchants of distant lands could meet in congress and commerce. Assad remembered the Greek his mother had washed linens for: kindly and garrulous, an oil merchant who spent his mornings engaged in haggling and his afternoons spooling lies to whomever would listen, children especially. He told stories of his travels – tales of giant birds and fish the size of small islands, of one-eyed ogres and talking apes, of flying carpets and sinister djinn – stories which always degenerated into mad caperings and bawdy songs about the whores of Sarandib. The Maydan had been his stage.

Now, even by the soft light of the moon, the place looked as cheap and mean as the old Greek's wife: two ramshackle tenements rose from the uneven earth, the ground at their feet jumbled with refuse and choked with weeds. Waist-high tussocks of sedge grass rattled in the faint breeze.

Look beneath, Musa had said. *Look beneath*. Assad frowned. Beneath what? Beneath the tenements? Beneath the ground? Beneath some marker he had yet to see? *Look beneath . . .*

Assad prowled deeper into the Maydan, skirting heaps of smashed pottery and scatterings of yellowed animal bones. He stopped again and listened, his hand resting lightly on the carved ivory pommel of his salawar; raw hatred pulsed through the hilt – a sharper vibration than any he had felt in a long while. The blade hungered. It thirsted for blood, for slaughter. Baring his teeth in a bestial grimace, the *Emir* of the Knife exerted his will over the blade's burning rage; the effort caused his biceps to bulge and thick ropes of muscle to writhe between wrist and elbow.

In that instant, with his senses heightened by ancient wrath, Assad caught a hint of movement on the periphery of his vision. He sank to a half-crouch and peered through a fan of sedge. A dozen yards away, a dark shape disengaged from the deeper shadow between the tenements. A shape clad in black, its lower face muffled by a scarf. It straightened visibly as another figure seemed to emerge from the very ground – surely rising from the entrance to a cellar or the like which, given Musa's dying admonition, made perfect sense. This figure, too, was black-clad, but with close-cropped hair the colour of heavy gold. Words passed between the two; the first figure nodded vigorously and drew a knife while the other turned and scanned the expanse of the Maydan before returning into the ground. Assad had the impression of a hard and angular face, a Frankish face, with skin bronzed by the sun and pale eyes that glimmered with a strange inner light.

The Heretic.

Assad loosened his blade in its sheath. With measured steps, taking care never to rise above a crouch, he slowly worked his way around the edge of the Maydan. He passed wraith-like through deep wells of shadow and came in behind the lone sentry, who squatted in the lee of the nearest of the two tenements, perfectly still save for a twitch that caused a flicker of moonlight to reflect from the blade of his drawn knife. And in that position the sentry remained, even as Assad rose up behind him like a spectre of Death.

The man stiffened at the cold caress of steel on his neck, the blade's razored tip touching his flesh where the skull met the spine. 'How many fedayeen remain below?' Assad whispered in his ear.

The sentry shook his head, pale with fear and yet defiant.

'Your end can be swift.' Assad increased the pressure on the hilt of his salawar. Blood oozed as it sank a hair's breadth into the sentry's flesh, provoking a sharp intake of breath. 'Or I can make it so you linger in misery. The choice is yours. How many?'

'To Hell with you, dog of Alamut!' Before Assad could stop him the sentry hurled himself to the ground, the point of his own knife jabbed against his sternum. Assad heard the pommel scrape on stone; the man groaned and writhed, flopping on to his back like a speared fish. The knife stood out from his chest. Blood glistened, beads of onyx on the sedge grass.

Swiftly, Assad knelt and clamped a hand over the man's nose and mouth. Iron fingers stifled an agonized cry. The sentry's curved blade had missed his heart, and the bloody froth boiling in his throat promised that his suicide would be neither quick nor painless.

'Idiot,' Assad said. 'The knife cut into your lung. You're going to die, but if you tell me what I want to know, I'll make a swift end of your suffering. Keep silent and I will leave you here to drown in your own blood. One last time: how many fedayeen remain to your precious Heretic?'

The sentry's eyes pleaded for a quick death; he nodded. Assad lifted his hand away. An explosion of bright crimson jetted from the man's nostrils. The wretch gurgled and choked. 'S-Six,' he managed, around a mouthful of blood. 'Six remain . . . you're – you're a dead man, dog of A-Alamut! My master – my master knows – he k-knows you're c-coming . . . !'

'Good. It is your master I seek.' In one smooth motion, Assad wrenched the knife free of the man's sternum and hammered it down again with the precision of a surgeon: upper chest, left of centre.

Gasping, the man shuddered and died.

Assad rose to his feet and padded over to where the Heretic had vanished. As he expected, there was an entrance carved into the earth, a jagged cleft, its raw edges hinting at recent excavation. Slowly, Assad circled it. Moonlight filtered into the dark spaces. On one side, knotty planks and timbers shored up the earth; on the other, he saw the beginnings of an ancient stone wall, pitted and etched with fantastical figures. Crumbling steps followed it down into clotted shadow. There was something buried here, something hidden over the centuries by Nile silt and blowing sand. Something older than Cairo. *But what?* This was no cellar; Assad was certain of that, not with the totems of an older Egypt decorating its stonework. Such images, animal-headed and profane, were anathema to Moslem, Nazarene, and Jew alike. Even if the locals had claimed this as their own they would have first effaced its walls. No, this was forbidden ground . . . a place where the sins and heresies of the past boiled to the surface, where a sense of dread conjured by the devilish friezes was reinforced by the eager knives of the Syrians.

The perfect bolt-hole for the thrice-cursed infidels of Massaif.

Savage fury vibrated through the Assassin's hard-muscled frame, twisting through tendon and sinew as he descended into the earth. He made no attempt to muffle the sound of his approach. Down forty-two uneven steps, the heels of the Assassin's boots scuffed and thudded until he reached the bottom of the cleft. A faint breath of air trickled out around the edges of the curtain-hung entry. Scowling, Assad's fingers knotted in the thick fabric, and with a savage jerk he ripped the curtain free of its fastenings. The dim glow of a lamp shown from deeper within, through a yawning doorway.

'Heretic! We have business, you and I!' Assad's voice reverberated about the antechamber and out into the hall beyond, giving the Assassin some inkling of the dimensions of the place. 'Show yourself!'

The echo faded, unanswered; Assad crossed the antechamber and crouched by the doorway, ears straining to catch any slightest hint of an ambush: the scuff of a foot; the rasp of steel on leather; the whisper of fabric. Anything that might betray the locations of the remaining fedayeen and their master.

Columns as tall and thick as the cedars of Lebanon filled the next room, a stone forest lit by small clay lamps, dim and widely spaced. Still, it was enough light for Assad to see by . . . and more than enough to create wells of impenetrable darkness between the columns. The Heretic and his fedayeen could be hiding behind any one of them, Assad reckoned, waiting for him to either pass by or to turn and show them his back.

The Assassin straightened. Though outnumbered and on unfamiliar ground he still had the advantage: he was the *Emir* of the Knife; every myth, rumour, and half-truth attached to that name would come shrieking to life as they waited there in the dark. Fear would squat like a misshapen gargoyle on the shoulders of the Heretic's men, blunting the edge of their murderous zeal. Fear of *him*. The Assassin's scarred face settled into a resolute mask, cold and brazen; like a conqueror, he strode through the doorway and into the columned hall.

'Heretic!' Assad roared.

Stronger light flickered from his left, a reddish glow that spilled out through an intricately carved doorway and into the columned hall. Assad's eyes narrowed. A figure stood in partial shadow beneath the graven lintel with his hands clasped before him like a pious Nazarene. This man was older than the Heretic, a hairless pate and greying beard framing dark vulpine features.

'Where is he, old man?'

The fellow did not reply.

Assad moved between the columns. Years of stalking human prey had honed his senses to predatory sharpness; he knew after a handful of steps that he wasn't alone. From both sides he could hear the faintest whisper of calloused feet on stone. Assad caught the flicker of pale flesh, twinkling with sweat, and smiled. 'Six little fedayeen cowering in the dark. You are wise to fear me, dogs. Bring forth this Heretic of yours and perhaps I will allow the rest of you to live.' Cloth rustled. Ruddy light glinted off bared steel. 'Do you hear me? Bring him forth!'

'The Hammer of the Infidel!' the old man muttered, staring at the blade in Assad's fist. Gnarled fingers twitched, as though he longed to reach out and caress the watered steel, to stroke the ivory pommel. 'The spirits did not lie!'

Assad froze; suspicion clouded his scarred face. Never since bringing the blade down from the high Afghan Mountains had he met someone who knew its name. 'What spirits, old man? How do you know that name?'

'I hear its voice, as you do,' the old man replied. 'I hear *his* voice. Listen to him howl! Still he rages against the injustices done to him, against the betrayals and the broken promises, unaware that his is a vengeance that will never be consummated.'

'And who is *he*?'

Assad regretted the question even as he uttered it. Instantly, comprehension sharpened the old man's stare; a cold smirk twisted his thin lips. 'Do you test me, or do you truly know nothing about the blade you carry? Gods below! You don't know, do you? The

Hammer's history, its antecedents: such things are as alien to you as the meaning in these carvings!'

Assad bristled. 'I know enough!'

'Do you?' The old man laughed. 'It seems I have overestimated him, Badr.'

The Heretic emerged from the darkness at the old man's side like a creature born of shadow. His close-cropped golden hair caught the dim lamplight, pale eyes ablaze with contempt. 'He is artless, master.'

'Indeed, he is. The djinni of the blade merely toys with him. It deserves a stronger master, a more appreciative master.' The old man turned away. 'Kill this fool and bring the Hammer to me.'

The death sentence hung in the air for a score of heartbeats. Assad met the Heretic's pale-eyed stare without flinching, sizing up the man who casually drew a Frankish dirk from the small of his back. A half a dozen paces separated the two; Assad weighed his chances of reaching him and dealing a killing blow before the fedayeen, who were inching closer in the darkness, swarmed over him. The Assassin reckoned it would be suicide. Still, his muscles tensed. The blade in his fist throbbed with ancient hatred, its pent-up rage shredding every cell and synapse as it threaded his nerves with red-hot wires.

Blood, the steel sang to him.

Time slowed, thickening like honey on a cold winter's morning. A single heartbeat elongated into a caricature of eternity, and in that long moment of absolute stillness a series of disjointed images impressed upon Assad's consciousness: a carving of a man with a falcon's head lit by wavering lamplight; eerie blue eyes flicking right and left; tendons flexing as the Heretic tightened his grip on the hilt of his dirk, his weight shifting in anticipation . . .

Blood, the steel cried.

Suddenly, the *Emir* of the Knife laughed, a sound like the swift footsteps of Death – and as he laughed, he struck. With a panther-ish twist Assad sprang to his right, his salawar sweeping out before him. Flesh parted beneath its damascened edge; a Syrian who had strayed too close staggered, gurgling and clawing at his severed jugular as he fell to his knees. Assad barrelled past him to ram his shoulder into a second attacker's midsection. The man catapulted backwards, breath *whooshing* from his lungs; his spine crunched against a column and he sank to the ground.

The point of a Syrian dagger ripped through Assad's khalat, ploughing a bloody furrow along his ribs. The fighter who dealt the blow loosed a savage howl of triumph – a howl which abruptly changed to a death rattle as Assad's flickering riposte split open his skull like an overripe melon. Wrenching his blade free of the toppling corpse, the Assassin wheeled to meet the rush of the remaining Syrians and their master.

Shadows danced on the walls as the dead gods of this ancient land, graven in stone, watched the tableau unfold like spectators in a blood-soaked arena. Assad faced three fedayeen, black-turbaned murderers with fists upraised and knives gripped white-knuckle tight. A fourth lay at the base of a column, writhing in agony and fighting for breath. Of the Heretic, Assad saw no sign. Yet, in that flash-frozen sliver of time he apprehended the tactic of his enemy, for it was one he had himself used to good effect, one he had learned from Daoud ar-Rasul: *If your prey would prefer a fight, then blunt his sword with the flesh of the Faithful.* The Heretic would wait until the fedayeen had exhausted him before moving in for the kill.

Inshallah, Assad thought. *So be it.*

Assad did not slacken his pace; even in the full knowledge his own doom might be upon him, he did not hesitate. His veins blazed with hatred not wholly his own as he waded into the Syrians' midst, gore dripping from his blade and the stench of fresh-spilled blood yet in his nostrils.

The soldiers of Massaif were well trained, and they fought with the reckless bravado of men who held no fear of death. But against the fury of the *Emir* of the Knife, all their training and all their bravado accounted for nothing. Forged in the crucible of war and honed by the masters of Alamut, Assad moved with blinding speed, never still, his every step perfectly timed and without hesitation.

A maelstrom of steel rasped and whickered around him. A knife flashed past, a spirited lunge gone awry; Assad sidestepped and caught the man by the wrist of his knife-hand. His own blade fell like a butcher's cleaver, severing the fedayeen's arm at the elbow. The man screamed and reeled away, clutching the crimson stump to his body. Assad slung the amputated limb in the face of his nearest attacker.

As the Syrian recoiled from that grisly missile, the *Emir* of the Knife twisted and smote his remaining companion a terrible blow, hammering aside the long knife he hastily flung up in his defence. Assad's salawar crashed down full upon the man's left shoulder, splintering the bone and sending great gouts of blood spurting from the wound even as it drove him to his knees. A pitiful moan escaped the dying man's lips.

The last of the Heretic's soldiers chose that instant to spring; thinking *now* was the opportune moment to sheathe his knife in Assad's heart, before the Assassin could drag his blade free of the crumpling body. But his was a deadly miscalculation. In a spatter of gore, Assad tore his Afghan sword-knife from the soon-to-be corpse and pivoted; he caught the Syrian in mid-leap, committed to his attack and unable to check his momentum. Steel flashed in the gloom. There was an instant of impact followed by a fierce cry as the two men crashed together, their straining limbs intertwined.

But it was the *Emir* of the Knife alone who rose up from that deadly scrum. Blood dripped from his face and hands; it made slick the ivory hilt of his salawar, which sprouted from the fallen Syrian's chest like a steel spike. The fellow's ashen lips writhed. '*Allahu akbar,*' he whispered, again and again. 'God is great.'

'And there is no God but He,' Assad said, planting a foot on the Syrian's shoulder and prizing his blade free. The man shivered, death freezing his features in a rictus of horror.

Flames of vengeance flickered in Assad's eyes; he glanced up, his gaze raking the shadows. 'Heretic!' he roared. 'Why do you hide? Come out and let us settle our accounts! Or is it that you only kill beggars and women?'

A sudden gust of air, hot and stale, flowed out from the doorway where the old man had been standing. It extinguished a few of the lamps scattered about the columned hall and caused others to sputter. Darkness thickened. Assad turned, staring at the elaborately carved doorway that led deeper into the ancient temple. *Was there another way out of this accursed place?* The possibility wrenched a sulphurous oath from the Assassin's lips. Perhaps the fedayeen had sacrificed themselves so the Heretic and the old man – *master*, he had called him – could make good their escape. 'God curse the coward's bones!' Assad started for the door.

'You take much for granted, Emir,' said a silky voice from the shadows, dripping malice. 'You presume fear when none exists, and you presume I am at your mercy when, in truth, you are at mine.'

'Am I?' Assad stopped; his eyes narrowed to fiery slits. The voice came from somewhere behind him. He cocked his head to one side, straining to catch the slightest sound. 'Am I at your mercy, al-Mulahid – or whatever your name is? If that is the truth, as you say, then I bid you to prove it. Come. Show me the quality of your mercy.'

There was no answer. Assad pivoted slowly in the oppressive silence, his nerves screaming, his senses whetted to razor-sharpness. The coppery reek of blood hung like a shroud in the still air; shadows flickered around the remaining lamps, dim pools of light that illuminated the carved columns but little else. Piteous sobs from the last of the fedayeen left alive, his legs twisted and useless, shattered the eerie stillness. Assad shifted his weight . . .

The blow came with little warning – a faint whisper of cloth, a displacement of air. Before Assad could wheel to face these sounds, his left shoulder exploded in searing agony. A blade, no doubt a long Frankish dirk, sliced through taut muscle and skittered off the bone of his shoulder blade. Assad staggered, teeth clenched against the pain, and lashed out with his salawar. The ancient blade slashed empty air.

The Heretic's mocking laughter echoed through the columned

345

hall. 'There. You see? Such is the quality of my mercy that I could just as easily have cut your throat.'

Hot blood soaked the back of Assad's khalat. He said nothing, but slowly backed into a circle of light cast by one of the remaining lamps, shaped like a terracotta pitcher and sitting slightly above the level of his head on a crude wooden ledge spiked to a column.

'Have I stunned the great *Emir* of the Knife to silence?' The gloating voice came from Assad's left. His nostrils flared; the Heretic was close . . . but just outside the reach of the light.

Unless the light moved.

Quick as a snake, Assad thrust his salawar out, hooking its tip in the lamp's finger-hold. The Assassin twisted and slung the lamp to the ground a few paces to his left. Pottery shattered; the flaring wick sparked a conflagration of oil, a brief inferno that bathed this portion of the hall in a greasy orange glow – and revealed the crouching form of Badr al-Mulahid, poised to strike.

Assad sprang, heedless of the wound in his shoulder. The Assassin did not waste precious breath with curses or taunts; the time for words was long past. He leapt the pool of flaming oil and met the Heretic in a swirling tempest of steel.

The Afghan blade in Assad's fist sang a paean of hatred; its rage was the voice of the dead – the voices of a thousand souls slain, forever trapped in a web of unrequited vengeance and ancient sorcery. Savage fury drove the corded muscle of his arm, but there was nothing random or reckless in Assad's attack. Far from it. A cold and precise intellect guided stroke after hammering stroke.

The Heretic gave ground amid the rasp and slither of steel. His dirk, its eighteen-inch blade the work of an Italian master, was no less deadly than Assad's salawar, nor was the pale-eyed killer's skill any less impressive. He shifted, his body swaying away from blows that would have split him from crown to crotch.

Slash and parry, thrust and riposte: their blades flickered in the dim light, grated together, and sprang apart. The Heretic feinted, cutting at Assad's face before turning it at the last instant into a stab for his heart; Assad batted his enemy's blade aside and countered with a furious upward rip. The Heretic danced back from that blow.

The air in the columned hall grew close and hot from their exertions; both men panted, sweat streaming down their faces. They stood now at the spot where the battle had begun, inside the ring of slain fedayeen. The Heretic took advantage of the brief lull to scoop up a fallen dagger. He dropped into a knife fighter's stance, his dirk held pommel first, its blade close against his forearm; his purloined dagger he kept low and angled for a disembowelling strike.

Dark eyes aflame, the *Emir* of the Knife lunged and then stopped short with a loud stamp of his foot. It was an old cavalier's trick – one he learned from a Persian swashbuckler in Basra – and it caught the Heretic off guard. Badr recoiled, ready to parry a thrusting blade; even as he did so, Assad swept in and brought his salawar crashing down with every ounce of power in his knotted shoulders.

Desperately, Badr al-Mulahid raised his dirk to fend off the blow. The hardened edge of Assad's salawar snapped the Italian steel of the Heretic's dirk; it sheared through flesh and bone, severing the Frank's forearm in a spray of blood, and continued down to bite into the juncture of his neck and shoulder.

Badr al-Mulahid reeled. A sudden pallor tinged his features; eerie eyes widened in a mingling of shock and disbelief. The Heretic's knife clattered to the ground. He reached up and grasped the blade jutting from his upper chest, heedless of the bright gore cascading over his fingers.

'I . . . I hear them,' Badr croaked, glancing up. 'Voices. T-They call to me . . .'

'Then go to them, spawn of Shaitan!' A welter of blood, and Assad wrenched his blade free, spinning it in a tight circle – a circle that ended with jarring impact and the sound of a butcher's cleaver splitting a haunch of beef.

The Heretic's pale eyes dulled; slowly, his head rolled off his shoulders and struck the stones with a wet crack. His blood-spattered body stood there a moment longer before toppling sidewise.

'Allah.' Assad wrung sweat from his brow; he stared at his fallen foe. Blood from the wound in his shoulder dripped down his left arm. Already the limb was stiff; pain made it increasingly difficult to move. Still, he had one last Syrian to account for. The old man the Heretic named as his master.

'Come out, greybeard.' Assad turned and staggered to the carved doorway, its posts and lintel still limned by a faint ruddy glow. 'I have no call to harm you.'

Assad paused, a supernatural thrill crawling down his spine. The glyph-etched walls of the room beyond were black as soot and cut with a dozen deep niches, each one sheltering the nearly identical statue of a man wearing a serpent-browed headdress, his pose rigid, his angular beard unnatural, his eyes cold and hawkish. *Was this the god of this accursed place?*

The Assassin shook his head to clear his mind of distraction. *There is no God but Allah*, he reminded himself. Aloud, he said: 'You have no need to hide, old man.' Light seeped around the edges of another curtained entry. He heard nothing beyond it. The air was thick with the stench of slaughter, but underlying the stench of blood was the aroma of oils and unguents, dust and salt, and the none-too-subtle hint of decay.

Assad scowled, ripped the curtain aside . . . and recoiled from the overpowering stink that billowed from the room. *What deviltry . . . ?* Inside, a trio of copper lamps cast their ruddy light over low tables cluttered with bits of stone and scraps of paper, with frayed rolls of papyrus and half-burned candles, with delicate alabaster jars and vases of murky glass. A gold knife sat atop a bundle of dried herbs; pots of ink stood beside a mortar of heavy stone that looked better suited for grinding flour than for mixing . . . what? Assad could make little sense of any of it. Was the old man an alchemist of some sort? A concocter of potions and poisons? Assad stepped over the threshold . . .

. . . and stopped short; by instinct, he tightened his grip on his salawar.

Bodies lay scattered across the floor of the small chamber. Six were ancient, like desiccated manikins of wood and leather swathed in crumbling cerements of age-blackened linen. A seventh body reclined among them like the Devil's own courtesan: a naked young woman, her eyes open and staring; in the cool, dry air her mottled flesh was just beginning to show signs of putrefaction. The eighth and final corpse was familiar to Assad: it belonged to one of the men he had killed in the Rub al-Maiyit, the one with the infected eye.

The Assassin's jaw clenched in revulsion. The old man was no alchemist. He was a defiler of the dead – a necromancer. And he was gone. Assad saw no sign of him. *How?* The chamber was small; it afforded few places to hide and no other exits. *How did he escape? A hidden door?* With a muttered curse, Assad drove his salawar point-first into the top of one low table – upsetting a pair of jars whose human-headed stoppers were fashioned from alabaster – and moved to snatch up a copper lamp. This place and everything in it should burn, but something the old man had said stayed his hand. *History . . . antecedents: such things are as alien to you as the meaning in these carvings.*

Assad turned slowly, studying the walls. Carvings covered every inch, creatures and glyphs chiselled in stone. His eyes shifted from the walls to the items on the tables. Many of the same symbols he saw repeated. What was the link between these carvings and the old man's presence here? What meaning . . . ?

Weariness left Assad's limbs cold and leaden; the ache of his lacerated shoulder dulled his thoughts. He blinked and shook his head. Whatever the old man's plans might have been, the Assassin had little doubt the death of the Heretic and his fedayeen had disrupted them. The advantage lay within his grasp now. And wherever the necromancer's powers had spirited him off to, Assad would find him and send him on to a well-deserved grave. For that to happen, however, he would need fresh eyes and ears.

He would need the King of Thieves.

Assad's lips set in a thin line, a humourless smile; he sighed, staring at the blood-stained ivory djinni grinning up from the pommel of his salawar. Abu'l-Qasim would need a peace offering.

9

The King of Thieves slept uneasily. Sweat beaded his brow. Moaning, he thrashed against his bedclothes; one hand flailed about, hitting a pottery wine jug that stood atop a low table near his divan. It toppled, rolled off, and struck the tiled floor in an explosion of terracotta fragments and wine lees. The sound jolted Abu'l-Qasim from his restless slumber.

'No!' he cried out, his hands flying to his throat. Abu'l-Qasim ripped away the bandages to touch the thin laceration left behind by Assad's blade, relieved to find it unchanged. In his nightmare, something had tried to claw its way out . . .

Abu'l-Qasim sank back against the cushions of his divan. Through shuttered windows, dawn's grey light suffused the air of his bedchamber with rising warmth. He closed his eyes and listened at the sounds filtering in from outside: the furious barking of a dog; wagon wheels rattling on the hard-packed street; babbling voices; and, in the distance, the blaring of trumpets. It was too early for such a cacophony.

He heard a slight knock at the door to his bedchamber before it creaked open; pottery crunched under the soles of soft slippers. Abu'l-Qasim felt a stab of anguish; as a little girl, Zaynab would often steal thus into his room, her soft voice begging him to take her up on the roof so she might watch the sun rise.

A hand touched his shoulder. 'I beg your pardon, effendi.' It was his Berber spymaster.

'What is it, Derna?' Abu'l-Qasim opened his eyes. Derna looked dishevelled, heavy-eyed, as though someone had just roused him from slumber, too. His face was the colour of curdled cream.

'The army of Damascus, effendi! Just as you forewarned! They came up from the south and circled around the city during the night!'

That explained the noises, the trumpets. With a sigh, Abu'l-Qasim flung off his bedclothes and got to his feet, his careworn face settling into a mask of resolve. 'Fetch my stewards and send for my captains. I want the doors to remain open and food prepared for any who desire it. Put forth the word, Derna: all who seek succour are welcome in the house of Abu'l-Qasim.' Abu'l-Qasim's eye flickered to a settee at the foot of his bed, where a tray covered by a wicker dome awaited his pleasure. He gestured. 'Take that away. I will let you know when I am ready to break my fast.'

Derna's narrow eyes crinkled in confusion. 'Of course I will take it away, effendi, but I did not bring breakfast to you. That must have been brought in last night.'

'What?'

'It was here already, as Allah is my witness.'

Abu'l-Qasim's beard bristled with suspicion. His gaze slid from Derna to the tray; carefully, he reached out and raised the wicker dome. Its contents gave off the metallic aroma of spilled blood. Behind him, he heard his spymaster gasp. 'Allah preserve us!'

Abu'l-Qasim grunted in equal parts surprise and perturbation.

A severed head lay on the tray; its angular, Frankish features clean-shaven, its close-cropped hair the colour of heavy gold. Eyes a pale shade of blue stared through half-closed lids. From between its lips protruded a roll of papyrus. This Abu'l-Qasim took; gingerly, he smoothed the papyrus out and held it so he could read the two words written in a firm hand upon its surface: *As promised.*

Below this, daubed in blood, was the sigil of an eagle, its wings outstretched. He had seen such a symbol before, among Zaynab's things. It was the mark of Alamut.

Derna wrung his hands. 'What means this, effendi? Is it a threat? A warning?'

Abu'l-Qasim crumpled the papyrus in his fist; turning, he walked to the window and nudged open the shutters. A Nile breeze carried away the smell of blood. Outside, the rising sun turned the dusty sky above Cairo into a canopy of orange and gold. Pigeons rose like a smoky cloud and wheeled over the domes of the distant palace. Brazen-throated horns continued their clamour, calling soldiers to their posts; fear rustled through the streets as self-appointed heralds spread news of the advancing army like bearers of a plague. Yet, for all the promise of chaos the day held, Abu'l-Qasim's heart felt suddenly light, unshackled. 'He kept his word.'

'Effendi?' Derna said.

'The *Emir* of the Knife kept his word. He brought me the head of my daughter's killer. Take it down into the courtyard, Derna. Spike it to a lance and put it where everyone can see.'

Derna bowed. 'It will be as you wish, effendi.'

And breathing deeply of the morning's breeze, Ali abu'l-Qasim – whom the folk of Cairo called the King of Thieves – smiled.

The Sixth Surah
Lion of Cairo

1

The surgeon hunched over Assad's lacerated shoulder was a smooth-faced eunuch, slender and severe in a khalat of green silk and a turban-wrapped fez; he approached the stitching of flesh with the single-minded intensity of a master tailor. Assad clenched his jaw as the eunuch sluiced cool brine over the wound, inspecting its edges with a critical eye. Salt water tinted with blood spattered the golden travertine underfoot.

Stripped to the waist, Assad lay on his stomach on a stone bench, beneath a keel-arched portico of a pleasure kiosk standing alone at the heart of a jewel-green garden. Early morning sunlight slashed through a haze of dust; heavy serpentine columns upheld the graceful arches, striping the flagstones with alternating bands of light and shadow. Assad heard the eunuch mutter to himself about the dust as he readied a curved golden needle attached to a length of catgut thread.

From the corner of his eye Assad caught the Caliph pacing. The young man wore the rich white robes of his office, his undervest and silken girdle sewn with gold and silver thread; his bulbous turban sported a brooch of electrum inlaid with mother-of-pearl, a snowy egret feather bobbing above it. He turned suddenly, hands clasped at his back and his brow furrowed. 'You will not tell me what happened?'

'It was a personal matter, my lord. A thing of no importance. It is done, regardless.' Assad winced as the surgeon began knitting the two sides of the wound together. 'Is it true you've received an embassy from Shirkuh?'

'It is.' The Caliph crossed the portico to stand by one of the columns. The garden around them was unnaturally quiet; no insects trilled in the rising heat, no birds sang; the grit kicked up by the army of Damascus drifted south on the light breeze. It settled over Cairo like a shroud, obscuring distant domes and minarets and adding a touch of jaundice to every leaf, bough, and blade of grass.

'And?'

Rashid al-Hasan looked askance at the Assassin, a petulant curl to the young man's lip. 'Oh, it was a personal matter. A thing of no importance. It is done, regardless.'

The eunuch surgeon chuckled. Assad shot a frosty glance over his shoulder. 'Leave us.'

'I have not yet finished—'

'Leave!' Perturbed, the fellow tied off the ends of his half-drawn sutures and stood. He bowed to the Caliph before withdrawing from the kiosk. Assad sat up on the stone bench; he winced as he flexed his shoulder. 'My master has a saying. "Where goes Alamut, so goes Massaif." I got this rooting out a nest of those God-cursed infidels who thought to set themselves up in the Foreign Quarter.'

'I do not understand,' the Caliph said. 'Is this Massaif a rival of al-Hashishiyya?'

'They are al-Hashishiyya, or they were. Massaif is a mountain-top fortress in Syria, my lord.' Quickly, Assad sketched out what he knew of this decades-long war between the two Assassin sects. He told the Caliph of how, in the time of Hasan ibn al-Sabbah, Alamut had established a mission in Syria to combat the rising influence of the Turks, and how a schism erupted after Ibn al-Sabbah's death – a schism fuelled by the Syrians' thirst for wealth and power. 'Massaif has become a den of traitors and renegades. They seek to supplant the Hidden Master's dominion with that of their own chief, the so-called Old Man of the Mountain, even as Alamut seeks to crush them under heel.'

The Caliph looked sharply at Assad. 'Allah! Could these Syrians – these Assassins of Massaif – could they have been allied with Damascus? It cannot be a coincidence that they were here in Cairo even as an army from Syria stands upon our doorstep.'

Assad recalled their eerie lair, with its scattering of ancient corpses and the stink of necromancy, and shuddered. *It's as though they were looking for something.* 'Though I cannot say for certain, my lord, I don't think their presence here had anything to do with Shirkuh – or with Amalric, for that matter.'

'Perhaps you are right.' Rashid al-Hasan said nothing else for a long moment. He stared out over the silent garden, his eyes haunted by things he had seen over the past days, over things perpetrated in his name. Lines of concern etched his youthful brow as the weight of his office pressed down upon him. Finally, he stirred. 'The Book of Allah tells us: "If the enemy incline towards peace, do thou also incline towards peace and trust in Allah." Shirkuh has requested a parley tomorrow, an hour before the noon prayer.'

'Where?'

'The Pearl Pavilion, on the Nile's banks beyond the Qantara Gate, away from his army and out of bowshot from the walls. We will each bring two-score men – advisers and officers, slaves and stewards. I'd like you to be there, of course.' The Caliph trailed off, chewing his lip; suddenly, he said: 'Do you think it was foolish of me to accept Shirkuh's offer? As I see it, what harm is there in listening to the man? He's made no violent overtures. His men have shown restraint in dealing with people and property beyond the walls . . .'

Assad stood, a simple act that wrenched a groan from his lips. His muscles ached from sole to crown, the gash along his ribs throbbed, and his shoulder felt as if his surgeon had threaded it with sutures of white-hot wire. He craved a cool goblet of wine, a good meal, and a few crumbs of opium. But more than that, he craved sleep. 'I would not call it foolish,' Assad said, 'but don't be gulled by this show of peace, my lord. Shirkuh wants Cairo; his master, Nur ad-Din, wants Cairo. But in order for the Sultan of Damascus to appear to his followers as the saviour of Islam, the Mother of the World must remain whole and unspoiled. And while Shirkuh cannot afford to have Cairo become a second Ascalon, Amalric of Jerusalem is under no such constraint. He will gladly pull Cairo down brick by brick if it means putting an end to the Moslem threat on his southern border. I imagine the prospect of wholesale slaughter appeals to Amalric – and Frankistan will surely echo with paeans of glory for he who razes Cairo.'

Rashid al-Hasan shivered. 'Our choices, it seems, are little different from those of a plump summer hare: do we let ourselves be spitted on the huntsman's shaft or crushed in the jaws of his hounds?'

Assad walked to the portico's edge, one hand braced against the fluted marble shaft of a column. 'We're not hares, my lord,' he said after a moment. 'And we have a third choice. After the sun sets, with your blessing, I will slip from Cairo and go out among the Damascenes. I will strike Shirkuh down where he sleeps. Once they are leaderless, it will be easy to sway his men into fighting for you when the Nazarenes arrive. A common enemy creates a common cause.' Rashid al-Hasan folded his arms over his chest; unconsciously, he started to gnaw at the pad of his thumb. Assad sensed his hesitation. 'Does this trouble you, my lord? If you're worried about the stain such an act would bring to your honour—'

'No,' the Caliph said quickly. 'No. My honour is secondary to Cairo's survival. I worry that perhaps our survival hinges upon the good graces of Shirkuh ibn Shahdi, upon keeping him alive. Consider this: I have generals aplenty, but who among them can lay claim to Shirkuh's experience? His battlefield knowledge? Even combined, their skills fall well short of his. Ten thousand more men will not improve our chances if those in command have not the talent to prosecute a war against the Nazarenes.' Rashid al-Hasan shrugged his thin shoulders. 'In my heart I agree that the course of action you counsel is wise, but I cannot give it my sanction. Not now. Shirkuh is worth more to me – worth more to Cairo – alive than dead.'

'As you wish,' Assad said, sagging against the column. His vision blurred; he rubbed his eyes, pinching the bridge of his nose as he stifled a yawn. Exhaustion and his wounds were taking their toll.

Concern wrinkled the Caliph's brow. 'Come, my friend, I have kept you from taking some much-needed rest. I will have my chamberlains prepare you a room.'

Assad shook his head and motioned to the shaded heart of the kiosk, where travertine gave way to thick carpets strewn with cushions and pillows. It was a nest where lovers might meet or where men of rank might sit together in private. 'This will serve my needs well enough, my lord.'

'You're certain?'

Assad staggered to the bench and caught up his salawar, the ivory-hilted Afghan blade wrapped in the blood-stained folds of his tunic. He stared suddenly at the long sword-knife. Despite its leather sheath and the draping of grey cotton, he could feel a renewed sense of hatred radiating from it, stronger, sharper, an insatiable yearning that coiled serpentine through muscle and sinew. *You are Death incarnate,* the knife said, its harsh voice lancing through Assad's skull like a blade of jagged ice. *You know what it is to thirst for blood, for flesh; you know what it is to desire a death with such singular purpose that nothing else matters – not your life, nor the lives of those closest to you. You know revenge . . . you know . . . you . . .*

'Assad? You look pale. Shall I recall the surgeon?'

The Assassin glanced up. 'No,' he said after a moment's hesitation. 'No, my lord. I am all right – or I will be, with a few hours' sleep. Perhaps then I can offer you some worthwhile counsel.'

'Your counsel is ever worthwhile, my friend,' the Prince of the Faithful said. 'Rest for now, but seek me out once you have slept your fill. I would continue our conversation . . . and perhaps learn something of your master.'

Assad bowed as the Caliph retreated back to the palace. Alone, the Assassin retired to the well-carpeted kiosk where he eased himself down on to the thick cushions, his salawar in arm's reach. He shut out the endless parade of questions that whirled through his brain: from the meaning of the cursed glyphs beneath the Maydan al-Iskander to the nagging uneasiness that he had not heard the last of the Heretic's master; from the approaching horde of Nazarenes to what fate might befall the Caliph should Shirkuh gain the upper hand. He ignored them all and instead fixed his attention on the dusty green leaves of a willow tree growing near the edge of the portico, visible through the door of the kiosk.

And to the hypnotic sway and rustle of leaves, Assad fell asleep.

2

In the fields northeast of Cairo, a mile and more from its ponderous gates, the army of Damascus squatted like an iron-shod beast. The pawing hooves of ten thousand horses threw thunderheads of dust into the sky, a sickly yellow haze that drifted south on the breeze. Steel flashed like lightning as mailed Turkoman scouts emerged from the dust clouds to survey the city's walls. Alert, patient, the army settled into the grass like a predator and waited for the right moment to spring.

Yusuf ibn Ayyub cantered back down the road, along ancient dykes and over wooden bridges that spanned reed-choked canals. He squinted through the dust to catch a glimpse of the landscape through which the army had travelled, so different from the pastures and fields of Damascus. Here, everything was dry and brittle. The land itself, pale and sun-bleached, reflected heat like a furnace. Hawks circled overhead, lost in the haze.

Ahead, the road skirted jumbles of mudbrick sprouting between groves of spiky date palms. Stonework jutted from the sandy soil: fallen columns and plinths; crouching lions with the heads of men, their features effaced by time and wind; obelisks of reddish granite, cracked and broken like rotten teeth. Amid these bones, these relics of a long-forgotten age, stood Shirkuh's command tent: a fly-rigged pavilion of striped linen that snapped in the breeze.

The place was a hub of activity. Messengers came and went; grooms and water-bearers tended the horses while their riders relayed terse missives to Shirkuh himself. It impressed Yusuf that his uncle did not rely on adjutants to manage his affairs; from scouting reports to where best to dig latrines, Shirkuh personally handled his army down to the least detail.

Yusuf dismounted and handed his horse's reins to a nearby groom; slapping dust from his trousers, he walked through a cordon of Turkoman guards to where Shirkuh stood beneath his pavilion, leaning over a makeshift table whose surface bore a crudely sketched map of Cairo done in charcoal. A pitcher of khamr and a cracked pottery bowl waited at Shirkuh's elbow.

'Make sure your men know better than to bathe in those canals,' Shirkuh said to one of his atabegs. 'A crocodile can drag a man under quick as that.' The commander snapped his fingers; at the edges of the pavilion, several other Turkoman officers – older men who had accompanied Shirkuh to Egypt in years past – nodded sagaciously.

A grin split Shirkuh's craggy face as he caught sight of Yusuf. The Kurd's voice boomed: 'What say you, nephew? Does this place where we are to parley meet with your approval?'

'It is adequate, uncle, though I would not have chosen it. It rests too near the river and a veil of greenery obscures it from casual view. I would have offered to meet the Caliph in a more open spot.' Yusuf frowned. 'This is why the task of speaking on your behalf should have fallen to me.'

Shirkuh raised an eyebrow. 'And run the risk of them recogniz-ing you and taking you hostage? No, Yusuf, your counsel is too valuable to me. There will be other ways by which you might yet earn glory.'

'There are people for whom glory is no more important than sand, uncle.'

'Indeed. In that you are too much like your father, my staid and pious brother, Ayyub.' Shirkuh poured a measure of khamr into the bowl, raised it in salute, and drained it in one gulp. He smacked his lips in relish. 'Tell me, Yusuf: is the accumulation of glory not pleasing to Allah?'

'It is, if it serves to exalt His name,' Yusuf said. Nods of assent rippled through the Turkoman officers. 'But a man who seeks to adorn himself with glory for no reason other than his own foolish vanity is no better than a whore who paints her face and proudly displays the golden rewards of her sin.'

Shirkuh's good eye shimmered with unaffected delight. 'And that, my nephew, is why I did not send you forth into the lion's den. To lose you would be to lose my very conscience.'

'And what of your backbone?' A harsh voice lashed out from behind the wall of Turkoman officers. Men parted, allowing Dirgham entry to the pavilion. 'Have you lost that, Shirkuh ibn Shahdi?' Clad in a blue khalat and gold-embroidered undervests, the former vizier of Egypt was a head taller than Yusuf. His salt-and-pepper hair and untamed beard lent him the aspect of a fierce desert prophet; he spoke as much with gestures as with words, as though the wild contortions of his hands helped his tongue retain its silvery edge. 'Why do we not attack? Have we not travelled across the desert, endured thirst and horrible privation, for this very moment? And yet, here we stand, admiring the city from afar like pilgrims! Fulfil your obligation to your lord in Damascus, Shirkuh, and lead us into battle!'

Shirkuh refilled his bowl. 'I would parley first.'

'Parley? By most holy Allah! You would speak with the Serpent in the Garden of Unimaginable Delights? For that is what Jalal al-Aziz is: a serpent. His words will beguile a simple soldier like you, my lord. His voice sows confusion even among the mighty.'

'I accept the risk,' Shirkuh replied coldly. 'Simple soldier or no, I would speak with our brother Moslems ere we come to blows.'

'Then you are a fool!'

At this, one of the atabegs – a grizzled officer sporting a forked beard shot through with grey – took a menacing step towards Dirgham; his lips peeled back, teeth bared, as with one sinewy hand he drew his curved yataghan from its sheath. The sword's razored edge caught the bright sunlight. Dirgham recoiled with a gasp, startled by the naked hatred that gleamed in the man's eyes.

But a gesture from Shirkuh brought the atabeg up short. 'Put that away, Uzbek. Has being driven into exile with naught but the clothes on your back taught you nothing, Dirgham? It behoves a beggar to be humble, and not to answer generosity with insults.'

Anger suffused Dirgham's features. To the lords of Damascus, he was ever the Beggar of Cairo; it was an appellation he was powerless to quash, for it was one born of truth. He had nothing – not a horse, not a dagger, not a single stitch of clothing upon his person – that wasn't the product of Sultan Nur ad-Din's generosity. Shirkuh wanted him to remember that.

With difficulty, Dirgham bent his neck in a stiff approximation of a bow. 'Perhaps my words were ill chosen,' he said through gritted teeth. 'But that does not change matters. Your master sent you to crush Jalal al-Aziz, not to parley with him! Do your duty or step aside!' Dirgham whirled and stormed from the pavilion.

Grim amusement tugged at the corner of Shirkuh's mouth. 'That one still thinks his nemesis awaits the full measure of his wrath.' Those of his officers within earshot, Uzbek included, grinned; they had heard the tale of Jalal's demise already. Shirkuh gestured after the retreating vizier with a jerk of his bearded chin. 'Keep an eye on him, Yusuf. Dirgham's aspirations might drive him to mischief, especially since he deems his plan greater than mine.'

'And what is your plan, uncle?'

Shirkuh pursed his lips. He canted his head and fixed his good eye upon Yusuf. In its dark depths, the younger man saw the familiar gleam of reckless ambition. 'We took Atfih without striking a single blow. Why not Cairo as well?'

3

From the garden just inside the Emerald Gate, from a gilded iron bench in the immense shade of a plane tree, Parysatis watched the day pass. She sat on a mass of silken pillows that the Caliph's slaves had prepared for her, a small ebony table resting at her elbow; a tray of honey cakes and a linen-shrouded goblet of pomegranate juice, its golden surface beaded with moisture, awaited her pleasure. Parysatis ignored the refreshments. Her attention never wavered from the gate.

The Emerald Gate faced north; on a clear day Parysatis could have seen the crenellated heights of the Bab al-Nasr, the Gate of Victory, rising in the distance, towering over Cairo's ramparts as easily as the latter towered over the Soldiers' Quarter. Today, the air thick with strangling dust, she could barely see the far edge of the parade field that lay beyond the open gate.

A score of Massoud's men stood guard, conical helmets and heavy mail flashing in the hazy sunlight. Scarves muffled their noses and mouths as they scrutinized everyone who passed through the Emerald Gate. Palace eunuchs – lesser chamberlains and functionaries – enquired into the business of each and every person who stepped foot on palace grounds. Some, like the entourage of the chief cadi of al-Azhar Mosque, who the chamberlains escorted in with great pomp, were shown to a place where they might refresh themselves before their audience with the Caliph; others – the merchant-princes seeking special tax dispensations in light of the coming war, or the adventurous nobles seeking a warrant of command in the Fatimid army – found themselves shunted aside, forced to wait with a thousand other petitioners desiring but a moment of the Caliph's time. The remainder of the throng, the commoners and those fellahin dispossessed by the sudden arrival of Shirkuh's army, made it no further. The eunuchs drove them away with curses and threats.

Parysatis sympathized with this last group most of all. They were simple men caught in the merciless vice of war: tradesmen, labourers, and farmers from Fustat and the southern suburbs, separated from their families by chance and pressed into the Caliph's service by necessity. Most only sought permission to have their wives and children brought inside the city walls; barring that, they begged for the Caliph's blessing to leave Cairo, to abandon the city in hopes of ushering their families to safety before Shirkuh struck.

She wondered what the Damascenes would do to them, to those left outside the city, after the truce engendered by tomorrow's parley came to an end. Would Shirkuh leave the poor unmolested as he had the merchants of Fustat, or would his army circle the city and drive the masses before them, killing the men and damning the women and children to lives of bitter slavery? A palpable sense of desperation hung over Cairo. Desperation and fear. Parysatis tasted both in equal measure. But her deepest fears were not for herself, but for Yasmina, who still had not returned.

'I sent a man to enquire after your girl among the servants of Ali abu'l-Qasim,' Massoud had told her that morning. 'They claimed not to have seen her since the day of Zaynab's murder.'

'If she's not there, then . . . then where would she be?'

Massoud tugged at his beaded moustache. 'Al-Karafa, perhaps,' he said at length. 'It is the cemetery on the road to Fustat, not far from the old mosque of Ibn Tulun. Abu'l-Qasim's son and two of his wives are buried there.' Parysatis wanted to go; she wanted Massoud to provide an escort to al-Karafa, but the Circassian responded with a brusque gesture of denial. 'Impossible. We cannot even open the gates to admit the families of those poor wretches.' Massoud raised his chin to indicate the fellahin who clamoured at the Emerald Gate. 'We are under Shirkuh's scrutiny, lady. Thus far, he has acted with admirable restraint, but only Allah knows how long his benevolence will last. So we do nothing to provoke the dog until we know for certain what his true intentions are.'

'I cannot leave Yasmina alone out there!'

'We're not even certain she is out there, lady. That's the problem . . . we do not know *where* the girl has gone. For all we know she might have found a bolt-hole here in the city, a place where she might lie low and grieve.' The Circassian amir pursed his lips. 'What I can do is send a few of my men out to scour the streets for her. This, at least, will give them something to do while we await Shirkuh's pleasure. And, if it be Allah's will, perhaps they'll find her.'

So as a handful of men searched the streets and alleys of Cairo, Parysatis kept a resolute vigil over the Emerald Gate, the only entrance to the palace the White Slaves of the River had not shut and barred. Of course, the Gate of al-Mansuriyya remained open; those tall, keel-arched doors of cedar and gilded iron provided a direct route from the Bayn al-Qasrayn to the Golden Hall. Reflecting its importance, that way was off limits to all save the amirs of the army and of the palace, their officers and their messengers. No, if Yasmina returned to her – *when she returned*, Parysatis corrected – it would be through the Emerald Gate.

The day trudged on, flurries of commotion punctuating the long stretches of indolence: the clash and clatter of mail as the guard changed; the song of the muezzin as the sun reached its zenith and again as the shadows lengthened; the ghostly bells of Fustat's Coptic churches, calling their frightened parishioners to the altar. Parysatis watched as the wise men of the city – the imams and cadis, shaykhs and sharifs – arrived to take counsel with the Caliph and then left again, their faces no less grim for the effort. She watched the tide of fellahin rise and ebb, their hope that the Caliph might grant them leave fading with the daylight. Parysatis' hope faded, too, as dusk settled in with no sign of Yasmina.

'Where are you?' she whispered. Desperate tears welled at the corners of her eyes. 'Please, come back. Allah, please—'

'May I sit with you?'

Parysatis jumped as a familiar voice spoke from behind her. She turned, wiping tears away with the heel of her hand. Rashid al-Hasan stepped closer and leaned against the bole of the plane tree. The Caliph was dressed simply in a galabiyya of loose white linen, without belt or sash, and a turban-wrapped fez. Slippers of gold-embroidered leather protected the soles of his feet. Parysatis made to rise, but Rashid waved the gesture off.

'I'm sorry,' he said. 'I did not mean to startle you. May I sit?' The woman nodded and brushed pillows aside to make a space on the bench for the Caliph. 'When I didn't see you this afternoon, I thought perhaps you had returned to the harem. Then Massoud told me where you were . . . and why you're holding vigil here. Is there still no sign of your friend? What is her name?'

'Yasmina.' Parysatis sighed. 'And no, nothing yet, my lord. I've racked my memory for an answer to where she may have gone, some hint from her past as to where she might find a small measure of comfort, but to no avail. I am at my wits' end.'

'Is there anything I can do?'

Parysatis raised her face, her eyes meeting the Caliph's; she saw nothing patronizing in his expression. Indeed, the stern set of his jaw convinced her that the Prince of the Faithful would reorder the heavens for her if she but asked. Quickly, Parysatis averted her gaze. 'No, my lord. No. I thank you for your kindness, but my troubles are of little consequence compared to the troubles afflicting all of Cairo. You have enough to worry about without my making demands of—'

'And yet,' he said, cutting off her protests, 'where would I be if you had chosen simply to look the other way, to go about your own business and not get involved in mine? We both know the answer. Jalal's intrigues have left us in desperate straits, to be sure. But for the moment I've done all I can to soothe what ails Cairo. Give me a chance to do the same for you.' The Caliph raised one hand in a gesture of summons; a chamberlain standing a respectful distance hurried forward and knelt.

'Command me, Most Excellent One.'

'Send a robe of honour to Ali abu'l-Qasim, who dwells near the Nile Gate, and send along with it our condolences on the loss of his daughter, Zaynab. She did us a great service and it is one we shall not forget. Further, tell Abu'l-Qasim we would consider it a personal favour if he were to focus his considerable resources on discovering the whereabouts of the girl Yasmina. She, too, has done us a great service and her safety is of the utmost concern.' Rashid al-Hasan dismissed the chamberlain with a nod and returned his attention to Parysatis. 'If Massoud is right, this Abu'l-Qasim has more eyes and ears than even my own spymasters. He will find her, I'm sure of it.'

'Thank you, my lord,' Parysatis said. Tears glistened in her eyes; on impulse, she clasped the Caliph's hand to her lips and kissed it. He did not recoil, as she feared he might. Indeed, her body trembled as he caressed her cheek and gently wiped away her tears.

'May . . . May I ask a kindness of you?' he murmured.

'Ask anything of me, my lord.'

'For tonight, at least, I wish to be known simply as Rashid. Not "my lord", not "O Caliph", not "Excellent One" nor "Prince of the Faithful" . . . just Rashid. Can you do this small thing for me?'

'Yes, my—' Parysatis smiled suddenly. 'Yes . . . Rashid.'

'Would that you smiled more often,' he said. 'Have you eaten? Something light, perhaps. Come; let us pass the evening in comfort and without pretence. I would hear the tale of your family, and as payment I will tell you the scandals of mine.' He stood.

Parysatis' smile faltered. Unsure, she cast a worried glance at the gate. 'What if Yasmina returns . . . ?'

'We will not be far, and besides, my chamberlains know she is to be shown into my presence immediately.' Rashid al-Hasan offered Parysatis his hand. 'Will you join me, if only for a short while?'

After a moment's hesitation, she glanced away from the gate to meet the Caliph's gaze. She noticed a tightness around his eyes, no doubt born of anxiety over the coming days, but Parysatis recognized something else, something deeper: a desire for a thing he had never experienced, a thing made of gentleness and passion. One night of normality out of a thousand days of madness, that was all he was asking for. *And he's asking me to share it with him.* Parysatis' smile returned as she took the Caliph's hand and rose to her feet.

'You have a scandalous family . . . Rashid?' she said, still unused to calling him by name.

The young man chuckled; slowly, he escorted her into the garden, where the sound of their passage silenced insects in mid-chirrup. 'Glorious and Almighty God! I am an opium addict whose followers perpetrated a palace coup against my vizier, and still I would be accounted among the tamest in a long line of Caliphs stretching back to al-Mu'izz li-Din Allah.'

Parysatis laughed. 'My father, may Allah hold him in His favour, used to spin me stories of his youth here in Cairo . . . and his adventures with your own sire.'

'Truly? I have not heard this. Do tell . . .'

4

The sun hung in the blood-red sky like a misshapen disc of copper, its edges blackened, its face radiating waves of excruciating heat over a landscape ravaged by war. Thousands of corpses littered the streets of Ascalon, a carpet of hacked and riven flesh. Mothers clutched their children; fathers and brothers clutched shattered spears and broken swords. Tattered yellow and green banners once carried with pride by Ascalon's defenders now rustled like ghosts on the hot wind.

As a ghost, too, did the dark figure of a man drift through the multitudes of the slain, the flash and glitter of his gold-chased mail incongruous in this gore-blasted wasteland. He followed the dry wind, followed zephyrs of dust through deserted squares and down winding streets; past fire-gutted buildings looted by victorious Nazarenes. The wind led the man to the city's heart, to where a ruined mosque squatted in the middle of a broad square.

Here the man stopped, one hand falling to the carved ivory hilt of an Afghan sword-knife that jutted from his sash. His brows drew together as he swept his gaze across the mosque's crumbling portico; higher, he peered through the dusty haze at a dome scarred by endless bombardment. Fury racked his body. Fury as hot and relentless as the coppery sun. He bounded up the shallow steps and burst through the open doorway. Inside, shadows swirled like smoke from a funeral pyre; shafts of murky copper radiance lanced through ruptures in the domed ceiling. The man caught sight of a figure pacing the periphery of the chamber, a lean wraith clad in a surcoat of grimy white cloth who warily avoided the columns of light.

The man's wrath made him fearless. He crossed the threshold, his voice profaning the silence. 'Why?'

Instantly the silhouette stopped and spun towards the door, falling into a predatory crouch. It snuffled the air like a hound on the trail of a hare.

'Are you deaf?' the man said. 'I asked you why! Why Ascalon?'

'Why?' the figure replied, its voice hard, guttural, and full of rage. It crept forward, still in a crouch. 'Because God willed it.'

'God?' The man spat. 'Your God holds no power here!'

'Lignum crucis, Signum ducis,' it muttered, coming closer. 'Sequitur exercitus quod non cessit, sed praecessit in vi Sancti Spiritus.' Closer, sidestepping a shaft of light. Menacing eyes glittered and sinew creaked. Still, the man displayed no trepidation; he stood motionless, his knuckles whitening around the hilt of his blade.

'What is that you babble?'

Now, with only six paces separating them, the figure straightened. This close, the man saw a design in blood caking the chest of the figure's surcoat: a cross, red on white. The man's eyes narrowed, his nose wrinkling. The stench of death clung to it.

'Behind the wood of the Cross,' it hissed. 'Behind the banner of the Chieftain follows the army which has never given way, marching in

the strength of the Holy Spirit. God wills it!' The Templar threw his head back, howling his rage as it sprang upon the man. Ancient steel rasped on leather even as searing cold talons dug into his throat . . .

5

The rasp of a whetstone echoed like a drawn-out sigh through the cavernous Golden Hall. Inside the Caliph's alcove, the Seat of Divine Reason looming above him, Assad sat on the lowest level of the dais with his back to the alabaster wall. He held his salawar up in the morning light and squinted down the length of the blade, looking for the slightest imperfection in its cutting edge. Unsatisfied, he resumed his ministrations. The oiled whetstone hissed.

He had risen with the sun, drawn from sleep with a curse on his lips and fury in his heart. It was the nightmare – the same familiar nightmare that had troubled him for years. Even now, hours later, he could recall shreds of it: the shattered ruin of Ascalon, the stench of death, the hateful presence of the Templar. Yet this time the nightmare was different. *Why was I not afraid? Was it because you were with me?* Assad scrutinized the blade once more. *What was it the old man had said? 'I hear his voice . . . he rages against the injustices done to him, against the betrayals and the broken promises.'*

'How did he know?' Assad muttered. But whatever haunted the salawar made no answer beyond the faint, ever-present vibrations that coiled along his arm. The question of the Heretic's master troubled Assad like no other. Who was this man, this necromancer eager to blacken his very soul by consorting with the dead? What purpose brought him to Cairo? And, more importantly, where was he? 'I have slain the wolves,' the *Emir* of the Knife whispered, 'but let the lion escape, it seems.' He smoothed the whetstone over an almost imperceptible nick in the blade.

Sunrise had brought with it a stifling heat; sticky with sweat and crusted blood, Assad had staggered from the kiosk where he'd slept, traversed the silent garden, and pressed into his service one of the palace's ubiquitous eunuchs, ordering from him a bath, food, and a change of clothes. The man responded admirably. Two hours later, Assad emerged from the hammam with his hair and beard trimmed and oiled, his skin freshly scrubbed, and his left shoulder bound in clean linen. A bowl of stewed mutton and a flat loaf of bread had taken the edge off his hunger, while the eunuch had replaced his grimy clothes with the finery of a Fatimid officer: silk, linen, and gold over a hauberk of fine mail. He rejected the thick-nasalled helmet the eunuch had offered, opting instead for a simple steel cap . . . something easily hidden under the folds of his turban.

And thus had he retreated to the Golden Hall, to think and to partake of the chamber's delicious cool while waiting for the appointed hour of the Caliph's parley with Shirkuh. Beyond the curtain, beyond the Hall's gold-crusted doors, Assad could hear the rising din of Cairo's embattled populace. There was a desperate energy in the air, no doubt born of a belief that frenetic activity could stave off imminent doom. Messengers scurried to and fro; soldiers brought in reports from the city's walls, while scribes of the chancery compiled tallies of what remained in the granaries and magazines. Chamberlains issued contradictory orders to the legion of eunuchs serving them, bellowing to be heard over the incessant bickering of courtiers and petitioners.

Assad seemed the sole island of calm inside the chaotic palace walls. His sojourn in the East had taught him that worry served no purpose, and only fools frittered away their day trying to second-guess the will of God. Allah wrote each man's destiny at birth; inevitably, that destiny included the cold hand of Death. Assad could no more change that than he could change the course of the sun, so why allow himself to become overwrought? His end would come, in its own time.

The Assassin glanced sharply at the niche behind the Caliph's throne. Over the *slish* of stone on steel he heard a faint *click*: the sound of a latch on a hidden door. He remained perfectly still as the rear of the niche swung inward.

Rashid al-Hasan's voice echoed from the secret passage: 'To think I sat so close and never imagined its existence. But not every niche hides a door, does it?' He stepped out, turned, and offered his hand to Parysatis.

'No, not every one,' she said. 'But with few exceptions, all the doors I have found are in these niches. I wish I could have found them all, but to stay gone from the harem too long was to risk Lu'lu's wrath.'

'Lu'lu!' Assad heard a note of anger in the Caliph's voice; woven in with it, the Assassin sensed a confidence that had not been there before. 'That creature will bedevil you no more! His days as Chief Eunuch of the Harem are numbered! This I promise.'

Parysatis sighed. Her hands smoothed away a wrinkle in the Caliph's undervest, brushed a phantom bit of dust from the chest of his snowy khalat. 'Rashid, please. You make me regret telling you the tale. I have no love for Lu'lu, but he is excellent at managing affairs and much beloved by your aunts. He only needs guidance. Your guidance. Grant him clemency and give him a chance to prove his worth to you.'

'Perhaps.'

'Besides.' She flashed an impish smile. 'Does not "Rashid the Just" have a better sound to it than "Rashid the Merciless"?'

The Caliph laughed. 'Either one rings superior to "Rashid the Obscure". Still, I should make an example of someone, at least. Why not Lu'lu?'

'Please, Rashid . . .'

After a moment the young man nodded. 'As you wish, then. I will practice leniency on this harem despot of yours. But – and I will brook no argument on this! – I do not want you returning to Lu'lu's demesne until I've had a chance to set this right. Honour me as my guest . . . and allow me to bask in the life you bring to my cold apartments.' Gently, he stroked her cheek with the back of his hand.

'Well, if you will brook no argument,' she said, capturing his fingers with her own, 'then I shall not argue. But what will your advisers say?'

'Nothing,' Assad said, rising up from the base of the dais, 'for he is Caliph and he does as he pleases.' Parysatis gasped, her eyes widening in surprise; Rashid al-Hasan whirled. Wrath flickered across his hollow-cheeked visage, but upon seeing it was the taciturn Assassin who interrupted them the Caliph whistled a sigh of relief.

'By God, man! Are you the spawn of cats, sired by the wind?'

A thin smile curled Assad's lip. 'So some might say.'

The Caliph gestured to the scarred emissary of the distant Lord of Alamut. 'Should some ill befall me, trust this man, Parysatis. He has proven himself worthy beyond reproach.'

The young Persian woman cocked her head to one side, glancing curiously at Assad. 'You are the Sufi from the Hejaz . . . but are you not also the slayer of Jalal al-Aziz?'

'I am many things, lady,' Assad replied, offering her a slight bow. To the Caliph, he said: 'The appointed time draws near, my lord.'

'Of course.' Rashid al-Hasan turned back to Parysatis. 'What was it your father used to say? About luck?'

'That luck is the result of good preparation,' she said.

'And am I prepared?'

There was a frankness to Parysatis' gaze as she smoothed Rashid's khalat one final time. 'You are the Pillar of the Faith, a Prince of the Sons of Ali descended from the favoured daughter of the Prophet himself,' she said softly. 'Who is this man who would challenge you? Who is this Shirkuh?'

The Caliph exhaled, his shoulders squared, pride stiffening his spine. 'Bless you, daughter of Ibn Khusraw, and thank you.'

'For what, my lord?'

'For your company . . . and for reminding me of who I am.'

Parysatis smiled, her eyes moist. Nodding, Rashid al-Hasan

gave her hand a squeeze, then he turned and descended the dais in a swirl of white linen and cloth-of-gold. The tall Assassin held the silken curtain open for the Caliph, who passed from the alcove and into the domed Hall without a backward glance. Though his features were yet thin and pale, Rashid al-Hasan nevertheless wore a mask of iron resolve.

'If murder remains out of the question,' Assad said, falling in beside him, 'have you decided how else we might lure your enemy into a pact of friendship?'

The Prince of the Faithful glanced sidelong at him. 'A good question. I've given it some thought.'

6

The Pearl Pavilion was a league from Cairo's walls, at the heart of an unkempt garden overlooking the reed-choked banks of the Nile. Built upon a foundation of limestone blocks quarried from the temples of Old Egypt, the Pavilion's walls were formed from thick columns of milky alabaster that supported a dome of carved wood and stucco; traceries of vines and flowers intertwined with delicate calligraphy. Sheer panels of translucent linen fluttered between the columns, while unlit lamps of filigreed glass hung from ceiling beams.

Shallow steps led up from the Nile's bank; here, in the shade of a knotted cypress, Massoud's boot heels clacked on stone as he paced, his hand toying with the hilt of his sabre. The Circassian smoothed his bead-heavy moustache. 'I don't like this,' he muttered again. 'This place . . . it is a perfect spot for an ambush. What's to stop Shirkuh from ringing this grove with his cavalry and burning us out like escaped slaves?'

'Nothing, save his word,' Assad said. The tall Assassin sat on a thick cypress root, idly stirring the leaf-mould with the tip of a crooked twig. Though he presented the picture of nonchalance, his eyes betrayed a sense of wariness.

Massoud snorted. 'His word? Come, now, you're not so naive as to believe he would keep his word, are you?'

'It's not a question of naivety,' Assad replied. 'It's about knowing your man. Shirkuh ibn Shahdi is a cavalier, noble by breeding if not by birth. In the souks of Palmyra they still tell the tale of his exile from Tikrit. They say he spilled the blood of a gentleman who insulted a woman of Shirkuh's acquaintance. This is not a man who gives his word lightly.'

'Still, I don't like it.'

Assad rose to his feet. 'You don't have to like it. Just make sure your men know what's expected of them.'

'They are prepared. You need not worry about that.' Thirty-four of Massoud's finest soldiers guarded the Pavilion, inside and out; veteran swordsmen who wore steel chain beneath their silken khalats, and who carried round shields inlaid in gold with the blessed words of the Prophet. To bring their company up to two-score, the Caliph himself had selected a pair of chamberlains, a revered jurist of al-Azhar Mosque, and a scribe whose task it was to record the words and deeds of the participants.

A brazen horn announced the arrival of the Damascus contingent; as one of the two chamberlains rushed out to guide Shirkuh and his men to the Pavilion, Assad and Massoud returned to the Caliph's side. Inside, a breeze off the river ruffled the linen panels. Rashid al-Hasan sat on a low divan strewn with pillows, the grey-bearded jurist at his right hand and the scribe at his left. The young monarch's new-found confidence remained unshaken; he sat erect, composed. He nodded to Assad, who took up a position behind and left of the Caliph's divan.

They did not have long to wait. Through billowing linen, Assad spotted a column of men approaching the Pavilion: gaunt Turkomans who had long since traded their sheepskin jackets for coats of mail, sinewy hands resting near the hilts of their yataghans, the curved swords favoured by these dwellers of the

Asian steppe. At the head of the column, escorted by the Caliph's chamberlain, came three men; two were Kurds who shared a family resemblance – Shirkuh, Assad reckoned, and a younger kinsman – while the third was a fox-faced Arab, his wild eyes agleam with the light of fanaticism. His terrible gaze raked the Pavilion as though searching for someone.

Shirkuh gestured for his Turkomans to remain outside the Pavilion; with his kinsman, the Arab, and a pair of grizzled officers, the Kurd who was Nur ad-Din's right hand ascended the shallow steps on the heels of the chamberlain. The latter bowed three times before hurrying forward to fall prostrate at the Caliph's feet.

'O Most Noble One! O Prince of the Faithful, who strengthens the religion of God, I present to you the honourable al-Amir Asad al-Din Shirkuh ibn Shahdi! By his side stands the son of his brother, Yusuf ibn Ayyub, and the captains of the Army of Damascus. With them comes Dirgham, once of Cairo, my lord.'

Rashid al-Hasan dismissed the chamberlain with a nod. 'The blessings of Allah upon you, Shirkuh ibn Shahdi.'

'And may His beneficence shine upon the descendants of blessed Fatimah for the length of your days, O Caliph,' Shirkuh replied, bowing. 'We have—'

'Excellent One,' Dirgham interrupted, 'has your office been so reduced that your vizier forces you to treat with us in person, as though you were selling baubles in the souk?' The Caliph stiffened; Shirkuh's face purpled. Turning his head slightly, he tried to silence the Arab with a growl. Dirgham, though, was having none of it. He shrugged off Yusuf's hand as the younger man sought to restrain him and took a step forward. 'Such insults to your august person should no longer be tolerated! Send for Jalal al-Aziz, my lord! Give us both a blade and we will let Allah decide the issue!'

The silence that descended over the Pavilion was all but absolute, broken only by the rattle of leaves and the soft *scritch* of the scribe's pen. A humourless smile flirted at the corners of the Caliph's mouth. Finally, he turned and gestured to one of his chamberlains. 'An excellent idea. Fetch my vizier. He and Dirgham should be reacquainted.'

The chamberlain bowed and scurried to the rear of the Pavilion, where one of the Circassians passed him something; crossing to where Dirgham stood, the chamberlain placed his burden on the floor at the other's feet. It was a round, covered basket, tightly woven of reeds and caulked with pitch.

'Though,' the Caliph continued, 'the issue of your respective claims on my power has been rendered moot.'

The chamberlain lifted the lid. Dirgham recoiled at the stench rising from inside the basket. Nestled in a bed of discoloured silk, the severed head of Jalal al-Aziz, mottled and bloated with putrefaction, stared up with milk-white eyes. Dirgham gasped for breath, lips writhing as he sought to form coherent words. 'M-My . . . My lord! I—'

The Caliph raised his voice. 'You have done Cairo a great service, Shirkuh ibn Shahdi, by returning this traitor to us. And though you come girded for war, we bear you no ill will. No doubt you and your benevolent master, Nur ad-Din, fell prey to the curse of silver upon Dirgham's tongue . . . for Allah the Most Merciful knows it drips falsehoods like poison.'

'I protected you!' Dirgham shrieked, spittle flying into his beard. 'When others would have gladly used you for their own ends, I thrust my neck out for you! And this is how you repay me? With lies and baseless accusations of treachery?'

'Is it a lie that you would plunge Egypt into war for the sake of revenge?' the Caliph said. 'Is it a lie that you hoped to use the swords of Damascus to regain your lost prosperity? To assuage your bruised pride? This man has played you for a fool, good Shirkuh! Give him to me, and I will see he meets the end he so abundantly deserves!'

Shirkuh stroked his beard. His good eye flickered from the Caliph to Dirgham and back again. Beside him, Yusuf stirred.

'Is it not written, uncle, that he for whom the door of righteousness is opened should take advantage of the opportunity, for he knows not when it may be shut against him?'

Shirkuh glanced sidelong at Yusuf; slowly, he nodded. 'My nephew is a man of uncommon wisdom, and I would do well to heed his advice. But I cannot simply hand Dirgham over to you. Something must be given in exchange.'

Dirgham whirled. 'Idiot! Nur ad-Din will have your head!'

'What is he worth to you, good Shirkuh?' the Caliph said, ignoring Dirgham's outburst.

'To me, nothing. To my master, Nur ad-Din, he perhaps has some small value – as a curiosity, nothing more. Still, it is the principle of the thing, you see.'

'I do. Let me propose this, then: in exchange for your pledge of peace and cooperation, I offer you the position that Dirgham covets so. I offer you the robe of vizier – not my sole vizier, mind you, but a place of honour, nonetheless. Thus will my enemies become yours . . . and for the moment I hold Dirgham as chief among my enemies.'

Shirkuh and Yusuf exchanged incredulous looks. 'For peace, you say? And cooperation?'

Dirgham backed away. 'Do not be a fool! Do you not see? This is how the Partisans of Ali repay loyalty! You have an army, Shirkuh – use it as your master intended!'

'Enough!' the Caliph barked. 'What say you, good Shirkuh?'

Assad saw a slow smile twist the older Kurd's lips; he smoothed his beard, a calculating gesture. Finally, Shirkuh nodded. 'I say let your enemy trouble you no longer, my lord. Uzbek.'

Dirgham barely had time to recoil from Shirkuh's dismissal before the fork-bearded Turkoman officer, Uzbek, leapt in and hammered a calloused fist into the side of his head. The Arab staggered under the sudden blow; Uzbek seized him as he fell, turned, and dragged the former vizier from the Pavilion. Through panels of sheer linen, Assad watched as the lean and leathery Uzbek hurled Dirgham to the ground at the feet of the scowling Turkomans. The Arab shrieked a litany of curses that changed to pleas for mercy. Both fell on deaf ears. A yataghan flashed in the dusty sunlight; it rose and fell, Dirgham's screams cut short by the sounds of steel rending flesh, of vertebrae crunching.

The Caliph watched the execution in utter stillness, his eyes like chips of black ice. After the deed was done he glanced over at the scribe who, though pale with shock, had not ceased his record. 'Let it be written,' the Caliph said, 'that on this day, Dirgham of the Lakhmi Arabs met his just and proper end. Let him remain unburied and unmourned as a warning to those who would betray Cairo.' He turned back to face Shirkuh, but before he could say anything more a horse came crashing through the dusty undergrowth outside the Pavilion, its rider screaming incoherently.

The Caliph shot to his feet. Around him, the soldiers of Cairo reacted instinctively, drawing steel and baring teeth in defiance. 'What madness is this?' Massoud bellowed, thrusting himself in front of the Caliph, while Assad – his face set with murderous purpose – aired the edge of his salawar and sidled closer to the scowling Shirkuh. Steel hissed as fierce Turkomans sprang to their lord's defence.

'Wait!' Yusuf ibn Ayyub forced his way between the two groups. 'Wait. Listen!'

The horseman gasped, gesturing back towards Shirkuh's camp. 'An army is coming . . . coming up the valley from Bilbeis. Jerusalem. They fly the banner of Jerusalem!'

'Jerusalem?' Shirkuh whirled to face Rashid al-Hasan. 'What madness, indeed! Is this your doing? Would you lull us into complacency while your Nazarene allies cut our throats?'

'They are not my allies,' the Caliph snapped, prodding with his booted toe the basket holding the severed head of Jalal al-Aziz. 'But his. I feared as much. No doubt when word reached Jalal that you had set out for Egypt, he sent envoys to Jerusalem. Amalric has ever been eager to add Cairo to his kingdom. The Infidel is upon us, Shirkuh. Do we quibble among ourselves, or do we make ready?'

Such was the earnest honesty in the Caliph's voice that not even Assad could discern his lie: that he had not been aware of Jalal's blasphemous alliance beforehand. Shirkuh's good eye bored into the young Prince of the Faithful; he looked him up and down, seeking some outward sign of treachery. After several long moments, the Kurdish general barked with laughter. 'God's teeth! You have the right mettle, O Glorious One! I swore your enemies would become mine, and that dog of a Nazarene, Amalric, is the enemy of all righteous men. Let our forces join to send him shrieking back to his master in Hell!'

7

Trumpets blared along the Turkoman lines; whirring kettle-drums fired the blood of the ferocious steppe-dwellers, stoking their lust for slaughter to a fever pitch. Assad saw dervishes among them, wild-eyed men bereft of armour who swung bright silken banners embroidered with the sayings of the Prophet over their heads, and who chanted '*Allahu akbar!*' at the tops of their lungs. Steel rippled as men thrust lance and sword to heaven.

'*Allahu akbar!*'

A guard of a dozen Mamelukes surrounded the Caliph; Assad stood near, holding the reins of his borrowed horse while the younger man added his awe-struck voice to the fury of the Turkomans. He had insisted on leading Cairo's forces out himself, to personally hand command of them over to Shirkuh. Assad thought it curious that the one-eyed Kurd had only requested fifteen hundred men from the Caliph – with the caveat that they all be cavalry, well armoured and mounted on swift horses. Still, Rashid al-Hasan obliged him by giving over the remaining five hundred Jandariyah led by their captain, Turanshah, with another thousand drawn from the Sudanese mercenaries. Allied officers clustered around Shirkuh, listening as he laid out his plan for the Nazarenes.

'*Allahu akbar!*'

The sun was well past its zenith, and the heat of afternoon lay like a stifling blanket over the Nile Valley. A mile distant, across a sandy plain where the cultivated lands touched the desert, Assad could discern the vanguard of the Nazarene army, their harness flashing like lightning through a haze of dust. Nigh-deafened by the roar of the Turkomans, Assad nevertheless gave ear to Shirkuh even as he watched the enemy fan out into a line of battle.

'*Allahu akbar!*'

'. . . are tired from their march, thirsty, and unprepared to fight. Amalric thought to find a fretful city on the verge of capitulation, with an unseen ally plucking the strings of power in a song of submission. He did not expect to find an army facing him. He did not expect the lords of Damascus to join with the lords of Egypt!' The gathered officers bellowed their approval. Shirkuh calmed them with a raised hand. 'Blessed Allah saw fit not to grant Amalric a surfeit of imagination where the waging of war is concerned. He is predictable. Even now, he arranges his lines as he always does: his cursed knights in the centre with his infantry defending each flank. He will try and use his horsemen as a carpenter uses a wedge, to split our formation. I am of a mood to turn his conceit against him.'

Shirkuh drew a dagger and knelt in the sand. He sketched out a series of lines; then, gesturing to his nephew, he said: 'Yusuf, take the left wing. Dismount four thousand of your men and have them dig their heels in against the Nazarene infantry. Load the remaining thousand with as many arrows as their horses can carry and send them against Amalric's flank. I will do the same on the right. Harry them without mercy, Yusuf. Force them to wheel and we will crush them in on themselves. You, sons of Cairo, you will have the centre. Nay, do not cheer so, for you will bear the brunt of Jerusalem's cavalry charge.'

Turanshah stepped forth from the knot of Cairene officers, grim and deadly in the plain grey mail he had adopted since his fall from grace. 'You honour us, Amir Shirkuh. Let Allah witness my oath: we will not falter.'

The Kurdish general grinned. 'Ah, but I *want* you to falter. When Amalric's cavalry presses you, fall back. Draw them off in pursuit. The Nazarene will break his own lines to keep up.'

A slow smile spread across Turanshah's face. He salaamed and returned to his place. Shirkuh stood; he stropped his knife against his trouser leg to clean sand from the blade before sheathing it, and then swept his sobering gaze over the assembled officers. 'It is a soldier's duty to risk all in battle. If any among you fear death or slavery, then I say you are fit to serve neither Sultan nor Caliph. Go home, if fear threatens to unman you; put down the sword and take up the plough. Raise goats. Stay with your wives for you have no place here among true men, if indeed true men you are. I go to fight! Will you come? What say ye?'

The officers responded with one voice, a roar that echoed across the plain: '*Aye!*'

'Take your marks, then,' Shirkuh bellowed, vaulting into the saddle, 'and may God grant us a swift and easy victory! *Allahu akbar!*'

'*Allahu akbar!*'

'We should return to the city, my lord,' Assad said, nodding to the Caliph as the collected officers dispersed to their posts.

'Aye, he's right,' Shirkuh said, reining in beside Rashid al-Hasan. 'It's about to get a damn sight less safe here, Glorious One. Prepare your city. Should we falter in truth – or should Amalric prove tougher than usual – his heathens will be pounding on the gates of Cairo by supper.'

'I have great faith in your ability, Shirkuh ibn Shahdi,' the Caliph said. 'Despite our differences, I pray Allah bless you and keep you . . . and may He grant you victory over the Infidel.'

'*Inshallah!*' Shirkuh echoed. With a shout and a flash of drawn steel, the one-eyed Kurd bolted away, dust swirling in his horse's wake.

Assad swung into the saddle; his horse whinnied, stamping its hooves and tossing its head. He leaned over to pat the mare's neck when something in the distance caught his attention: a flash of light, a shimmer of gold. Assad straightened, shading his eyes with the flat of his hand. Across the plain, at the forefront of the Nazarene lines, the standard of the Latin Kingdom of Jerusalem rippled and danced: an ornate golden cross on a silver field. Beside it rose and fell the dour emblem of the Templars, a pennon half white and half black. The sight of it fired the blood in his veins. *The stink of Ascalon choked him, the stench of charred flesh and viscera, the reek of corpses left to rot under the merciless sun.*

'Allah smite those sons of bitches!' Rage made Assad's voice steel-cold and harder than flint.

'The Franks call that rag Beauséant in their uncouth tongue,' Yusuf said, coming abreast of the Assassin. He smoothed his beard to cover the grimace of distaste twisting his thin features. 'But in Syria we know it as the standard of the Devil himself. You are familiar with the Order of the Temple?'

'Aye, I know their handiwork. The siege engines at Ascalon flew that ill-fated banner.' Assad stared hard at the distant pennon. Unconsciously, he stroked the pommel of his salawar, sinews twisting with the familiar burn of hatred still raw after fourteen years.

Fourteen years, and not a day had passed without some phantom reminder of Ascalon's death. Even the carnage Assad had wrought in his guise as the *Emir* of the Knife paled by comparison to the senseless slaughter of those dark times: days spent fighting off wave after howling wave of Nazarenes who sought death in service to their crucified messiah; nights spent huddled in the lee of a shattered wall, ankle-deep in a broth of blood and piss, kept awake by the creaking of Templar war-machines – and by the flesh-rending impact of their crude missiles. And that cursed piebald banner . . . Assad's jaw clamped shut; the muscles in his neck knotted. Allah, how he hated that scrap of filth! Day and night it had fluttered over the siege-works, a constant reminder that a swift and ignominious death was but a stone's throw away.

Now the piebald banner had come to Egypt. To his homeland! Should Shirkuh fail, the same machines that breeched the walls of Ascalon would batter Cairo to dust. The same threat; the same spectre. *But I am not the same man.* The Assassin bared his teeth in a cold and mirthless smile. *I am the* Emir *of the Knife, the Fist of Alamut. I am Death incarnate.*

'Who leads these Templars?' Assad snapped.

Leather creaked as Yusuf leaned forward in his saddle. Lips pursed, he considered the pair of standards: Jerusalem and Temple. 'With Amalric on the field,' he replied at length, 'I expect they have dispatched their chief warmonger. *Ya sidi-Arnat* is what we of Damascus call him. Arnaud de Razès is his name in the tongue of Frankistan. If it serves Allah's purpose, may his fall be as swift as his rise.' Yusuf straightened. Horns blared; across the field, the host of Jerusalem surged forward. 'Look, they come. You had best get the Caliph to safety.'

The bronze curb bit jangled as Assad wheeled his mare about, the seed of a plan forming in his mind. He nodded to the Caliph. 'Come, my lord.'

The younger man eyed him with great curiosity. 'What was that about? What bedevils you, my friend?'

'It's nothing. A memory of Ascalon. Quickly, now! We must get you to safety before the arrows fall.'

The Prince of the Faithful frowned at the mention of Ascalon, but following Assad's lead he spurred his horse to a gallop, his guard close on his heels. Soldiers parted; the men of Damascus cheered his passage no less stridently than did the men of Cairo, their glittering weapons thrust to heaven. The Caliph raised his hand in benediction.

Leaving the raucous host behind, the cortège rode south in silence. They passed through Shirkuh's camp, through his sparse – and sparsely guarded – baggage train, where merchants and would-be camp followers had come from Cairo to ply their trade among the Turkomans. *Sutlers and whores.* Assad studied this with no little interest as he and the Caliph's entourage cantered down the road; the seed of his idea was beginning to take root . . .

A distant roar caused Rashid al-Hasan to rein in his horse. The animal stamped and snorted; the Caliph twisted in the saddle to stare at the thunderheads of dust rising over the battlefield. Assad heard it, too: faint cries intermingled with horn blasts and the basso rumble of drums. 'Blessed Allah! It has begun,' the younger man muttered. 'It is only a matter of time, now. Will we know the outcome by nightfall, you think?'

'Perhaps,' Assad said. 'And perhaps sooner. Go quickly, my lord. Your guard will see you safely back to the city.'

'You're not returning with us?'

'No. I have a new task in mind.' Assad dismounted and stripped off his turban and his helmet; he unwound his sash and shrugged out of his khalat. This left him clad only in a mail hauberk, white linen trousers, and boots of supple leather. 'A task that, given my master's orders, I've decided I cannot leave to chance . . . or to Shirkuh.'

'But are you not charged with securing my safety?'

'After a fashion,' Assad replied. He glanced around at the White Slaves of the River who guarded the Caliph, at the style of their armour and the manner of their dress. 'You there,' he said to one whose harness was simplest of all. 'Lend me your coif. I need a belt, and a straight sword with a plain hilt.' The soldier looked to the Caliph, who nodded his assent. The first Mameluke drew off his mail hood while another unbuckled his weapon and handed it over to Assad. That done, the Caliph waved his guards away.

'What do you mean, "after a fashion"?'

'My orders have always been twofold: dispose of any who would do you harm, and sow fear among your enemies. Win or lose, Amalric needs to be reminded there are some things no number of swords can defend against. *Inshallah*, I can think of no better instructor than the one standing before you.'

Rashid al-Hasan swore. 'Don't be a fool, Assad! Even for you, Amalric's death is no spur-of-the-moment undertaking.'

'My lord, does the messenger kill his intended recipient? If he does, who will hear what he has to say? Not his recipient's kinsmen, for they'll be too intent upon vengeance. No' – Assad bared his teeth – 'there is another, one who stands at the King's shoulder, whose death will serve our purposes.' The Assassin settled his borrowed sword on his left hip and tucked his salawar into his belt. Finally, he drew the mail coif over his head. It was a simple disguise, but one that rendered him indistinguishable from any number of native-born Nazarene soldiers who fought under Amalric's banner. Satisfied with his appearance, Assad swung into the saddle.

'No! I forbid this!'

Assad shrugged. 'Forbid all you like, my lord, but my mind is set. If I have not returned by dawn, then it is likely I shall not return at all. Remember what I've told you. Send secretly to my master, tell him what has befallen, and he will surely send you all the aid you require. Be wary of Shirkuh! Beneath his beard and bluster lurks the heart of a serpent. A victory here today will only serve to embolden him.' Assad's horse pranced, sensing its rider's anticipation to be away. 'I must go. *As-salaam alaikum.*' He touched his heels to the mare's flanks and the animal sprang forward; the grace and power of its Arabian blood was undeniable. With a wild cry, the *Emir* of the Knife vanished in a maelstrom of dust.

'*Alaikum as-salaam*, my friend,' Rashid al-Hasan muttered. His heart suddenly heavy, the Prince of the Faithful turned his horse towards Cairo, where the domes and minarets of the Mother of the World shimmered, beckoning him home through waves of brutal heat.

8

'*God wills it!*'

Precipitated by that strident roar, the knights of the Order of the Temple led the charge against the centre of the Moslem line, against the serried ranks waiting beneath the gold-and-yellow pennons of the Fatimids. The earth shook with the thunderous impact of their horses' hooves; steel-clad riders gave tongue, screaming a holy paean so God might hear them over the shriek of trumpets and the rumble of drums. At their head, snapping in the artificial gale, the Templars' piebald banner seemed an impoverished rag alongside the gold and silver of Jerusalem. Behind them, Amalric's infantry struggled to keep pace.

Through the billowing dust, Yusuf ibn Ayyub witnessed the headlong charge of the Nazarenes – rather more like a controlled stampede in the enemy's direction. What struck him most, though, was the display of courage by the men of Cairo, who stood unflinching as the steel fist of Christendom bore down upon them. The young Kurd's sword flashed in salute to their unparalleled valour before turning into a gesture for his trumpeter. A horn blast skirled over the Turkoman lines; as one, Yusuf's half-wild archers unleashed a hellish rain of iron.

A single Turkoman, trained from birth in the traditions of horse-archery, could loose five arrows in the span of time it took a horse to travel ten paces; a thousand such Turkomans, loosing in unison, could hide the face of the sun behind a veil of black-feathered shafts. Now their arrows scythed through the Nazarene lines, volley upon volley, puncturing leather and mail and flesh. Riders toppled from the saddle; horses stumbled and screamed, crashing to the dusty ground to foul the legs of their fellows.

Still, the Nazarene charge did not falter. Their voices sang out: '*God wills it!*' And perhaps He did, for as the third Turkoman volley lofted skywards the lances of the Order of the Temple splintered against the shields and bodies of the men of Cairo. Through a haze of blood and grit, Yusuf heard a terrible sound, like the wet snap of bone coupled with the grinding rasp of metal upon metal, the whole punctuated by screams, guttural shouts, and cries to Allah for mercy.

Yusuf ibn Ayyub, though, had little time to appreciate their sacrifice. Preceded by the desultory sniping of their own archers, a wave of Nazarene infantry came baying through the haze. Mail-clad giants with bristling blond moustaches swung their axes alongside dark-eyed Norman swordsmen and savage native spear-men from the Christian strongholds of the Lebanon. Howling like wolves, their eyes alight with holy fervour, Amalric's soldiers struck the Turkoman lines with deafening impact.

Spears cracked and shivered; swords beat upon shields; axes crushed helmets and the skulls underneath; blood spewed from riven throats and poured from pierced entrails, turning the ground underfoot into a scarlet morass. The stench of a slaughterhouse filled the air. Curses and prayers, grunts and screams rippled along the lines, competing with the deafening crash of steel upon steel.

And like a wave upon the rocks, the warriors of Jerusalem broke against the Moslem bulwark.

9

Assad rode as though the Devil himself gave chase, pushing his sweat-lathered horse mercilessly through the afternoon heat. Loose rock and scree rattled under the animal's hooves as it thundered down the bed of a long-dry wadi that cleft the hills at the desert's edge. By ridge and ravine, Assad worked his way around the site of the battle, keeping the road from Cairo to Bilbeis always on his left-hand side.

The name of the Templars' master swirled through Assad's mind, the Assassin's plan for him coalescing around it. *Ya sidi-Arnat. Arnaud de Razès.* Provided he survived the battle, this de Razès would serve as a scapegoat for the dog-king of Jerusalem – a message Amalric could not deny: win or lose, his campaign was at an end. This Templar . . . his flesh would be the wax; Assad's blade, the stylus.

Would that I could destroy them all. Assad gritted his teeth. *Every last one of them. Let them suffer as the folk of Ascalon suffered.* But he squelched the desire for vengeance, that craving for blood no less distracting than the lust for a woman. Vengeance could not be his purpose. Not now. Not with the fate of Egypt hanging in the balance. He would cleave to his original commission to sow fear among the Caliph's enemies.

I am Death incarnate.

Still, in the back of his mind, Assad heard his old mentor's voice, his tone one of sharp rebuke, though not without its usual dollop of patience: *and what if your prey falls on the field, in the first exchange of blows? What then?* Rather than despair, the *Emir* of the Knife's dust-streaked face settled in an iron mask of resolve. Alive or dead, de Razès' fate meant little. Another Templar would take his place, and that man would become his target. The message was all that mattered. The message and its delivery . . . For that, he had to get close to Amalric.

Some five miles north of where Moslem and Nazarene clashed, Assad drew rein as an errant breeze brought him the telltale scent of wood smoke and ox dung. He dismounted and clambered to the crest of a low bluff. Dropping first to a crouch and then on to his belly, he wriggled across rock and scrub until he was able to peer out over the Nile floodplain. A scant two hours of daylight remained. Squinting against the westering sun, he saw the river in the distance, its surface the colour of molten copper. Closer, reed-choked canals were emerald slashes alongside the brown of patchwork fields, their rows already stripped clean of this season's crops; a village straddled the palm-lined road from Cairo, houses of mudbrick and thatch crowning a flat hillock fringed with dusty sycamores. A slender minaret rose above the trees.

And all around, encircling the village like a peasant army, sprawled the baggage train of the King of Jerusalem.

Assad grunted in satisfaction. Unlike Shirkuh's Turkomans, who were born to the saddle and bred to make do with the barest necessities, Amalric's army required the efforts of a small city to ensure its survival. Hundreds of wagons surrounded the village: ox-drawn wains that conveyed the army's tents and pavilions, its utensils and tackle, its provender and perishables. Drovers tended to the lowing oxen while farriers and squires made ready to care for the cavalry's weary mounts once the battle ended. Smoke curled from the temporary forges where armourers and black-smiths plied their trade, adding to the miasma rising off the ovens and roasting pits. Assad saw gangs of villagers pressed into service hauling water and digging trenches. Their Nazarene overseers paid them little heed, though; instead, they fixed their attention to the south, where plumes of dust marked their King's battle against the Saracen.

With predatory patience, Assad studied the enemy encampment; he noted the ebb and flow of individuals and the dis-tribution of matériel. He marked the wood-gatherers engaged in building bonfires against the coming night, and the draymen who shuffled the heavier wagons to the edge of camp to create makeshift ramparts. He paid special attention to the pairs of men-at-arms who stood sentinel around the perimeter. As he expected they were not the cream of Amalric's soldiery, but rather lightly armoured irregulars or veterans too old to fight in the vanguard . . . hale, to be sure, but nearing the end of their usefulness. Assad stripped off his borrowed coif and tossed it aside. From what he could tell, the men who remained with the baggage train wore no mail; neither would he.

As the Assassin backed away from the bluff's edge – routes of infiltration already taking shape in his mind – movement off to the south caught his attention. Instinctively, he dropped flat against the chalk-dry earth. Through the dust and lengthening shadows a single horseman raced up the road, Jerusalem's colours fluttering from the tip of his lance. Horns blared from sentries at the camp's edge; the commotion drew men from every quarter, men who shouted questions to the rider as he passed, his destination no doubt the small square and mosque at the centre of the village. He bore news of the battle, but was the news good or ill? Denied answers, even the sentries joined the press of men streaming after the rider.

Determined to take advantage of the sudden lapse in the camp's vigilance, Assad scuttled across the ground. He did not have time to retrace his steps, to find a simpler way down on to the plain; near at hand, a deep crevice cleft the face of the bluff. The Assassin cast a quick glance across the plain, then swung his legs over the crevice's edge and recklessly lowered himself down, oblivious to the forty-foot drop. To a man who had survived alone in the high Afghan Mountains, where the wind howled and knives of ice carved canyons through the black limestone, the fissure's cracks and outcroppings created no more a hindrance than did a rickety ladder. In places, Assad's mailed shoulders scraped stone; his booted feet dislodged showers of rock as he fell the last few feet to the Nile floodplain.

The Assassin rolled and came up into a crouch. Sweat burned his eyes. He breathed heavily, flexing his fingers to work the cramps from them; the muscles in his thighs and back ached. Fresh blood seeped from the lacerations he'd received at the hands of the Heretic. In the distance a ragged cheer sounded from the Nazarene camp – a sign the rider's news must surely favour Jerusalem. Assad, though, was unmoved, undeterred. *The message is all that matters.*

Rising, he unbuckled his sheathed sword and tossed it into the crevice. Next, accompanied by muffled curses, he wriggled free of his mail hauberk. This left him clad in a jupon of faded green-and-gold brocade – sweat-stained and spotted with rust – his trousers, and boots. Baring the edge of his salawar, he cut a strip of leather from the hauberk's hem and used it to tie back his tangled black hair. Not a perfect Frank, true, but he trusted the coming night to camouflage the worst of his flaws.

Assad caught up his blade, sheathed it, and set off across the plain with the loping stride of a hunter. He kept to the swathes of waist-high sedge grass that divided the naked brown fields, vaulting narrow canals overgrown with reeds; his passage dislodged a flock of herons who took to wing amid sharp cries of indignation.

It took longer than expected, but Assad reached the edge of the

Nazarene camp as the sun dipped below the far horizon. The sky above was aflame, shades of fiery red and orange and umber fading to the deep velvet of night. Stars flared to life, pinpricks of light in the evening haze. Assad bolted from a thicket of sedge and skidded to a crouch alongside one of the perimeter wagons. Panting, he listened to the chaotic sounds of Amalric's camp.

Shouting voices and the creak of wheels marked the departure of scores of wagons, doubtless bound for the battlefield to recover the wounded and the dead. The Assassin glanced out from beneath the wagon's bed and saw the return of smaller donkey carts that had accompanied the army. At one time they had carried casks of water, sheaves of arrows, and lances; now they were laden with groaning bodies. Torches blazed, casting murky light over the pale and hollow-eyed faces of the injured. Weary horsemen clopped alongside, barely acknowledging the throng of camp followers who barked questions and pressed clay cups of water into their hands.

Unnoticed in the confusion, Assad rolled beneath the wagon and came smoothly to his feet. He blended into the mob of camp followers, who spoke a mixture of Frankish and Arabic, until he found himself walking alongside one of the donkey carts.

A young foot soldier clung to the side of the cart, forced into a sitting position by the sprawled bodies behind him. Mail hung in tatters from his narrow shoulders; he winced at each bump and jostle, cursing in Arabic, one bloody hand clawing at the broken shaft of an arrow jutting from his side. He would have ripped it out had Assad not caught him by the arm.

'Don't,' the Assassin murmured. 'You'll only make it worse.'

The soldier sighed and nodded.

'Tell me, brother: are we victorious?'

The soldier raised his head. A glancing blow from a mace had splintered his left cheek and brow, blinding that eye. He tilted his pale face to look at Assad; blood dribbled from the corner of his mouth. He blinked, spat. 'I . . . I d-don't know . . .'

10

The sounds of slaughter faded with the sun's light. Cries for succour replaced the crash of steel as a temporary truce was called; Moslem and Nazarene put aside their differences and set about caring for the wounded – and tending to the dead.

Yusuf ibn Ayyub regarded the harrowed ground through eyes brimming with weariness and pain. The young Kurd's helmet was gone, ripped from his head by an axe-wielding Nazarene. His khalat and mail hung in tatters. Gore clotted his arms, his hands. It stiffened his beard and gave his countenance a ghoulish cast in the guttering torchlight. Yusuf walked with the aid of a splintered spear shaft; the same lance thrust that pierced the meat of his thigh had slain the horse beneath him. His second horse had gone down with a cleft skull.

Initially, the battle unfolded as Shirkuh had predicted, but the Nazarenes proved themselves no less resourceful in a pinch. Their lines held; the men of Cairo failed to draw Amalric's centre away while a reserve of light cavalry kept Shirkuh's own horsemen from flanking the enemy infantry. What should have been a lightning rout turned instead into a hard-fought draw.

Heaps of corpses marked the Turkoman line: bodies entangled in death; hacked mail reflecting daggers of light; beards jutting heavenward; hands clutching broken sword hilts. Spears and lances, some trailing scraps of colourful cloth, erupted like grotesque saplings from the bloody ground; a harvest of spent arrows grew from the flesh of the slain. Exhausted Turkoman soldiers saw to their injured brethren, helping stand those who could and carrying those too wounded to move. Yusuf witnessed reunions and tragedies in the eerie twilight: fathers and sons embracing; brothers kneeling around the body of their slain elder; old friends lending one another a shoulder as they wept for dead saddle-mates.

'Yusuf.'

The young Kurd turned. Shirkuh stood behind him, drawn and haggard. He, too, bore the bloody signs of battle.

'What happened, uncle?' Yusuf said. 'Why did Amalric's lines not break as you foretold?'

'Perhaps he and I have crossed paths once too often, and now he knows better than to underestimate me. Perhaps his skill has improved. Or perhaps we simply did not fight with the full measure of our hearts. Only Allah knows for certain. Come, Yusuf. Let the surgeons see to that leg.'

Yusuf waved away Shirkuh's concern. 'There are others worse than I.'

'True, but let them bind it properly so you may still be of use to me. We have much yet to do. Our victory—'

'Victory, uncle? What victory? Amalric yet lives; he yet has an army at his fingertips, and he yet bedevils Egypt. Calling this a victory is premature, at best. At worst, it reeks of hubris.'

'Ever my conscience, eh?' Shirkuh grinned. 'Tell me, if you remember, what task did our Sultan – may Allah hold him ever in His favour – saddle us with? Was it the destruction of Amalric of Jerusalem? No, boy! Though Nur ad-Din would not look askance on a gift such as Amalric's head, that is secondary to why we are here.'

'I remember,' Yusuf said. 'We are here for Cairo.'

Shirkuh's smile widened. 'For Cairo! And therein we have our victory, for am I not a newly minted vizier of that great city? The Caliph will open his gates and welcome us back with open arms!'

Yusuf ibn Ayyub limped to his uncle's side. 'What will you do with this new-found goodwill? Will you strike?'

'There is no need for haste in these matters,' Shirkuh said. He offered Yusuf his arm to lean upon. 'No need at all. We will see first to the Nazarenes; then we will let Cairo simmer for a few weeks while we regain our strength. Give the people a chance to become accustomed to our presence.'

'And then . . . ?'

'There can only be one ruler in Egypt, Yusuf. Only one.' Shirkuh ibn Shahdi's grim smile widened. 'And I intend for it to be me!'

'*Inshallah*, uncle. *Inshallah*.'

Arm in arm, the pair faded into the star-flecked night.

11

Amalric of Jerusalem returned from the battlefield in a towering rage. He did not seethe against his soldiers, who had acquitted themselves admirably; nor did he rail against his situation, which was a damn sight better than he had any right to expect. No, Amalric reserved his rage for the man who rode at his right hand.

The blond-bearded King of Jerusalem twisted in the saddle, glaring at the Master of the Temple, Arnaud de Razès, whose black surcoat was stiff with Saracen blood. 'What do you mean, we should pull back to Bilbeis?'

'Bilbeis is a more defensible location,' replied Arnaud, a raw-boned giant of a man whose blue eyes gleamed with murderous piety. His face was like a mask of hard leather stretched over a frame of gristle, and it bore a tracery of old scars, some wrought by steel and fire, others by the ravages of Time. His greying moustache bristled. 'Its walls—'

'I didn't come to Egypt to occupy a shit-hole like Bilbeis! God's teeth, man, we have Shirkuh on the defensive and you advocate running away? Merciful Christ! What has become of the fabled courage of the Templars?'

'May God forgive you your blasphemy, milord,' Arnaud said, his voice low and measured. 'As for my brothers and I, we endeavour to balance courage with truth . . . and the truth is we no longer have the manpower to prosecute a proper siege.'

'The Devil take your "proper siege"! All we need is one weakened gate and the courage to take it by force. We've flung the dice, de Razès. Now it's time we seized our winnings.'

'Milord, be reasonable! We can no more—'

'Reasonable? War is no place for reasonable men!' As if to prove his point, King Amalric spurred his horse into the village square. Paved in yellow sandstone and shaded by a fringe of well-kept palms, this place was the centre of life for the Saracen peasants; their mosque, appropriated by the Templars to be their barracks, opened on the square, as did the inns and caravanserais the Frankish nobles had seized as part of their spoils. Now iron cressets spilled ruddy light over what had become Jerusalem's makeshift court. All around, exhausted and bloodied King's men awaited his pleasure, the barons of the realm who had pledged their flesh to Amalric and their souls to God; with them were retainers and men-at-arms, common soldiers and camp followers. Cheers went up at the sight of their King.

Amalric raised his hand for silence. 'Men of Jerusalem! Blessed soldiers of the Cross! Today, I saw in your hearts the spirit of our forefathers – the prowess of Duke Godfrey, the ferocity of Tancred, and the piousness of Adhemar!' The recitation of these names, heroes of the past who had spearheaded the Great Crusade, sent ripples of pride through the listeners; their cries redoubled. The King stroked his beard sagaciously and waited for their voices to subside. After a moment, he continued. 'God, in his inscrutable wisdom, did grant us victory over the filthy Saracen. Shirkuh's back is broken, his ragged host much reduced! Upon the morrow, I will march to the gates of Cairo and demand its surrender. Should they refuse, I will pull those gates down with my bare hands if need be. Will I stand alone in this?'

'No!' his men, noble and commoner alike, answered with a resounding din. 'No!'

Amalric raised himself up in his stirrups. In his battle-scarred mail and blood-spattered surcoat, with his sandy hair and beard and fierce-eyed stare, he looked every inch a warrior-king of legend. He swept his notched sword from its sheath and thrust it at the star-flecked heavens. 'For God and for Jerusalem!'

'*For God!*' The square erupted, a thunderous roar of

approbation matched only by the rattle of wood and steel. Torchlight flashed from spearheads, from shield bosses, from helmets as the soldiers mimicked their King's gesture, stabbing their fists to the sky. *'For Jerusalem! For Amalric!'*

'Let us look to our wounded and make ready for the dawn!' Amalric turned and made his way back to where de Razès waited. The Templar's face remained impassive. 'This,' the King spat. 'This, by God, is why we are here! I'll hear no more talk of retreat. Have your machines and your Templars ready to move at first light. Do you understand?'

'I do,' Arnaud de Razès replied through gritted teeth. 'Forgive my impertinence, milord.'

'Tear the gates of Cairo off their hinges for me and all will be forgotten.'

'It will be as you wish.' Bowing at the waist, the Master of the Temple took his leave. Amalric spared him a final, withering glance before succumbing to the half-drunk and clamorous demands of his barons.

And no one – neither King nor baron nor common soldier – paid even the slightest heed to a scar-faced man in faded green-and-gold brocade who drifted into the shadows alongside the mosque.

12

Assad studied his quarry through hate-slitted eyes. Though he could make out little of what passed between King and servant – and he understood the Frankish tongue far better than he spoke it – he recognized royal displeasure when he saw it. A grim smile rose unbidden to the Assassin's lips. Amalric's disdain for the old man did nothing to sour his usefulness to Assad's cause; indeed, he rejoiced in the knowledge that the last words spoken between the two would be words of harsh rebuke.

The Assassin drew deeper into shadow as Arnaud de Razès dismounted in front of the mosque, tossed his reins to a waiting groom, and stalked through the arched entryway; he called for wine in a voice harsh and full of wrath.

An instant later, Assad was in motion. Turning, he sprinted down the narrow alley to where a two-wheeled cart waited, empty and wedged into place, its poles driven into the ground. Assad darted up the angled bed of the cart; he leapt from its apex, twisted, and caught the crumbling edge of the mosque's roof. He hung there for a split second, hissing at the sudden pain in his shoulder, and then pulled himself up into a crouch on the rooftop. Abraded fingers touched the hilt of his salawar in silent benediction.

The mosque itself was a squat cube of whitewashed mudbrick surmounted by a shallow dome of peeling green stucco. Its area doubled, however, with the inclusion of an arcaded courtyard, paved in the same yellowish sandstone as the village square. At the far corner of this courtyard, a curious minaret towered above the village; its staircase spiralled along its exterior, an imperfect replica of the minaret belonging to the mosque of Ibn Tulun, south of Cairo.

From this vantage, Assad could see the lights of the King's pavilion away to the north, positioned on the edge of the village where it might receive the benefit of a steady breeze. What's more, the Assassin had walked the ground between unchallenged; at times his enemies even greeted him, blind to the fact he was not one of them. *That* was the Nazarenes' great failing: they were on guard against a force of Saracens, but a single man who knew how to blend in – especially one who looked no different from a native Maronite or Jacobite Christian – could move about at will without raising an alarm.

The day's heat still radiated off the brickwork on the mosque's roof. Carefully, Assad crept forward until he had a clear view of the courtyard below, its stones bathed in soft yellow light from lamps hanging between arches along the arcade. At its centre, under an awning of sun-faded blue cloth, a fountain burbled in a circular basin. Easily, Assad caught sight of de Razès. Servants had stripped the Templar Master of his blood-crusted surcoat and were helping him out of his armour; a dozen brother-knights stood near at hand.

'He means to press on,' de Razès was saying. 'And we have little choice but to accompany him.'

One of the knights shook his head. 'A fool's errand!'

'Do not slander your King!' The chief of the Templars sighed; with a grimy hand he massaged the bridge of his nose. 'In my heart I agree with you, but Amalric is no fool. He simply lacks his brother's patience.' He gestured to the knights. 'Go. Prepare the siege train. We move on Cairo at dawn.'

'For God's sake, we will do it, milord.' His men bowed and went about their business. Some returned to the arcade, where they mended mail hauberks and sharpened blades, while others hurried from the mosque to rouse the Genoese and Armenian mercenaries of the siege train – the stewards of those devilish machines that pierced the heart of Ascalon. Assad bared his teeth. If he had more time, he would pay those sons of whores a visit, as well.

Below, a brown-mantled servant brought de Razès a stool. 'Will you eat, milord?'

'I have no appetite. Pour me another cup of wine and have done.'

The servant did as ordered, and then withdrew to a discreet distance. For some time Arnaud de Razès sat in the shadow of the fountain's awning, sipping his wine as he brooded over the day's events. Assad, though, did not have the same luxury. Time was of the essence. So, moving with infinite patience, his body low against the roof, he worked his way down to the narrow ledge that ran around the top of the courtyard wall. Decorative crenels, like teeth of broken brick, afforded him slight cover; dripping sweat, he crab-crawled towards the far minaret, the only way down from the roof that offered any hope of concealment.

Assad was wrestling with how to strike quickly and remain unseen when abruptly Ya sidi-Arnat stood. He slung wine lees from his empty cup and tossed it to the waiting servant. 'Fetch the chaplain,' he said. 'After I take in the night air, I would have him hear my confession.'

The servant bowed and scurried off to do his master's bidding. De Razès turned; with hands clasped behind his back, he walked towards a door in the corner of the courtyard. A door that led to the minaret's spiral stairs.

Assad dared not believe his eyes. No servants followed the Master of the Temple; no brother-knights offered to join him. For a few moments, at least, Arnaud de Razès would be alone and out of sight of his fellow Templars.

For a few moments, Ya sidi-Arnat would be vulnerable.

The Master of the Temple vanished through the doorway; with a renewed sense of purpose, Assad scuttled the last few yards to where the minaret's foundations rose from the courtyard wall. The Assassin squatted on his haunches with his back pressed against the waist-high balustrade of solid brick and listened to the measured shuffle of the Templar's feet as he mounted the stairs. De Razès passed him by, oblivious to his presence; a dozen steps later he gained the summit of the minaret.

Noiselessly, Assad vaulted the low wall and dropped to a crouch on the stairs. From below, he heard the faint snores of sleeping Templars and the soft footfalls of their servants; from above, a resigned sigh from de Razès.

The Assassin's hand drifted to the hilt of his salawar, its rage and hatred calling to him. *No*, his own good sense cut through the din, *the others might hear*. With titanic effort, he let go of the blade and instead reached up to untie the thong securing his long hair. The tough leather was thin and damp with sweat, but long enough to wrap once around both hands while still leaving a span between – sufficient to whip around a man's neck. Cat-like, Assad padded up the last few steps to the minaret's balcony . . .

. . . and beheld Arnaud de Razès leaning against the railing. He was staring away north, as though trying to pierce the purple fabric of the King's pavilion and read his mind. The Templar must have seen something from the corner of his eye – some brief flicker of movement – for he turned his head suddenly and muttered in perturbation: 'Yes, what is—'

Before he could register alarm, the *Emir* of the Knife was upon him.

Assad struck first with the heel of his foot, a crushing blow that caught the Templar in the side of his knee. Bone and sinew parted with an audible snap; de Razès gasped, stumbling against Assad as his leg gave way. He opened his mouth to loose a bellow of agony even as the leather thong drew taut around his throat. The two men went to the ground like lovers in an obscene embrace.

'*Allahu Akbar*, O Master of the Temple,' Assad spat, his voice carrying no further than his victim's ear. His back to the Assassin, Arnaud de Razès gurgled and thrashed, eyes distended, the veins standing out on his temples as he clawed at the makeshift garrotte. 'God wills it.' With a savage wrench, Assad cinched the cord ever deeper into the soft flesh of his enemy's throat.

The struggle for life was draining from de Razès' limbs with every breath denied him. His feet struck the balcony railing; his heels drummed against the brick. Spasms racked his body as only a croaking hiss escaped his crushed larynx. Suddenly, the Templar's rigid frame relaxed; Assad felt him go limp, tongue lolling from his open mouth. After a few more seconds, the Assassin slackened his grip. He caught his own breath and listened for sounds of commotion coming from the courtyard below.

Nothing.

Then, nodding to himself, he bared the edge of his salawar.

13

'*Amalric . . .*'

The King of Jerusalem stirred on his divan and jerked awake, drawn from his exhausted slumber by . . . by what? By a disembodied voice? Or was it simply the soft cry of a bird coming from somewhere outside his pavilion? Regardless, the blond-bearded monarch yawned and rubbed his bloodshot eyes.

The silken walls of the King's pavilion soughed and sighed; poles of carved cedar creaked in the soft night breeze. A small golden lamp, its wick burning sweetly scented oils, cast a flickering glow over carpets and velvet tapestries, over a desk laden with books and papers and a wooden stand supporting the royal panoply. Impenetrable shadows danced in the corners of the pavilion.

Seeing nothing amiss, Amalric was on the verge of rolling over and surrendering once more to sleep's embrace when a tiny imperfection – a thing out of place – caught his attention. He blinked, looked again. If his thick-nasalled helmet, with its circlet of gold, was resting atop the wooden stand, then what was that sitting on the edge of his desk?

The King grunted and clambered to his feet, naked but for a long shirt. He shuffled over to his desk. Rubbing his eyes once more, he stared down at the object someone had left for his perusal.

An object that dripped blood.

Amalric recoiled. 'Christ and the Saints . . . !'

It was a man's head. What's more, the King recognized its waxen countenance, though slack and colourless in death: *Arnaud de Razès*. A cry of alarm rose into the King's throat, but before he could give tongue to it a shape boiled from the shadows at his back. It struck him across the shoulders, a massive weight that drove him to his knees. Amalric felt iron fingers knotting in his hair . . . and he felt the cold touch of steel at his neck.

Something clawing and horrible fluttered down his spine, something that did not care that he was a king of men; something that stripped away his courage even as it settled in the pit of his stomach. He dared not utter so much as a whisper for fear of angering it even further. The King's eyes rolled heavenward.

'Speak,' a voice hissed in his ear, 'and Jerusalem will be poorer by a king. I bring you a message and a warning from my master, a young shaykh of storied lineage who dwells on a mountain-top by the shores of the Caspian Sea. He bids me tell you, Malik al-Morri, that Egypt is not for you. Leave here. Cease your foolish struggle and be content with what lands you possess. That is my master's message. His warning is thus: should you force his hand, should you ignore his wise counsel, should even the least of your siege engines come within sight of Cairo's walls, then he will send me unto you once more – and the head I take then will not be the head of some God-cursed Templar, but rather one of royal blood. Perhaps yours . . . perhaps your son's. Do you believe I speak the truth?'

Amalric swallowed hard; slowly, he nodded.

'Pray, then, O King of the Latin Franks. On your son's life, pray your god grants you wisdom and health, for if I return you will have neither.'

The King felt the steel lift from his neck; he felt the fingers loosen their hold on his scalp. Velvet hangings rustled. On the soft carpets, faced by the severed head of the Master of the Temple, Amalric remained kneeling, not daring to move until the unaccustomed spasm of fear passed.

Quietly, he prayed.

14

The splash of water, louder than the familiar burble of his fountain, easily roused Rashid al-Hasan from his bed. A tomb-like silence had settled over the East Palace during the night; the White Slaves of the River maintained their diligence, patrolling its halls and arcades, its courtyards and gardens. Hand-picked cadres stood rigid guard over the gates while, across the Bayn al-Qasrayn, the West Palace was ablaze with light and raucous noise. Turkomans mingled with Sudanese, with Syrians. They drank to the shades of the dead, to the health of the wounded, and to the victory of their commander.

Already, the Prince of the Faithful sensed the walls of ambition rising around the hero of the hour, the swaggering Kurd, Shirkuh. *Let him have his triumph*, Rashid had decided, retiring to his apartments where an anxious Parysatis awaited him. They passed the night in conversation, only withdrawing to their separate beds when her kohl-rimmed eyes became heavy with sleep.

Rashid's own slumber had been fitful, at best, his dreams haunted by the faces of men slain in his name, by the groans and pleas of the injured soldiers who returned by the wagon-load from the field of slaughter. Not even Parysatis' soothing presence could allay his nightmares.

Now, repeated splashing piqued the Caliph's curiosity. He rose and drew on a silken robe. Grey light filtered through the lattice-worked doors leading out to his garden; tendrils of morning mist drifted under the threshold to dampen the tiles of his floor. Shivering, Rashid al-Hasan eased open the doors and stepped into a world of fleece and velvet.

Dawn was not far off, and a heavy fog reeking of the Nile lay over the domes and minarets of Cairo. The Caliph walked barefooted in the wet grass until he could see the stone basin of the garden fountain.

'Assad? Is that you?'

The figure sitting on the fountain kerb turned at the sound, water dripping from his fingers. 'Aye, my lord. I didn't mean to disturb you.'

The younger man waved off Assad's concern. 'My sleep was disturbed long before now. Are you injured?'

Assad chuckled. 'Scrapes and bruises, my lord . . . and a gigantic thirst.' He leaned down and scooped water into his mouth.

'I'll have something brought—'

'Don't bother. This water is cool enough for my needs.' Assad sighed and splashed a handful in his face, sluicing the dust from his beard. His fingers lingered over his jagged scar.

Rashid al-Hasan walked to the fountain's edge and sat. He looked up, watching as the sky above grew light, the fog glistening and opalescent. After a moment, he said: 'Your task . . . was it successful?'

'It was. I expect the visit I paid to Amalric, and the gift I brought him, soured the sweet nectar of victory on his lips. Unless he's more of a fool than I imagined, I suspect the Nazarene will trouble you no longer after this night.'

'Shirkuh will be crestfallen.'

Assad raised an eyebrow. 'Ah, Shirkuh. And what should we do with the Kurd now that his importance to Cairo's well-being has become moot? Should I pay him a visit as well?'

'Not yet. I would prefer to try and deal with him myself before I resort to other means. If I could win as staunch a Sunni as Amir Shirkuh of Damascus to my cause . . . well, what better way to prove my worth in the eyes of Allah – and in the eyes of your master?'

Slowly, Assad nodded. 'As you wish, my lord. But I will be watching him, and if Shirkuh makes one untoward move against you, then I shall do my master's bidding and send the bastard to Hell.' *And with him that elusive necromancer, the Heretic's master*, he added to himself.

While either man lived, the Fatimid Caliphate of Egypt was in jeopardy, body and soul. In truth, Assad reckoned the young man at his side more imperilled now than when he was at the mercy of his vizier. No longer was he merely an empty robe, an ornament waiting to be put on display by ambitious men; he was Caliph in fact as well as in name. He wielded the power in Cairo, and that alone would draw in conspirators against him as a lamp draws insects. To keep him safe, Assad would need to call upon every ounce of cunning he possessed, every trick and instinct. Everything. His hand dropped to the hilt of his salawar. Hatred coiled and seethed; tendons cracked as ancient rage threaded through muscle and sinew. *I am Death incarnate*, it whispered.

So am I, the *Emir* of the Knife replied. *So am I.*

Epilogue

Wheels creaked in the mist.

A laden donkey cart plodded down a narrow road, little more than a rutted trail that followed the overgrown banks of the Nile. Two men walked alongside, rag-pickers from Cairo clad in tattered galabiyyas, their skins burned as black as an Ethiopian's by the relentless sun. Both were furtive; their eyes slipped from palm-trunk to sycamore-bole as if every shadow held unseen menace.

Still, for all their wariness, neither man saw the dark-cloaked figure step into the middle of the trail until their donkey balked and brayed. A second figure joined him, slender and child-like.

'Merciful Allah!' swore the taller of the two rag-pickers, a man whose past transgressions had earned him a slit nose. 'That's how you get your precious throat cut!'

The newcomer ignored him. 'You have brought the body.' It wasn't a question. The rag-pickers exchanged worried glances. Slit-nose shrugged; the other scratched his scraggly beard.

'Well, it's like this: we didn't know which body you wanted, so we just brought them all.'

'All?'

'Seven of 'em. That hole-in-the-ground you sent us to was a regular slaughterhouse.' Slit-nose shuddered. 'Allah's mercies, but I wouldn't want to meet the devil who did that.'

'Let me see them,' the cloaked figure said.

Working in unison, the two rag-pickers peeled back the splotched canvas covering the bed of their cart. The donkey shied at the sudden stench of blood, at the reek of bladder and bowel. Stacked haphazardly in the cart were seven corpses clad in black, their exposed flesh pale and waxen; one, sprawled ignominiously on top of the others, lacked a head and part of an arm, a horrible wound gaping in its chest.

The cloaked figure cursed softly, shook his head.

'This is the one. He had a knife . . . a Frankish dirk . . .'

Slit-nose grumbled and spat as he fished the hilt-shard of a broken blade from the small of his back. From his sour look, it pained him to hand it over. In turn, the cloaked figure motioned for his smaller companion, who mechanically stepped forward and accepted the broken knife-hilt.

'You'll pay extra for the others?'

'You will be rewarded,' the figure said, turning away. Again, the rag-pickers exchanged glances; a look of greed flickered between them. 'Yasmina.'

At the mention of her name, the slender Egyptian was in motion. Her cloak fluttered from her shoulders as she darted forward, the hilt-shard a blur as it passed beneath Slit-nose's stubbled jaw. A rooster-tail of blood fountained from his now-exposed jugular. Wide-eyed, he sank to his knees and clutched in vain at his slashed arteries. The second rag-picker bellowed, clawing for his knife; as his blade cleared its sheath, the girl danced close and brutally rammed the jagged shard into the hollow of his throat.

She held him upright, impaled, while he gagged and sputtered on his own blood. After a moment the rag-picker toppled, the knife-shard tearing free of his flesh. Yasmina turned to the cloaked figure of Ibn Sharr.

'Was that enough, master? Have I not proven myself?'

Ibn Sharr stared dispassionately at the two still-quivering corpses. 'Not yet, child. Perhaps in time you will have proven your worth. For now, though, we must find Ta-Djeser. Come, child.'

'What about the bodies?'

'Leave them,' Ibn Sharr said, a cryptic smile spreading across his grim countenance. 'I have what I need.'

Yasmina paused. She looked back over her shoulder, past the cart and its grisly burden, past the riven corpses, and imagined she could see the gleaming palaces and mosques of Cairo. The nighted streets of the Mother of the World had taken both the mother of her flesh and the mother of her soul. And for what? Yasmina sighed. There needs must be a blood-price. A reckoning.

As Zaynab suffered, so must I . . . and so must they all. It is Allah's will.

Turning, she followed the necromancer into shadow.

Author's Note

The genesis for *The Lion of Cairo* lay not in the annals of history, but rather in the pages of such pulp-era magazines as *Adventure, Argosy,* and *Oriental Stories*; in the wild tales of Robert E. Howard and Harold Lamb, and in that compilation of bawdy and exotic stories known to western audiences as *The Thousand and One Nights*. The Cairo presented herein is not the city of history, but rather the Cairo of Scheherazade – a city where the fantastic occurs around every corner; a city steeped in its own history, where the magic of ancient Egypt meets the mysticism of the desert. Some elements of the city are contemporary to the twelfth century, others are imaginary, still others are drawn from diverse historical periods: columns scavenged from Egyptian temples sit cheek-by-jowl with the carved façades of the Mameluke sultans, which overlook gardens laid out by the Fatimid caliphs, with the whole protected by walls erected during the reign of the Ayyubids. It is the Cairo of fable and legend, and I've taken egregious liberties with its topography, its character, and its people for the sake of story.

Readers wishing to learn something more of the true character of Old Cairo need only look to Jim Antoniou's *Historic Cairo: A Walk Through the Islamic City* (The American University in Cairo Press, 1998); I also found Michael Haag's *Cairo Illustrated* (The

American University in Cairo Press, 2006) and *Cairo: The City Victorious* by Max Rodenbeck (Knopf, 1999) extremely helpful.

In order to build a fantasy world that evoked the vanished era of the Crusades, I found myself consulting a wide variety of texts, both historical and modern, from Philip Hitti's excellent translation of *The Memoirs of Usamah ibn-Munqidh* (Columbia University Press, 2000) to Roland Broadhurst's *The Travels of Ibn Jubayr* (Goodword Books, 2001) to Amin Maalouf's *The Crusades Through Arab Eyes* (Schocken Books, 1984). In particular, *A History of Egypt in the Middle Ages* by Stanley Lane-Poole (Methuen & Co., 1901) and *The Assassins: A Radical Sect in Islam* by Bernard Lewis (Oxford University Press, 1987) proved most invaluable. As always, I am to blame for any misreading or omission of fact.

Acknowledgements

The tale of the *Emir* of the Knife owes its existence to quite a few people: to Josh Olive, first among readers; to Darren Cox, who made sure my plots and intrigues weren't totally ridiculous, and who provided a second set of eyes; to Wayne Miller and Kris Reisz, the oldest of friends, who ensured I didn't make an ass of myself – often by exploiting those times when I did; to Constance Brewer, Meghan Sullivan, Gabrielle Campbell, and David S. De Lis, who helped keep the gnomes at bay; to Russell Whitfield, for the loan of his Arabic-speaking stepfather; to Howard Andrew Jones, Deuce Richardson, Tom Doolan, and the late Steve Tompkins, who kept me going with their infectious enthusiasm.

Most of all, though, Assad owes his life to two men, both storied cavaliers in their own right: my editor, Pete Wolverton, and my agent, Bob Mecoy. Mecoy epitomizes the gentleman-agent: a tireless advocate, shrewd publisher, and hilarious raconteur rolled into one; he's never too busy to answer a question or explain the publishing process for the umpteenth time. Across the desk from him, Pete is every inch an editor in the classic sense: gracious in manner even as he pores over endless drafts in search of the best bits contained in each, making suggestions and reining in the worst of my excesses. His notes on what would become *The Lion of Cairo* read like a masterclass in how to write a novel. To both men I owe an impossible debt of gratitude, not only for their expertise and passion but for their formidable patience.

And last, but far from least: to all the readers who have followed me from tale to tale – it is you who make this task of writing a joyful experience. To each and every one, my heartfelt thanks.

ABOUT THE AUTHOR

Scott Oden hails from the hills of rural North Alabama. His fascination with far-off places began when one of his brothers introduced him to the writing of Robert E. Howard and Harold Lamb, and his obsession with the ancient world when a school teacher showed his class slides from the great Tutankhamun exhibition. He started writing his own stories aged fourteen but it would be many years before anything came of it. Following a brief fling with academia and the usual roster of odd jobs – from delivering pizza to working at a video store – Scott now writes full time. His first two historical novels, the acclaimed *Men of Bronze* and *Memnon*, are available in Bantam paperback.